IN AND OUT OF STEP

CHRISTINE M. KNIGHT

Copyright © 2010 Christine M Knight

ISBN: 9780994628602

HIGHLIGHT PUBLISHING
ABN: 71212072993
PO Box 187, Fyshwick, ACT 2609 AUSTRALIA
TEL: +61 2 6108 3624
www.highlightpublishing.com.au
email: info@highlightpublishing.com.au

The right of Christine M Knight to be identified as the Author of this Work is asserted in accordance with the Australian Copyright Act as amended and the Copyright, Design and Patents Act 1988 UK as amended

This edition (third) published by Highlight Publishing in September 2016 (ISBN: 9780994628602)
Second edition published by Highlight Publishing in 2012 (ISBN: 9780987434838)
First edition published in Australia by Sid Harta Publishers Pty Ltd in 2010 (ISBN: 9781921642500)
Second print published by Sid Harta Publishers Pty Ltd in 2011

The right of HIGHLIGHT PUBLISHING to be identified as the owner of the cover design for 'In and Out of Step' is asserted in accordance with the Australian Designs Act 2003 as amended

Cover design: Luke Harris
Typesetting: Working Type Studio
Marketing design: Working Type Studio Melbourne (www.workingtype.com.au)

pp. 496

National Library of Australia Cataloguing-in-Publication entry
Creator: Knight, Christine M., author.
Title: In and Out of Step / Christine M Knight.
Paperback ISBN: 9780994628602   eBook ISBN: 9780994628619
Subjects: Women Fiction
Women Identity--Fiction
Dewey Number A823.4

ATTN OVERSEAS READERS:
Christine M Knight uses the British spelling and language conventions.

About the author

An Australian, Christine M Knight is a
published author of fiction, poetry, short
stories, and blogs. She also composes
music. A graduate of Macquarie
University, Christine travelled extensively
overseas and lived for three years in the
United States — San Antonio, Texas and
Montgomery, Alabama. Married to an
officer in the Royal Australian Air Force, Christine has settled
in the Canberra region. A writer, public speaker, and teacher,
she continues to have a varied and enriching life.

Author website: www.christinemknight.com.au

Other fiction by Christine M Knight
The Keimera Series
Life Song   Book 2
Song Bird   Book 3

Christine M Knight's first set of novels, The Keimera series,
are loosely related in that they draw on a pool of characters in
that world. The novels are not necessarily sequels one to the
other. Each novel functions as a standalone story.

Acknowledgements

Special thanks to my principal readers for their untiring support and willingness to discuss the tough issues: my husband, Wayne, and my dear friend, Eva Campbell — in you I trust.

Thank you to my children, Erin and Alistair, whose unwavering faith in my skills sustained me throughout the writing process.

Thank you to Terri Caldoreon (nee Gaines) of San Antonio Texas for input into issues centring on female perspectives and for feedback as a reader in the early drafts.

Thank you to my husband, Wayne, and my brother, David, for help in research.

I would like to thank all those teachers in Australia and Texas USA who have shared their experiences with me over the years, providing me with themes and issues.

Appreciation is expressed to HG Nelson and Roy Slaven whose style of banter I've used to provide insight into collegiate interaction.

'The Loch Ness Monster's Song' © Edwin Morgan; Carcanet Press

'Do Not Stand at My Grave and Weep', Mary Frye

NSW Rape Crisis Centre

NSW Rural Fire Service

The New Braunfels Fire Department, Texas

This book is for my family

Glossary

ADFA is an acronym for the Australian Defence Force Academy. It is located in the nations' bush capital, Canberra.

Arvo is Australian slang for afternoon

The Australian Bicentennial occurred in 1988. The novel is set between 1988-1990.

BHP (today known as BHP Billiton) is a global mining group that includes steelworks such as those based in Wollongong south of Sydney. In Australia, it is the top producer of iron ore and coal (thermal and metallurgical).

Bloke is Australian slang for an ordinary man

Chook an Australian term for chicken. It is sometimes used as a nickname.

CWA is an abbreviation for the Country Women's Association. It is a non-profit, non-party political, and non-sectarian organisation for country and city women. Members work for the welfare of all women and children through representation to all levels of government, undertaking fundraising events, providing networking opportunities and teaching life skills.

Dux is Latin for leader. It is the title given to the student with the highest overall academic score in the graduating year (Year 12) of high school. The American equivalent is valedictorian.

Esky is used in Australia as a generic name. It more correctly is a trademark owned by Coleman Brands Pty Ltd and which specifically identifies an Esky brand name icebox cooler.

Federation refers to the process by which the six separate self-governing British colonies of New South wales, Queensland, South Australia, Tasmania, Victoria, and Western Australia formally joined together to form one nation, Australia, in 1901. http://youtu.be/tjlj3KKKAlA

Federation architecture is the style prevalent in Australia in 1901. A limited range of colour schemes were used prior to WWII because of the narrow range of pigments in paint.

Fella is an informal word for a male that is not age specific. It can also be used as universal term for either gender.

HG and Roy are a comedy team whose parody of sport commentary gained them a wide fan base and popularity across Australia. http://youtu.be/wY9aBjste5E

The Herald (also known as the Sydney Morning Herald or the Saturday Herald/Sunday Herald) was the oldest continuously published newspaper in Australia at the time when 'In and Out' is set. It is a supersized broadsheet newspaper.

H.E.C.S is short for Higher Education Contribution Scheme. It is an interest-free federal government free loan to Australian students who attend Australian tertiary education institutions and pays university fees. It becomes a tax when a student defers repayment until after study is completed. Repayment begins when the student's taxable income reaches a set level post study.

Keimera is a fictional town that incorporates features from three New South Wales towns: the coastal town of Kiama, rural towns of Camden and Goulburn.

Mate is used when a person is trying to achieve some kind of rapport. Originally, it referred to male relationships. By the late 1980s, anyone could be a mate.

MASH was a novel by Richard Hooker, later a feature film, and then a long running American a TV series. http://en.wikipedia.org/wiki/M*A*S*H_(TV_series)

The MASH trophy as used in 'In and Out of Step' is a parody of the above image and the two fingered gesture. This gesture is regarded as an insult in Australia, New Zealand, South Africa, Ireland, and the United Kingdom as the gesture signifies 'f*** off'.

The Melbourne Cup is the premier thoroughbred horse-racing event in Australia held on the first Tuesday in November each year. It is widely known as 'the race that stops the nation.'

Minties is an Australian iconic brand. It refers to a white, chewy, square mint-flavoured lolly in a wrapper (candy). A long running and very successful advertising campaign linked a wide range of everyday experiences (good and bad) with the catch phrase, 'It's moment like these, you need Minties.' After viewing the attached link, overseas readers may better appreciate the embedded joke on page 193 of 'In and Out of Step'. http://youtu.be/pFF3KNJH6JY

Mungo Jerry was an English rock group See http://youtu.be/yG0oBPtyNb0

Nong is Australian slang and is used as a mild and/or endearing insult. It means a bit of a twit, or idiot. Nothing too mean or horrid is meant by calling someone a nong.

Port Kembla is a major seaport south of Sydney NSW that was established in the late 1890's to facilitate the export of coal from the mines of the Illawarra region. Major steel works were subsequently established in the area.

Robert James Lee 'Bob Hawke AC GCL (born 9 December 1929) was the 23rd Prime Minister of Australia from March 1983 to December 1991 and therefore longest serving Australian Labor Party (ALP) Prime Minister.

RSL is an abbreviation for Returned Services League. Anyone who served in the Australian Defence Force (ADF) is eligible for full membership. The RSL provides vital advocacy services and support for all current and ex-serving ADF personnel as well as a club where people can meet and socialise.

Sloppy joe is an Australian term for a sweatshirts, windcheaters, sweaters or sweats.

A squatter's chair is a comfortable timber chair. The back is hinged at its base with the back of the seat. The inclination of the back is adjustable using a tube that is notched into the back of the timber arm rests.

A squatter was a grazier who had taken over a large bit of land without paying for it. They employed station hands known as 'blackfellas' to do a lot of the work.

'Sway' is used at the end of the novel to symbolise the relationship between Cassie and her mate. Ideally, the final scene would have closed on the lyrics.

TAFE is an abbreviation for Technical and Further Education. TAFE provides students over sixteen years with an alternative pathway to study that includes vocational courses as well as traineeships for industry and Defence. The learning and social environments are very different to that found in high schools. TAFE also provides night courses for mature aged students returning to study who did not graduate from high school.

The Rape of Persephone
http://www.mythicarts.com/writing/Persephone.html
http://www.youtube.com/watch?v=x5V67tY_Kh8
https://en.wikipedia.org/wiki/The_Rape_of_Proserpina

Trackie-daks are the bottom half of the tracksuit, not the whole. The whole tracksuit is the trackie. A tracksuit (made from stretch material or velour) is very commonly worn in Australia.

Toey is Australian slang for being on edge or excited or nervous.

The Sword of Damocles is an allusion to a legend (http://en.wikipedia.org/wiki/Damocles) by Paul Selton to comment on Talbut's precarious situation and the dangerous nature of the 'game' that he plays.

Tunnel has two meanings. Literally, it is a passage, often underground. In Australian surfers' slang, tunnel is used derogatively to refer to a woman; it reduces a women's value to her sexual organ.

Wee Waa is Australia's major cotton growing area. http://www.weewaa.com/Document1.aspx?id=217

A whiteboard is a name for a glossy, usually white surface. It replaced blackboards in Australian classrooms in the late 20th century. Erasable nonpermanent markers are used on it instead of chalk. As a matter of interest, in 2011, Smartboards have replaced whiteboards in many Australian schools.

Character List

The Sleight Family (rhymes with slate) and significant friends	
Cassie	Central character, a ballroom dancer, and first-year-out English teacher posted to Keimera High School
Leonie	Cassie's older sister
Nancy	Cassie's mother
Tom	Cassie's father
Jake Dominguez	Son of close friends of Sleight family, Cassie's childhood sweetheart
Melissa Pratt	Daughter of close friends of Sleight family
Madison House	
Significant secondary characters	
George Madison	Patriarch and owner of Madison House (a historically significant mansion from the 1800s in colonial Australia)
Minna Madison	Wife of George Madison, Michael's mother, Keimera alderman and past mayor of the township
Michael Madison	Heir to Madison House, only son of Minna and George Madison

Terry Kirkby	Boyfriend to Mavis Mills, a banker
Gary Putnam	A close friend of Terry Kirkby and one of Mavis Mills' admirers, active member of surf lifesaving movement in Keimera
The Mills Family	
Mavis Mills	A major secondary character, a gregarious country girl who aspires to make it as a singer
Marg Mills	Mavis' mother and a friend of the Madisons
Trevor Mills	Mavis' father and a friend of the Madisons
Keimera High School	
Significant secondary characters	
Keith Coachman (aka The Hitman)	Head Teacher of the English faculty
Mark Talbut	2IC of the English faculty
Paul Selton	Senior teacher within the English faculty and aligned with Van der Huffen
Valen Van der Huffen	Senior teacher within the English faculty and aligned with Selton
Rajes Chandran	Senior teacher within the English faculty, one of three women posted into the previously all-male English faculty in 1988

Samantha Smith	A teacher within the English faculty, one of three women posted into the previously all-male English faculty in 1988
Vince Pearce	An Art teacher at Keimera High
Minor characters	
Graham Fuller	English teacher and aligned with Talbut
Pothole (aka John Pothall)	English teacher
Doggy Barker (aka Rob Barker)	Deputy Principal of Keimera High School
Ewan Cameron	Principal of Keimera High School
Meri Bennett	A seventeen-year-old girl in Year 11
Tina Schwartz	A mature age Year 12 student
Chris Williams	A seventeen-year-old boy in Year 11
The Keimera Ballroom Dance Community	
Kate Denford (aka Ken)	Past girlfriend of Michael Madison, a ballroom dancer, active member of surf lifesaving movement in Keimera
Martin Jones	Ballroom dance teacher in Keimera

Life:
strands of colour,
separate yet interwoven.
Each hue
influences the weaving,
defines the other.

A complex tapestry:
indiscernible when close;
recognisable only at a distance.

Chapter 1

As she drove south from Sydney, Cassie Sleight wondered, How many people make decisions based on the emotion of the moment? Fed up with her impossible situation, when she had seen a means of escape the year before, she had taken it. Ticking the box *anywhere in New South Wales* on her application, she had left it to chance where she ended up in the approaching Bicentennial year. Cassie hoped now that she would not regret acting on that impulse.

With her view framed by her car window, Cassie turned off the highway toward Keimera. The road still glistened from the night rain. Tall, Norfolk pines marked the boundary of the harbour park on her left. A long string of shops stretched down the street on her right. Cabbage tree palms grew out of the footpath every few yards and shaded the shopping strip. Purple and white agapanthus bobbed in the morning breeze at street corners. There wasn't any sign in the town of the drought that gripped the hinterland.

Uplifted by the beauty of the township, Cassie drove slowly past the pink Federation post office, looking for a sign to the school, and then turned right toward the foothills. The street leading to the school was typical of coastal country towns. It was wide with a row of trees creating pools of shade down the centre.

Little of the school was visible from where Cassie parked. In fact, the place looked deserted. Aware that it was almost nine, she steadied herself by checking her make-up, scant though it was, in the rear-vision mirror. She settled her dark hair, hating the way the curl had tightened with the humidity. Not for her, the big hairstyles currently in vogue.

After locking the car door, she looked down at her clothing: a simple white shirt, a flowing denim skirt, and her favourite black shoes. She looked the part. All she had to do was be it. Teaching is another form of dance, she thought, a simple matter of learning the steps and getting in time to the rhythm of school life. I can do this.

With her footsteps echoing in the school driveway, Cassie looked for signage. She found a portable blackboard with ambiguous writing where the driveway opened into the main quadrangle.

Double doors? Which ones? There're lots, Cassie thought, scanning the area. It was then that she noticed the assembly dais much like the one used at her old high school. Given the conformity of school layouts, Cassie assumed that reception was in the far left corner obscured by the dais.

She was right. Pausing to visualise a confident entrance, she took a deep breath and pushed the opaque glass doors.

Inside, people stumbled, domino like, into one another. 'Hey, watch it!' protested a number of voices.

'Sorry.'

A man in jeans and a blue striped shirt near Cassie rubbed his shoulder while the dowdy woman next to him complained about the damage to her shoe and toes. Cassie looked at the crowd. Many of them wore variations of denim though a number had opted for beige or brown shorts, socks, and sports shirts. Had the school population grown in size or was there a big turnover in staff?

'Excuse me,' Cassie said, her path blocked. 'I need to get to the reception desk.'

Nothing happened.

'Excuse me,' Cassie spoke louder and tapped the shoulder of the man in front of her.

He turned and looked at her. His, 'Do I know you?' unnerved her.

'No … I'd just like to get through, please.'

Other eyes now focused on Cassie. She felt her cheeks quivering, swelling, reddening but knew it was mostly an illusion. When she was twelve, she had actually consulted a mirror and discovered that what others saw had little to do with her sense of self when under stress. Ignoring the speaker, she edged her way through to the centre glass cubicle and willed the red to subside.

The grey-haired receptionist, apparently deaf, took her details.

'Why hasn't that old mare been pastured?' It was a male speaking from somewhere nearby. Cassie looked at the receptionist. She obviously had not heard.

'I had to tell her four times!' the speaker continued.

Registration completed, Cassie waited, wedged between a pipe of a man and a barrel of a woman. Neither was inclined to talk. She glanced around the small room, looking for a friendly face or for someone who felt as lost and unsure as she did. Unsuccessful, she worked for self-possession through distraction.

Looking at her shoes, Cassie realised shoes were the only remaining link to her life as a dancer. Was that why she loved them? That day's shoes were from Spain and Flamenco in style. She loved the filigree lacework over the toes. The ratio between heel, arch, and ball was perfect.

A booming male voice read out three names, 'Chandran, Smith, Sleight.'

The crowd parted like the Red Sea allowing two women to enter the office to the right of the receptionist but it closed on Cassie. Exasperated by the deafness of the people in her path, she resorted to tapping, edging, and finally vigorously elbowing a route.

Stepping into the office, signed as Deputy Principal, she saw a man in the centre of the room. His dark hair was slick. His manner oozed authority. She assumed he was the Deputy Principal but soon realised her error.

The Deputy sat behind a paper-littered desk. His face resembled that of a basset hound, and he seemed small compared to the man before him. Cassie suppressed a smile when she heard the Deputy addressed as Mr Barker. Unfortunate name, she thought.

Cassie studied the two other women. They formed a sharp contrast to one another: a middle-aged Indian with beautifully coiffured hair and wearing a green sari, and a peroxide blonde whose dress hugged her full figure.

The Deputy Principal spoke, 'I assume you're Mrs Chandran.'

Rajes Chandran graciously inclined her head.

'I'm afraid that's where my powers of deduction end. Which of you is Sam Smith?'

'I am,' said the blonde, 'but I prefer to be called Samantha.'

'I see that you were a mobile teacher for six months at Wollongong. But you're a local though, right?'

'Yes. Wollongong was a long commute.'

'Hopefully, your probation paperwork will arrive in the fullness of time. And as for you, m' dear,' the Deputy now spoke to Cassie, 'years of education equip me to deduce that you are Cassandra Sleight.'

'Yes, sir,' Cassie replied, missing the attempt at humour.

'You realise that your probation is for a year? Keith

Coachman here is Head of English and History and your immediate supervisor. Apart from whole-of-school staff meetings, I'll have little to do with you apart from leave forms. You see Keith for everything else. I hope your stay with us is a long one, ladies. Unlike other faculties, Keith seems to have problems holding onto his female staff.'

'A matter of professional dedication. Literary subjects involve a lot more work and can't just be taught from a text book.' Coachman was dressed in a khaki suit, white shirt, and bow tie. 'Your orientation material, ladies, is upstairs.'

'And how many men does your department boast?' Rajes asked.

'Eleven.' Coachman directed his next comment at the Deputy. 'I had hoped repeated requests for a larger staff room would've been approved for this year.' He looked intensely at the Deputy. 'I'd like to tell the men we're moving in before classes resume.'

'Oh … I thought … the Boss decided that classroom pressures are too great. You'll have to stay put.'

'They won't like that especially with three girls to cram in. We're not sardines you know. At this rate, we might even start behaving like lemmings!'

'Not my decision; take it up with the Boss.' The Deputy Principal, sensitive to the potential for confrontation, shifted the papers on his desk.

Coachman weighed up the wisdom of a skirmish.

'On your way out, Keith,' the Deputy said without looking up, 'tell Jim I'm ready to see his new Science staff. I'll see you noon at the executive meeting.'

'Twelve?' Coachman's voice had an unexpected edge to it. 'I thought the meeting was at ten. Is it still in the Boss' office?'

'No, um …' The Deputy Principal's face flushed.

Coachman's brow beetled. 'Another of Rhonda's stuff ups?'

The Deputy hurried on, 'Oh well, I guess she's been pretty flat out down here. The venue has been changed to Home Ec. Kitchen 3. The Boss has decided to keep the Inner Sanctum clear of meetings this year. Don't forget to send Jim in with his new Science staff.'

The Deputy shifted the papers on his desk again. Cassie looked at Keith Coachman. Something was happening here. She didn't understand.

Coachman suppressed his quip, swept past the women, and headed toward his domain. The women followed in brisk pursuit.

The rest of the day was a blur of information and a muddle of impressions.

During the drive to the boarding house, Cassie sifted through the day's images. The staff room was cramped and hot. The men were a defensive pack obviously resentful of female intrusion. The English Head appeared to be a control freak. The identities of her colleagues were a jumble. Overwhelmed by the number of names she would have to learn, she did the maths: five classes times thirty students. God! That is one hundred and fifty names to know and identities to work out. Eleven men in the faculty, not to mention the rest of the staff! How will I ever remember them all?

Chapter 2

'Tea, George?' Minna Madison sat in a large wicker cane chair. She was a small woman who liked to think of herself as plump rather then overweight. Plump suggested an attractive, soft ripeness of the figure like in Rubens' paintings. George, her husband, thought of her as having a Mae West figure without the 'Come up and see me sometime' attitude. Minna loved life and everything in it.

Politically active since her twenties and on the local council as an independent, Minna had been the mayor for a number of years until the party machine ousted her through a series of unfounded accusations. Her regular, insightful articles written for the local newspaper extended her influence in the community, adding to the other aldermen's resentment. By contrast, her role as Branch President of the local Country Women's Association had been unchallenged and lengthy.

'I'm fine with this one, love,' George replied. 'I don't like the chances of those rock fishermen if their bait is what I think it is.' He had thinning grey hair and the characteristic oversized beer belly common among many older Australian males. He sat in a squatter's chair, binoculars glued to his face.

'I'm worried that we haven't heard from Mike. Tell me again what you said to him.'

'I can't remember the exact words, Min.'

'Don't expect you to. Just the salient points.'

'I told him about the vacancy at the newspaper but left it

to him to see the advantages compared to labouring.' George returned to his scrutiny of the anglers, moving to the southern end of the verandah.

Minna leant back in her chair and chewed her right thumbnail in contemplation. George had said so much less than she had wanted. With Mike, less was better. She knew that now.

It had taken Michael's unannounced departure north to teach her that. He'd left in anger and inflicted six months of sleepless nights and anguished days on them because his whereabouts were unknown. In the three years that followed, they saw him a mere handful of times. Minna felt the alienation in each courteous visit from him. Mike held her at a football oval's distance but not so George. His failure to understand her feelings strained the marriage.

'Min, one of them has caught something. A bloody snapper! Bigger than a politician's ego.'

Dimly registering George's conversation, Minna's thoughts were fixed on the past. Clever, athletic, and very social, Michael had been headstrong as a sixteen year old. He was restless when left to his own resources and always wanted to be out-and-about.

Minna's arguments with Michael mostly stemmed from what she thought of as misused time. She felt study had to be a priority. He was capable of being school dux. He should be dux. He would not be if football, dancing, and his mates continued to distract him. The scenes between them had been loud, emotional, and hurtful. Michael would not be steered. Needing defence, he had used knowledge of his parents' relationship problems as a weapon against his mother.

George had stood by mute, which Michael interpreted as censure of Minna. George's silence had infuriated her, as did its effect on Mike. She had fought battles on two fronts and lost.

The loss added to the rift between husband and wife that both masked with talk about the inconsequential and mundane.

Rattling around the expanse of the house, they had tried to cope with its sudden emptiness, each in their own way. George found comfort in increased workload while Minna turned her energies outward into the community. The only positive that Minna saw in her son's abrupt departure was the severing of his relationship with Kate Denford.

'Min, you're not listening to me!'

'I am. Something about a fish being landed. I'm glad someone got what they were fishing for.'

'Huh?'

Upset, Minna said, 'I need my sunnies. Won't be a tick.' Would she ever get over that grief, she wondered as she entered the house. She had hoped Michael would return with George the week before, and with that return, her hope for reconciliation be realised. Now, she thought, it might never happen.

Aware of his wife's upset, George wondered what he hadn't said.

On her return, Minna was again in control. 'And how was your day?'

'I've been wondering lately if the real killer of the elderly is boredom. Fishing, bowling, and relaxing aren't what I'd thought they'd be. What do other old men do with their lives once they retire?'

'You're not old. It takes time to adjust to changed circumstances.' She felt her emotions bubbling just below the surface and tried to cover them by pouring another cup of tea.

'Not for me, thanks. What I lack is a sense of purpose. Reasons to get up in the morning. You've got them. I need them.' George stood. 'Want a hand with the washing up before I go down to the pub, love?'

'No, thanks, I've some council work to do first. This will hold until the dinner wash up.'

'Righto. Dinner at seven?'

'Yes.'

Minna watched George saunter across the expanse of lawn at the front of the house. There wasn't any point trying to help him. An ideas man, he prided himself on finding solutions often before a problem presented. It was for that reason that they had taken in boarders after Michael's departure.

With land rates in Keimera spiralling upwards and worried that their income would expire before they did, George had persuaded Minna to rent rooms in their sprawling home, build up their nest egg, and enhance George's potential superannuation payout. Three of the four vacancies had filled quickly. The house again echoed with the clod of adult feet and the chatter of young people, distracting the Madisons from their son's absence.

On his way into town, George realised that his marriage had foundered on daily ritual and the pressures of life. They had been dry-docked, and he had not realised it until his retirement the year before. Since then, he had analysed his marriage, determined what was wanting, and how to refit it. The repair to the hull, all things going well, would be that night.

Chapter 3

Rounding the final curve leading to Pipers Point, Cassie caught her breath at the sight. Madison House, a white two-storey colonial mansion, dominated the crest of the peninsula and was the only house visible.

Pulling over, Cassie reread the directions on a small piece of paper that had bookmarked the street directory.

The reality of Madison House was far different from her expectation of a small family home with a room to let. It was obvious even to Cassie's uninformed eye that the house was historically significant and represented something of the former pastoral glory of the region. Why would someone who lived in a house like this rent rooms? As a child, she had wondered what life in such a house was like. Now she would find out.

Cassie looked back down the road before she pulled out. The view was fantastic with uninterrupted views of the town's harbour, its marina, and the southern coastline.

The driveway snaked up to the rear of the house, past two acres of terraced gardens that swept down to the cliffs. A large shed that at one time had housed tractors and other farm equipment now housed a car. To the right stood a garage.

Pebbles crunched under foot as Cassie walked toward the back verandah. A number of doors opened onto it. Unsure as to which door to knock at, she hesitated.

At that moment, Minna stepped onto the rear verandah. 'Yes?'

'I'd like to speak to Mrs Madison.'

'What can I do for you?'

'I'm Cassie Sleight … your new boarder.'

'Oh … I didn't expect you until much later. How's your friend?'

Random images from the past weekend came to Cassie's mind. A hospital gurney whisking Jake past his parents to the lifts that led to the operating rooms. His wife, Melissa's distress, 'It's all your fault, Cassie! Why did you call? I thought you'd accepted you were no longer in his life. Go away, and stay away for all our sakes! I never want to see you again; never, never, never ever again!'

Minna, disturbed by Cassie's distracted silence, said, 'I didn't mean to pry.'

'Oh … you weren't.' What could she say to close the matter without appearing rude? 'He's … on the mend.'

'Good. What do you want to do first: have a cuppa or see your room?'

'Tea would be great.'

The kitchen had wooden floors, a centre workbench, and a large Oregon table to the right of the room. Windows provided a sweeping harbour view.

'Something smells delicious, Mrs Madison …'

'Chocolate fudge. I'd rather you called me Minna. Everyone does.' She used a long bamboo skewer to check the fudge. 'One of the joys of having people in the house again is cooking.'

As they chatted, Minna studied Cassie. Striking eyes offset an attractive face that lacked the gilt of make-up common in her age group. Her discreet dress gave insight into her personality; in an era when women flaunted their physical attributes, Cassie covered hers.

Information about Keimera, the history of the family and

the house laced Minna's conversation during the tea ritual. Suffering from information overload, Cassie had zoned out of the conversation until Minna mentioned her work.

'How long have you been in politics, Minna?'

'Twenty years or so.'

'Wow! … You don't look like a feminist.'

'I'm not, at least not in the sense I think you mean. I was very much a part of my time, but then as now, there were many types of women … and agenda. Let's see your room, shall we?'

Feeling corrected, Cassie followed Minna who said over her shoulder, 'You'll meet my husband, George, tonight and the other boarders tomorrow. They won't be home till late.'

Three different shades of green summed up the décor of Cassie's huge room. The lower wall panels were a medium green broken by a dark green picture rail with a lighter green on the walls above it. The ceiling had ornate patterns and was a brilliant white. Small stained glass panels featured in the French doors that opened onto the upper verandah. Furnished with old world charm, the furniture was solid wood, not veneer like Cassie's room at home. The head and foot of the bed had a carved tulip panel in the centre. White netting edged in lace fell in graceful folds from a hoop that was suspended from the roof.

'Oh, I just love the bed.' Cassie sank onto it. 'I've always wanted one like this. The canopy is fantastic.'

'It's not really a canopy, love. It's a mosquito net, and you'll need it in summer.'

'But you've got fly screens on all the doors.'

'I know, but in old houses like this, there are still lots of mozzies, and no matter what I do, they thrive. I wish it was as easy as the advertisement says. You know, one flick and they're gone.'

'Anyone in the rooms next to mine?'

'Mavis is to the right. She's gone out to dinner from work tonight with our other boarders, Terry and Gary. You'll like her. Everyone does. The boys are great too. The other room is my son's, but he lives in Sydney. He's home sometimes. Your bathroom is down the corridor. I hope you don't mind sharing.'

* * *

Homesickness was something Cassie had anticipated but not the gnawing sense of loss. She forced herself to concentrate on the Madisons' conversation during dinner. Their teasing banter was very different from the way her parents behaved. It reminded her of the way she and Jake interacted.

She corrected herself, had interacted. Would she ever get over that?

'Not hungry?' George asked Cassie, noting the way she was playing with her food rather than eating it.

'Not really. The food is delicious though!'

'So dessert is out of the question then?' Minna asked.

Cassie nodded.

'George and I shouldn't either.'

Cassie laughed at George's reaction, one of mock deprivation.

'One look at your waistline, George, and Cassie knows you've had too much pass the lips already. C'mon, help me clear the table.'

As the trio shared the washing up, a body-resonating clap of thunder heralded the breaking storm. Minna sent George and Cassie to various parts of the house to secure it.

The upper floor echoed with the thud and rattle of blinds

and windows as Cassie raced from one room to the next, leaving hers to last.

From the upper floor, she called out, 'All secured up here. I've just my room to do.'

'When you've done, join us in the lounge,' Minna said. 'I'm not sure what's on the telly.'

'Thanks, but I've got things to do.'

When Cassie entered her room, the curtains were flapping wildly. After closing the windows, she found fragments of a cherished vase, a gift from Jake, over the floor. Distressed, she collected the pieces, placing them on a sheet of newspaper that somehow had missed the earlier disposal. She had unpacked her treasures first, out of anxiety about how they had survived the trip, but now regretted that decision.

Overwhelmed by an emotion, which she could not dam, Cassie sat on her bed. What is wrong with me? she thought. I haven't cried since …

When her grandfather died a few months before her sixteenth birthday, she had not cried. At his funeral, the rest of the family had been awash with emotion. Her mother had been inconsolable and leant on her father. Leonie, her older sister, make-up tear-tracked and mascara running, had tried to provide support to Cassie who looked ill, but as the emotion of the service built, Leonie's grief had given way to sobs. During the wake, Jake, Cassie's soul mate from childhood, had found her sitting silently in her grandfather's closet, inside Pop's dark blue overcoat.

Nor had she cried six months later after her first sexual encounter. Then as in the weeks that had followed Pop's funeral, she had suffered a terrible numbness followed later by headaches but not tears.

Now though, her distress flowed. Despite having chosen

exile, Cassie had not counted on how much she would miss her family: her mother's knack of saying the wrong thing when she tried to be helpful, her father's heartiness in the face of either of his daughters' distress, Leonie's advice, often unwanted but nonetheless motivated by love.

Disturbed by the unleashed emotion, Cassie worked to calm herself. She recalled her grandfather's words, 'You always have a choice.' For Pops, life had held only challenges, never obstacles.

Cassie said aloud, 'I'll make it work.' So she sought distraction by opening her last two boxes, records and a player, packed years earlier when she had ended her relationship with Jake and resurrected before leaving home.

Record player resting on her desk and plugged into the socket underneath it, Cassie chose Ravel's *La Valse, une poème choréographique*.

The music started quietly with the rumblings of the basses. Gradually, the other instruments joined in song, building in passion, drawing Cassie into the music. Without thinking, her hands and arms extended rhythmically, a visual expression of the melody. It felt good to express herself this way again.

Led by the violins, the orchestra and Cassie extended the movement into an enthusiastic waltz. As the waltz changed into whirling, emotions denied for so long found release. She felt like a trapeze artist working the highwire with a safety net. The explosion of energy at the end of the track matched her mood. With tears streaming unheeded down her cheeks, she sank to the floor.

Listening to the storm and the next track, *Le Jardin Feerique*, Cassie's breathing became calmer and her emotions quieter. She stretched out, rolled over, and looked at the ceiling. She liked the clarinets in this piece. I might be happy here, she thought.

Rising with the first movement of *Sonata for Violin and Piano in G Major*, Cassie looked out her window at the storm. The atmosphere created in the music sharply contrasted with it. I've been the reverse of this for years, she thought.

Downstairs, Minna sheltered inside the rear kitchen door wondering about the identity of their unexpected visitor. The exterior lights, which were on a timed switch until eleven, distorted the size of the approaching man, making him seem huge. With his coat pulled over his head to shield him from the driving rain, he rushed to the verandah.

'Bloody awful night!'

'Michael!' Minna wrapped her arms around him. 'George, it's Mike!'

'I know,' George said as he came up behind her.

'You expected this?'

'Known about it since Mike came down for his interview. Been killing me keeping the secret.'

'He got the job?' To Michael, she said, 'Really? Oh, Mike!'

Michael nodded.

Aware of surging emotion that threatened to overpower her, Minna said, 'That's great! Let Dad help with your bags.'

'What about making your famous scones, Mum, while I unpack?'

It was hard for Minna to contain her joy over her boy being home. As always, her mood somehow came through in her cooking. The scones rose to spectacular new heights. When she broke one to test it, the scone was light and delicately textured. She whipped the cream, lacing it with a touch of icing sugar. She scanned her preserves and jams for Michael's favourite – strawberry. She set the kitchen table with love and then went upstairs.

Usually indifferent to the first floor mirror that faced the stairs, Minna came to a standstill in front of it. It was always a shock to see herself these days. Would she ever get used to seeing this woman? In the angled study of her face, there were still glimpses of the way she mentally saw herself. Time and age were overtaking her though. Distracted by the effect of gravity, she headed to Michael's room, passing Cassie's closed door.

George had advised forging a new relationship with Michael and avoiding a rehash of the past with its minefields. Minna's instinct, however, told her that unless issues were resolved, they tainted the present.

At the door of Michael's room, she reassessed her impulse as she watched him unpack. A rogues gallery chronicled his football and dance achievements. Trophies lined the cedar dresser. Mosquito netting furled back and looped up high above the bed head.

Michael had changed from the boy she knew. He looked like her brother had at that age with the exception of the facial hair. She really did not like his beard, no matter how well trimmed.

'Scones ready?'

'Yes, but they're too hot for cream yet. Mike, I er … I just wanted to say …' Minna steadied herself with a deep breath. 'I regret very much what happened between us.' A surge of unexpected emotion caused her to pause. 'Socks still in your bottom chest drawer?'

'Uh huh.'

Using the commonplace to calm, Minna added, 'In all the yelling, I lost sight for a while that I … I love you. I never meant anything that I said in temper.' She was crying. 'Do you forgive me?'

'Mum!' Michael crossed and hugged her. 'There's nothing to forgive. It takes a lot of love to stick at it when someone behaves like I did. You never gave up. Dad's right about me finishing off my HSC at TAFE down here. Only fools knock back opportunities when they present themselves.'

My George is a gem, Minna thought, but she said, 'Your dad and I use a communication board kept in the kitchen now if one of us leaves the house before the other gets up. Saves worry.' Trying to be upbeat, she said, 'Well ... let's have those scones.'

'The scones, right!'

Michael kissed her on the cheek. 'I love you.'

* * *

After packing her records carefully in the bottom of her wardrobe, Cassie closed the door. She looked at the vase fragments resting on the newspaper. It really could not be pieced together. There would always be leaks. Consigning its fragments to her waste paper basket, she felt the regret of an adult farewelling childhood.

Crossing to her bed, she stepped on a small fragment of vase that she had missed. Extracting it, she thought, I really should vacuum. She found the laundry, which was adjacent to the kitchen and the rear verandah, and discovered an ancient vacuum cleaner. Cassie was halfway up the stairs and had crunched her foot twice underneath the vacuum when Minna, George, and a man entered the foyer from the lounge room.

'Room not to your liking?' Minna asked.

'It's fine, but the wind ... a vase is smashed.'

'Well, that's too heavy for you to carry. Mike?'

He responded by taking the steps two at a time.

'I really don't need any help.'

'Nonsense! Mike, Cassie is a teacher and our new boarder. Arrived this afternoon. Now, George, what did you want me to look at?' The elder Madisons disappeared into the lounge room.

Cassie looked up at Michael who stood on the step beside her. He was a head taller, lean, and muscular.

'Thanks, but I really can do it by myself.'

'Never any doubt about that. Let me help anyway. I've been out of Mum's good books for a while now. Acts of thoughtfulness may get me back in. So, where are we taking this monstrosity? She's had it since the Dark Ages.'

'My room is to the left,' Cassie said, disturbed by her response to him, 'the second last one in fact.'

Cassie trailed behind him with the nozzle, distracted by the hose that threatened to trip her progress.

Over his shoulder, Michael said, 'You don't look old enough to be a teacher.' He stopped unexpectedly.

Cassie bumped into him. 'Oh!' She felt her cheeks reddening. In her imagination, they were ballooning too. She clamped the lid on her nervousness, apologised, and stepped back. She hoped her voice was steady. 'You can put it down just there, thanks. I can manage the rest of the way.'

'Fair enough.'

'I thought you lived in Sydney.'

'Moved home tonight.'

'You must feel good then. It's hard being away from home.'

'Sure is, but it helped me work out what was important. Hope you like it here.'

He headed downstairs while she wheeled the cleaner into her room.

Chapter 4

Fragments of the past splintered Cassie's sleep. She woke around two and remained awake until just before dawn. With a couple of hours until her alarm went off, she fell asleep.

Sunlight streamed in through her bedroom windows; colours danced wildly across her bed and walls. Cassie struggled to throw off the weight of sleep, aware dimly that she had to get up. She raised herself on one shoulder and looked around for her alarm clock. Focusing was difficult. She climbed out of bed, threw on a dressing gown, grabbed a towel and the outfit she'd chosen the night before, and headed for the bathroom.

Knocking, Cassie called, 'Are you going to be much longer?'

'No,' came the muffled reply, 'just finishing my teeth.'

The door opened. A clean-shaven man stood before her, a towel wrapped around his lower torso. His body was tanned and perfectly sculpted.

'Oh,' Cassie said. Having grown up in a predominantly female household, she was unused to semi-naked men let alone one using her bathroom. Who was he anyway? she wondered.

'Sorry, slipped into old habits. I hope I haven't made you late.' He rushed past her without waiting for her reply.

'No, I've heaps of time,' Cassie said to his back.

* * *

The school buzzed with excitement. It was a splash of blue and green chequered skirts, white shirts, and grey shorts. Students streamed out of buses, cars, and off bicycles. They filled the driveway and poured into the main quadrangle, which was an obstacle course of hand-hammered balls, handball warriors, and rival tournaments.

Cassie took a deep breath, climbed out of her car, and wove her way through the tangle of teenagers. She visualised a poised, sophisticated woman. A thousand eyes bored into her. She slowed her breathing and prayed that she did not blush.

The stairs leading into the English block were congested with students.

'Excuse me, would you mind moving so I can get through?'

'You in the right place, Miss? This is the English block entrance. The Home Economics stairs are over there and the Music and Art are near the main office.'

'I know. Now, would you mind moving?'

Legs moved and an aisle appeared amidst the sea of bodies. Halfway up the stairs, she heard snatches of adolescent conversation.

'Geez! Tail bait in English, again!'

'Fun and games ahead, boys.'

'How long do you reckon this one will last?'

* * *

Coffee mug in hand, Cassie stood at the staff room window that overlooked the quadrangle. Teachers trickled through the quadrangle and into the administration area, but she did not recognise any of them.

The Deputy Principal and Keith Coachman stood on the stairs outside the administration area in intense discussion.

Approaching staff, noting the duo, detoured, taking a circuitous route through the doors leading into the English area.

The behaviour of a cluster of girls to the right of the quadrangle snagged her attention. They stood in a semicircle around a teacher, his long brown hair held loosely by a leather strip in the fashion of the seventies despite it being the late eighties. His behaviour in the group reminded her of Jake. Memories spilled unexpectedly at the thought of him.

Girls had discovered Jake in Year 7, his confidence and roguish smile the lure. They clustered around him like fish in a feeding frenzy. Cassie had felt as if her minnow friend was in shark-infested waters. It had been difficult relinquishing her place to breasted girls who mocked her for immaturity. So she drifted away to the grassed lawns earmarked as havens of girl gossip. On the bus trip home, Jake had sought her out, draping an arm over her shoulder, mostly around her neck, and reproached her for abandoning him. That had been enough for her, then. She had been happy.

And what am I now? Cassie wondered. She sipped her coffee and grimaced at the bitterness that had become stronger with the cooling. Watching the man with the teenage group below, she felt a surge of dislike for him. His swagger as he left the group flagged him as a lothario, a type she preferred to avoid.

Rinsing her mug, Cassie wondered when the others would arrive. The staff room was a sea of desks. Conditions were cramped, made worse by an oversized, rectangular table assigned to her.

The men, when they arrived, were noisy. They acknowledged Cassie's shy greeting but then ignored her. Camped in clusters around the centre table, their conversations interlaced and centred on cars, women, and the coming year's football team. Feeling overwhelmed, Cassie withdrew to the window again. She found being ignored comforting. It gave her time to learn about the men as they were, without the show some people assumed with strangers.

It seemed the men only used surnames to address each other. The most commanding of the men, dark skinned but not quite black, sat at a desk above which stretched an Aboriginal flag. The men called him Selton. Although only medium build, he dominated the room mostly because the other men deferred to him.

Standing next to him was the man she observed earlier in the playground, Talbut. Based on the facts of the story he was telling, he was definitely like Jake: an alpha male, irresistible to women, and cocksure. She hoped Jake never talked about her in that way.

Mistaking Cassie's attention, Talbut winked at her. She blushed, hating herself for doing so, and looked out the window.

The other women arrived.

Samantha Smith took a direct route to her desk, edging passed the men, a feline quality to her movement. Coming literally abreast of Talbut, Samantha said, 'Ah, I see you're not happy with your morning shave. And you are?'

'Mark Talbut, 2IC. Pleasant though this moment is, it's my duty to tell you that staff should be on site thirty minutes before the bell.'

Rajes Chandran chose a longer route to her desk, one with fewer encounters. Cassie liked her quiet dignity.

Talbut said, 'We need to get rid of this centre table. Traffic flow needs to be easier.'

The other men responded disjointedly.

'Can't do without it.'

'Need it for meetings.'

'Book returns.'

'Moderation sessions.'

'Reporting.'

'Lunch.'

'It's the only desk big enough for the Herald.'

A tall pale man dressed in black, Van der Huffen, gestured at Cassie. 'Isn't it her desk now?'

'That's not good enough,' Selton said.

'Luck of the draw, mate,' a nondescript unidentified man said. 'Coachman pulled the women's names out of a hat yesterday morning. Best that can be done until we get a new staff room.'

The morning bell rang, and the faculty became a flurry of crushed activity.

Outside the staff room, the corridors teemed with students. Some milled outside classrooms while others pushed their way through to distant rooms. The men strode up the corridors while the women followed, with varying degrees of confidence, in their wake.

It was a difficult day for Cassie. She lacked presence in her classes and battled spot fires of misbehaviour unsuccessfully. Lacking the power that came with knowing individuals, the group defeated her. By the day's end, the disorder of her classroom's furniture reflected her lack of control.

Downhearted, the heat of the car made her feel worse. She regretted now the lack of air-conditioning. Her father was right. Excluding it had been a false economy.

Driving through the town, Cassie felt an overwhelming urge to go home. There was just too much change in her life. Too much that was confronting. She wanted the comfort of family in spite of all its flaws.

Shelving her plan to explore the township, she headed back to Madison House. The thought of small talk with strangers added to her sense of loss.

The sea breeze was a welcome relief from the overpowering heat of her car.

Seeing her reflection in a kitchen window, Cassie realised she looked a sight. The order of her curls had been destroyed in the drive.

Aware now of the returning tide's song, she thought a swim would be better. Exercise always helped when she felt bad. Did she bring her swimmers though?

Voices from the front of the house carried to her. She so did not want to deal with strangers now. She felt frazzled. Needed space. Did not feel like being civil.

Crossing from the kitchen into the foyer as quietly as she could, Cassie reached the stairs before she was noticed.

'How did we miss you coming up the drive?' Minna called. 'Why don't you come outside and join us?'

I don't want to, Cassie thought, but she did anyway.

At the sight of Cassie, George said, 'You look like … windblown and hot. Maybe a swim would help?'

'That was my plan.'

'Have a cuppa first,' Minna said. 'Personally, I've always hated the feeling of drying salt on skin on the walk back to the house.'

'Walk?'

'It's what we all do here,' George said. 'Parking's an issue down town and at the pool.'

'Oh.'

Minna continued, 'And you remember Michael?'

Cassie focused on the clean-shaven man before her. 'Oh, that was you this morning? You look … younger.'

'Hair loss has a way of changing age, hasn't it, Dad?'

George scratched his head. 'Hasn't changed my good looks.'

'Michael's landed a job with the local newspaper,' Minna volunteered.

'Congratulations,' Cassie said, accepting a cup of tea without any intention of drinking it.

'Look,' Michael began, 'I'm going out soon to catch up with some old school friends. I can give you a lift to the pool if you like. The walk back is pretty good, sea breeze all the way.'

'Thanks. Michael or Mike?'

'I answer to either.'

'I won't be long.'

* * *

The rock pool was deep with currents that provided Cassie with pleasurable resistance as she swam. The area was crowded, but most people floated in the shallows. Cassie enjoyed the power of slicing through the water. It felt like velvet against her skin. Spent, she emerged from the water and towelled herself down, uncaring that her one piece was outdated. She now felt up to meeting the other boarders. Towel wrapped around her, she began the walk back.

The beeping of a car horn brought Cassie up sharply. 'Michael, what're you doing here?'

'My plans changed so I thought I might as well give you a lift. You should've seen your face when Dad suggested the walk back.'

She laughed, aware that she could not remember the last time she had done so spontaneously.

'I'm not really as slack as that. In fact, I like walking.'

Driving through the township and unready to return home just yet, Michael said, 'Feel like an ice cream?'

'Looking like this?'

'Sure. People do it all the time in seaside towns. It's not like anyone knows you yet. A parking spot! Looks like we were meant to stop.' Without waiting for a decision, he swung his car into the angled park position.

Resenting what she saw as highhanded behaviour, Cassie said, 'I haven't agreed.'

'I know, but it was worth claiming the spot while you made up your mind. Notice the engine still running. If you'd rather go back now, we can.'

'Oh ... that's very considerate of you.'

'Not really. It's a natural reaction. That sort of thing was an issue between my parents when I was growing up. I think Dad was mostly a modern man, but he inherited attitudes from his father that Mum challenged. I couldn't help but learn the lessons he learnt.'

'I haven't thought about my friends much since I left,' Michael continued as Cassie and he found seating, ice creams in hand, outside the Great Australian Ice Creamery situated in the main street. 'I guess I assumed life for them was the same old same ol'. Stupid really, given the way the town's grown.'

'Not stupid. It happens with migrants all the time. They carry a memory of home as it was and not how it is evolving. How could it be otherwise?'

'Well, I've been home a handful of times though not to catch up with friends.'

'So what made you leave in the first place?'

'I thought my parents were too controlling. School seemed to be a waste of time. I soon wised up though it was hard to admit it.'

'It takes a lot of strength to face the reality of ... mistakes ... and to go beyond them.'

'Speaking from experience?' Michael asked.

Cassie nodded. It occurred to her, with unexpected insight, that when she thought of Jake it was as he had been and not as the person he had become.

'You don't strike me as the rebellious type, Cassie.'

'Oh, I wasn't, not in the usual sense. I wanted ...' She thought of the arguments with Jake: melodramatic scenes followed by Jake tearing up the driveway on his bike, then later in his yellow Morgan – a dust cloud marking his departure; the reconciliations: his heart-felt apology as he stood on the other side of the front door screen, the joy of reconnection; the attempts to go beyond the type of relationship their parents had. 'I knew what I didn't want but not much more.'

'And now?'

'Well, I'm here, not knowing what's around the corner, and a bit scared I've made another mistake.'

'If you have, you can always go back. That's the good thing about boarding, isn't it? You can walk away any time without worrying about leases, furniture and all that other stuff.'

'So what made you come home?' Cassie asked.

'Heaps of things. I was sick of labouring all day and doing TAFE at night. Dad told me of a job with the local paper so I jumped at it. I'll be finished my HSC this year. Journalism might be an option. I thought this job might be a foot in the door for a cadetship.' Popping the last of his ice cream cone into his mouth, Michael asked, 'Seen much of the town?'

'I've been here two days and most of that time at work. I like the look of it though.'

'We could have a wander before heading back.'

In the stroll down the main street, Michael outlined how the town had changed in his absence. Cassie enjoyed the camaraderie and the lack of expectation. Catching sight of her reflection, she did a double take. Her hair had dried and reminded her of a clown's wig. She wasn't fussed but amused by how different she looked. It was good to be just two people talking without shared baggage and expectations.

Chapter 5

Humming, **Minna put the final touches** to the dining table for that night's dinner to celebrate the prodigal's return. She had been dubious about George's plan to take in boarders but had agreed to it anyway. She had questioned his assurances that Michael would return. How many times, she wondered, had she wrongly doubted him?

'Wow!' Cassie said, standing on the threshold of the now empty room.

The dining table seated twelve. Made from cedar, the table-top gleamed. The chairs had intricately woven tapestry cushions and sculpted backs. An antique sideboard, that would have been too large for contemporary houses, stood against the wall opposite the French windows. Moulded cornices decorated with an embossed grape and vine pattern concealed the join of the fifteen-foot ceiling to the walls. A huge oriental rug protected the highly polished floors from the drag of the chairs. Clearly, life had been lavish here in the past.

'Bloody great room, isn't it?' Gary said, edging past her with the first bain-marie for the sideboard. He ran his hand along its carved ornate detail. 'Makes you want to work in wood, doesn't it? C'mon, there's a lot more to come. We all lend a hand here.'

* * *

With her curtain of long black hair, Mavis Mills exuded personality as she sat at the end of the table, retelling a yarn about a recent surf club competition that she had watched with Terry Kirkby and in which Gary Putnam had participated. Responsive to fashion trends, she wore a fitted black top and a red flouncy, short skirt over black spandex leggings. The telling of the yarn seesawed between Mavis and Gary, with both adding embellishments the other had omitted.

An avid surfer and lifesaver, Gary, like Mavis, enjoyed telling a good yarn. He tolerated Mavis' additions and corrections in good humour. His Hawaiian shirt, acid washed jeans, and a left pierced earring marked him as a man of fashion.

Cassie thought they seemed well matched and a fun couple. So it came as a surprise to her during the meal when she realised that the quieter male boarder, Terry Kirkby, was Mavis' boyfriend.

Terry in appearance seemed to be a conservative man. He was, however, master of a worldly air and listened in tolerant amusement to the yarn, treading the fence of dispute when Mavis and Gary differed over the facts. He did not understand the drive to use their lives as performance material, but he kept that to himself.

Appealed to by both, Terry hummed and hawed in mutterings. Neither Mavis nor Gary waited for confirmation. They relaunched into the telling, laughing at each other's comments and jumping in when the other paused for breath.

When the meal ended, Cassie was surprised when the men joined automatically in clearing the table and the washing up. The men she knew would never have dreamt of such a thing.

In the kitchen, Michael said quietly to Cassie, 'You were pretty quiet at dinner. You okay?'

'I guess I'm nervous about tomorrow. Besides, I don't compete.'

'Another difference between us,' Michael said. 'I love the adrenaline that comes with competition.'

'That's not —'

Mavis interrupted them, speaking to Cassie. 'Why don't you come to the pub with Terry and me later?'

'Another time. I've heaps of prep to get through before school tomorrow.' She did not add that without it she would be unable to avoid the chaos of the classroom that she had experienced that day.

Unable to bear the throbbing, walled-in heat of her bedroom any longer, Cassie gathered her work and moved to the lower front verandah.

The onshore wind provided pleasant relief from the heat, the only negative: the feasting mosquitoes. Cassie wished that she could quash her longing for home as easily as she squashed the mozzies. She needed to talk to someone who understood her. She considered phoning Leonie but rejected the idea because of privacy issues.

Mid evening, the screen door creaked. Cassie looked up.

'Will it disturb you if I have a smoke? I don't like polluting the house,' George asked.

'It's your verandah … I'm sorry, I didn't mean to sound rude.' She returned to her work.

George faded into the night. The scrapings of the squatter's chair broke Cassie's concentration. She looked up and watched George fuss with the angle of his chair.

'Why are you sitting over there?' Cassie asked.

'Don't know if the things they are saying about passive smoking are true, but prevention is better than cure.'

'Oh … that's … um … very considerate of you.'

George tamped the tobacco in his pipe.

The cicadas' chorus mingled with the strains of the television. Cassie worked in silence. The surf hushed over the rocks at the base of Pipers Point.

The screen door creaked open again on Mavis and Terry.

'God, it's stifling inside!' Terry said to no one in particular. 'Gary and Mike are playing darts out back. We're off to the harbour park for a while and then the pub.'

Mavis spoke to Cassie, 'It's beautiful down there this time of night and a lot cooler. The pub is air-conditioned as well. You sure you don't want to come?'

'Thanks, but no. I've still got some work to finish.'

The couple disappeared into the night, their voices floating back on the evening breeze. Cassie remembered times when she had been in similar accord with Jake: hunting for crabs from under rocks at the seaside, sharing fish and chips down at the Richmond shops, working on their dance routines after school. She missed him. Did he ...? Why do this to yourself? an inner voice asked. The past is the past. Stay with the present.

'I said, sometimes a worry is halved by sharing it,' George said as he puffed on his pipe.

'I'm sorry, what did you say?'

George removed his pipe and considered Cassie. 'Kids difficult, were they?'

'That's one way of describing them.'

'Beginnings are mostly overwhelming. Add to that the wit and parry of human interaction and ...'

'I'd hardly call today wit and parry,' said Cassie as she thought back on the day.

The day had been horrible.

Irrespective of the age group, Cassie's experience was the

same. Students, sitting in conversational cliques, ignored her. Restless boys played piggy-in-the-middle. The noise, similar to the cacophony of a poultry shed, echoed and carried to quieter classrooms. Standing at the front of the class wanting to do something, Cassie did not know how to make herself heard, let alone gain control.

In the staff room at lunch, the men's perspective added to Cassie's humiliation.

A member of the shorts and long sock brigade said, 'And so another love hate relationship renews itself.'

Someone said, 'Let's hope this year's honeymoon lasts longer than Mrs Smith's banana.'

Cassie turned to see Samantha flush, her banana poised mid mouth.

'I prefer Ms, thank you,' Samantha said.

Talbut, of the trim and taut swimmer's build, said, 'Damn it, Fuller! You've ruined the vicarious ecstasy of her eating. Really, some sensitivity is required now there are women on the team.'

'Honeymoon?' Samantha asked, covering her banana with its peel before putting it on her desk. A little later, she put it in the bin.

'The first week or so the kids are subdued while they get your measure. Then you see their true colours.'

'Well, to all you fans and bandwagonists,' Selton said raising his coffee mug in a mock toast, 'this season will undoubtedly test the mettle and pluck of our recruits.'

'Their grit and resolution in the heat of battle,' Van der Huffen added, his signature colour of black already a distinguishing characteristic to the women.

'Let's hope education doesn't get a bad rap because of …' Selton added.

'Inexperience? Ineptitude?' one of the men offered.

'More like dubious allocations,' Selton finished.

Cassie was relieved that her lack of control in her classes eluded comment.

'Most uncharitable of you,' Van der Huffen responded, looking at Talbut and his group of men, 'in word and planned deed.'

'Shabby,' Selton added.

'You follow our drift?' Van der Huffen said to the men, 'A reflection of the ignoble spirit that drives —'

'Give it a rest,' Fuller said. 'We get it! You're not party to that book.'

'Were Selton and I ever?'

'And sadly the wheels are already wobbling on the faculty wagon,' Talbut said. 'So ladies, how did you find your classes?'

Cassie, like the other women, was as closed as a poker player when the stakes were high. She did not get an opportunity to discuss the female experience in private before the other women left for the day.

Returning to the present, Cassie stared at the flickering lights on the harbour waters, the sea's surging against the rocks a background sound. When next she spoke, it was more to herself. 'Maybe I'm not the right personality for teaching.'

'Been thinking the same about myself and retirement,' George said.

'Oh, sorry, forgot you were there.'

'Why the doubt?'

'I was more ignored than heard today. I felt so … inadequate … demeaned.'

'You didn't look upset this arvo.'

'I felt terrible though.'

Packing up, Cassie thought about her reaction to the day.

It had been quite different from Samantha Smith's, her voluptuous colleague, who had been loudly angry about the way her
classes had behaved. Anger seemed to inject Samantha with
energy that enabled her to return her to the classroom battle.
By contrast, Cassie had seen the day as just one more thing
in her life to endure. What should her reaction have been?

'Cassie, I reckon kids are much like fish. They avoid the
hook. A fisherman, new to an area, should observe the locals,
learn from them, and only then set up his line for casting. Fish
don't bite straight away. They nibble at the bait before getting
hooked. Perseverance is the key to success, y' know.'

'I've been saying that to myself since … It helps hearing
someone else's perspective though. Thanks.'

Minna came to the screen door, 'Supper in five minutes
in the kitchen.'

On a rare impulse, Cassie hugged George.

Taken aback, George asked, 'What's that for?'

As embarrassed as George, Cassie tried for a calm that she
was far from feeling. 'For listening and caring.'

On the way upstairs, Cassie thought about the future. Her
life, like a road, had curved. From what she had experienced
at the school, it looked like she was travelling up a mountain:
the roads icy, visibility poor, the ascent steep, and beyond …
uncharted country.

Chapter 6

Stressed, often nauseated, described Cassie during February. Her stomach knotted in the morning as she left the staff room and headed downstairs to her timetabled room. Her mantra was, 'Where there's a will, there's a way'.

In the first week, the student collective worked effectively against Cassie, ignoring her presence. Paper planes and a variety of small objects flew around the room. Students clumped together, talking at volume. Feet were up on tables. Chairs tilted backwards precariously against walls. Unable to make herself heard above the general din, she wrote the work on the board and then moved from one desk to the next, from group to group. Bodies deflected and walled her out. In breaks, she decided against returning to the staff room; she dreaded wisecracks about her incompetence.

During the last lesson of that week, thwarted and ashamed, Cassie slumped against the classroom wall, looking into the quadrangle. Elsewhere, she could see classes at work. Feeling like dust on a shelf, she wondered about the key to cooperation.

Looking at her students, Cassie's depression lifted with the dry realisation that she was audience to a form of performance art. They are, she thought, *A Study in Disruption*. Then what am I?

In the face of Cassie's quiet despair, her class was indifferent. Their egocentricity awakened her appreciation of the black comedy in the situation. I could be called …? What?

Dance Novice replied an inner voice. But I've never been a wallflower though, she thought and re-entered the battle.

When the bell signalled the end of the day, her students rushed for the door, ignoring her. All over the school, students streamed into the quadrangle, down the driveway and onto buses. In similar fashion, staff throughout the school collected their bags from staff rooms and headed home or for the pub.

Anticipating criticism from her colleagues, Cassie delayed return to the staff room. A silence, unnatural in the school day, settled in the building. As she entered the deserted, concrete stairwell, Rajes came down.

'Oh!'

'Cassie, I thought I had missed you. Do you feel up to celebrating the end of our first week at The Salty Prince?'

The unexpected kindness unlocked the strongbox containing the turmoil of Cassie's emotions: the indignity of that first week in the classroom, her deprecating self-assessment, the final months leading up to her departure, the sense of loss: family, Jake, her image of herself as a teacher.

'I think Selton summed it up best today when he told Samantha that the beginning is like slogging uphill in a landslide of mud during heavy rain.' Rajes smiled sympathetically at Cassie. 'We have all been through it and survived.'

Cassie's suppressed emotion released itself in tears.

Rajes put her arm around Cassie and sat with her on the bottom stair.

The tears changed to sobs. Frightened by the magnitude of her emotion, Cassie battled for control. This was not the sort of woman she wanted to be – powerless like her mother and the women of that generation! Cassie fought against the distress.

A cleaner entered the building, took in the women with

concern, and moved on after Rajes responded silently to a voiceless query.

Unaware of that brief exchange, Cassie focused on the tempo of her breathing. Counted the inhalation, increasing its depth with each breath. Thought about the hardness of the concrete step on which she sat.

'My first week teaching in Australia was a nightmare too. I can't tell you that this week was the worst. I can say that if we work hard and are true to the task then we can make a difference even though we may never realise the scale of it. Samantha had a good cry before she left. She asked me to tell you that she would see you next week. You're not up to coffee, are you? Would you like company while you pack up?'

'No.' Cassie's voice reflected her returning calm, but the emotional undercurrents were still audible. 'Have a good weekend.'

'Oh, all right, and you too.'

On her way upstairs, Cassie considered her dislike of emotional outbursts. As a child, she had seen her mother resort to tears when all else had failed with Cassie's father. It didn't work though. It just made her look pathetic. Today, Cassie did not feel demeaned but cleansed and something bigger … relieved.

* * *

The weekend passed quickly, divided between sleep, schoolwork, and the distraction of the Madisons' banter. As for the other residents, they were out of sight and mind. Cassie's only contact with them was at the evening meal when they shared competing stories about the day. A phone call home helped Cassie ease the emptiness caused by separation from the people she loved. That became the box, the structure for that part of her life in the weeks that followed.

In the second week, the pattern of student defiance continued but with more exaggerated behaviours. Cassie, however, had a small but significant win; she realised that lunch and recess breaks were useful allies. When the bell rang, she stood in the doorway blocking the exit.

Daunted but unmoveable, she held up a makeshift A3 sign: SILENCE NEEDED BEFORE DEPARTURE. It came slowly. The first time she attempted it, fifteen minutes of the recess passed before she achieved her objective.

'From now on,' Cassie said, 'you'll get out on time if you've made an effort to do the work. Anyone who hasn't will be kept in. You can do the work in the scheduled break. That's only fair given you took the break in class time.'

'You can't do that!' was the response from a press of boys pushing forward but stopping short of contact.

'We have a right to recess. You'll get in trouble if we don't get a break!' said a loudmouthed girl with huge blonde hair, wider than she was tall. Her peer group bleated their agreement.

Again, Cassie held up the sign.

'Oh, you'll get a break but the minimum required under the law and not the full time that kids who work get.' Cassie made a mental note to confirm that time constraint with Rajes.

There was a breath of time between the end of the detentions and the beginning of the next block of lessons. Energised by the glimmer of control over her classes, she raced up the stairs, found the staff room almost emptied, grabbed her work as well as a quick drink, and sprinted back to her room. She saw little of her male colleagues beyond the blur of the rush. Samantha shared a wry comment whenever they passed, usually eliciting an unexpected laugh. Rajes, serene in her progress, always took time for encouragement.

For lessons that were not followed by a break, Cassie used the same tactic but made up a detention list. She issued late slips with non-compliance as the reason for the delay to the next class. At such times, she often faced two classes: the incoming and the outgoing, the thud of student feet signalling arrival. Throughout all of this, she maintained a positive demeanour despite feeling weighed down. With the room finally empty, Cassie restored the upturned tables and chairs before the next war for control began.

As different classes cycled through recess and lunchtime detentions, the number of students complying in her classes increased. With that, the nature of lessons changed. Cassie still wrote an overview of the lesson's work up on the board but added photocopies of the actual work as handouts. Finally, the student wall of resistance cracked when some of the kids decided they would rather be outside with their friends.

That win continued to be outweighed by Cassie's inability to sustain on-task behaviour for any length of time. Once she had moved to another section of the room, those making a show of work stopped and joined in the disruption. To combat this, she maintained a constant circuit, influencing whomever she could.

In the third week, when the bell rang for recess or lunch, the press of bodies continued to confront her. Though feeling intimidated, Cassie refused to give way. The A3 sign was still the only means to achieve silence.

Silence gained, she said, 'I'm going to monitor what you get done in fifteen minute segments. Anyone who doesn't get enough work done will be on detention. I'll initial your books at each check to avoid last minute shows of work, and from now on, wait at your desks until called for the exit check. The bell is my signal not yours! If you try to leave without being called, you'll be the last to be checked.'

As each student gained exit rights, Cassie made a point of praising work done, no matter how little, and set each student a personal goal for the next lesson. It was also an opportunity to learn student names. In the margin of a log, which she kept so that her progress comments would be meaningful, she penned a visual clue to prompt her memory when they next met. She found satisfaction in the dynamic change, small though it had been.

At the end of detentions, Cassie calmed herself with a deep breathing exercise that she had used prior to dance competition. Being centred was more important to her than a break and a cuppa. It was essential for maintaining her mask of quiet containment in front of her classes. Besides, she found the staff room too cramped for her physical comfort as well as suffocating in those hot summer months.

At the end of each day, Cassie returned to the staff room to find everyone gone. Relieved and alone, she sat quietly for thirty minutes or so, collecting herself before she left.

Conforming to a weekly pattern, Cassie phoned home collect. Her parents now knew of her battle for control in the classroom, the pride she took in small victories, and the toll it was taking.

'It's not a matter of giving up, Pumpkin,' Tom, her father, said on the other end of the phone, 'but a matter of changing the battlefield. There are plenty of schools up here. Come home and end this exile.'

'I'll think about it, Dad.' And Cassie did, in every lesson throughout the rest of that month.

* * *

In the tradition of generations before them, George and Minna had afternoon tea on the front verandah in the summer months. For Cassie, it was a period of respite from her workday stresses. Driving away from school, she found herself looking forward to it. In the languid moments over iced tea, she enjoyed their talk about town. It provided a window into a life very different from anything she had experienced. Their disagreements were games of verbal sparring ending in laughter.

As for the other occupants of Madison House, she continued to see little of them beyond the continued camaraderie of the evening meal.

At night, Cassie's preparation for the next school day consumed her. She had to find the key to being an effective teacher.

Minna, looking in on her one night, said, 'We work to live, Cassie, not live to work.'

'I know, but teaching's not like normal jobs where you go to work and the work is there waiting for you. Apart from working out how to teach the stuff, I have to invent it. And then there's marking.'

'Well if you have to spend so much time on it why not work on the verandah with us after dinner,' Minna said. 'You're not getting to know anyone here.'

'Okay, I'll think about it. If you don't mind, Minna, I've got to get this done if I'm to get any sleep tonight.'

When sleep finally embraced Cassie, it was hot and restless. At times, nightmares possessed her. On some level, her mind recognised it as the past revisited. A reassuring inner voice helped her break free. Don't cry. It's the nightmare. You're okay. You can pull yourself out of it. You can! Wake up! Wake up!

Why, she wondered as she lay awake listening to the song of the surf, why have these nightmares returned? The best sleep, deep and dark, was in the early hours of the morning. It ended too soon with the jarring ring of her bedside alarm.

* * *

During the slow crawl through February and into March, a hard core of recalcitrants worked against Cassie in each class. In detention, they refused to work and waited her out. Time ultimately was on their side. At an impasse, Cassie realised she needed to change tactics. The problem: to what?

The solution grew out of her need for relief from the classroom. She realised that the hard long slog for control might take the year. Without food and strong coffee, the battle would be impossible to sustain.

Committed to breaking the resistance, Cassie checked off her detention list. 'From now on, all you have to do is give me ten minutes of sustained silence and stillness. I'm timing each of you.'

When students attempted any kind of disruption or distraction, she said with the façade of compassion, 'And you were going so well too. What a pity! I'll have to restart your time.' That ticked the individual off. Time divided the peer group.

Aware that her tactic might fail if they all continued to leave together, Cassie pretended that one boy, Mick Fryor – the weak link in 10G, achieved the goal. Near enough was good enough in this context. He swaggered out of the room with a smug last look at his peers. That departure triggered an unexpected change in Year 8 and 9 students. Randomly, they settled and worked off their time. Each departure weighed the scale of control in Cassie's favour. The whir of overhead fans could finally be heard.

The leaders of the resistance from each year group waited out the legal amount of detention time and left with a throw-away comment like, 'That bitch is a lousy teacher!' or 'That tunnel needs to be taught a lesson.'

'Tunnel?' The surfer's slang initially lacked meaning for her. Slowly over the day, she understood. Shocked, she wondered about the culture that produced such an image. No wonder she was having trouble with the boys.

* * *

'It's got me beat,' George said to Minna, turning off the television. 'I don't think we can say anything to Mike about hitting the books.' A clock chimed twelve in the background.

'I'm frightened that the past is repeating itself, George,' Minna said, returning her mug to the coffee table.

'It won't if we react differently.'

'But what if he blows this chance?'

'Then he obviously doesn't want the opportunities that come with study. I told Mike he could live life as he wants, Min. I can't go back on that.'

A door closing sounded from the kitchen. Leaning side-ways, Minna said, 'Shush, it's Mike.' She reached for a maga-zine in the rack beside her chair.

Looking at the wall clock, George said, 'Didn't expect to see you back so soon.'

'Didn't you? It is midnight, Dad. No comment from you, Mum?'

A test or a challenge? Minna wondered. Michael seemed to her to be in a playful mood. Should she risk it? She was aware of George's thought directed at her though he did not look that way.

'Nothing much,' Minna said, 'other than your dad and I need to cut down on how much coffee we drink. We've been too wired to sleep.'

'That why you're up?'

'No doubt about it. I think I'll make us some warm milk, George, to help us sleep. Michael?'

'I'll pass,' Michael said.

Chapter 7

'**M**anagement of student behaviour,' Coachman said in his fortnightly interview with Cassie that Monday morning, 'rests primarily with the classroom teacher. Strategies should take into account student differences, natural justice principles, and child protection guidelines.'

'But even the best lesson fails if a teacher can't get them to listen and cooperate. I need help.'

'You don't know that, now do you? As a probationer, your role is to take direction. Stimulating lesson plans are the solution to your problem. I see none of it in this.' He gestured at the detailed work before him. He handed her a wire bound booklet. 'In there you'll find prototypes of effective lessons. Use them as a model.'

'I didn't mean that sort of help.'

'If you can't stand the heat, get out of the kitchen. As for intervention, that will only occur in dire circumstance.'

'And what exactly constitutes that?'

'You are dismissed, Miss Sleight.'

Looking at him, Cassie refused to be treated like a schoolgirl.

When she did not move, Coachman said, 'If you want to stay at this school, you'll have to stand on your own two feet.'

* * *

The cost of a phone call, Nancy Sleight thought as she accepted reverse charges, is measured by what is accomplished.

'The kids are awful, Mum. My boss is the original chauvinist.'

'Perhaps not the original one, Cassie.'

'You're right. He's not that old, but, Mum, he's out of touch with the changes of the last twenty years.'

'Do you remember me telling you and Leonie what Grandma told me about life?'

'What's that got to do with …?' Cassie put a stop on her impatience. There was intent behind the comment. She just had to wait until her mother arrived at it. 'Why?'

'Do you remember it?'

Cassie repressed the urge to parrot the answer. She waited.

'That as long as men and women have been on the earth that women had always been water and men stone.'

'Yes,' Cassie sighed wearily, 'I know.'

'That holds true even in the workplace. Water goes around barriers, adapts to the landscape, and in turn the landscape is shaped by it. The result: spectacular landscapes. We want you to come home,' Nancy paused and checked that Tom was out of earshot, 'but I think it's important you persevere. Men have a complexity that you need to appreciate if you are ever to see their real worth. Don't run away. Come home to be recharged, but stay the course. Then come home for good. You'll be a stronger woman.'

Nancy hoped that Cassie would develop tenacity from the experience. She worried about her daughters' futures given their unrealistic expectations of men. Unless there was a change in them, they would miss out on happiness.

The three-minute warning beep sounded. 'That's been twelve minutes; your dad will have a fit! Really think about what I've said, Cassie. Love you.'

'Thanks for listening, Mum. Love you too.' Hanging up, Cassie wondered why it couldn't be two ways with men expected to adapt to women too.

* * *

'And so Persephone emerges from Hades,' Samantha said as Cassie entered the staff room.

'Oh, hi! What did you say?'

'How did another day in hell go?' Samantha sat at her desk, student workbooks piled to the right and left of her. Her olive green skirt and fitted white shirt emphasised her figure.

Cassie dumped her materials temporarily on her chair, ordered her desk, and pushed her colleagues' discards to the far end of the table. 'I'll feel better when I have some control of at least this part of my school life.' She looked at the information on the huge staff whiteboard above the desks to her left. 'Do you understand any of that wider school stuff?'

'No. I work on the assumption that I'll be told when I miss something. I'm about to make a fresh pot if you feel like a cuppa.' Samantha did not, however, move.

'Thanks. Not into teabags?'

'I believe in having the real thing.'

'Oh, Persephone, I get it! I hope my story's different from hers.'

'No dark god in your life determined to have you?'

Unsettled, Cassie said, 'As a kid, I used to think it such a romantic story. Not now.'

'You've got to admit that sort of passion is attractive.'

'Not if it's unwanted.'

'Personally, I like to be lusted after.'

Lust and desire. Cassie knew that heat. Memory flickered

… Long blades of grass in her sightline. Fingers trailing over her face, body.

Cassie shook off the memory. 'There's a drive in lust to possess that overrides the other person's right to choose.'

'Do you think?' Samantha said still at her desk.

'Look at the story of Persephone, any version. Hades was the prime player. He took what he wanted. His passion plunged her into a world she wasn't prepared for and didn't want to go to. How frightening must that have been? And then the months of darkness! No thought by him of what she had lost.'

Samantha looked at her, head askance. She considered probing the experience behind this interpretation but decided against it. 'My Gran was always big on the tea ritual. She liked the time it took and called it meditation. I doubt the quality of the teabag experience. Seems to me that you'd benefit from the calm of the tea ritual.'

Cassie laughed. 'Is that your way of asking me to make it?'

'I'm giving you the choice of making it. Gran said that the objective of the tea ritual is to live in the moment and focus on the sense appeal: the sound of the water as it comes to the boil, the effect of light on water as it flows from one point to another, the aroma of the leaves, the silence as the tea steeps.'

'When you describe it like that how can I refuse?'

'Exactly!'

With her shoes kicked off, her legs stretched out to the adjacent chair, and savouring the tea, Cassie said, 'This is nice.'

'The tea?'

'That and having company. How come you're still here?'

'My car's in the workshop for two days so I have to wait for my hubby to get me.' Samantha luxuriated in the unaccustomed space. 'It's good to stop. I'm still crashing after work. Steven hates that I'm asleep when he comes home. What about you?'

'I get tired, but don't seem to relax enough to sleep properly. I'm running on adrenaline.'

'That's like a sugar high, right?'

'Yes, sugar causes a release of adrenal hormones.'

'Sure you're teaching the right subject?'

'I'm not sure that I should be teaching at all.'

'You and me both, but money keeps us here, doesn't it? What else could you do?'

When a child, Cassie had thought that she would be a dancer. In the adult life she imagined, she starred as a modern-day Ginger Rogers. That childhood daydream disappeared the day her nightmare was born. Dark memories seeped into her now despite the daylight. She had to keep the lid on that emotional box and so tuned back in to hear Samantha say, 'You need to surface for air a lot more than you do. Bonds in the staff room are as important as control in your classes.'

'I'm not comfortable in here.'

'And you never will be unless you make the effort, Cassie.'

'I don't like people in my personal space.'

'Yes, but you can make it work for you. Flirtation and the promise of something more has always been a valuable tool for women since God knows when.'

'That's so not me, Samantha. My sister flirts, but I don't think that's why. Men still in cliques?'

'At times, but there is … fellowship? I think that best describes it. They play a competitive game of quotes that is fun. I'm not sure whether they are pretentious or just really knowledgeable. I listen in awe, not that I let them know it.

You'll find it's a lot better now than at the start. Talbut is inclusive not to mention incredibly supportive. Make the effort to spend more time here in the breaks.'

'I'll try.'

'Not good enough. Make it happen. You're acting like teaching is a prison sentence without time off for good behaviour. Even God took a break.'

'So what's your advice for getting more time off?'

'Use the system.' Samantha waved a wad of A4 pages at her.

'What're they?'

'Behavioural records.'

'Did I miss that in the orientation?'

'No. Talbut told me about it one afternoon down at the pub. Everyone chills down there Fridays. Talbut invited me. He is a useful man to know, charming too. You should come too. Here, have a read; it's one of my early entries.'

Cassie looked at the record sheet. 'I get the foot stamping too. How does this work?'

'When kids build up enough documentation, they get after-school detentions with the Head Teachers and stay there until a significant change is seen in class. It works. Sid used to be a horror. Now he's intermittently awful, but I've hope he'll evolve.'

'Where do you get the time for this?'

'Before school. I arrive after the cleaners at six and sometimes return to school after I've had a sleep, and work till lockup. My husband thinks I'm nuts, but then he's not at the chalkface. A system is only as good as its users, Cassie. Talbut will help if you ask. Once he saw how distressed I was, he came into my classes, got them settled, and reminded them how warnings, timeout desk, and detention were really the road to suspension.'

'Didn't that reinforce the boys' perception that women are weak?'

'Don't know. Don't care. What matters is that with Talbut's backing I have some control. Talbut says that the only things that work with the hard cases are the arvo detentions and caning.'

'Caning? Bullying bullies isn't an acceptable solution.'

'Implementing consequences is not the same as bullying. Talbut says that for some it is the only brake that halts the behaviour.'

'I doubt that!'

'Don't tell me you're one of those "violence breeds violence" types. It doesn't, and I know that for a fact!'

So, you've experienced violence in your childhood too, Cassie thought. Growing up, Cassie had thought her family the exception, not the rule. Both Leonie and she had been exposed to violence, a lot of it in their childhood, because of their father's heavy drinking. They had heard it but not seen it. That exposure had led to an abhorrence, not endorsement. How true was that moral teaching? Cassie wondered. Was the aggression in her classes the result of their background or something else?

Papers thrust at Cassie brought her out of her reverie.

'This is some stuff that I found useful.' Samantha paused. 'And I didn't mean to be hostile. It's just my disgust at …' A horn sounded in the quadrangle. 'My husband! Talk to Talbut. See you.'

At Samantha's request, Talbut stayed after work the day following Cassie's conversation with her. When he materialised from behind the staff room door where he'd been scanning the faculty resource bookshelf, Cassie jumped, dropping books she'd been carrying.

'Sorry, didn't mean to startle you. Sam said you like weak tea, no milk and sugar. That right? If so, I've one on the sink for you.'

As she sipped the tea, which was a little too strong for her liking, Cassie described her experiences and strategies to date. Talbut sat at the centre table, arms outstretched on the desk, hands clasped, listening and occasionally nodding. He struck her as a man of reason and compassion.

'What you don't know is that Coachman and his cronies regularly offload the worst classes on incoming staff. I argue against it every time, but Selton and Vander always win out.'

'What?'

'You and the other women were set up. It's been a pattern here for some time. It happens at lots of schools.'

Cassie faintly remembered the Deputy's reference on the first day to Coachman's difficulty in keeping female staff.

'As for Coachman's crap about your problem being the result of ineffective teaching, forget it. Survival and success is dependent on establishing clear behavioural parameters and consequences if they are crossed. As I said to Sam, make the system work for you, and the battle is won.'

'Yes, she's filled me in.'

'Did she? … Well, you can relocate up to two of the little beasties to me at any given time.'

'That's really kind of you.'

'You'll find that when they lose their peer audience …'

'They're disempowered.'

'They hate it. Of course, you will need individual lesson plans and work organised in the eventuality that such relocations are needed. Can't have anyone claiming the kids are being denied their educational opportunity, not that they do any work when they are in class.'

Buoyed by the possibility of respite, Cassie headed for the car park with Talbut. He directed her, left hand gently placed in the middle of her back. His praise at her uncomplaining persistence was like the first rain after a long drought.

'Sam's shortcoming as a teacher is that she's hot-headed and reacts as a victim. You, my dear, have been stoic in your lack of complaint. Like I said to Sam, I'm more than happy to function as your unofficial mentor.' Talbut closed the car door for her.

'Thank you so much. I don't know how I can repay you.'

'Tit for tat.'

'Yes,' Cassie said not really understanding his meaning.

Master of all he surveyed, Talbut watched her drive off before he sauntered back to the staffroom.

Driving toward the township, Cassie thought about Samantha's reference to Persephone. Cassie could see the parallels. She was not out of that dark land yet, but she had begun her journey. She had no intention of surrendering control to anyone again.

* * *

In search of female companionship that Saturday morning, Mavis stood in the doorway to Cassie's room surveying the pile of books on the floor, the scatter of papers, and Cassie's wilting body over her desk. Mavis had liked the look of Cassie from their first meeting but keeping Terry happy was a priority that took up most of Mavis' free time. With Terry away that day on a business trip, Mavis had time on her hands. The French doors that led onto the verandah were wide open. A warm breeze billowed the translucent curtains.

'Are you okay?'

Cassie jolted back to her surroundings; her vision blurred. 'I'm just tired. I must've dropped off.'

'You're always working. I thought teaching was supposed to be a cushy job.'

'I wish.'

'Hmmm. Being a perfectionist isn't always a good thing.'

'Perfectionist? I'm trying to survive. I've gone back over all my lecture notes.' Cassie gestured to the pile of paperwork on the floor, many of which had been disturbed by the breeze. 'There isn't anything that tells me how to get out of the minutia of lesson prep.'

'Can't you leave the work till tomorrow? The elves aren't goin' to steal it.'

'I wish.'

'Talkin' might help clear your head. What's your boss' advice?'

'Nothing constructive other than a paternal hand pat and a suggestion that I'd be better suited to a career as a secretary. He seems oblivious to the fact that teaching has been a female path forever.'

'In high schools? The only women teachers when I went to Keimera were in Art, Music, and Home Ec. I always thought women taught primary school and men … look, is anyone else approachable?'

'Yes, Talbut and the women.'

Propped on Cassie's bed, Mavis said, 'I remember Talbut from when I went to school. Smooth as.'

Cassie waited for the comparison to be completed.

Mavis continued, not understanding Cassie's expression. 'He married a girl from my year group after a hot and steamy flirtation. So what did they suggest?'

Distracted by Mavis' revelation, Cassie asked, 'Who?'

'Talbut and the women.'

'Oh, I'm following Rajes' advice on control techniques.' Cassie smiled. 'She's a lovely woman. Talbut's been a great help the last two weeks, explaining jargon and documentation processes. Detention is still my middle name though.' Relocation of kids to Talbut would be her final resort.

'Huh?'

'I have kids on detention every day.'

'So you punish yourself as well as them?'

'That's about it, Mavis.'

'Then you definitely need a break!'

'I can't afford the time.'

'Sure you can. Not having a life hasn't worked so far. What's to lose?'

'Nothing when you put it like that.'

'C'mon then, let's get out of here. Keimera is a great place this time of year.'

Cassie looked at her room, realising she needed to live beyond it. 'Okay.'

Mavis linked arms with Cassie as they walked downstairs. 'I missed the luxury of a close female friend. I used to talk to my mum about stuff, but we're a bit out of step these days. Maybe we could talk sometimes about … y' know, about relationships.'

Sharing, it was what Cassie missed most. Being alone is disempowering, she thought. It was a throw away thought, but its truth hit her, literally stopped her mid-stairwell.

'Somethin' wrong?'

'No,' Cassie laughed, 'Just further confirmation that I'm on the right track.'

* * *

Weekends in the warmth of autumn brought out the day-trippers. Keimera, despite its distance from Sydney, was a popular destination. A carnival atmosphere pervaded Keimera that warm Saturday afternoon.

Local artists had set up a gallery alongside the footpaths that crisscrossed the parkland between the main street running parallel to the ocean, and the road that led north to Sydney. On the retail side of the main street, outdoor cafes were packed.

Blues music filled the air. After buying double-scooped ice cream, chocolate and macadamia from the ice creamery, Mavis and Cassie headed down to the grassed foreshore. A marquee and stage dominated the area and a large chalkboard outlined the afternoon program.

'Isn't this great?' Mavis said, visibly excited.

'The music?'

'All of it!'

'It really is!' Cassie restrained her urge to walk in time to the music.

'Hey, Mr Infield, good to see you up and about again,' Mavis said.

'Legs are better than the rest of my body.' He did a little jig to demonstrate. 'When're your parents comin' into town again?'

'Not sure.'

'Tell your dad ...'

Mavis followed Mr Infield's gaze but could not at first see what had distracted him.

'Second thoughts, I'll speak to him myself. Have a good one, Mavis.'

'Bye.' Mavis looked after him thoughtfully. She watched him cross the road to a familiar white Commodore. Her father leant against his car, indulging in his love of chocolate ice cream. It was a simple pleasure and one that father and daughter had relished whenever they came to town.

Mavis choked with emotion. She had waited a long time for just this opportunity.

'I'll be back in a tick,' Mavis said to Cassie. She threaded her way through the crowd, delayed by people she knew. All the time, Mavis kept her eyes on her father. Of her parents, he was the softer, the more forgiving. Her mother had been the disciplinarian and her father the peacemaker. She needed him onside if she was to have a chance with her mum.

Usually, Mavis enjoyed the intimacy of life in a small town, but the delay of friends and acquaintances irritated her now. Within speaking distance of her father, she saw her mother struggling with white plastic shopping bags. Her father disposed of his ice cream in a nearby bin so that he could help Marg, his wife.

Trevor said, 'You said it was only a few things you were getting.'

'I know, but ...' Marg saw Mavis first.

Dimly aware of the people around her, Mavis closed the distance. 'Mum. Dad.'

'Mavis,' her father replied. Marg was at a loss for words. She had imagined their first meeting as an emotional reconciliation; blame pushed aside.

Trevor took the bags off his wife and moved to the boot. 'Give us a hand with the key will you, love?'

In reflex, Mavis crossed to her father unaware that he had been talking to Marg. She extracted the key from the tangle of the stretched plastic bag handles and his fingers, flicked the automatic release button, and lifted the lid.

'Thanks.'

Marg remained transfixed to the spot, silent.

'You're lookin' well, Dad.'

'Feelin' it.'

'Stayin' for the festival?'

'No interest in that sort of thing these days.'

It was an awkward moment filled with hundreds of things that needed to be said but weren't.

Trevor turned his back on Mavis; she was devastated.

'You're lookin' well,' Marg finally found her voice. 'I looked on the flyer, but your name wasn't there.'

'I haven't had enough time to build up my repertoire, not with work and all.' Mavis looked at the back of her father's head as he moved to open his car door.

'Maybe next year?'

'Maybe.'

'Have you got time for a cuppa?' Marg asked looking around for a suitable venue. She remembered that the Lions had a tea tent set up over near the street artists.

'Oh, I'd like one, but I've left my friend down on the grass. I'd have to let —'

'Don't bother,' Trevor said. He did not want to see Terry. 'I've got a man comin' about some land. Ready, Marg?'

Wide-eyed, Marg looked from husband to daughter. Her life had escaped her like this, at someone else's demand. With dignity, she looked at her husband and then crossed to Mavis and embraced her.

It was an awkward moment. Shocked by her father's rebuff, Mavis received the embrace but did not reciprocate.

Marg fought back the tears that came with what she saw as rejection. 'Always remember we love you.' Marg climbed into the car. She used the business of door closing and window wind down to push away the distress. 'Come home and visit. Bring anyone you want.'

The Mills drove out of town in silence, stoic in their distress.

After a while, Marg, her voice tight with emotion, said, 'How could you?'

The miles sped past in tense silence.

* * *

The reality of 'As ye sow, so shall ye reap' had never been clearer to Trevor Mills, Mavis' father. Reviewing each stage of his life as the car sped homeward, the result was the same.

His father had lived on the fringe of family life well into Trevor's teens because farm life consumed his father by day and the pub by night. When his father had tried to become more involved in the family unit during Trevor's teens, Trevor had rebelled and rejected that involvement. For Trevor, his father's interest had come too late.

When Trevor married Marg, they had begun their life on assumptions. They had not planned how to live, they just did. Patterns were set in place that could not be broken.

Osmosis-like, the world around Trevor had changed in the sixties. Working long hours in relative isolation, he knew little of life beyond the farm and less about the dynamics of other families. It was not the sort of thing he talked about at the pub. As pub life changed and gender segregated areas disappeared, Trevor spent less time there; mostly, he thought, because Mavis had become a little person and cried when he went anywhere without her.

A doting father, Trevor had not said, 'No,' to Mavis till her teens despite Marg's voiced concern. Although money had been in short supply, the Mills gave Mavis what they could. Trevor put off replacing gates with cattle grids, rewiring sagging fences, and general building maintenance. Trevor and Marg went without the niceties of life using what money they had for Mavis' music tuition, a first class piano, and a quality guitar - a Maton.

Slowly, Trevor had sold off parcels of their land to developers to keep the property going and to give Mavis a chance for a better life. Each sale though had cut into Trevor's heart; his forebears' collective spirit was buried in the land they had battled nature to hold.

That pain was offset by the pleasure he found when Mavis starred in high school musicals, performed at the annual City and Bush Schools Spectacular, and was selected for camps run by the Conservatorium of Music in Sydney.

That pleasure faded under the strain of Mavis' teenage years. Though Trevor understood her need for friends, he did not understand how anyone could over-book weekend activities. He was hurt by Mavis' failure to understand that he lacked the time, money, and inclination to rush her from one thing to the next.

Anger overtook Trevor when Mavis persisted in playing her disco music loudly— the Bee Gees were popular at the time—but he left the discipline to Marg while he escaped outdoors to work. At fifteen, when Mavis tried to transform into her icon, Blondie, Trevor and Marg argued privately before Marg had the strength to curtail her daughter's dress excesses.

With the unexpected dive in her school grades, Trevor told Mavis in quiet, measured words, 'We can't afford tutoring, but you'll have it. How can —?'

Mavis had covered her ears with her hands, and walked off singing *Heart of Glass* loudly.

'Why?' Marg had asked. 'Why is she like this? Surely, other girls' parents aren't as casual about their daughters as Mavis claims? Have the times changed that much?'

Trevor lacked answers. For the first time, he wondered, Was this the crop they had planted?

Over the next few years, Trevor suffered Marg's broken heart and hid his own.

Then Mavis had become involved with Terry Kirkby. Mavis had been eighteen at the time and had recently been employed as a singer at the Keimera pub. The only positive about Terry was that he put a brake on Mavis' imitation of Madonna.

Trevor objected to Terry on several grounds. From the beginning, his relationship with Mavis was full on. Her circle of friends decreased the longer she was with him. Terry talked big, but he behaved in a small way. He claimed to earn a lot of money and yet, aside from the car, there was little evidence of it. An expensive date for him was going to the movies. Mavis believed him when he said that he would support her so that she could pursue her career in music when he gained sufficient seniority in the finance industry. Her parents thought it was talk. Finally, he was eight years older than their daughter.

From Trevor's experience, people who came on hot and fast lacked staying power. They had known many people like that in their youth. At the six-month mark, this seemed to be the case with Terry. He stopped seeing Mavis after her performance at the pub on Friday nights. Her father had to pick her up. Terry's time with Mavis on Saturdays reduced to half a day. When he was visiting the Mills, he referred to his friends and experiences. The Mills wondered why Mavis had not been included. They chided her for being too available and for settling for less than she deserved.

When the Mills shared their concerns with Mavis, it backfired on them. She shut down, accused them of being controlling and living their failed lives through her. 'Terry thinks so too,' she had said.

Looking back, Trevor saw the harvest came from teaching Mavis that only her wants mattered. They had assumed reciprocity without taking time to cultivate it. That was how he came to terms with her behaviour before she left home at nineteen.

That Friday night, Mavis had left for work as usual but had taken a duffle bag with her. The Mills waited a good part of the night for her return. Then Trevor drove into town and around it on the off-chance that he might see her. He phoned in on the hour to see if she had come in. This proved more difficult than anticipated as most phone booths had been vandalised.

Saturday was a nightmare for them. The Mills did not know where Terry lived. They lacked contact details for Mavis' few remaining friends.

Saturday night, Trevor drove back to Keimera to the pub to see if his daughter was at least alive. He watched her performance from the shadows of the bar; anger replacing relief. To his disgust, Mavis was at her vibrant best.

Without speaking to her, Trevor returned home. His resentment at Mavis' ingratitude grew with each mile.

Sunday was a silent hell. Shock immobilised her parents that night, when Mavis returned, packed her things, left her cross-stitch, and moved out.

* * *

Sitting on a dappled stretch of grass, Cassie listened to the music, enjoying the festival spectacle. It seemed to her that everything and everyone moved in time with the music. It feels good to be on the edge of the scene, she thought. She frowned. Why don't I feel like Melissa did?

As a child, Cassie had been in the thick of it. Melissa had been the observer despite her vocal protest. Why don't I feel like that? Cassie wondered. An inner voice replied, Because you choose to be on the outside here. You were as unhappy before you left.

For Cassie, the afternoon passed languorously with Mavis periodically standing to chat to people she knew. Unused to her, she failed to note Mavis' quietness or her feigned moments of brightness when people stopped to chat. Occasionally, Cassie tuned into what was being said.

'I don't really have that big a blues list,' Mavis said to one couple who inquired why she wasn't on the bill. 'Besides, I don't write songs like that.'

'So you're an artist?' Cassie asked when Mavis sat down.

'Of sorts. I sing at the main pub Fridays and alternate Saturday nights. You should come down sometime.'

'When I get the time.'

'Hi,' Mavis was on her feet and distracted by her friends when the Seltons approached.

'G'day, Cassie.' Selton's deep tones were unmistakeable.

She scrambled to her feet.

'This is my wife, Mary, and this,' he patted his wife's emerging pregnant stomach, 'is our long awaited son.'

'Or daughter.'

'Congratulations.'

Mary looked at her husband; this was a battle she had thought won. 'All that matters is that baby is healthy and whole, either sex will be fine. Right, Paul?'

'I know … healthy and whole that's what counts, but the Seltons have always had boys first. Unlike Henry VIII, I know how a child's sex is determined. No harm in being optimistic, eh?'

Cassie smiled. Their interaction reminded her of her grandparents, one always qualifying the remark of the other, irrespective of the audience.

Mary refrained from further comment.

'You haven't seen the Chandrans have you, Cassie?' Paul asked. 'We're supposed to meet somewhere around here before dinner at the pub.'

'No, sorry.'

The Seltons chatted with Cassie for a while and then moved on. In parting, Selton said, 'If you see Rajes, tell her we're strolling down to the marina and then back to the pub by the road. You're welcome to join us if you want.'

It felt good to be included and yet not be under obligation. 'Thanks, but Mavis and I have the afternoon planned.'

As they moved off, Cassie heard Mary say to Paul, 'You're putting way too much pressure on me when you go on about the baby being a boy. As for him becoming a barrister and helping win our ancestral rights for land … Way too much to put on any child.'

'But Mary …' The rest of Selton's rejoinder was lost as they disappeared into the crowd.

In the process of sitting, Cassie noticed Talbut at the other end of the park. At a distance, she again saw Talbut's likeness to Jake. They both had presence in a crowd. Talbut's stance was different though. He did not settle back on his heels as Jake did but appeared watchful, definitely not relaxed despite the setting. There was an intensity in their manner with women that went beyond awareness. Watching Talbut standing close to Samantha, Cassie remembered the sense of intimacy, the feeling of being valued. They were physically different though. Jake's Spanish heritage was imprinted on his handsome features.

Interested in people, Cassie continued watching the couple, noting their separation when a second man joined Talbut and Samantha. The husband, Cassie guessed: a tall thin man with the slight stoop of someone who had never been comfortable with his height. He wrapped a possessive arm around Samantha's waist. She seemed to enjoy the obvious tension between the two men.

The contrast between the men was sharp, making Talbut's confidence appear as cockiness. He has allure. She realised she had been wrong to let his likeness to Jake shape her perception of him. He was willing to empower her rather than wrest control from her as Jake had done.

Talbut excused himself from the pair with what Cassie now recognised as a distinctive lean in and hand touch manoeuvre. He sauntered off towards the Lions' sausage sizzle but a bevy of adolescent girls intercepted him. The girls were alike in dress and manner: short snug skirts, tight shirts with revealing necklines, and standing a little too close to Talbut for it to be respectable. They definitely came on to him. Funny, Cassie thought, men are like birds, always puffing up in the presence of the other sex. Talbut is used to being 'the big man', and he likes it! Most people would.

Talbut left the girls, again the lean and touch gesture, and joined the sausage sizzle line where he greeted more townspeople. He appeared to be respected.

'Well?' Mavis said, back on the ground next to Cassie. 'Feel like heading back to the house?'

'Sure.'

Chapter 8

'**M**r Coachman, may I speak to you?' Cassie asked, coming into the staff room that recess, late as usual.

Coachman glanced at her, noted that she was a woman on a mission, and said, 'You know the rule. No shop talk during breaks.'

The men, with whom Coachman sat, continued their conversation in the background.

'But this is urgent,' Cassie persisted.

'Not now.'

'But there must be times —'

'This is my break,' Coachman interrupted. 'You have Monday interviews to discuss work with me.'

Manoeuvre mangled, Cassie thought. With her access to her desk blocked by the men sitting around it, Cassie considered retreat to the library but rejected the idea. Looking at Selton because he seemed to be the most responsive, she waited. He reacted by standing and moved into the corridor saying, 'Okay, you mob, make way.'

Amid complaints, Cassie edged her way to her area at the centre table. The men who had been sitting around it, moved up to one end.

'Typical of women,' Talbut said. 'Can't let a man have a moment's peace.'

Samantha looked at him sharply.

'I don't get your point,' Cassie said.

'Ah, that's the problem, Cassie,' interrupted Talbut, 'but any one of us would be pleased if you did. We'd line up in fact. It would contribute significantly to my own satisfaction.'

'What?' Cassie said, not understanding.

Most of the men laughed, not Selton or Van der Huffen.

'Oh!' Getting the inference, Cassie frowned at Talbut who preened himself, pleased with the response from the men. She did not like this unexpected side of him. Did not like people who got a laugh at another's expense. Focusing now on her workspace, Cassie saw the discard of crates and some of her things on the floor and under the table.

Gesturing at her things on the floor Cassie said as coolly as she could, 'Didn't anyone notice this or did you all just step over it? I don't care what this table used to be, it's my work station now!' She held down her distress by drawing on a pre-competition breathing technique before she picked her things up.

Van der Huffen initiated the transfer of books and crates from Cassie's table. He passed them to Selton who stacked them outside the staff room. She smiled appreciatively at them before picking up her things.

'So what's the duff on a bigger staff room, Keith?' Selton asked.

'I'm keeping up the pressure. It's a matter of understanding the big picture.' Coachman registered the relocation of the books outside the staff room. 'You can't leave books in the corridor!'

'I'll have two kids from my next class move them to the book room,' Van der Huffen offered.

While restoring order to her table Cassie said, 'As for innuendo, Talbut, don't direct it at me. It's offensive.' She sat down, aware that she was quivering inside.

'Bravo,' Rajes mouthed wordlessly to Cassie.

'Excessive sensibility is inappropriate in the workplace,' Coachman said to Cassie. 'You need to develop a sense of humour. I thought women of your generation were supposed to be sexually liberated.'

'We are,' Samantha said, looking up from her work, 'but among other things, we've also gained the right to draw the line, and since 1984, there's been a law to protect that right.' She smiled sweetly at Coachman.

Surprised by Samantha's support, Cassie also looked at her, but Samantha had returned to her marking.

The other men withdrew into private conversations.

* * *

Sitting on the top verandah step, Mavis cackled every time she won a hand of Gin.

'There's nothing like a sensitive winner,' Terry said, nudging her in the ribs.

'Don't; I'm ticklish!'

'Are we playin' cards or what?' Gary asked.

The front screen door opened on Minna. 'Guess who I ran into today, George? Martha Mays.' Minna set down the supper tray at the table where Michael and Cassie were working. George sat across from them.

'C'mon, fellas, you're not scared of losing another game, are you?' Mavis said.

'Hhmm!' George grunted distractedly without looking up from the paper he was reading.

'No point playin' when someone's on a lucky roll,' Gary said.

'You know her. She's the eldest Walsh daughter, married …' Minna continued.

'How ungenerous of you, Gary; it's sheer skill. No luck about it! Terry, talk him into another hand.'

'Who did she marry?' Minna scanned her memory of genealogical records.

'No idea,' George replied.

'Shuffle the deck real good, Terry,' Gary said, 'and we'll cut twice just to be sure.'

'His family settled here after the Black Friday fires in Victoria. When was that?'

'1939,' George said. 'You don't forget fires like that even if you only read about them in the papers. The New South Wales 1951-52 summer season was a shocker as well. I reckon we're heading that way again if the drought doesn't end.'

'Oh, it doesn't matter who she married, the thing is you know her,' Minna continued.

'Know a Nev Mays, used to be on the volunteer fire brigade with me.'

'That's him! Well —'

'Nev planned for retirement ten years before he bit the bullet! Knew exactly what he'd do with the rest of his life. Should look him up.' George stood. 'Wonder if he's in the phone book?' He crossed to where Minna stood.

'You can be so exasperating!' Minna said.

'Don't know what you're on about, woman.'

'You don't listen to me, George.'

'We've been talking, haven't we?'

They went inside, their voices low in argument.

'Read 'em and weep, fellas,' Mavis chortled, 'Gin again!'

'No!' both men spoke in unison.

'That's it!' Gary threw his cards in.

'Let me see,' Mavis said innocently. 'That's eighteen hands I've won tonight! You have been creamed! Annihilated!

Terry, Gary, I've news for you,
From the style of your playin' you haven't a clue.
Luck and skill are at my command,
I've been ready for your cards hand after hand.'

Michael met Cassie's amused gaze and held it. Self-conscious, she returned to her work, allowing her hair to fall forward shielding her face. She regretted that retreat immediately, feeling like a silly schoolgirl. Cassie was aware of Mavis standing nearby, the rhythmic beat tattooed by her on the verandah rail, and her chant.

'Chance and opportunity abandoned you men.
It's time you admitted I'm the Boss, my friends.
I have dazzled, rattled, and out-gamed you both.
It's time you conceded you're burnt, you're toast.
When you're hot, you're hot! When you're not, you're not!'

Cassie forced herself to look at Michael. 'How's life?' she asked.

Mavis' chant and her interaction with Terry and Gary receded into the background.

Michael replied, 'Great! I managed to find some old friends and pick up more or less where we left off. You seeing light at the end of the tunnel yet?'

'I'm getting there.'

'If you don't take real breaks, Cassie, you won't make the distance.'

'That the logic behind your late nights, is it? I'm surprised your parents haven't said anything to you. If you don't put time into study, you'll only ever have a job. Kiss the thought of a career goodbye.'

'Nuh, life has to be lived while working toward goals, not put off until some distant endpoint. If you don't have the skills to cook the dish then you shouldn't consider being in the kitchen.'

'What?' Cassie bristled. He sounded like Coachman.

'If I can't keep the balance between work, study, and play then maybe I'm chasing the wrong goal. Uni will be heaps more demanding than school. If it takes me all my waking hours to get good results, I'm not going to cut the grade there, am I?' Aware of the tension between them now, Michael said, 'I'm going to see *Rain Man* next weekend. Why not come along?'

'I'll think about it.'

'Even God took some down time, Cassie.'

Meanwhile, Mavis' chant came to an end,

'Well, my friends, you'll have to catch me first.

I'm fitter and faster, you won't match my burst.

When you're hot, you're hot! When you're not, you're not!'

With that, Mavis ran off across the lawns toward the town. The men followed. Hoots and laughter faded as the trio moved out of sound and sight.

Chapter 9

Home! Cassie felt a growing peace as each mile brought her closer to her family. The road sang in excitement as her white car sped out of Windsor, passed the air force base on her right, through the arch of plane trees that lined the Windsor-Richmond road. The leaves were thinning, a prelude to the skeletal starkness of winter.

The car slowed as it skirted the edges of Richmond, the railway station to her left. Picking up speed as town gave way to country, Cassie headed toward the Hawkesbury River, sprawling homes surrounded by lush pastures to the left, the polo field on the right.

The shopping complex at North Richmond was typical of small country settlements: a post office, shops, a petrol station, and the obligatory pub. It was early and her parents, creatures of habit, never went out before ten.

Cassie pulled up at what looked like the original corner store and bought her mother some flowers and her dad the Saturday Herald. She chatted with the owners about local events and gave an impressionistic sketch of teaching with emphasis on the positives. As she walked back to her car, she thought about the spin she'd put on her life. It's like when people ask, 'How are you?' They don't want the truth. It's a gesture of camaraderie not interest. It doesn't count as lying, not really.

The Sleight home was an old house that had grown with

each generation. A fresh load of blue stone gravel covered the dirt driveway that ran steeply down to the two-acre home paddock. Cassie parked on a flat gravel stretch to the left of the house – the visitors' area.

Imagined homecomings are often unrealised and so it was with Cassie's. The joy she felt was not mirrored by family who rushed out to greet her. There was warmth in the sun though as she crossed to the front door. She liked the way heat splayed out from one spot on her back. It was going to be another beautiful autumn day.

Argument, fierce and hot, spilled from the house. Her father sounded in right form. Without entering, Cassie visualised the scene. It was a chilling dance.

This version of her father was brutal in his language, huge in his gesture and movement; volume was the preferred weapon of assault. Her mother's responses were controlled and selected. She sheltered under a cloak of martyrdom occasionally twisting out of it like a matador uses his cape to deflect the bull's charge. The killing sword, a list of grievances partially forgiven but not forgotten, cut her father's ire. From his tone and the drop in volume, Cassie knew that her father was bloodied. The battle would continue until one gained superiority, another sort of kill.

A reflex of calmness woven from twenty-two years of family life shrouded Cassie. She hated their emotional excess. It led nowhere and damaged everything. What was the point?

Leaving the flowers and newspaper at the front door, Cassie walked along the verandah, selectively peering through windows, avoiding her parents' notice. Where was Leonie? Unsuccessful, Cassie remembered Leonie's childhood reaction to parental argument. Where Cassie would remain in the house, neutral and choosing the time to dispense cups of tea and impartial solace, Leonie would flee to the gum tree at the edge of the eastern side of the home paddock. Cassie had stayed with her parents thinking of herself as a kind of talisman that warded off the excess of conflict heard when she was younger.

Striding across the paddocks, Cassie regretted wearing sandals. Her toes were wet.

Which tree? Cassie wondered, looking aloft.

'You didn't actually expect to find me up there, did you? Chucked the job in?'

'Where are you?' Cassie said looking around. 'And, no, I haven't. Coming home was an impulse thing.'

'You do things on impulse? Interesting.' Leonie, a blonde genetic variation of her sister, wearing striped pink and brown pyjamas and farm boots, trudged up from where she had been sitting on a recently felled log. 'I doubt I could shinny up that thing anymore.'

They exchanged the perfunctory kiss of sisters.

'Coming back to the house?' Cassie asked.

'Are they still arguing?'

Cassie nodded. 'What's it about?'

'Money and drink. Apparently, Mum tried to put a halt on Dad's spending and drinking in public when they were out last night. I don't know the exact details. Dad came home fuming and ready to blow. You know what that's like!'

'The tension is as thick as treacle.'

'Cold treacle. They went to bed, same room, and I thought, Age has mellowed them. Boy, was I wrong! Dad woke livid. They've been going at it hammer and tongs since six. What stage are they up to?'

'The heat's going out of Dad. Mum's scored a few covert hits. Another hour maybe. Want to go for a coffee?'

'Like this?'

'You can wear something of mine. C'mon.'

At the car, Leonie rifled through the clothing options. 'This is all so … so … monotonous! When are you going to tune into fashion?'

'Then I guess we're staying here.'

'No way!' Leonie selected a denim skirt, white shirt and a red scarf. 'When did you start wearing red?'

'Jake gave it to me.'

'Do you mind then?' Leonie wove the scarf artistically around her flowing curls.

Cassie did but did not say so, surprised Leonie liked anything of hers. Standing there, Cassie realised that she disliked sharing.

'What a mouth!' Leonie laughed.

'Don't wear my scarf like that.'

'Why not? I thought I had a Grecian effect going?'

'You do, but … actually, I don't want you to wear it.'

'Fair enough.' Leonie pulled the scarf off her hair and handed it to Cassie who carefully folded and pocketed it.

'Finally a benefit in being bigger than you: I love the way this skirt hugs my bum.'

'It fits well. I don't know if any of my bras will …'

'Don't need one.' Leonie took off her pyjama top. 'I've got great boobs!'

'Leonie!' Cassie said looking around. 'Someone might see.'

'So?'

'How is it that you're comfortable with your body, and I'm not?'

Leonie breathed in as she buttoned the shirt; it was a snug fit. 'Don't know. Don't understand a lot of things about you, but then again, I've only recently started to understand myself. Well, let's get out of here.'

As Cassie drove to North Richmond, Leonie said, 'Maybe it's a chromosome thing.'

'What?'

'There are genes for eye and hair colour, nose size, body shape, internal qualities like being a nurturer or aggressive, possibly even the careers that we're drawn to. Genes might even be responsible for how we dress.' Leonie warmed to her topic. 'Look at birds and their plumage for instance. Teachers could be like them.'

A collage of teachers, male and female, passed through both women's minds. Cassie laughed. 'The educator's,' Cassie spelt the next word, 'j.e.a.n.o.m.e.'

'A sad attempt, but hey, you haven't run with an idea like that for years!'

'Of course I have.'

'Not for years. You're a shadow of the girl you once were.'

Cassie frowned. 'You think?'

'I do, often. You were such a fearless, feisty girl, Cassie.'

The centre of her own world, Leonie had not given much thought to Cassie as they grew up. Like most older sisters, she had found her sibling and her playmates more nuisance than companions.

Unbidden, memory intruded on the present.

* * *

'But Mum …'

'For goodness sake, Leonie.' Nancy stood underneath the clothesline at the side of the house fighting the winter wind and pegging out school uniforms. 'Is it so hard to play with Cassie, Melissa, and Jake?'

'They're kids!'

'Off with you, or you'll not be going to the movies tomorrow with your friends.'

'But it's cold.'

'Last time I tell you, Leonie, …'

'Okay, I'm going, but I'm getting a book first.'

'I'm holding you responsible if anything happens to them.'

'It won't.'

By the time Leonie returned, the trio had run well ahead across the paddocks. When she caught up with them, Cassie and Jake were in full adventure mode. Sheltering in the lee of the hillside, Leonie watched her sister and friends play.

The bite of winter certainly had little effect on Cassie and Jake's games. Matched in indomitable spirit and rugged in woollen jumpers, they scaled monster trees, teeter-tottered on bikes along dam edges, and gallumped through paddocks, startling rabbits while cattle ruminated in the bending grasses.

Melissa, timid and more interested in playing Barbies than adventure, lagged behind them, complaining. Under pressure from Leonie, Cassie and Jake modified their games to Hide-and-Seek so Melissa could play.

* * *

Winnowing through her memory file, Leonie realised that there had been a change in Cassie in her mid-teens. At the time, she had been relieved that Cassie had given up imitating her dress style and had been unconcerned about the underlying reasons for the devolution into oversized clothing. There had been a behavioural change too. Looking back now, she saw that Cassie had shut down emotionally and become less communicative.

What had happened? Why had the robust personality

become muted? And how had Cassie lost out to Melissa? Melissa of all people! Leonie wished she held more of the jigsaw pieces to her sister's story.

'So what do you think?' Cassie asked as they sat in the outdoor area of the local café. 'Leonie?'

It took a moment for Leonie to reframe her thoughts. 'Sorry. I was thinking about something else.'

'Is there something wrong with me when I switch off emotionally in a conflict situation?'

'I think it's good you can keep your cool. Your classroom is really a power struggle, isn't it? The kids win if you lose it.'

'But I don't choose to be calm. I just am, and I seem to be stuck in that mode a long time. Then, sometimes after I've survived it all,' she paused, aware of emotions surging within, 'I get emotional, really emotional, and cry. It's like I'm feeling okay, I'm in a safe place, and then out it comes.'

'Geez, I'd be worried if you weren't reacting that way! A good cry is therapeutic. I always feel better after one. As for the calm, in your situation, it's an asset.'

'You think? There's not something dysfunctional about me?'

'Of course not! Being calm in a crisis is good. I think years of living with Dad equipped us with that reaction. Mum made such a big deal of us tiptoeing around, careful of what we said, and how we said it when he was in one of those moods. Remember what that was like?'

'Yes.'

'Last night when I was waiting for him to blow, I was quietly tense, somehow detached. The house felt like … you know that tension in the air before a storm breaks?'

Cassie nodded.

'Like that.'

'Maybe our childhood was training for me to be a teacher.'

'If teaching is like Dad in his younger days, then you'd better get out before you get hurt.'

'I'm not ready to do that. Maybe when I'm in control and it's a choice, not an escape.'

Leonie grimaced. 'Still stuck on that?'

'It hurt.'

'I meant to help, Cassie. Walking off when you're uncomfortable, changing topic, not standing up for yourself, not fighting for —'

'Was walking out on John an escape or a realisation and acceptance of a truth about you?'

'Acceptance, but you won't catch me walking out of places or trying to avoid events just because John is there. You won't find me seeping sadness when I think no one's looking. Look, someone has to have this talk with you. Dad and Mum sure won't. I've thought about this a lot lately. What sort of woman do you want to be?'

'I intend dealing with age through plastic surgery.'

'Don't be glib with me, Cassie. I mean the authentic person.'

Silence.

'Neither of us, Cassie, have been good at communication. Mum's queen of the stuff-ups, and Dad's so into 'I'm the man' he doesn't listen. I see now I mirrored their relationship with John. We shared the flat and expenses but never communicated, not about the things that mattered anyway. The sex was good, but I wasn't interested in his life or work nor he in mine. I think that's where you went wrong with Jake and why Melissa won out. If there's anything Melissa does well, it's talk and show her feelings, especially for Jake. Communication should be a course at school.'

'I think it's called English.'

'But that's more about literature and stuff, not what I'm talking about. Oh God, there's Marnie Royston!' Leonie picked up a menu and feigned interest. 'Cassie, don't look so conspicuous!'

'Would you like me to hide under the table? Trying to avoid attention actually draws it to you.'

'Table's too small. You could —'

'You're saved; she's heading to the car park. What's your problem with her anyway? You used to be friends.'

'We still are, but she just got engaged and talks of nothing else. She gloats.'

'That could be just your perception because it's a sore point.'

Leonie considered Cassie. 'If I tell you something, I don't want you to tell the parents or, for that matter, give me your opinion.'

'Geez, what is it?'

'John proposed.'

'What? When?'

'We met last week at Bellini's to talk things over.'

'That's good then, isn't it? You want to get married.' Taking in Leonie's expression, she asked, 'Don't you?'

'I did, but not with John blackmailed into it. When I asked him what he thought marriage meant, he said it was a legal commitment that entailed giving us two-way rights to possessions and income. He misses me and wants me to move back so his life is back on track. Not one word about love. Can you believe it?'

'Well ... yes, he's always been pragmatic. A simple remark about it being a nice day led to a detailed description of the climatic conditions. You thought that endearing once.'

'More fool me then for not understanding what those values meant for us in the long term. I want a man who wants to share his life and everything in it with me. I do not want separate lives with some shared moments like it was. I want passion, not just affection. I made a big mistake moving in without talking about where we were headed. I just assumed we wanted the same thing.'

'So you told him no.'

'I was so angry!'

'You had a fight?'

'I'm not like you. I was disgustingly sensitive at the time but got mad later.'

'And now?'

'I've worked out a five year plan, and I'm not looking outside myself to find happiness. Damn! What's she doing back here? It's bloody Marnie again! C'mon, let's go. Look the other way!'

As the car travelled up Terrace Road, Cassie asked, 'How long are you staying at home?'

'Don't know. It's a chance to save for travel and work on my design business. It's heaps easier than working and trying to keep on top of housework. Dad has remodelled a couple of rooms so I have my own apartment. I'll show you next time. They're in chaos now.'

Cassie frowned. She had always thought Order should have been her sister's middle name. Even when Leonie had moved in with John, her approach had been systematic and organised. In fact, Leonie had stopped John's chaotic unpack and the pile of things he'd been creating. 'We're not living in a dump, John. If we don't have a place to keep it then it's out of here and in the bins.'

Was Leonie out of step now despite all her show of being attuned to life's rhythm? Should she broach it with Leonie now or talk to their mother first?

Leonie continued unaware of her sister's distraction.

'Giving up my dreams to pay bills was the first crack in John and my relationship. I just didn't realise it at the time.' Cassie tuned into her sister's conversation as Leonie said, 'Anyway, I'm at peace with my choice, finally. Mum was a bit worried there for a while about the mess and all, no panic attacks or oesophageal spasms thankfully. We had one of those circuitous talks of hers; it helped me sort out what I want. I do not want to confuse matters now with telling them about John's proposal. It's great being home, and apart from the current blue, all has been quiet on that front.'

With a strong feeling of déjà vu, Cassie parked on a flat gravel stretch to the left of the house.

* * *

'Hey, look who I found at the front door!' Leonie called out to her parents.

No response.

'Mum! Dad! Where are you?' Leonie called as the sisters walked through to the rear of the house.

'Out back,' Nancy called.

Tom was on his knees working in the vegetable patch, and her mother was sitting on the verandah reading the local newspaper to him. 'There are very real concerns about the funding of local infrastructure. For years, the single carriageway between Windsor and Parramatta has been inadequate despite the increasing population of the area. The Local Government and the Shires Associations encourage all ratepayers to support their campaign in lobbying State and Federal Government to increase ... Cassie! What are you doing here?'

'I missed home. Mum, these are for you. Dad, I got the Herald.'

Leonie took the flowers into the kitchen in search of a vase. The Herald took up residence on top of the local newspaper which lay on a small wooden table near Nancy.

'The weekend?' Nancy asked.

'Just till Sunday morning.'

'It's too far to travel for one day,' her father said.

'On a regular basis, you're right, but this is a treat, Dad. I've really missed you, all of you. Can we have a group hug?'

'You're a little old for that, Pumpkin, aren't you?' Tom asked.

In that moment, Cassie felt vulnerable. Was it always to be like this, she wondered, rejected by the men she loved?

For Nancy, the memory of the first time she had initiated the group hug played as backdrop to the present scene. Furious with both girls over a scratched record, Tom had raged at them throughout that winter's morning despite Nancy's best efforts to calm him and shield them. His temper had finally spluttered into silence, as was the pattern of his explosions, midafternoon. Cassie had sobbed her heart out in the bedroom while Leonie had disappeared as soon as her father had lost interest in them. By evening, Tom had regained his equanimity and with it an expectation that his daughters should mirror his mood. They, however, had been emotionally bruised and guarded.

Aware of the fragility of the evening's peace, Nancy had called for a group hug. The girls had come to her willingly. Tom had resisted but eventually succumbed. Nancy was not sure why but suspected that it had something to do with the ultimatum that she had finally given him a few months before. Tom had accepted the hug as tentatively as a child baiting a worm on a hook for the first time. In the intervening years, he had joined the group hug with a show of protest. Despite that, Nancy believed he now enjoyed these moments. After all, it was the only time he was close to his girls.

'No one outgrows the need to feel loved, Tom,' Nancy said. 'It's lovely to have you home, Cassie.'

* * *

Boldness resurfaced in Cassie on her return trip to Keimera. As a child, in dance and in games with Jake, she had willingly risked failure and embarrassment in order to win. She decided to discard Coachman's blueprint for effective lessons. If teaching was going to work for her, it had to be to her choreography.

As the Keimera lighthouse loomed into view, Cassie realised that the knowledge her family were always there in the background gave her strength. Although she and Leonie preferred to solve their own problems, there was a tacit understanding that the family was a safety net. No situation was truly impossible. As adults, she and her sister had different roads to take but family were only ever a phone call away.

Focusing on her journey, Cassie decided to implement an idea that had been evolving for the last few weeks. It could be a series of lessons, she thought. Excitement and not the usual rush of anxiety warmed her.

Chapter 10

Monday, Cassie arrived at school an hour before the rest of her colleagues. Her first stop was the photocopier room. As she surrendered her place to an unidentified teacher, Van der Huffen, sleek and trim in black from head to toe, entered.

'Good morning,' Cassie said to him. Does this man ever wear anything else? she wondered.

'Any day that we are privileged to work at the chalkface is a good one,' Van der Huffen replied dryly.

'I hope I feel like that one day,' Cassie said.

Van der Huffen assessed her. She really needed a hand on a cap to catch things that went over her head.

Bruce Cliff, who was the Creative Arts and Languages Head Teacher and one of the sport shirt and shorts brigade, said, 'A hope that each one of us has experienced one time or another.'

Oh, mockery again, Cassie thought, it is everywhere. I should think before coming in. She filled out the photocopier register faithfully.

Amused, Van der Huffen observed her scrupulous tallying.

'We should pay the Department for the privilege,' Bruce continued.

'I believe that many of us already are; the coin is sweat, fat, and tears.'

Cliff looked down at his ample girth. 'Got me in two

words: fat and tears. I lucked out this year: I drew the short straw on the dregs of Years 9 and 10.'

'Bad luck, mate.'

Cassie left.

Van der Huffen moved to the photocopier as Cliff crossed to a workbench behind him to staple his class sets of copy.

'At least, I was in there with a chance. My people don't like the way allocations are done in your area let alone —'

'Take that up with Talbut, he's 2IC, or if you have the balls, take it up with Coachman.'

'But, mate –'

'Nice to see you noticing the effect of my workouts.'

'Huh?'

'Or is it the cut of these trousers?'

'Don't like being the butt of your games either.'

'Disappointing! I thought it was my butt that had your admiration.'

'And I hate this … whatever you English teachers call this sort of talk! Can't for the life of me work out why you do it. It puts a man off. … I'll take it up with Talbut; he is the best of your lot.' Cliff left without filling out the photocopier register.

Chuckling, Van der Huffen returned to photocopying only to experience frustration with a paper jam.

Aware that she was running out of time, Cassie set up an overhead projector, wrote a cryptic message on the board, and rearranged the configuration of desks in her room. On them, she placed A4 pages with an overview of the lesson direction, a sheet of butcher paper, and pens. She was excited about her plans for the day. Like Edison with his light bulb, the key to success might be a two thousand step process. She hoped not though.

The first bell rang, signalling assembly in ten minutes.

Cassie locked her room and walked back to the staff room. She had time for a coffee before the school carousel began. At the staff room doorway, she reconsidered that idea. The room seemed full.

'Fingerling in the waters,' someone said loudly.

Van der Huffen, from behind Cassie, said, 'I don't resemble that! Just as well my sword is sheathed and at my desk.'

'Yes, but the hilt is visible,' Selton said.

Confused, Cassie puzzled over its meaning.

'A belated sense of fairness,' Van der Huffen replied. Then to Cassie, he said, 'After you, m' lady.'

That comment raised eyebrows among the other men. Cassie wondered at Van der Huffen's intent as well. Was he flirting with her? God, she hoped not. He was so old.

Samantha, absorbed by her own preparations, had tuned out to the dialogue but not the movement. 'Hang on; this would be a good time for me to leave.' She brushed passed Talbut at the door, a slinky quality in her manner. Her smile reflected a sense of intimacy and comfort, the sort that friends of long standing share.

'Morning, one and all,' Talbut said. 'Nice tail.' He said to no one in particular as he watched Samantha walk down the corridor.

'Personally, I prefer the tale of the Sword of Damocles,' Van der Huffen said.

'Those who live under the sword,' Selton began.

'Need to reconsider their taste,' Van der Huffen ended.

Cassie knew something was wrong but not exactly what. Van der Huffen's cryptic criticism of Talbut continued. Talbut squared off for battle as men do but was stopped by Rajes' arrival.

Arriving and taking in the scene, Rajes said, 'Isn't it a little too early for testosterone flexing?'

Amid groans and a range of mild expletives, those men in direct line to Rajes' desk either exited or stood aside to let her pass. Conversation for the remaining time in the staff room was fragmented and mundane.

On the way downstairs to assembly, Selton said to Van der Huffen, 'So what brought you out of the corner?'

'R.E.S.P.E.C.T.'

'Please tell me you're not going to sing, V.H.'

'Got a problem with my voice, P.S?'

'More with our silence, V.H.'

'You seeing Talbut from the women's perspective too?'

'I am, V.H. The man's got seriously fucked up since his wife walked out.'

'Your lack of eloquence speaks volumes. So, what are we going to do, P.S?'

'I'll have to think about it, eh?'

The school assembled in classes organised into year groups. Each year group was recognisable from their variation to the uniform as well as the height difference. Staff moved down the class roll lines, marking attendance. During announcements from the Deputy on the dais, staff teaching the first session were permitted to leave.

Year 9, a group of academically capable students, lined up noisily outside Cassie's room. A few of the taller students peered over the glass panelling in the top half of the wall and ran a commentary on what they saw.

Pleased with their interest, Cassie crossed to them. As they entered, she gave each student one of five coloured cards. They looked at the setup while dumping bags on the floor, the unrhythmical thud sounding around the room.

As Cassie launched into a series of questions about language and communication, her class looked downward, scrunching as low as possible. The lack of hands did not matter. She passed onto the lesson's next stage, flicking on the overhead projector. The first transparency just had *The Loch Ness Monster's Song* and a related picture.

'Never heard of that song,' a fat boy at the back of the room said to his scrawny male neighbour. 'Anyone heard of this Edwin Morgan?'

'With songs like that, he's not gunna make it into the charts,' called out a boy who sat with his arms folded and body slumped back in his chair.

A girl, her confidence bigger than her stature, called out, 'God, I hope she's not gunna sing to us!'

'It's not a song in that sense,' Cassie said, 'and by the time we've finished this work, I think you'll be impressed by the poem. Now …'

While the class stared at the projection, Cassie read the song with attitude.

'It don't mean nothing! Shit; it's just jumbled sounds from the alphabet! Why do we have to do this?' said a disembodied voice to the left.

'Is he right?' Cassie asked, looking at her class.

About half of them grumbled agreement with the dissenter.

'Ed, you look like you disagree,' Cassie said.

Regretting that he had raised his eyes, Ed said, 'Some of it makes sense. I thought it sounded a bit lonely in the beginning but then the sound changed; all the g, r, and d sounds made it sound like the creature is angry. At the end, I reckon it's submerging.'

His peers sat back with a collective, 'Oh.'

'I think so too.' With comic exaggeration, Cassie repeated the last line, 'Blm plm, plm!'

The class laughed. It was not that harsh, derogatory

mirth directed against someone that adolescents often indulge in, but rather the sound of delight, sincere and appreciative.

'Any other clues to what else is being said or happening?'

The original dissenter said, 'It's asking a few questions.'

'And, and,' said an undersized, mousy-haired girl sitting directly in front of Cassie, 'Look, there's an exclamation mark!'

'Well done,' Cassie consulted her seating plan, 'Evie.'

In an aside to Ed, the girl said. 'I think the creature's excited about something … the harder sounds don't automatically mean it's angry.'

Ed shrugged off her comment.

Moving around the room, Cassie issued worksheets as she spoke, 'I want you to group with people of like coloured cards, agree on a workstation, and complete the task related to the song.'

As Evie moved to join his group, Ed mumbled angrily the disputed lines.

'Geez,' his target replied, 'just cause I disagreed …' In reaction to his smirk, she added, 'Smart arse!'

Movement in the room was relatively quiet by past standards and non-threatening. There was a lot of noise, but it stemmed from cooperation.

Following group discussion and presentations back to the class, Cassie told her students to form pairs for the next task. She moved quickly around the room issuing envelopes. As she did this, she had the loudest student, Tom Cullen read the second task aloud: the development of a gibberish conversation to be presented to the class with the details in the envelope kept secret.

There was an initial reaction of, what the?

'Anyone here ever upset someone?' Cassie asked.

Hands shot up around the room.

'Was it the words you chose or something else?'

The silence of the confounded held in the room. Cassie controlled her urge to jump in and end it. Finally, the hand of the mousy girl in the front row edged up tentatively.

As Cassie asked, 'Evie?' the girl was in the process of withdrawing it.

Evie looked hesitantly across the room at Tom Cullen as she spoke. 'Friday, Tom didn't make it into the room. It's not because of what he said, not really.'

The texture of the silence changed. Interest had entered the room.

'Mr Gunerson said Tom's attitude was calculated for offence and not for Maths.'

'So what did you do, Tom, do you know?'

'Nup.'

'Would you mind replaying the situation for us?'

Inclined to decline, Tom absorbed his so-called mates' smirks, interpreted them as superiority, and so agreed.

'No sweat. What do you want?'

'Go outside. Think about what was going on Friday and how you were feeling before you went to Maths. Then come in and act as you did then.'

'Right. Gotta have my bag though.' He swung it over his shoulder and left the space with his habitual swagger.

Expectation meant all eyes were focused on the doorway. Time passed without Tom's return.

With a calculated walk of nonchalance, Cassie crossed to the door and looked down the corridor. It was empty. Walking back to her desk, she considered how this incident could be explained to Coachman. In a moment of wonderment, she looked at her class. 'Well …' Cassie began.

The laughter was spontaneous, the class reading the situation. Then Tom materialised in the doorway and waited for attention. With a gum-chewing swagger, he crossed to Cassie, eyeballing her for a few seconds.

Safe within the re-enactment situation, Cassie appreciated the way he claimed power and challenged her. Something she could use, maybe? Would she ever feel that confident?

In the silence, Evie said softly, 'Mr Gunerson said, 'Good morning, Tom'.'

Cassie nodded her thanks. 'Good morning, Tom.'

'What's it to you?'

Tom went to his desk, swung his leg over the chair while dropping his bag. He leant back, assessing Cassie. She held his stare. Thank God he didn't try this on with me, she thought. Aware of the room's stillness, she asked, 'So what did Tom communicate?'

Silence. This was an arena no one was eager to enter.

'Anger or challenge?'

Silence.

In an attempt to get her lesson back on track, Cassie pretended insight. 'I reckon he was angry before the lesson and that affected how he reacted to Mr Gunerson. It wasn't a good morning at all, and he thought Mr Gunerson was prying.'

Tom now looked out the window. His jaw pulsed.

'And so a bad day got worse. Thanks for your help, Tom.' Cassie noted the flush creeping up Tom's neck. 'Throughout the ages, conflict has happened not just because of what was said but because of how. In this next section of work, we're looking at how people communicate. We'll begin with oral work and then explore the how in writing. Okay, ten minutes to develop the paired task before showing it to us.'

Mid lesson, non-threatening laughter filled the room.

Cassie relaxed and enjoyed herself. With each student pre-sentation, she deftly focused her class on aspects of the communication process. Time passed so quickly that the class voiced their surprise when the bell rang.

Chapter 11

Midnight chimed. Returning from the kitchen with coffee in hand, Michael paused in the doorway and watched Cassie who sat on the floor wrapped in a blanket. The room was paper chaos, but he knew, from the condition of his own room, that there was order of a sort.

He cleared his throat, 'The kettle's boiled.'

'Thanks, I was going to have a break soon. You've saved me some time. Love your trackie daks by the way.'

'I'm a true suburban dag.'

He was anything but a dag. Urbane and pliant, he appeared to be at ease everywhere. Another quality he shares with Jake, Cassie thought. Charming men, I can do without them.

'It's cold in here. How much longer are you staying up, Cassie?'

'Another hour or so.'

'Why let the fire die out then?'

'I don't have time for fires, Mike.'

'Fair enough.' He left.

A little later, Michael returned with the log bag, entered the room, and rekindled the fire.

'That's a kind thought, Mike, but there wasn't any real need. I'm cosy.'

'Well, I'm not. I hate the way weather swings leading up to Easter. Any objections if I bring my work down and finish it here?'

With the fire flaring back into life, Michael dropped a leg over an armchair and slipped into it. 'I'm working on an essay about Slessor's poem *Sleep*, Cassie. Do you know it?'

'Uh huh.'

'I like his use of the Hades motif to organise his ideas.'

'It's clever.' She continued to block him out with work.

'My teacher couldn't explain how the motif holds up for the second stanza. He reckons that's the shortcoming in the poem. Mind if I run a few ideas past you?'

Surprised, Cassie looked up. Jake never asked her opinion on anything. She gave it, but he didn't want it.

'Well?' Michael asked.

'Sorry, I was distracted. Go ahead.'

'Won't be long, just need my notes.'

And I might as well get a coffee, she thought, as she headed off for the kitchen.

On her return, Cassie found Michael on the floor, sifting through his notes, positioned between the fire and her. For the rest of the hour, he outlined his ideas and argued passionately about them. Cassie played devil's advocate, and in doing so, they discovered the nuances of the motif.

Contentment warmed Cassie. She liked the physical and mental closeness forged by a common interest. She enjoyed discussion and loved the excitement that came with discovering another perspective.

As the clock chimed one, Michael leant back against the armchair, satisfied. He resisted the urge for a cigarette, a bad habit defeated with difficulty. 'I'm wrapping up, Cassie. You should too given it's a school night.'

'Yes, Dad.'

'I mean it, Cassie. You burn the candle at both ends. No one can keep that up for long.'

'And you don't?'

'Not on work and study. There's a lot to be said for relaxation and having fun though. You need to get out.'

'I will once I'm on top of my work. And since we're in counselling session, you need to —'

'Truce.' Michael held up his essay, laughing. 'I don't have a white flag, but will this do?'

'Okay.' She returned to her work.

Sitting now in his father's favourite armchair, Michael closed his eyes for a time. He felt a satisfaction that he had previously associated with the effect of nicotine, the same settling calm. He wished TAFE sessions were as good as this one had been. He liked talking to this girl. She was different. Tiredness percolated through him.

Time passed.

Brought back to wakefulness by the clock chiming the half hour, Michael asked, 'You almost finished?'

'No. You don't have to stay up on my account.'

'I'm not.'

As he watched her, he noted the contrast between Cassie's skin and the random curls that defied the control of her hastily made chignon. Her boat-neck, blue cashmere sweater emphasised the roundness of her shoulders. He thought of Kate who now seemed angular. Kate definitely had an edge to her; a polished sharpness that focused him like a tuner did with a television aerial.

'All you seem to do is work, Cassie. You using it to hide from life?'

'What?'

'Just a thought. Kate's thought really.'

'Kate?'

'An old girlfriend … friend now.'

'How odd that you talk about me to her or anyone for that matter, Michael.'

'Not really. She's interested in how things have changed here. Kate has an opinion on everything. It's one of her many charms.'

'Remember telling me you'll live your life your way?'

'Not in those words.' Michael anticipated what was coming.

'What I do is not your business.'

'It is if you keep me awake at night, Cassie.' Then in response to her expression, he explained, 'You cry in your sleep sometimes. Is it work or something else?'

'Most probably work. As the kids say, 'It sucks!' Sorry, I don't have time for this.' Cassie made a show of being engrossed in her work.

'Do you have a mentor you can talk the work stuff over with?'

'Sort of. The women I work with are a comfort.' She blocked Michael by focusing on her work.

He moved closer, stretching out on the lounge behind her. He was intensely aware of her.

'Go to bed, Michael, don't fall asleep here.'

'I will once I've unwound. If I don't, my mind won't shut down.'

'I'm a bit like that.'

Lying there, Michael found pleasure in the hiss and sigh of the fire. 'Open fires have such an appeal, don't you think?' He inhaled with the air of a connoisseur. 'Some woods have a distinctive fragrance ... or is that you?'

'It's the wood. If you're going to stay here, at least be quiet so I can finish.'

Toying now with the curls at the nape of Cassie's neck, Michael asked, 'You're a beautiful woman. So what are you interested in beside work? Maybe we share similar interests.'

'Sleep for one, and I'm not going to get any if you don't leave me alone.' She brushed his hand away. 'Go away, boy, you're bothering me.'

Affronted, Michael left.

Watching his retreat, Cassie wondered about her reaction. She had been keenly aware of him, unsettled by his proximity and interest. Despite that, she experienced an odd sense of loss.

Chapter 12

Coming to an unexpected halt at the bottom of the school stairs that Thursday morning, Cassie realised that there was a blockage mid-stairwell. Groans and complaints echoed up and down the stairwell as students continued to push forward.

Cassie raised her voice to quell the surging masses. It lacked the stun-gun quality of the men but was imposing nonetheless and achieved her goal. Minutes later, the flow resumed. At the top of the stairs, the student masses swerved away from the staff area and towards the classrooms.

'G'day, beautiful,' said Talbut when they met in the corridor. 'You solved that bottleneck effectively.'

'I thought so.'

They walked toward the staff room.

He rested a hand on her arm, stopping her. 'It's a pleasure to see my protégé's firm hand at work. I'm perfectly happy to provide other opportunities for such focused handiwork.'

Flustered, Cassie said, 'That's very kind of you.'

He smiled. 'This fluttering dove quality of yours is most appealing.'

'I have a wider personal space than most people.' She stepped away from him.

He grinned. 'Do you?'

'Yes.'

'As I said, most appealing.' He opened the door to an empty staff room.

Cassie caught herself in a moment of hesitation but pushed past it.

Talbut leant in and lightly guided her, his hand in the small of her back.

Her entrance masked the uneasiness Cassie felt at being alone with him. 'As I said, you need to give me more space.'

He laughed.

'And I'm not interested in you so I'd prefer you dropped the … er … whatever you think you're being.'

'I'm just playing with you, Cassie.'

For the rest of the session, Cassie focused on her work, retreating that way. She shelved her plan for shopping after work. The changes she planned in her clothing would bring unwanted attention.

Memory, the sort that's always there in the background, whispered to Cassie: hide, retreat, aren't you tired of a past littered with escapes? She stared at the books in front of her. At the time, she had rejected Leonie's perspective; now its truth resonated, again.

As time passed, Cassie forgot about Talbut. In a reflex response to his movement, preparation for his next class, she looked at him. 'Oh!'

Talbut's face flushed. 'You make a hard man of me.' He turned his back on her.

The door opened. At a glance, Samantha took in Talbut as he approached her. 'Good to see you're pleased to see me, Talbut.'

'How could I not be? However, you're mistaking the fit of these damn trousers for desire."

'That's very pointed of you.'

Talbut laughed, closing the door behind him.

'That man oozes masculinity. I don't think there is anything sexier than a man who is open about his feelings.' Samantha fanned herself. 'He makes me hot!'

'Aren't you supposed to be on class?'

'I've walked out on them, Cassie. I can't make it to recess.'

'You should see Coachman then. The class has to be covered.'

'Useless. All his focus is on what happens. He ignores the subtext that goes with it. Can't you take them? Please?'

'All right, but you owe me.'

* * *

Later that day, raucous male voices echoed in the quadrangle adjacent to Cassie's room. Feet thundered on the polished floorboards in the corridor. Standing in her doorway, Cassie watched as the twenty-eight boys from 10G lurched to a halt in ramshackle disarray in front of her. She waited for silence.

Settling for a parody of it, she directed her class to enter. Shirt-tails out, socks at half mast, bags used as battering rams, they charged into the room. Boys propped on windowsills and hung half in and half out of the windows. They called out ribald comments to peers visible elsewhere in the school.

The three leaders of the class ringed her, chanting in a round, 'So what're we doin', huh?' They closed in on her in a menacing dance.

Panic pushed against Cassie's sense of personal control. She looked beyond the trio to the rest of the boys. They pushed misbehaviour to the limits, rudeness to extremes. Lessons with them were a bizarre caricature of what she'd been told to expect in training; this class was the ugly and repugnant. Amused by the thought, she found the power to relax.

Cassie looked at the ringleader, Glen Dobbs, a solid block of an adolescent, who seemed to Cassie more adult than boy. With a calm that she was far from feeling, she said, 'And a good morning to you too. Decide where you're going to sit, please, and unpack. Today's work is on the board.' Then she looked at the rest of the class. 'Sit down and unpack, or you'll be here at lunch; you must have better things to do with that time than spend it with me.'

'There ain't nowhere to sit in here,' Glen Dobbs said loudly.

For a moment, there was silence and stillness. Then there was frenetic industry as desks, chairs, bags were tossed into the quadrangle. The noise was deafening.

Appalled, Cassie masked it. She needed a cooperative candidate to go for help. There wasn't any. Aware that she could be in trouble for leaving the room unsupervised, she headed to the classroom next to hers. She met Coachman mid corridor. He passed her without a word.

At the doorway, Coachman's eyes swept the room. His voice tolled like a deep bass bell. The boys froze. 'Get all of that back in this room through the door in an orderly fashion in the next five minutes. I'm timing,' Coachman made a show of checking his watch, 'from now!'

Boys scurried out of the room, their faces transformed into masks of compliance.

'I'll take the class for the rest of this lesson, Miss Sleight. Go have a coffee. I hear that you rarely get the chance. We'll have an interview later.'

Feeling ashamed as much by the dismissal as by her inability to control the class, Cassie packed up her things with a quiet dignity that she was far from feeling. As she walked down the corridor, she noted the grim procession of furniture. She felt like laughing but did not.

The staff room was empty. A scattering of resource books and five crates of novels covered Cassie's centre table.

After heaving the boxes onto the floor, Cassie sat down. Her skin burned and her stomach churned. It's okay to be upset. I should be upset. Nothing I'm going through is reasonable. She focused on the boxes. I wonder how they'd feel if they found this stuff dumped onto their desks.

Thought turned into action.

After relocating all the crates, Cassie crossed to the staff typewriter, loaded the triplicate paper, and began the student behavioural records. As she typed, the confrontation translated itself into shaking and rising nausea. She finished the first record, left for the bathroom, and in the tiled coldness of that space, dry-retched.

Back at the typewriter, Cassie visualised herself in a glass dome, untouchable. She could not afford to give in to emotion again. The paperwork had to be completed. She had to deal with Coachman later. A long day was ahead of her.

With the bell for lunch, Cassie faced a dilemma: wait for Coachman or meet him back at her classroom.

Selton's arrival decided the matter for her. 'You're up here early. Had a good morning?'

'Not really. Coachman took my class.'

'Reached the dire circumstance stage, eh?'

'If you call discovering 10G's vocation may be as furniture removalists, possibly weight lifters for the 1992 Olympics, maybe even shot putters or discus throwers if I stretch my imagination and visualise hard.'

'What a pity the others aren't here to witness your transition from innocent to wisecracking smart arse. Let me make you a cuppa. No, I insist!'

Coachman appeared at the doorway seconds later. 'I'll see

you in my office after school, Miss Sleight.' He left, her compliance assumed.

Selton said. 'Was it tea or coffee?'

'Coffee, white, no sugar.'

Over the next ten minutes, the rest of the staff dribbled back to the staff room. To Cassie it felt like a staged invasion. The sheer number of people continued to overwhelm her as it had on her first day. In fact, when she thought of them, it was as a collective and not as individuals.

'Someone's got up the Hitman's nose,' one of the first men to arrive said. His arms were full of books. 'He's hotter than the smelting furnaces at Port Kembla.'

'Nice image!' Selton said, flicking a look at Cassie. 'Where did you get it?'

'My dad works for BHP.' His books were dumped on the centre table and slid toward Cassie's area.

'C'mon!' Cassie said, trying to avert the book slide and on the edge of tears.

'Sorry, habit. Any idea who's in the shit?'

Selton answered, 'Could be any one of us, mate.'

Another male teacher, rotund and gravel-skinned, arrived and pushed his way through to his desk.

'For God's sake, Pothole, give a man a chance,' said the previous arrival. 'This sort of closeness is harassing. I'm not that way inclined, you know.'

More staff arrived in staggered sequence. Groans and complaint dominated the next ten minutes mingled with protest about unwanted book crates on desks.

'All accounted for, I think,' said the last man to enter before he edged to his desk. 'Easter can't come fast enough for me. The weeks are dragging!'

'Not like your cigarettes!' said Samantha, coming into the room.

'Speaking of Easter,' said Pothole, 'who feels a need for chocolate?'

There was a murmur of agreement followed by the tossing of Mars bars, Snickers, and other variations on a chocolate theme around the room from the faculty filing cabinet stash.

Silence crowded the English staff until the shrill ring of the phone.

Van der Huffen answered. 'Hang on. I'll ask. Anyone know where Talbut is?'

'I passed him on the way out to playground duty,' Pothole said. 'I'll check the roster.' He ran his finger down the list posted on the wall. 'Lunch 1: Oval 2.'

Van der Huffen relayed the information and then hung up.

'So, why are you called Pothole?' Cassie asked.

'Because he's always in the road,' replied the men in unison.

Selton looked at his male colleagues, decent blokes he had worked with for years. The year so far had been down right awful for a lot of them. He picked up a pen, tapped his coffee mug, and made much of clearing his throat. 'It's time, is it not, VH, for the first Fickle Finger of Fate Awards for this year?'

A number of the men drew their seats into an arc.

One of them said, 'I've missed this!'

Selton continued, 'Will one of you blokes reach into the trophy cabinet and collect our most prized possession?'

'Where?' a disembodied voice asked from behind his desk shelving.

'Treasured in darkness,' Selton said, 'beneath legendary waters, kept secure for its guardians to lift it from its hiding place and bring forth light and thereby renew the keepers of knowledge ...'

'He means the sink cupboard,' Van der Huffen said without looking up from his work.

'Okay, fellas,' Selton continued, 'careful getting it out of the trophy case. Don't throw it, mate, bear it here with all the dignity you can muster.'

'Age has not wearied nor the years condemned …' intoned one of the men.

'Wrong ceremony, you nit!' Van der Huffen said. 'There are some things we do not mock! Don't you know the essentials of the script yet?'

'I believe, ladies and gentleman, that we need a moment of silence to refocus,' Selton said.

The men passed the trophy one to the next in mock awe. The construction, inspired by the MASH hand, was a grotesque travesty of it.

Cassie and the other women watched.

'Neither time,' Selton continued, 'nor coffee spills has sullied its celebrated surface. VH, I require your assistance.'

'I've got essays to mark,' Van der Huffen said without looking up.

'They can wait.'

'No, they can't.'

'C'mon, mate.' Selton aimed the first of two scrunched balls of paper at him. It bounced off the back of his head. The second glanced off his right shoulder and into the wastepaper bin.

'Great shot!' a number of the men spoke as one.

'C'mon, VH, I require your wit, your glib turn of phrase, your silver-tongued patter, your ability to wing it …'

'It's about time you gave laudatory recognition to my gifts.' He looked at the timetable taped to the right corner of his desk. 'I guess a break won't hurt.'

The trophy passed to Van der Huffen who intoned, 'Once more, dear colleagues, we gather to recognise and reward the mishaps, the misfortunes, and adversities of our faculty. PS?'

'Thank you, VH. Our esteemed and oft-time revered leader, Coachman, has drawn in our team's players, young and old. His play has been magnificent. Each time the ball's been passed to him, he's made a try. The spirit of the opposing team is crushed, and gloom straddles the locker room.'

'Exactly, PS. It's unsettling to see such one-sided play, but the gloom is understandable. The faculty score remains at zero against Coachman's impressive twelve in the cauldron of Keimera High. I pass over to you, PS, as I reach for a sobering coffee here, a steadying coffee in the crushed conditions of this beleaguered room of weary professionals.'

Faculty score? wondered Cassie.

'Well, VH, from the multitude of games seen this term, we have four contenders for this term's Fickle Finger of Fate Award. The first contender is none other than a first time player, Miss Cassandra Sleight.'

Startled, Cassie felt her confidence sucked out of her, however, she tried to smile though her lower lip trembled.

'I hear, VH, that she's a young player who's been in the bin more often than out of it.'

'That right, Miss Sleight?' Van der Huffen asked.

Cassie nodded.

'I'm proud to say, VH, that youth has not muscled out age in this contest. In this battle,' the gravel in Selton's voice increased, 'in this tug-of-war for our Quirks and Jerks of School Life trophy. Our second contender is none other than that redoubtable, stalwart player, Fuller: a gambler for all seasons and a teacher for some. He has bared his coffee stained tusks to the world, muddled through a series of disasters, and stuck to the task of teaching, such as that task is.'

'That's a beautiful summation, mate; it's brought a collective tear to the eyes of the assembled multitude. And the other contenders?'

'Mrs … sorry … Ms Samantha Smith takes the third nomination having muffed the cushy job of timekeeper at the swimming carnival.'

Samantha's smile did not extend to her eyes.

'She must feel a bit of a goose, PS. I suspect she feels like the goose of all gooses. The mammoth goose of gooses.'

'Speaking of geese, who could overlook the honking distress of our last candidate, Ned Wright, who got so tied up in a practical lesson on revolution that his class left him bound to a chair while they shot through to recess.'

'I have it from a reliable source, PS, that The Hitman's opprobrium merited entry into The Guinness Book of Records.'

'Opprobrium? Bloody impressive word.'

'Which brings us back to a bloody impressive player, Ms Cassandra Sleight.'

'Young Cassandra, VH, was caught failing to cover the correct class last week. Apparently, she was following the schedule for another day.'

'I hear it was an admirable lesson, PS, even if it was the wrong class. Fuller's class have petitioned for a return performance. Best lesson they've had so far this year.'

Cassie smiled.

'I think we all commiserate with her misfortune in being intercepted in the corridor by the Hitman only a metre or two short from her real class.'

'Sounds painful, PS.'

'Painful? It'd be bloody excruciating, but we digress … Where were we?'

'Giving it to the woman …'

'Yes, we've got to give it to her, VH. She did not break. That earthquake, lower lip tremble that we've all come to recognise as angst in the face …'

'Angst? That's a bloody big word. It's profound in its implications.'

'It's a bloody big emotion. I hear, VH, that she's been approached by the Sydney papers for insight into the nature of school-kind. Now, as I was saying, our young player refused to surrender to angst in the face of defeat. She braved it out.' Selton's voice savaged the next utterance. 'She's got balls, VH, balls! Any man would be proud to claim them. My word, she's a worthy contender for our award. Over to you.' Selton sipped his coffee as he assessed their impact on the audience.

The satire continued with two male teachers nominated. The other men murmured their sympathy as the exploits were examined and mocked.

The roast ended with, 'That qualifies Ms Smith for this season's first Fickle Finger of Fate Award.'

'Speech, speech!' demanded the assembled.

'What can I say?' Samantha plumped her long blonde hair in the manner of a star and beamed a synthetic smile. 'I'd like to thank this faculty for their inspiration, the PE department for faulty equipment and, of course, the administration for their understanding and compassionate response to clocking the school's fastest swimmer at the slowest time of the day. I'd also like to thank my mum, my dog, Bozo, and my cat, Squeaky, for their support. Thank you. Thank you a thousand times.' Before sitting, she put her trophy on the pile of books above her shelf.

Selton tapped on his coffee mug. 'Before this coverage finishes, I've got to say this. I remember reading that Newton was fascinated by Ferris wheels. He noted that when one went up, it was above him, and that once it came full circle, it was just one point on a continuum. School life is very much like that.'

The bell rang and the staff dispersed to their classrooms, leaving Cassie and Samantha alone.

'Those men sure have a nerve, rubbing in our mistakes,' Samantha said.

Surprised, Cassie said, 'It wasn't meant that way.'

'They've spent too much time listening to HG and Roy. My husband recites their blather off by heart too.' Samantha touched up her lipstick and fluffed her hair. 'I need some fresh air. If Coachman asks, I'm off for the rest of the day and have signed out for a doctor's appointment.'

'You okay?'

'It's an excuse, Cassie. I just need to get out of here. I find Coachman's fortnightly analysis tough. Facing mistakes publicly on top of that is just too much.'

'I thought their repartee put things into perspective. If it's any consolation, you did your part well.'

'Bloody chauvinists!' Samantha said, snatching her handbag.

'I wish I was clever enough to do that sort of banter. I like them.'

'You'll learn!' The door closed, and Cassie was alone.

Waiting for the end of day bell, Cassie distracted herself with the pile of marking on her desk.

Toward the end of that session, Selton entered. 'I gave my Year 12s an early mark. They've an assessment task due tomorrow and could use the time better at home.'

At the sink, he looked at the stains on his coffee mug. 'About time I cleaned this.'

'What is it with you men? All your cups are so grimed. Some even have signs of mould.'

'Good for the immune system. Perhaps it's our small protest against the political correctness and sterility of our times.'

'Coffee cups?'

'Gotcha, Cassie.'

'And you do it so well.'

The bell rang. Cassie waited five minutes for the thud of adolescent feet to leave the upper floor.

'Wait,' Selton said, waving a tea towel in her general direction, 'I endow you with the quick comeback. You've already got courage.'

Cassie looked at him quizzically.

'I've got a fairy godfather thing going.' He paused. 'Obviously read one too many stories to my six year old niece last night. Good luck!'

Cassie laughed and left. The buoyant mood carried her to Coachman's office. He leant back in his worn leather chair, waiting for Cassie to explain herself.

Am I becoming desensitised to this colour assault? she wondered, taking in Coachman's brownish yellow sports coat that hung over the back of his chair, his blue-grey chequered shirt, and green tie. He must be colour blind, Cassie thought. His whole family must be!

Given what Coachman perceived as Cassie's contrite silence, he decided to take the initiative. 'Good lesson session one with your Year 9 Monday.'

'What? How do you …?'

'I was on that session next door to you. I was intrigued with the lack of noise so I watched for a while.'

'But I didn't see you.'

'You were caught up in the performance. Well done! With patience, you may even get somewhere with 10G.'

'From all accounts, no one has ever got anywhere with

10G! I need help with them; they haven't become problems overnight. It's common knowledge none of the men wanted to teach them. Why, for God's sake, was it structured as an all-male class anyway? And how could you dump them on a newcomer, someone who lacks status and the authority that comes with it?'

'I delegate allocations to my senior staff. I don't micro-manage. And I don't explain myself to anyone, let alone a woman! Consider your load a rite of passage.'

'Rite of passage!' There was so much Cassie wanted to say, but she could not think quickly enough.

'Kids get tougher every year. It's not a job for the faint-hearted. This way you work it out faster and move on to a career suited to your temperament.'

Cassie looked at him. 'Maybe they get tougher because of the downgrade in your expectations when they have female teachers? A conditioned response works both ways, you know.'

'You can go,' Coachman said, focusing on paperwork, her departure assumed. Cassie stood her ground. She intended to be resolute this time. She had mismanaged her last attempt to resolve this problem and would not do so again.

Apart from the sound of pen on paper, the quiet and still-ness in Coachman's office reminded Cassie of a pre-storm atmosphere.

Coachman looked up from his desk. 'I've nothing more to say on this matter.'

'But I do!'

'You may go, Miss Sleight.' A vein pulsed in his right temple.

'Dobbs should be on after-school detentions. He is in trou-ble everywhere! Why did you put a block on it?'

'The boy shouldn't suffer because of the inexperience of his female teachers.'

Cassie choked.

'I spoke to the other Heads. Dobbs was moved into Maths and Science classes with male teachers last week. He won't be as unsettled now he has only one woman to cope with. Don't overlook his improvement because of your prejudice over his earlier behaviour.'

'My prejudice?' Cassie collected her thoughts. She could not lose this battle. 'The system should not be selective. Dobbs repeatedly broke the rules; he knows it and so do all the other boys. More than that, he has been offensive, deliberately! I followed your direction and documented everything! There has to be a consequence, otherwise, I'll face anarchy.'

Coachman looked at Cassie as if she was a tiresome child. 'An overreaction; is it that time of month, m' dear?'

'Don't patronise me!'

'You've overstepped the mark, Miss Sleight.'

Cassie shook her head in disbelief.

'You're dismissed.'

'Not yet, Mr Coachman. Respect, and the expectations that go with that, filter down through the staff to boys like 10G. This is not just my problem. It's yours too, and I expect your support, not just for me, but for them as well. What chance do they stand of holding a job if we let them get away with such behaviour? Society expects us to make a difference.' She paused. 'I will! Have you? How wide has your reach been?' Cassie left, walking as tall as she could.

Chapter 13

Friday night, the weather forecasters agreed that New South Wales was having an Indian summer. There was little prospect of relief for the drought-ravaged countryside. Bushfire threat levels remained at extreme. Cassie turned the television off and drifted out to the front verandah.

Waves hushed on the harbour rocks. A motorcycle roared through the township and faded into the distance. The household water system hissed as it replenished its tanks. The house creaked.

'I thought you'd retired,' Cassie said looking at the bundles of work carefully organised around George on the verandah table.

'From paid work five days a week,' George said. 'I'm on the board of Keimera Care. They manage the local retirement village and nursing home. I'm going to make a real difference there, especially the home. It's not enough to feed, toilet, and medicate our infirm elder citizens. All the money goes into medical staff and virtually nothing into diversional therapy. All those empty hours! No wonder their minds go; it's the only way they can escape the boredom!'

'Pretty harsh, George.'

'Appalling is more like it! Respect for human dignity means doing more than taking care of the shell that houses the spirit.'

Cassie could see the truth in what he said. It also applied to respect for self. She had been in denial of hers. Was she masochistic like her father said? It was something she would have to think about. 'So you're not working on the Lions Club's Revive and Survive project?'

'That too.'

'You are busier than salmon in cold water.'

'And what do you know about that?'

'Heaps. My dad and his mates are addicted to fishing; as kids we had no choice but to go where the fish swam.'

'Feeling upbeat, are you?'

'Yes, but I can't take credit for the line. It was something my sister used to say. Want a cuppa?'

'Love one.'

'What time will Minna be back?'

'She won't be home till the small hours. Schmoozing is the key to survival in local politics.'

'Why didn't you go with her?'

'Minna let me off the line this time. She knows I don't like that lot after how they treated her a few years back. Got on top of the work, have you?'

'Yes, but I'm still working on the control thing.'

Cassie wandered back into the house. Everyone her age was out.

Waiting for the kettle to boil, Cassie improvised a dance motif. It felt good to express herself in that way again. She realised that dance had been an anchor in her life. Its loss had definitely added to her suffering over the break-up with Jake. The present became the past …

1985. Tuxedos. Kilometres of tulle. A universe of sequins. An ostentation of plumes.

Cassie and Jake left the ballroom floor, crowded by well-wishers. First place in the Nationals! She could see their parents grinning back at them. Her mother's tears were visible even from that distance. She knew, before they spoke, that their parents would already be planning for the Australasian Championship.

Engulfed in family hugs, Cassie lost contact with Jake. He would avoid, she knew, his father's gloating ownership of his son's triumph. Raoul's attitude never upset her parents though it did her. Despite wide recognition of Cassie's talent, their parents and dance coach gave all the credit for their success to Jake's lead.

Time passed without Jake's return.

Lipstick-decorated and smile fixed, Cassie made small talk with the other people at the parents' table. She hid her concern at Jake's continued absence and returned to the dance floor with his father.

It seemed a long dance; the tables blurred; faces were indistinguishable; Cassie's cheeks ached. After it, she excused herself and escaped.

Well-wishers slowed her. Smiling at this person, shaking the thrust hands of that person, Cassie looked for Jake. After looking in the bar, she checked her make-up in the toilets and decided on fresh air to ease her headache. At least, that's what she told herself.

Outside, she passed parked cars and resisted the temptation to look inside. She pressed her temple, pinpointing the pain. She stopped. The car park was deserted.

It was on her way back to the hall that she saw them.

Jake's trousers were open, and he was re-buttoning his shirt. The girl, blonde and voluptuous, struggled with her bra hooks. Her flimsy dress was half-mast. Absorbed, they failed to register Cassie in the distance.

Standing there, Cassie realised that it was Melissa: blue

eyes, perfect teeth with a hint of gum, smiling back at her. Cassie was not in Jake's sightline.

Returning to the ballroom, Cassie's footsteps matched pace with her pounding heartbeat. The dance floor was crowded; the seated area around it congested. Her group's table was empty. With her legs threatening to buckle under her, Cassie pulled out the nearest chair. The room seemed unbearably hot.

Sometime later, Leonie, breathless and joyful, said, 'We're having a group shot over on the balcony. C'mon.'

Positioned with Jake, his arm around her waist, as the centrepiece in the grouping, Cassie survived the laughter and vivacity of the shoot with its eye-blinding flashes somehow. As the group separated, Jake pulled Cassie to him. 'I love you. This is just the beginning!' Cassie was unresponsive to his kiss.

Coming out of the embrace, Cassie registered Melissa's hard stare. Melissa reached for Jake as he passed her. Cassie did not hear what he said, but she saw Melissa's anguish as she stood alone, the crowd thinning.

Cassie said nothing about the car park incident then. She'd had enough though. There had been too many such incidents, too many girls. In the car park that night as their families separated, Jake said to Cassie, 'I'll come over tomorrow.'

'There are no tomorrows for us, Jake. I saw you with Melissa tonight. You're too much like your father and mine. No … don't touch me. We're done!'

For a while, Cassie got through life as if she was controlled remotely. Nothing moved her: Jake's pleas, her parents' haranguing, the arguments of their dance coach. Jake pursued her, and, for a while, Cassie toyed with the idea of forgiving him again, until it occurred to her that Jake was faithful only when he did not have her.

1988. The creak of the fly screen door made George look

up when Cassie returned with the supper tray. He looked disappointed. He covered with, 'I thought you were Min for a moment.'

'Sorry to disappoint. I offered the cuppa earlier …'

'Oh … thanks.'

Cassie considered the excess of civility between the Madisons throughout the afternoon and into the early evening. Was that how they fought? 'So how're things?'

'Isn't that my role?'

'Was I … did I get in the way this afternoon?'

'In this big old house? If Min or I wanted privacy, there are plenty of places we can get it. You weren't in the way. If anything, we used you as a buffer to get through the heat of an argument we'd been having before you came home. That gave us time to calm down and reflect on each other's perspective. And that's why I'm home.'

'Oh.' They were very different from other adult couples she knew. She doubted that any of them could reflect a partner's perspective. As they shared supper, Cassie decided to explore her record collection when she went upstairs. Maybe Santana. She loved that fusion of Salsa, Rock, Blues, and Jazz.

* * *

After luxuriating in bed Saturday morning, followed by a chat with Minna and George over lunch, Cassie decided to indulge in some personal reading. Rajes had recommended James Clavell's *Shogun*.

Sitting on the verandah, enjoying the warmth of the afternoon sun, Cassie wondered why Rajes liked the book. Cassie hated stories about the male experience with the sea.

Mavis and Terry returned from the beach with Gary an

hour or so before dinner. Cassie heard them coming up the hill: competitive and laughing.

Mavis paused to talk while the men disappeared into the house. 'We're goin' down to the pub later. Care to join us?'

'Later being?'

'About eight-thirty.'

'I'd love to.'

'It's goin' to be different from the scene you're used to in Sydney. We're country and all.'

'That's good. I didn't like the nightclubs my boyfriend and I went to … a bit plastic.'

'Here's hopin' things are different down here then,' Mavis said although there was doubt in her voice. 'So, you have a boyfriend?'

'Not any more.'

Mavis did not consider the force and coldness of Cassie's response. 'A recent break?'

Silence.

'Why did you break up? Was it because …'

'Do you mind, I'm trying to read.'

Feeling like cold water had been thrown over her, Mavis stood mute, aware belatedly of the earlier warning signal. She disappeared into the house.

Aware that her block to that line of conversation had sounded rude, Cassie said, 'Look, I'm not comfortable … Oh!'

On her way upstairs, Mavis' good humour was restored with the reflection that city girls were known to be reserved. Maybe, Mavis thought, it's because city people lack the privacy that comes with the space of country life and so guard the little privacy they have. There was a mystery there though, perhaps one solved once they were closer.

* * *

'But, George, of all the girls around here, why her again?' Minna said walking into the lounge room.

'Min, he's a man. It's his call.'

'I don't like her! So sweet to our faces, and yet you know she denigrated our relationship with him behind our backs. I'll never forget the sarcasm in her voice that day. 'Mummy's little boy, can't go anywhere without her permission.' Keeping us informed of his whereabouts was not getting permission; it was an act of courtesy.'

'Settle down. You're riling yourself up. Remember, Kate comes from a different type of family. They just weren't involved with their kids.'

'I need a Scotch and a soak. Thank God you put a spa in the ensuite. Let me know when that girl has left.'

Cassie closed her book. She told herself that she was thirsty and walked around the verandah to the rear of the house. Michael's car was still in the driveway.

The girl, a brunette bombshell, was flirting with Michael over a sponge cake and iced tea.

'Oh, hi,' Cassie said, pretending to be surprised, 'I got a bit thirsty outside.'

'Cassie,' Michael said from his seat, 'this is a good friend of mine …'

The interior door swung open and Gary entered. He came up short, obviously surprised.

'Didn't realise there was anyone here.' He gave a Mickey Mouse laugh and struck a casual pose. 'What are you doin' here, Ken?'

'G'day, Mike and I are mates. He used to be my dance partner.'

Dancing? Cassie looked at the woman. 'Where do you —'

'Does that mean you'll be dropping out of the club?' Gary spoke over the top of Cassie.

'Surf Life Saving is in my blood. I can do both.'

'Oh,' Gary did not attempt to disguise his disappointment.

'So where did you go for dancing?' Cassie asked, relieved she could get a word in.

'At the RSL,' Michael said.

'Here, in Keimera?'

'Yes. Don't look so surprised … Cassie, is it? This isn't a backwater, y' know.'

'I didn't mean —'

'Sure you did.'

'Ignore Ken, Cassie,' Gary said. 'She takes offence easy. I'm out of here.' He left. The back screen door closed slowly after him.

'Ken's an unusual name for a girl,' Cassie said.

'That's what the blokes at the club call me. They still have problems with women in the club. I'm cool with it though. My name is Kate Denford.'

'Kate?' So this is Michael's girlfriend. Noting the raised eyebrows of the young woman before her, Cassie said with emphasis on the surname. 'Kate Denford?'

'You guessed it, I'm Todd's sister, but don't hold that against me. I hear his Year 9 class have been real shits though he doesn't realise how it sounds when he talks about school at home. Keimera's a small town. Ready, Mike? See you.'

* * *

All women loved fashion or so Mavis thought until Cassie came to Madison House.

'Wait a tick, the southerly's come in. I'll need a jacket tonight. What about you?' Mavis asked, the tension from earlier that day forgotten.

'I've got a cardigan in the hall closet,' Cassie said.

'The one you were wearin' the other night?'

'Yes.'

'How about I lend you somethin' of mine?' Then in reaction to Cassie's expression, she added, 'It's so out-of-fashion! Was it a gift from your grandma?'

'No.'

'So why do you wear it? It's way too big.' Mavis raced upstairs. Cassie's mother and Leonie hated that cardigan too. She checked her clothing: baggy jeans, a long loose white shirt that hung to her thighs, her beloved gym boots. Fine for a pub, she concluded.

Music, a Tom Jones' oldie, drew Cassie to the lounge room.

Minna stretched her back after pushing the armchairs closer to the walls. George rolled up the rug. That done, they dragged it to the windows. With a courtly air, George extended his hand to Minna. They stepped onto their home-made dance floor.

Watching them, Cassie realised she really missed the ballroom dancing scene. Again, she saw the drift of her life since she had cut dance out.

As she waited, Cassie improvised in dance out of their sight. Hearing Mavis' footfall, she stood still, faking interest in her landlords.

'I decided on a change, Cassie. Here, wear this.'

Cassie took in Mavis' multi-coloured, layered ruffles attached to a waistband and her plunging, fitted green shirt. 'I'll say you have!' Then aware of the black leather jacket offered to her, she asked, 'Are you sure you want to share this?' There was beauty in its look and luxury about its feel.

Mavis nodded.

'It's too good; I can't borrow it.'

'Why not? We're friends, aren't we? It's special; you're special.'

'Look, I didn't mean to be rude when you asked about my boyfriend. It's just …'

'No sweat! Forget it.'

Moved and self-conscious about her appearance, Cassie said, 'Do you think I should change?'

'No use, I've seen your wardrobe, and besides, we're late. Here, I bought down this hip belt as well. You wear it like this.'

Other women would have been affronted. Cassie chose not to be. After all, she had heard similar criticism, a thousand times before, from her mother and sister. Besides, she really liked the feel of the leather jacket. As for the hip belt, she loved the way it transformed a plain shirt into something trendy. She checked herself out in the window reflection, pleased with what she saw.

'We'll be at the pub till closing,' Mavis said to the Madisons. 'Have fun you two. Cassie?'

'Oh, coming.'

As they strode down the hill through the Madison property, Mavis said, 'This is what I call invigoratin'. Feels like rain.'

'Sky's clear.'

'Look at that haze around the moon – definitely rain in the next few days. Well, what do you think of the fellas up at the house?' Mavis asked.

'I haven't had much to do with them. Why?'

'Just checkin' to see if I've got any competition over Terry.'

'You don't. He's a bit old for you though, isn't he?'

'Eight years isn't that big a gap.'

'It's not if you don't notice it,' Cassie said.

'Terry's different from the boys I used to date.' Images of them passed Mavis' mind-sight: gauche young men who were car obsessed, had hormones raging, and were hunters intent on sex. They had pulled and groped at her. The only thing Terry reached for was her chair or the door. He listened to her, expected her to have ideas, and made her feel valued. He thought and talked about issues bigger than the surf and football, and best of all he had an affluent future. 'In some ways, Cassie, Terry reminds me of my dad except Dad's not a collector.'

'Collector?'

'Of coins mostly, but he has a thing for cars as well, one car really.'

'I haven't seen it.'

'It's garaged in town. He only uses it for long trips. We prefer walking for stuff in town.'

'Oh.'

'Even though Terry restored his Austin Healy from scratch, he's not into men fawning over it or anything else for that matter. He doesn't need other blokes' envy for something to have value. He's like my dad that way. Reckon most girls want a man like their dads.'

'I don't.' Cassie regretted her moment of honesty.

'Your dad a bastard?'

'He's … not now, but … actually, he was. I don't want a life like my mum's.'

'We're sort of the same then. I want a better life too, but I can't go wrong with someone like Dad.'

The women walked in silence for a while before Cassie asked, 'Can you see anything wrong with wishing someone a good weekend?'

'Of course not. It's the Aussie salute.'

'That's what I thought, but whenever I say it to Talbut, he says, 'That's not a nice thing to wish a man'.'

'I don't get it.'

'Me either.'

'Now, I hope you won't take offence, but what's goin' on with your clothes?'

Taken aback by the directness, Cassie was silent.

'Were you really huge at one stage and just haven't got used to the smaller body?'

'No.'

'Your family from some sort of religious group that's got issues about the female body?'

Cassie laughed. 'No.'

'Well, why are you hidin' in your clothes?'

'I'm not hiding. I like to be comfortable.'

'You can be comfortable and fashionable. What you wear is a statement. Look at me. I'm proud of my assets. You should let me come shoppin' with you sometime or, at the very least, talk about how to accessorise. There's a sale on acid-washed jeans and jackets at Instyle. They sold out of my size, but there were a few smaller sizes left.'

'I'll think about it.'

'Right. That's my mum's way of sayin' no.' Mavis paused. 'I miss my mum.'

'Me too.'

'Yair, but you speak to yours every week.'

'So, what's stopping you?'

'Terry says that part of bein' my own person is livin' my own life without my parents' interference. If I talk to Mum, then she'll want to know about my life. Then I'll care about what she thinks and that'll stop me bein' my own person. I'll never grow up that way.'

Cassie frowned. 'It's good to be given different perspectives on things. Anyway, it's what parents do. What they say is just something to consider, we're not obliged to do it. How many people do you know who've cut their parents out of their lives? Not many, I'll bet! If you follow that line of thought, friends can only be mirrors. You and I couldn't even be friends; we're totally different! Sounds like Terry's possessive to me.'

'Really?'

Taking in Mavis' pleasure, Cassie added, 'But that's not a good thing.'

Chapter 14

The pub was panelled in walnut. The bar was long and u-shaped. A tiled floor connected the bar to the lounge which was various shades of red. Round tables and chairs surrounded a parquetry dance floor. The lights had an orange quality to them. The room was full of smokers.

Mavis wove her way through the crowd. She seemed to know everyone. Cassie followed her, uncertain and unsure. This was an environment that she had often seen in Australian movies but not experienced. She had only been to nightclubs with Jake and the local RSL Club with her parents.

'Didn't know you were workin' tonight,' a faded woman at a nearby table said to Mavis, 'we checked the board when we came in.'

'The owner's cut me back to one Saturday a fortnight. I alternate with a band; they start at ten.'

'Give us a song anyway, love? We won't be in next week,' the woman continued.

'When I've had a few,' Mavis said. She looked for Terry and Gary; they were perched at their favourite table near the upright piano.

'You did well gettin' us this table,' Mavis said, shedding her coat and taking Cassie's from her. 'Terry, ask Lil to hold these for us behind the bar. I don't want any burns or beer on them.'

'Is this place always as crowded?' Cassie asked Gary.

'Pretty much. Plonk yourself here,' Gary said, hooking out a chair with his foot. 'And your poison is …?'

'Lemon, lime and bitters, thanks.'

'A heavy drinker, eh, Cassie? Mavis?'

'Vodka and orange.'

'Put your money away, Cassie. Can't a man pay for anything anymore?'

The next hour passed quickly. Mavis and Gary again competed for the role of storyteller. Terry seemed content as audience.

Cassie considered him. He masked his insecurity at Gary's relationship with Mavis well. The telltale sign being his affectionate possessiveness in sitting closer to Mavis, his arm holding her to him, and his kissing of the palm of her hand as she shared attention with Gary. Cassie understood Terry's insecurity; Gary was more Mavis' type.

'What about the time you took the new surf boat out?' Mavis asked. 'You should've seen them, Cassie. They were full of it when they first launched the boat, but they couldn't handle the waves. They kept comin' back to shore.'

'It was rough surf …'

'It was, but that wasn't the problem. You were too busy posin' for the newspaper. When they finally did get out, Gary got knocked off. It made a great photo; he looked like he was in a spearheaded tackle!'

'Served me right,' he grinned. 'Hey, Mike! Over here. Of course we've got room for you and Ken. Nothing like being cosy.' He brushed elbows with Cassie. 'Nuh, it's Terry's shout, mate.'

'What about a song, Mavis?' someone from the bar called. Other patrons echoed that request.

'Love to. Any preference?'

'What about *Come Together*?' someone called from the bar.

'Great choice; can't beat the Beatles. I'll need some help with the backin'. Gary?' Gary was by the piano faster than a foot withdraws when it's stepped on cactus. 'Terry?' she called to him as he reached the bar.

Mavis sat at the piano and played a few chords as a warm-up.

'What're you waitin' for?' a woman near Terry called out to Mavis. Her hair was bottle blonde, and she was as thin as the cigarette she held.

'My man,' Mavis said gesturing to him.

'We'll get your drinks,' the woman said to Terry.

Terry and Gary struck a rehearsed pose.

'Okay, fellas?'

There was an expectant hush.

Terry and Gary vocalised the intro. It was deep and tuneful. 'Ssshhzzz, boong, dom, zoom, bongg; ssshhzzz, boong, dom, zoom, bongg.'

Mavis' voice was strong and pure: 'Here come old flattop …'

From the opening bars of the song, competing activity in the pub ceased.

The men threw themselves into the chorus. 'Ssshhzzz, boong, dom, zoom, bongg; ssshhzzz, boong, dom, zoom, bongg.'

Cassie was amazed at the clarity and vibrancy of Mavis' performance.

The dance floor filled, Michael and Kate among them.

'Go, Mavis,' someone from the audience called.

The music rocked as did the dancers. Michael and Kate danced a complex array of steps during the rotation of the floor. She stood close enough to him to feel his body warmth.

To Cassie, any choreography that allowed two people to

become one, through the fluid movement of the dance, was beauty in motion. She was struck by the primitive element in the beat, and the sensual heat between Michael and his partner. He was the stronger of the two dancers but lacked Jake's flair. Michael was good but not great. As for Kate, she was definitely an exhibitionist.

In the background, people were rapping on the bar and on the tables.

In the final chorus, the whole room joined in: 'Ssshhzzz, boong, dom, zoom, bongg; ssshhzzz, boong, dom, zoom, bongg.'

The crowd broke out in raucous approval when the song ended.

The trio remained at the piano for a bracket of songs.

When Michael and his partner returned to their table, Cassie said, 'Pretty good. Where did you learn?'

'We're not just good,' Kate interrupted, 'Mike's a potential champion if he has me as a partner.'

Cassie smiled. While there wasn't any place for modesty in competition, the woman overstated her skill.

Understanding Cassie's smile, Kate said, 'I don't feel like a drink after all. C'mon, Mike, let's dance.'

'I'm sitting this one out.'

'Suit yourself. There're plenty of blokes willing to dance with me. Your loss.' To prove it, she crossed to the bar, asked someone she seemed to know, and was soon on the floor.

'I hope that wasn't on my account, Mike.'

'And if it was?'

The directness made Cassie feel flustered. 'I guess I should say thanks then.'

'So, you dance?'

'Yes.'

'Not the bop and rock stuff, ballroom,' Michael said.

'As a matter of fact, I was —'

'I thought so; it's in the way you move. Would you like to dance, Cassie?'

'I'd love to but not this set. It'd upset Kate, and —'

'You don't even know her.'

'True, but we seemed to have started off on the wrong foot. I don't want to figure as anyone's rival as well.' Rival? Cassie couldn't believe she had said it that way.

'Cassie, I told Kate from the get-go that we're not picking up where I left off with her, romantically or otherwise. We're friends. I enjoy being with her because of shared history, nothing more. You'd be doing me a favour if you helped me reinforce that.'

'I don't want to be used as a shield either.'

The bracket of songs ended and the group, with the exception of Gary, returned to their table.

In an attempt to improve the relationship with Kate, Cassie said, 'I don't get the animosity Gary directs at you. He's usually so easy going.'

'A few years back, one of the women in the movement used the Anti-discrimination Act to force the Life Saving Club to open up the senior ranks to women.'

'Whoa!' Michael said and then after consideration added, 'That must have made them feel emasculated.'

'It didn't exactly endear women to them.'

'And they're still resentful?' Cassie asked.

'Yep.' Resignation and an element of defiance coloured Kate's response. Then more upbeat, she added, 'My dad's favourite saying is 'You might as well stand and fight because if you run, you will only die tired.' I am my father's daughter.'

Cassie liked Kate's courage and the philosophy underlying

her action made sense. Was that the way, she wondered, for women to achieve acceptance in a male-dominated institution?

Her thoughts drifted away from the scene.

Acceptance. She thought all of her teacher clothing was bought with that deliberate intent. Did she use clothing to hide? A mental review of her wardrobe showed a preference for denim and a subdued range of colour that made her commonplace. Her dress style was really camouflage. She preferred to blend into the background rather than claim a place in the centre of the picture.

Leonie's question resounded, Ever think about the sort of woman you want to be?

Different from what I am now, she thought. When she had time, she would work on the outer woman as well. She knew what her mother and Leonie thought was trendy.

'Are you ready to shove off?' Gary said to Michael and Cassie.

Michael and Kate stood. He looked at Cassie who was lost in reflection. 'Cassie?'

She looked up. 'Yes?'

Meanwhile, Gary's attention diverted. 'What the …?'

Cassie followed his sightline in time to hear Mavis' squeal and see her hug Terry, pinioning his arms to his body in her joy.

Mavis rushed over to their table. Terry followed grinning.

'Terry's just asked me to marry him, and I said yes.' She squealed again and grabbed Cassie's hands.

'Congrats, mate,' Gary said to Terry shaking his hand. To Mavis, Gary said, 'Felicitations on gaining the chain. I hope you'll be happy.' He attempted to kiss her.

Terry stepped in pulling Mavis to him gently but speaking in clipped tones with a sharp bite to the final word, 'That's a bit off, mate!'

'It was the old ball and chain joke. I was tossing up between that and marriages are made in heaven but so are storms.'

'I think shouting for the champagne for a toast will help you take your feet out of your mouth,' Michael said.

'Terry!' some women from the bar beckoned him.

'Won't be a moment,' Terry said, 'I just want a word with some people from work.'

'The next year and a bit are goin' to be so excitin'! I can't wait for the ring, the parties, the weddin' gown … ahhh!' Mavis squealed softly, unable to constrain her joy. 'I didn't realise what Terry was askin' me at first. He was a bit indirect about it. Guess how he did it?'

'Haven't a clue.'

'He said that since we make such good music together we should consider doin' it permanently. I told him that starrin' in a pub sing-along didn't mean he had a chance makin' a livin' out of it. He looked gobsmacked for a moment, and then he said, 'You dill! I want to marry you.' Isn't that romantic?'

'Well …' Cassie began.

'Oh, oh, I've worked out why Talbut is offended by the Aussie salute,' Mavis said.

'What?'

'You know, 'ave a good weekend. He's takin' W.E.E.K. to be W.E.A.K.'

'Oh.'

'It's sexual!'

'Oh!' Cassie was shocked but also impressed by the cleverness of the pun.

'Sounds like the man isn't gettin' it much.'

'You're not offended?' Cassie asked.

'My mum would be, but she's not out there in the workplace. Like my boss says, 'You've got to have a sense of humour.' You should hear the men where I work. It's a game men play and a lot better than their preoccupation with the size of their dicks.' She looked around for Terry. Her eyes hardened and her brows creased when she saw him charming some women at the bar.

'You've got a great voice,' Cassie said to Mavis.

'It's okay.'

'No, I mean it! Hasn't anyone told you you're talented? You should be studying in Sydney, not wasting your time in a pub.'

Mavis' attention diverted to Cassie; the truth resonated. Her smile manufactured, Mavis looked around the pub, seeing it as Cassie did. She had dreamed of being in the spotlight of the sun and ended up in the light of a waning moon. Then she saw Terry and refocused. Her insecurity nudged out the fleeting insight.

Cassie knew all too well Mavis' look. Jake's mother and hers assumed the expression whenever their husbands flirted. Cassie had guarded against it when Jake followed his father's lead. She knew even more the feeling: acid eating away the inner core of confidence. Was it always this way? Once possessed, always insecure?

Gary and Michael returned with champagne and glasses.

The popping of the cork brought Terry back to their table. A strained peace simmered between Gary and Terry.

'To the happy couple,' Gary said.

'To the most beautiful woman in the world,' Terry said.

Mavis' eyes became teary, but her spirits had revived.

Later that night, Cassie was preoccupied and deaf to the banter as the group walked back to Madison House. Mavis seemed to have it all together, but her comments about the male mentality troubled Cassie. Am I old fashioned? She didn't think so.

Cassie did not want to be a servile person with pre-sixties values. She did not think she was a prude though Coachman said she was. How could anyone confuse flattering attention with being groped? This was a dance she had to work out before she could manage the steps.

Chapter 15

A red-stoned circular driveway connected the grass lawns at the rear of Madison House to the huge barn where the cars usually parked. A florist's van now blocked a portion of that space. The delivery boy, shirttail out-hanging and cigarette balanced in the corner of his mouth, walked along the southern verandah after having knocked unsuccessfully at a number of the rear doors.

'Oi, anyone home?' He stopped midway down the verandah and peered in through the window. He continued his search, repeating his call. He looked at his watch – past knockoff time. On his return to the van, Mavis rounded the north-eastern corner of the house.

'G'day,' she beamed. Looking back to where she had come from, she said, 'You owe me five dollars, George. It wasn't my imagination. It's a delivery boy. I can manage it,' she called. Then to the boy in her receptionist voice, she said, 'Can I help you?'

'I've got a few boxes of flowers for you, that is, if you're Cassandra Sleight.'

'A few boxes?'

'That's right, lady. Can we hurry this up, I've got a home to go to, y' know?'

'Mind your mouth, squirt. She's not home yet. I can sign for them though, can't I?'

'It says the delivery must be to her personally.'

'In that case, you're in for a wait. Don't know when she'll be home. You see, she's a teacher, and the school's having their parent interviews this arvo. We don't expect her till seven. See ya.'

'Hold on.' The boy looked again at his watch. His face reflected his internal debate.

'Sign here. I can't stick around, and the boss said not to come back until this job was done.'

Mavis followed him to the van and watched, eyes agog, as he carried four large boxes into the kitchen.

'Four boxes! Wow! I've never got one.'

'Don't suppose there's a tip in this for me?'

'The only tip you'll be getting is in the garbage if you don't mend your attitude,' Mavis said. 'You're half my size, so don't think I won't do it.'

The boy scrambled back to the van.

Mavis fingered the card pressed inside the cellophane on one of the boxes. The message, 'Be with me, Jake.' appealed to her sense of romance. Wow! A real live romance under her nose!

There was a lot of speculation about the flowers over dinner that night, but interest was not high enough for everyone to alter their plans. Gary went to a Surf Life Saving meeting, Minna to the Country Women's executive planning meeting for the Australia Day fundraiser, and George to a Lions Club get together. Michael, true to his night pattern on weekdays, retreated to his room for study.

In the lounge room, Mavis had dozed off to sleep in George's winged armchair well before Cassie returned. The creak and bang of the kitchen door woke her. She wandered into the kitchen sleepy-eyed but brightened when she saw Cassie reading the card attached to the flowers.

'You're late, Cassie.'

'There was a rabbit on the road ...'

'You hit it?'

'No, I veered around it. It was stunned in the headlights. Then there was a frilled neck lizard ...'

'You should've run over them ... that's what the police recommend anyway. Want me to help with the flowers?'

'I can't accept them.'

'What?' Mavis exclaimed. 'Sure you can.'

'They have to go back.'

'But I signed for them, Cassie. They can't. I thought I was helpin'. Sorry.'

'Help me get them to my car. I'll take them back.'

'At this hour?'

'Oh!'

'Exactly!'

Cassie looked at the boxes. 'I could drop them off tomorrow on the way to school. C'mon, help me get them into the car.'

'But they can't go back! I signed for them; the delivery kid will get into trouble if you return them.'

'You signed?'

'Yes.'

'They can't go back. You signed!'

'That's what I've been sayin'.'

'Then they'll have to go in the garbage.'

'All of them?' Mavis stepped in front of the boxes. 'That's such a waste! My mum would be appalled, your mum too. You said she was talkin' about some such thing on the phone with you the other day.'

Cassie considered her options. 'Well, you have them.' She grabbed her bag, turned on her heel and left.

'Really?' Mavis looked at the flowers with delight. She flushed with a sense of ownership, of wealth.

The slam and creak of the kitchen door indicated Cassie's departure. Jolted to a wider situational awareness, Mavis followed Cassie. 'Where are you off to?'

'I'm not sure. I just ... I have to get out, away.'

'What's behind all of this ... this ... whatever it is you're feeling?'

Memory clicked in like the wheels aligning on a poker machine. Again, Cassie heard, Aren't you tired of a past littered with escapes?

'They're only flowers, Cassie.'

'They're much more than that. Not returning them is about the worst thing I could do. He'll think ...'

'You could write him a note, acknowledgin' the flowers and tellin' him you can't accept them. That you gave them to someone who could.'

Returning to the verandah, Cassie said, 'I could ... that's a good idea. Thanks.'

'G'day girls,' Michael said from behind Mavis. 'So, you've got a boyfriend, Cassie.'

'Not any more. I'm donating these flowers up to Keimera Care, but I'm not sure where it is. Mike, would you show me?'

'Oh,' Mavis said.

'No sweat,' Michael replied. 'I need a break from study anyway.'

Cassie continued, 'George said the other night they needed more flowers around the place.'

'I think, Cassie,' Mavis said, 'George was talkin' about replacin' all that concrete with gardens and about gettin' the residents involved in designin' an environment they'd like.'

'Doesn't matter. For a while the garden can come indoors.'

As Michael's four-wheel drive turned onto the newly built bypass that led toward town, he mentally debated how to broach the subject of the boyfriend.

'My granddad,' Cassie said, 'spent his last two years in a nursing home. He was a keen gardener until his stroke. After that … The nursing home had great gardens; he preferred sitting outside. Dad said he thought it was because the home had that old people smell, and Pops hated it.'

'I don't recall much about my granddad apart from a time when I was six. I remember him sitting on the front verandah puffing away on his pipe while I chewed on a hunk of bread with strawberry jam. He always wore a hat, the felt kind.'

'Oh,' Cassie said in a moment of warmth, 'Pops wore one too. When I think of him it is as he was before the stroke … dressed in dark grey trousers and a white shirt with rolled up sleeves.'

'It was sort of a uniform for that age group, wasn't it?'

'It sure was. Pops saw denim as a working class thing. He hit the roof the first time Leonie wore a pair of jeans. I didn't wear denim until after he died.'

'Because you were intimidated?'

'Out of respect. I loved him more almost than … I don't like upsetting people I love. Actually, I don't like upsetting anyone.'

'So what's the story behind the flowers then?'

Silence.

Michael turned into the township.

'Ever been in love, Michael?'

'What bloke hasn't?'

'I don't mean …' How could she say lust without sounding like she thought boys confused the two?

'Lust?'

Cassie nodded.

'You're judging me by the stereotype, Cassie.'

'Sorry, I —'

'No offense taken. I reckon most boys discover first love long before they awaken to lust. I know the difference. I thought I was in love, but it didn't work out.'

'Did you fall out of love?'

'Fall in love, fall out of love ... That makes it all sound so shallow. I was too young, and it all got too difficult. I still love for her though. No, don't look at me like that.' Michael laughed. 'I'm not as pathetic as that. I didn't say I was still in love with her.'

'I know exactly what you mean. It's such a relief to talk to someone who gets it. I still love Jake because of what we once shared but ... stuff happened, and it didn't work out. I've gone past being in love.'

'So you're getting rid of the flowers because you think it signifies ... what?'

'Jake can't let go. He wants to eat his cake and keep it too. It's not the right image, but do you get what I mean?'

'Are you sure? People send flowers for a host of reasons. A peace offering, a farewell perhaps?'

'As sure as I am that I'm sitting here. He'll take any risk not to lose ... he's used to ... I'm not saying he sees me as an object exactly ... more like ... I can't explain it without making him sound bad and without being unfair to him.'

'I get it; when you focus on an aspect of a person, you only see a caricature and not the real thing.'

'Like your Mum does with Kate?'

'There's so much more to Kate than what Mum sees. Jake could be like Kate ... she's not ready to let go of the relationship and what she gets from it.'

'That's Jake too.' Cassie studied him. 'And what about you?'

The sound of the blinker cued the turn left. 'Well, here we are.' He drove up the driveway and came to a halt. 'How do you want to do this?'

'Just give them the flowers.'

'No, Cassie, I mean do you want to ring the night bell while I get the flowers or vice versa?'

'Sorry, I forgot nursing homes lock down once it gets late. You ring.'

As they waited for the nurse to answer the doorbell, Cassie said, 'Thanks, Mike, for your help … and openness.'

'Anytime.'

* * *

Small Caramello filled Easter eggs were the order of the day for Cassie's Year 7 and 8 classes the last day of the term. Their pleasure at the gift embarrassed her. She had decided against giving any eggs to her Year 9 and 10s. They seemed too old for such things, however, two Year 9 boys, early arrivals to her class as the Year 7s filed out with eggs in hand, changed that view.

Ben Chivers and Joe Hackman had been all too willing to give up their status for chocolate. The rest of the class arrived before she had time to explain there weren't any for them.

Throughout the lesson, both boys worked hard: hands up in discussion, thoughtful contributions, on task in written work, their usual off-task banter silenced. Cassie felt downright mean as the lesson ended.

The class left with permission in typical haste, but the two boys lingered.

'Anything we can help you with, Miss?' Joe asked.

Cassie packed her books, wondering how to temper their

disappointment. As she dropped her pens into her plastic box, the one in which she had kept the chocolate eggs, she saw that by some stroke of fortune she had a few left.

'Well, you could take these off my hands,' she said selecting four eggs each for them.

'Gee, Miss, thanks,' Ben said.

'Wow! So many!'

'You worked really hard today. You deserve a reward.'

'Thanks!' both boys replied.

Climbing the school stairs that afternoon, Cassie thought about the cocoon stage from Good Friday to Easter Sunday. Had she been in a similar state since discovering Jake's affair with Melissa, focused on insulating herself from the pain of betrayal, from the sadness that came with it? Had she some-how got stuck? She did not want to be that girl any more.

* * *

Looking into the hairdresser's mirror, Cassie did not recognise herself. Her transformation went beyond anything that she had imagined. Reflexively, she ran her hand over her head. She felt naked, but smiled up at the apprentice hairdresser as the girl primped and fussed over Cassie's halo of curls, accentuating the forelock fall just above her right eyebrow with hair wax.

'Andre really is a master cutter! I just love the way he's used your hair in getting that diagonal look. Great design works with not against the material you work with, y' know. Your family won't know you.'

Never a truer word spoken than that, Cassie thought, reflecting on the changes in her confidence and attitude. The haircut made it possible for her to rid herself of the old Cassie who had always been there in the mirror looking back at her. That girl was gone. A new wardrobe would be the finishing touch.

'How do you think your boyfriend will react?'

Refraining from dispelling that assumption, Cassie said, 'What I am and how I look is not dependent on male approval. I am my own person.'

The girl reacted, nonverbally, with a whoa!

Cassie stood and waited for the girl to remove the protective cape. 'Thanks. I'll need some of that hair wax.'

Chapter 16

Easter came early April that year. It was unseasonally hot in the days with cold changes at night. In the hinterland, the landscape cracked as the grip of drought worsened.

Cassie revelled in the luxury of free time on Good Friday. She emptied the clothing from her wardrobe and dressing table and packed it in her suitcases with the intention of lugging them out to the garage for storage.

The thump and thud down the stairs broke the silence of the house but did not draw attention from the other residents who had decided on a late start to the long weekend.

As Cassie returned to the house, Minna and George parked on the gravel, the crush of stone under tyre giving way to the softer sound of stone under foot tread.

'You must've got up early,' Cassie said to them, waiting on the verandah.

'George likes the sunrise service and the community breakfast that follows. It's one of those shared things we do nowadays.' Minna reached for George's hand.

'They staged an outdoor drama this year,' George said. 'It's a pity Michael missed it.'

'The excitement of the children's faces as Jesus entered Jerusalem was so real. I felt like I was there.'

'Reverend Wehmann did a great job with the whole journey: poignant, chilling. Christ's despair on the cross really got to me. The rest of the congregation were in tears by the time he reached acceptance. Powerful stuff; it makes you want to try harder to justify that level of sacrifice. All in all it was a fantastic start to the day!'

The emotional excess did not sound great to Cassie.

'So, the others up yet?' Minna asked.

'Haven't heard or seen anyone.'

Back in her room, Cassie delved into the fashion bags that had been stored next to her dressing table the last week or so. Quality paper bags in distinctive colours with flamboyant labels collected carefully over days of exhilarating shopping.

New clothes for a new woman, Cassie thought, spreading out her carefully chosen wardrobe. She fingered the delicate cloth of her shirts, skirts, and dresses. Loved the rainbow of colour in her choices. She played model, trying this and then that on, parading before her mirror.

Looking at herself in the mirror Cassie committed to being more like Leonie, a sensual being at peace with the body in which she lived. I can't wait till she sees me tomorrow, Cassie thought. She imagined the scene: her mother's approval, her sister's praise, her father's disinterest. Now when they went out, she would not look the odd one.

The morning heat foretold a hot day.

Time for a swim, Cassie thought. Checking her appearance in the cheval mirror, Cassie saw the shorts were a snug fit, her backside good enough to be in a television commercial. Her legs were first class. Her bikini top was subtly visible underneath her translucent cotton shirt. She played with an 'on the shoulder' or 'off the shoulder' look but in the end compromised with one shoulder on and the other off.

* * *

Later that morning, Cassie lounged in the sun on the front verandah with Minna. They watched the local catamaran club trying to launch in the harbour. Unfortunately, the onshore winds were stronger than the outgoing tide and only a few cats had launched.

'I don't care what time Michael was out to. It's downright sinful to sleep the whole day away.' Minna clumped upstairs.

Cassie could hear Minna from where Cassie sat on the verandah. It sounded as if Michael was resisting to the last. A sudden thud on the floor accompanied with protestations told her Minna had pulled him out of bed.

The phone rang, breaking the morning stillness.

'Cassie, it's for you. Your mum,' Mavis called, having just come downstairs.

'Coming.'

'I've accepted the short hairdo now,' Mavis said as she handed the phone to Cassie. 'I'm sorry about my reaction earlier. You really do look fantastic.'

From the top of the stairs, Minna said, 'Mike, I'm serving your breakfast on the front verandah in five minutes. Hop to it! Sorry, Cassie, didn't realise you were on the phone.'

'Hi, Mum, I didn't expect to talk today … that was Mavis … oh, I changed my hair style … radical? That depends …'

Walking downstairs, Michael came to a standstill when he saw Cassie. In the process of saying, 'God, you look hot!' he registered her distressed stance so the final word remained unsaid.

Unaware of him, Cassie turned abruptly and faced the kitchen. 'But they've been married less than a year! I don't see how anyone can blame this on me.'

Michael stood still and therefore was unobserved. He thought of returning to his room but realised that if he did, his mother's pursuit would embarrass them all. He opted for continuing downstairs slowly, unsure of what he should do.

'But I only wrote to Jake once and that was after he sent me flowers. I told him not to contact me again ... No, Mum, I swear!'

As tense as Cassie, Michael debated clearing his throat. He did not want to eavesdrop nor did he want to frighten her if she turned around.

'I didn't tell you about the flowers earlier because ... I don't know why; I just didn't ... What? Why did Dad tell him I was coming home? ... That really puts me on the spot now, doesn't it? ... Can't you see how it will look? ... You think! ... Seriously, Mum, think about the number of times Jake and I have lost it with each other ... This term's been really draining. I just can't come home if there's even the slightest risk of histrionics ... Yes, well, I was looking forward to being together as well ... I'll miss you too. Love you.' She hung up, grabbed her towel and pulled it over her head.

Michael was behind her now.

Tears rolled down her face. She pulled the towel in closer. Life sucks, she thought.

Suppressing a laugh at the towel over her head, Michael crossed to the kitchen while Cassie was blind.

Thinking she heard someone, Cassie removed the towel and looked around, her hair messed up. Voices from the kitchen carried to her; she did not want to deal with people now. Grabbing her new Ray-Ban sunglasses from the hall table, she left.

Mavis, Minna and Michael sat in the kitchen, unsure of what to do.

'I think there's a romance to unravel.'

'Give it a rest, Mavis,' Michael said.

'Have your breakfast, love. We'll act like we didn't hear anything.'

'Do you really think she'll believe that, Minna?'

'We'll be the last thing on her mind.'

* * *

By noon, the day had turned windy. The flowerbeds at the front of the house wilted. Michael and Minna sat on the verandah in silence. He watched the waves crash on the southern rock pool through George's binoculars. The water foamed over the rocks, filling the pool. 'I might go for a swim.'

'Have fun.'

Michael walked to the harbour and through the park that connected the northern and southern peninsulas. The fishing fleet was returning; seagulls filled the sky, following the fleet. He stopped on the wharves to talk to some old friends from his high school days. Michael declined a pub-crawl invitation for Saturday night, and headed for the pool.

The water looked great; the foam was thick and the swimmers laughed as they bobbed in the waves. Michael stood on the concrete landing above the rock pool, stripped off his T-shirt, and flexed. A whistle from rocks to his right drew him over to girls he knew from TAFE: Sarah whose myopia blinded her to the fleshy ooze over her undersized bikini and Kara, a sizzling siren.

After chatting for a few minutes, Michael left for a swim. He would never understand why some girls dolled themselves up so much when they went to the beach or pool.

Having swum a few laps, Michael floated on his back, looking north toward the house. From the pool, he could see

Madison House's driveway and the back circle where they parked. It was empty. The sky was amazingly blue. He drifted.

Slowly, the direction in which he was floating changed. His vision dropped to the lawns on the southern point below the lighthouse.

Cassie's car was parked downhill facing north. She sat on the grass slopes.

He swam to the ladder and climbed out. After towelling off, he slipped on his T-shirt and headed toward her.

'Going so soon, Mike?' asked Kara. 'Why don't you come and sit with me?' She patted the place next to her.

The politeness of Michael's reply disguised his dislike of women who played the huntress. Give him forthright independent women like Kate or authentic women like Cassie any day.

* * *

At sea, a lone yacht battled, struggling to reach the harbour in the strong winds. There are many types of harbours in the world, Cassie thought. Where is mine?

The luminous sheen of Cassie's cotton blouse muted the floral bikini top under it. The wind played with her hair.

Michael stood behind her and wondered about his interest. He liked her determination though she worked way too hard. He admired her courage when it was clear she was under stress. Most of all, he was attracted by her lack of the usual female artifice.

Dropping down beside her, Michael said, 'G'day.'

Cassie continued to look seaward. 'What are you doing up here?'

'Nostalgia driven. When I was a kid, Mum and I would

come up here and eat a kilo of prawns. They're too expensive for that now.'

'Your hair's wet. What was the water like?'

'Great! Like swimming in champagne. The waves are rough, but that makes it all the more fun. Feel like a dip?'

By the time they had walked down to the pool, the waves were bigger. Heat seared the peoplescape.

Cassie stripped off and plunged into the pool.

She went deep, lost to the cool and the colour. Then up she came for air. She bobbed in the centre of the pool, enjoying the waves. The foam fuzzed around her.

Michael sat on the rocks on the ocean side of the pool. Waves crashed over him. Frothing white iced the rocks. It drizzled into the pool.

The waves continued to grow in size and strength.

A gigantic wave crashed over the rocks. It knocked Cassie against the land edge of the pool, winding her. She sank beneath the foam.

The waves towed her back toward the rocks. She gasped for air. Her lungs were fire hot, bursting. She gulped water. Air bubbles, miniature balloons, drifted upwards. Arms and legs churned in the water above her head.

'That was close!' Michael said as he resurfaced with her. 'You all right?'

Cassie clung to Michael, her head resting on his chest. As the stress faded, she became aware of his body. She looked up and realised that it was Michael holding her. 'Oh, it's you! I'm okay. I lost my bearings. I think I should head home.'

She climbed out of the pool, shaken and wobbly at the knees.

Michael followed. 'Hang on, I'm coming with you.'

They towelled off.

'You're bleeding,' Michael said.

Cassie's head popped through her shirt. 'Where?'

'Let me see.' He knelt. 'Your knee is grazed.' Using his towel, he applied pressure to the leg wound for a few minutes.

'There's no need, Mike.' Nonetheless, Cassie accepted his attention.

'As Mum would say, all better.'

'Thanks.'

As they walked to her car, they discussed her work and his HSC coursework.

Michael had never met a woman like Cassie before. She had a disarming air of innocence and shied away from games of allure. She was passionate about her work, cared for her classes, worried over their lapses in behaviour, and seemed preoccupied with making a difference.

Standing beside her car, Michael was acutely aware of Cassie: her scent and physicality, the way she moved as if to unheard music, her graceful use of her hands as she spoke. With only a broad impression of her past and the boyfriend she had left behind, Michael knew he wanted to know more about her.

* * *

Regret alienated Mavis from Terry as they drove away from the Mills' farm that Easter Saturday. Grief twisted Trevor's gut into knots as he trudged down to the milking sheds.

Trevor, one foot on a rickety paling fence, watched the ritual filing out of cows from the dairy and their meandering journey to the paddock and beyond. Bovines, Trevor thought, knew how to maintain social space and orientation. This combined with instinct allowed them to keep visual contact with one another and maintain herd membership. Could he learn something from cows that would help him keep his daughter in the herd? Marg looked to him for answers. He had none.

Inside the house, Marg converted her frustration and despair at the news of the engagement into energy, ordering her home; the only thing she had ever been able to control. Trevor was the king of discards, leaving debris in his wake.

A lifetime, Marg thought angrily, a lifetime spent battling the tide of disorder! Minutes, hours, days, months, years! A lifetime of telling him that it took the same amount of time and effort to put things away as it did to dump them. If she could not achieve that simple change in her husband, how, Marg wondered, would she ever reconnect with her daughter? She did not want to be a spectator to her daughter's life.

The loss of the prodigal was a weight too heavy for her to carry; it crushed her. Pain shot into her jaw, down her arm. Grief sat heavily on her chest, making it hard for her to breathe. She stumbled to a kitchen chair, chrome and vinyl. She knew the pain would pass with the help of a pill, taken from a bottle carried in her apron pocket. It always did.

Chapter 17

The evening shadows of Saturday lengthened into night.

'Oi! The Oakbank races are about to begin,' Gary bellowed from the living room. 'Hurry up, George, I've got drinks organised. What's keepin' you?'

'Beaudy!' Terry loped into the living room, having just returned from a day visit to Mavis' parents. He flopped into a nearby armchair. 'I didn't know any were bein' televised.'

'I'm savin' to go to Adelaide next year and see it live: steeple chasing, jumping, flat racing; what more could a man want?'

'That sort of race, eh? Why not go to the Bong Bong Picnic Races this November? It'd be a lot cheaper.'

'Not the same, mate. How was your day?'

'Strained. I've got nothing in common with those people, and I don't want to.' Terry looked over his shoulder to see if Mavis was within hearing. 'And to top it off, we had a hell of a row on the way back.'

Minna entered, having been upstairs. 'George not here?'

'Should be,' Gary said, 'I reckon he's in the kitchen. Can you tell him the races are starting?'

'George? George!'

'What do you want, love? Can you grab the second tray and bring it in?'

'Men!' Nonetheless, Minna did as asked and followed her husband.

'Miss anything?'

'Nuh. I reckon Oakbank rivals the Melbourne Cup in size and colour.'

'No way, mate,' Terry replied, 'the fact that it's not televised live proves that.'

'George, a word?'

'Can't it wait, Min? Gary and I … all right, when you look at me like that, guess it must be important.' He followed Minna back into the kitchen.

'I bumped into old Mrs Denford today.'

'And?'

'She seems to think Kate and Michael are an item, again. Would you speak to him about it?'

'No, it's his life. I thought we had all this sorted out?'

'But George?'

'No, Minna. He lives his life the way he wants even if it sticks in our throats.' He returned to the living room.

Muttering, Minna boiled the kettle. She knew her instinct in such matters was stronger than George's.

Car lights probed the growing darkness of the driveway, flashing in through the kitchen window. A moment of truth or a moment of restraint? Minna was not sure which she would choose.

Laughter, blended male and female voices, the tread on the gravel and then on the verandah announced their arrival.

Minna opted for restraint as the screen door opened. Cassie and Michael entered.

Relief on a scale not previously felt flooded Minna.

'Hello, you two. Didn't know you were out together?'

'We weren't,' Michael said. 'I passed Cassie on my way back from Kate's.'

'Oh. You were walking? Something happen to your car?'

'No, it was a beautiful day, and I felt like walking to Rajes' and back. Rajes wanted to drop me off tonight, but I particularly like walking and haven't been able to do much since I came here.'

'Too much time spent in the books,' Minna summed up.

'A necessity but that's changing. Anyway, Mike drove past and stopped. He insisted!'

'As if I could just drive by and wave.'

Cassie laughed. 'I guess not; I didn't expect the cool change so it was a relief to get out of the wind. Thanks.'

'Anytime.'

'Michael, a word?'

'Not now, Mum.' He caught up with Cassie on the stairs. 'Thanks for listening. Not everyone understands the drive to realise potential.'

'Probably because it means going outside the comfort zone. I've been doing a lot of that lately myself. It's amazing you're so clear on what you want from life. I'm still trying to work that out. I don't think it's teaching though.'

They arrived at her room.

'Cassie, *Rain Man* is still on. Do you feel like seeing it?'

'It's a long drive to Wollongong. Hey, weren't you going to see it weeks ago?'

'My plans changed. It's on at the RSL cinema in town. It's supposed to be a really good movie.'

'I'd love to but ...' Looking at her room, Cassie knew she was not ready to return to the grind. She was sick of it but even more fed up with being separated from her family. Being with Michael made her feel ... what exactly? She liked the unqualified way he showed his liking for her. He made her feel valued. Had she ever felt that with Jake? Not since they were kids. 'Okay. What time?'

'We can make the nine session.'

'Give me half an hour? I need a shower.'

'I wondered what that smell was in the car.'

'Such flattery will get you nowhere, Mike.'

'Then I guess we'll meet in the kitchen later.'

* * *

Wearing a dark blue tracksuit trimmed in white, Mavis lay in a foetal position on her bed. She hugged her childhood friend, an ear-torn bear. It had been a roller-coaster day. All attempts to establish common ground between her parents and Terry had failed.

Cassie's humming as she passed Mavis' room on the way to the shower sent a surge of resentment through her.

'You look disgustin'ly happy. A pity happiness doesn't improve tunefulness.'

'Did things go as badly as that?'

'Finally, a true note.'

Cassie stood in her doorway. 'Hey, I'm on your side. Continue biting at me if it helps.' Silence. Cassie crossed to her.

'I don't want to talk about it. Close the door on the way out.'

'Fine.'

An hour passed.

Mavis' bear sailed through the air into Cassie's room, falling onto the bed.

'Okay if I come in?'

Silence.

'I'm sorry about earlier. Cassie?' Mavis entered the room, realised it was empty, grabbed her bear, turned off the light, and left.

In her room, Mavis sought relief improvising on her

guitar in search of a melody that suited her latest lyrics. She strummed chords in different keys until she found an interesting tune. Then she experimented in picking out a melody line, making amendments yet again to her lyrics. The drive to match sound to lyrics blotted all else out.

When Michael's car pulled into Madison House driveway later that night, Cassie was aware that she didn't want their time together to end. She had enjoyed the physical contact that came with sharing little things: popcorn, the brush of their shoulders when seated, the moving moments on film, the coffee afterwards, and the like-mindedness on movie issues. She liked the way Michael smelt too. Enjoyed knowing she was attractive without feeling she was an object.

In the kitchen, Cassie initiated Michael into the beauty of the tea ritual with innovative embellishments. He laughed, charmed. Eventually, tiredness claimed her, and she went upstairs.

Michael joined his parents, Gary, and Terry in the lounge room. They were watching a report on the Iran-Iraqi war.

Minna beamed at Michael when he entered. George nudged her in response. She looked at George and, like many long married couples, read his thought.

* * *

Cassie lay in her bed, reading; tiredness having deserted her by the time she had changed into her pyjamas.

Mavis' bear sailed through the air in Cassie's room, falling onto the bed.

'What's he in aid of?'

'He's a reconnaissance expert. He wouldn't hear of me enterin' potential hostile ground without testin' for fire. Has his sacrifice been in vain?'

'I gather you're ready to be friends again.'

'I am.'

'C'mon in.'

Mavis flopped onto the end of the bed.

Cassie hit her over the head with one of her assorted decorator pillows. 'Idiot.'

'Well?'

'Well what?'

'Get it over with, Cassie; there's only so much joy I can stand. Who was the bloke?'

'There's no bloke, just Michael. Close your mouth before you swallow a mosquito. We went out as friends.'

'I don't think I could stand to see you when you're in love then.'

'I take it all is not well in the romance department.'

'Right there! Terry's never goin' to get on with my parents.'

'And?'

'I've thought about it the last hour or so. I have to accept it, just like he has to accept that my parents are important to me. I'll see them; he doesn't have to.'

'Sounds like a reasonable solution, Mavis.'

'Terry wants me to move in with him. You're doin' a good job of lookin' gobsmacked.'

'It's such a big step. Have you decided?'

'I'm not ready for any of that yet.'

'Sex is not like the first kiss that's for sure. My ... my first time it didn't feel very good. It was nothing like my girlfriends said.' Her brow creased. For a moment, she saw blades of grass.

'You okay, Cassie?'

'Sorry, I've a headache coming on. Where was I?'

'We're talking sex'.

Cassie nodded. 'It took time for me to enjoy it.' Cassie

hated the emotion, from who knew where, over matters she thought long since resolved.

Mavis looked at Cassie with concern. 'You okay?'

Cassie nodded. Her emotions were too raw for her to speak. 'Make sure it's your choice.'

Concerned, Mavis crawled under the bedclothes with Cassie, putting an arm around her. Sadness weighed Cassie down. So, Mavis thought, maybe her nightmares have something to do with this. She wondered if Michael had heard Cassie crying in the night. Bound to have, she thought, given his room is next door.

'I'm sorry, Mavis, I seem to cry at the weirdest times.'

'So how old were you the first time?'

'Sixteen.'

'I was eighteen.'

'But I thought you weren't ready yet.'

'For movin' in. I was hot for sex, still am.'

'Even at the beginning?'

'Sure, it hurt a bit, but orgasms are worth it. As for bein' in love, the sex is even better. Bigger is definitely better!'

'I so didn't need to know that about Terry.'

'Well, it's out there now.'

'Said the bishop to the actress.'

'What?'

'It's a school thing. Bad taste, sorry. I've been exposed to it so much, I've just absorbed it even though I've never thought it funny. So, why aren't you ready to make the move?'

'It's not how I imagined we'd start our home. When I said that, Terry said it was just a flat, an interim thing before we married.'

'And?'

'Livin' here was supposed to be an interim thing and now it's long term: three years to be exact. We might never set a date. It could become one of those things we try on. Y' know, like dressin' up in olden day clothes, havin' the picture taken, and puttin' it away as a keepsake, a faded picture.'

Cassie did not offer advice, aware that Mavis was using her as a sounding board.

'A lifestyle that's become a habit, a rut, one that's too hard to break out of. And then there's my mum's view: Why would anyone go to the trouble and expense of owning the cow if they could get milk without it?' Mavis now looked at Cassie in appeal.

Having rejected the thought, That cliché shows your mother does not understand the world we live in, Cassie said instead, 'I don't have any answers. All I know is that I don't want to be viewed as an object.'

'I'm talkin' about what makes a man commit to marriage.'

'I get that. The cow image … You're right, I went off on a tangent. Sorry. I really don't have a clue.'

'Who does? Can I ask you something real personal?'

Yes,' Cassie said guardedly.

'How did you decide what sex acts you would and wouldn't do?'

'I … what?'

'Terry's big on variety.'

Cassie tapped the image out of her head. 'We're not talkin' love making, are we?'

'No. We're talkin' about Terry gettin' it off, pure and simple in heaps of ways.'

'Just Terry?'

'A woman has to meet a man's needs if she wants to keep him, Cassie.'

'So my mother says, but I think it should work both ways.' Painfully aware of her own hang-ups, Cassie chose her words carefully. 'Specifically, Mavis?'

'I don't want to share the details, Cassie.'

'Fair enough. I think sex acts … are like a diamond … many faceted providing there is mutual benefit. What you choose to do should involve pleasure and be satisfying for both partners. If it isn't, then you shouldn't do it.'

Mavis nodded. 'So you're against feeding the man's inner beast?'

Cassie's eyes widened. 'Absolutely. When the beast takes over, a person can get hurt. Best never to waken it.'

'Too late for that, but maybe I can … feed it different, tame it?'

'I don't understand men at all, Mavis. I can't answer that.'

Chapter 18

Grey was the dominant colour for the beginning of the second term. The skies looked overcast. Rain threatened but rarely eventuated.

'Bloody old fart!' Samantha muttered as she entered the staff room at recess.

'What's up?' Cassie asked. She wore a moss green top layered over a red one, a striking belt, a fitted black skirt, and ankle boots.

'Well, this is a first. Never thought you'd be up here so quickly.'

'I've had a great start to the day.'

'Wish I could say the same.'

'Probation interview?' Cassie asked.

'No. The Hitman intercepted me on the way back from class. He says I'm unsuitably attired!' She wore a snug pantsuit made from salmon coloured suede. It had a strong tactile appeal. 'Attired – even his language is outdated. Do you see anything wrong with the way I'm dressed?'

'You look great! Do you mind if I touch? The material says, Touch me; touch me! Oh, it's so beautiful!'

'And I feel great in it; at least I did until … No, I am not letting the limitations of that old fart affect how I dress or see myself. You are right about the tactile appeal; it had the same effect on me when I saw it. I love your hair short and diagonal like that. Did I ever tell you? Is that a fresh pot of tea?'

'Yes, and it is. I seem to have everyone's stamp of approval.'

The next to arrive was Van der Huffen, his mood blacker than his clothing. 'The bloody nerve of those kids …' He dumped his books on the centre table and frowned at the ensuing landslide.

'I thought that dance over my claim to space was finished,' Cassie said to him.

'Sorry, habit.' He removed the books to his desk. 'What's a nice girl like you doing up here so early?'

'She's had a great morning. So what's ruffled your feathers?' Samantha asked.

'None of your business!' He selected a cigar from the top drawer of his desk and prepared it.

'You've got to be kidding!' Samantha said.

He ignored her.

Spirals of smoke trailed upward as nicotine seeped through Van der Huffen's system. He calmed.

'Well, I'm off in search of better company.' Samantha edged her way down the aisle, brushing passed Van der Huffen at his desk. She rested a hand on his shoulder. 'I wasn't prying, Vander. I'm sorry if I sounded flippant.'

He shrugged her off.

'Want anything from the canteen?'

The rest of the men, who had arrived in a crush, waited for her to exit.

'I traded the wagon in for a Mazda RX-7 with a limited-slip differential,' Talbut said to his male audience. 'I wanted something that made a statement.'

'You want people to think you're all flash and no substance?' Selton had dropped into his seat near the door.

Talbut flicked a look of disdain at him but otherwise did not react.

Samantha winked provocatively at Talbut as she pressed past him.

Talbut paused to appreciate Samantha's departure. 'I feel like a peach.'

'Out of season, mate,' Pothole said.

'I don't know about that. I may have a secret stash.'

'What was the trade-in?' Fuller, one of the older teachers, asked.

'I got the purchase price back.'

'Bloody fantastic, mate!' responded Fuller, bald and teeth stained from years of smoking.

'I'll say!' Pothole added.

'But wasn't it three years old?' Fuller's thoughts were on his own car and the return it might get.

Talbut nodded.

'Anyone remember to send a kid down to the canteen before the bell?' Fuller asked.

'Have you forgotten the Boss' decree?' a few male voices chimed in.

'Don't see what harm it does, not if it's in the closing minutes of the lesson,' Pothole mumbled. 'The runner gets a chance to buy as well and without the pressures of a student queue. It was a win-win situation.'

'Personally, I agree with the Boss' perspective that we're here to serve them,' Talbut said, adding as he looked at his mug, 'I guess I'm going to have to learn to appreciate a long black.'

'Speaking of me?' Van der Huffen asked, looking up from his work.

'Feeling a bit off, mate?' Talbut asked.

'Hard morning.'

'I usually enjoy ...'

'Cut it out, mate,' Pothole said. 'Whose turn to get the sugar and milk?' Pothole considered using milk chocolate to sweeten his coffee. 'How can we carry on?' He looked expectantly at his colleagues.

'Contrived, mate,' Talbut said.

One of the younger men said, 'I've got one! Lean on me, when you're not strong, and I'll be your friend, I'll help you carry on: Bill Withers: song writer, singer, guitarist.'

A collective groan deflated the speaker.

'C'mon, popular quotes are allowable!'

'No way, mate!' the collective responded.

'He's right,' Cassie said, 'the game is hard enough without excluding popular sayings.'

Aware that her colleagues looked stunned at her contribution, she added, 'Well it is!'

'M' lady speaks,' Van der Huffen said. 'So, you've decided to get off the fence, champion the underdog, and join us.' He looked at the men. 'Despite the fact that I have a perfect quote by Mahatma Gandhi on this matter, I think victory should be ceded to Ned.'

Again with the title, Cassie thought. Why? There wasn't anything flirtatious about his manner.

'Game, set and match to our championed colleague,' Talbut concluded as Samantha returned with a wire basket of goods. He stood at the sink having decided on a black coffee rather than miss his fix. 'Ah, lady bountiful has come to the rescue!'

Samantha said, 'If you guys keep eating like this, you won't get out of the door!'

'A weighty thought but not a curb to cravings!' said Pothole.

Taking in Talbut with coffee mug in hand, Samantha added, 'The canteen ladies insisted I bring up milk and sugar. I told them we had heaps.'

'You misspoke,' Fuller said looking around the room expectantly.

Selton said, 'No one will rise to that challenge, mate. No one says misspoke anymore.'

'Mark?' Samantha said. 'Could you give me some help in the book room? *The Pigman* is on the top shelf, and I'll need some help getting a class set for my next lesson. The steps seem to have disappeared.'

Cassie looked up. Was Samantha talking to Talbut? She noticed a few of the men making eye contact knowingly. What did they think was going on?

Talbut responded. 'No problem.' He winked at the men near him before following Samantha into the corridor.

'Lucky, bastard,' one man said.

An affair? Cassie thought.

* * *

Walking up the corridor, shoulders brushing, Talbut said, 'You look spectacular today, in full bloom.'

'Thank you, kind sir,' Samantha replied, caressing his arm as she did so. 'I do like the feel of your shirt and what's underneath it.'

'Come into my parlour,' Talbut said, his hand in a sweeping gesture as he bowed before her.

Samantha laughed. 'I like the gesture, but, Mark, your choice of words …'

The book room was a narrow space, the width of two people standing shoulder-to-shoulder but the length of a classroom. Talbut used shelving either side of the room as a ladder and stood spread-eagled as he passed sets of books down to Samantha. In three swift transfers, she had thirty.

'That's the lot!' Talbut jumped neatly to the floor close to Samantha.

'Thank you very much, kind sir. Anyone told you you're looking very Fabio lately? Working out a lot?'

'Sure am, and I'm prepared to turn your fantasy into reality. I like to eat peaches slowly, peeling the layers off.' His hand moved to her jacket zip and in one deft movement undid it, exposing her half-cup, black and cream, lace bra. Her breasts had a silk-like sheen.

'Very smooth, but I think it's best to stay in the realms of fantasy.' Samantha stepped back and attempted to re-zip her top.

'My package is well worth the unwrapping,' Talbut replied, putting a staying hand on hers. 'And you, my luscious peach, have captured my thoughts to such a degree it is hard to stand.'

'Mark, you've been such a good friend …' She removed her hand from his and zipped her jacket to the collar.

'I can be much more than that.' Talbut took her free hand and held it. 'As soft as velvet.'

'You've always been such a gentleman, sensitive to my feelings.'

'There is a strokeable appeal about you, Samantha. I particularly like this outfit.' Talbut encircled her waist, pulling her forcefully to him. One hand dropped to her behind, ample and firm. He pulled her into him. 'It is hard to resist peaches and cream.'

Samantha held herself back. 'Mark, c'mon, I've been flirting for attention but there wasn't any intention to …'

Talbut wondered why women always yammered on as a prelude to sex. 'A performance deserving of a standing ovation.' He released her; his hand moved to his fly; he unzipped it. 'I think we can contrive nicely in here with that wall as your brace.'

With a downward glance and a look of disdain, she said, 'Don't believe that twaddle which says women don't care about size; it matters. You may be a legend in your own mind, but you are not in mine. Get out of my space!'

The chill of her expression and the comment froze him. This was not how the hunt usually unfolded. Sexual freedom and the right to satisfy appetite had been the one perk for women that Talbut valued in his changing world.

Embarrassed, Talbut did not resist Samantha's exit.

* * *

Trembling, Samantha found herself back at her desk. Her head ached.

'You okay?' Cassie asked softly.

Samantha spoke in undertones for Cassie's ears only, 'Yes, Mark and I had … You could call it a disagreement, but the awful thing is that it is mostly of my own making.'

'He'll get over it.' Cassie wondered if what she said was indeed true. Would Talbut react like Jake? That which was denied Jake had added appeal.

'But I won't! It's a permanent rift!' Faced with her part in that play, she felt shame at her naiveté; she had thought of herself as a woman of the world.

Interested, Cassie waited for further detail but none was forthcoming.

In the silence of the staff room, Samantha knew she had to go home. She could not face her classes feeling as she did. Tears lodged in her throat, threatening to make her sick. Without a word, she headed for the front office to organise her sign out, leaving Cassie to wonder about the suddenness of her departure and the nature of the rift with Talbut. As she did so, Cassie noticed the surprised exchange of looks between the men who sat near them.

* * *

The storm lashed the coast for a week. High curling, white-capped waves broke onto the rocks. They crashed against the harbour wall, snatched loose fragments, and churned them in the foam and sand. Breakers geysered against the rocks below the Point. Winds wrapped themselves around houses and cars, attempting to rend and discard them as a child does wrapping paper at Christmas. Accidents and flash flooding took their toll up and down the coast.

The rural community shook their heads over the rain. It was too much, they said. Too local. The benefits would be short-lived. They were right.

The catchment areas inland received little rain. The Avon, Cataract, Cordeaux, Nepean, Tallowa, and Woronora dam levels continued to drop. City people did not seem to worry about the mighty Warragamba.

'Such a waste!' George said to Minna as they sheltered on the front verandah sipping tea, watching rain sweep the land-scape and ocean. George wore a heavy-duty jacket. Minna was literally rugged up.

'What are you up to today?' George asked.

'DamWatch has approached all the regional papers about issues over the Wingecarribee Swamp and Reservoir,' Minna said. 'There's some sort of a problem with the inflow of peat.'

'Not your usual sort of piece.'

'No,' Minna laughed, 'a consequence of my satire on political correctness. The Editor withdrew his support when the backlash came in.'

'How can you stand to work with those one-gobble turkeys?'

'Because there are bigger things in the community than ourselves. The Madisons have …'

'Yes, yes, I don't need to hear that spiel again.'

'George, please. I don't want your mother's predictions about me to become a truth.'

'You still smart from that? You're not really equipped knowledge-wise to write this sort of article, are you?'

'And that's why I had planned to drive up that way today …'

'Not in this weather, you're not. Roads are too dangerous.'

'Agreed.'

'And I'm going with you, Min. I've got a better head for technical info than you. Besides, it'll give us more time together. Lately, I've been thinking about how we're living. On the one hand, I appreciate the need to stave off age with being productive, but we're connecting less and less. Who knows …?'

'Don't jinx us by saying it.' She felt a surge of passion for her husband awakened by fear of losing him.

The beep of Cassie's car horn in farewell followed by the double beep of Michael's four-wheel drive signalled their departure.

'C'mon, George, time we indulged in some morning delight.'

Chapter 19

Movement to and from school was increasingly hazardous. Cassie wished she had taken up Michael's offer of travelling with him until the weather improved. Driving into town, she witnessed cars caught in squalls on the twisting bends that led into Keimera. Luckily, that morning, cars did not slide crazily into oncoming traffic nor take the plunge down the sea cliff onto the rocks.

As the school day began, sheets of rain swept across the quadrangle. The ground floor doors flapped wildly in the wind. Struggling to close them, Cassie became drenched. Shivering, she raced up to the washroom to its hot air, hand-drying machine. Uncomfortable with the cling of her clothing, a belted crimson knit dress but aware that she could not afford any more time, she returned downstairs.

Strident voices bounced off the corridor walls.

Passing the classroom next to hers, Cassie looked in and saw Talbut had Year 12 English; they were quiet and attentive. He crossed to the doorway. 'Where the hell have you been? You're late and that class is rioting. It's almost impossible to teach. Get them quiet, and hurry up about it!' He slammed the door.

If you couldn't teach, why didn't you get them under control? Cassie thought. She wished she thought more quickly and had the gift of the smart comeback.

Standing in her classroom doorway, Cassie was appalled at

the scene. 10G had transformed the room into a cricket pitch. Desks were stacked to either side of the room. The windows were smoky. The room stank, a combination of wet wool and body odour. The spate of wet weather had not dowsed their spirits. They were in their element: hyperactive, loud, faces distorted by ribald jokes at one another's expense. Closed windows and door made the noise deafening.

Catcalls and whistles greeted her appearance in the opened doorway. She ignored the leers and made herself heard above the din. The game stopped.

'Restore the room, and someone crack a window open; it stinks in here!'

A series of farting noises were delivered in reply. Cassie remained in the doorway.

'In five minutes, I want to see everyone seated where I assigned you last week with your books out ready for work.'

The boys clumped together in lewd groups, eyeing her with an occasional lewd comment directed at her.

Refusing to be baited, Cassie said, 'Do as I say or ...'

'Or what?' a blonde boy said as he threw a ball across the room to a peer.

'You'll all be coming back at recess for detention.'

The ball passed to another boy.

'Big deal!' said Bill Fryall, a hulkish boy at the back of the room.

'Get those desks and chairs back where they should be!' she said. 'Now!'

No one moved. She looked at her watch.

'You've got sixty seconds to do it.'

No one moved. As Cassie watched the second hand sweep time, she realised her error in talking to them collectively. Focusing on the weak link in the group, a weed of a boy, Cassie said, 'Do as I say, Mick, or you'll be the first to Mr Coachman's office, and I'll speak to your parents on the phone tonight.'

Mick visibly flinched and then moved to the window.

'Thank you. Not too wide.'

'Wayne, you're the second one on my list. Isn't that your mum in the canteen today?'

He pulled an upturned desk from the bottom of the pile, causing an avalanche.

Cassie narrowed her eyes, waiting for the din to subside.

'Tim, you're on Selton's football team, aren't you? What do you think will happen if I tell him you were not only non-compliant but defiant?'

Three other boys picked up desks and chairs as Tim did.

'Use commonsense, boys. You can't set up your desks there until there's space.'

The rest of the boys now stood together, a wall of resistance. The boys who had complied now watched the scene.

What else do I know about these boys? 'Didn't I see you outside Mr Coachman's office, Will? Something to do with defying Mr Talbut at recess yesterday? I can't imagine either of them would be happy to see you again.'

Will blanched and moved to the remaining overturned desks.

Glen Dobbs, short in height but big in ego, swaggered up to Cassie. 'We don't care about the Cockroach! You're weak, you mother-fuckin' cunt-lickin' bitch!'

'You could at least be consistent with the gender.' Cassie was amazed at her calm. Where had that reply come from? She was usually gobsmacked in confrontation. The room was quieter.

Will halted, his cooperation forgotten.

Dobbs looked at her, stumped. He did not understand her correction, but it established her intellectual superiority, and he hated her for it.

Dobbs gestured obscenely, a violent upward thrust. He sauntered around her with the leer of a man in a striptease bar. 'There are only two things about you that we're interested in; your tits and ...'

In tense, measured tones Cassie said, 'Leave the room, Glen.' She could hear the rain beating against the windowpane.

'Nuh!' He sat down and stretched his legs across a chair near him. 'I don't do nothing a tunnel says. Now, as for usin' —'

'I want everyone out. Go wait outside the English staff room.'

No one moved.

Cassie was very still as she assessed the situation. 'Do it! Anyone who stays will share in Glen's fate.'

To Dobbs and her surprise, the room emptied in record time.

Not knowing what to say, Cassie studied Dobbs silently. He looked back at her brazenly. Without flinching, she kept her eyes on him.

Lacking an audience, Dobbs' bravado deflated like air out of a high-flying, careering balloon. He no longer seemed bigger than her; for the first time, Cassie saw the boy inside the adult body.

Very quietly, Cassie said, 'I think you need to present yourself at the Principal's office.'

Cassie gambled and left the room on an adrenaline calm.

Upstairs, a subdued 10G were scattered down the length of the corridor.

Selton stood in the staff room doorway.

'Thanks for keeping them quiet,' Cassie said.

'This is how they came up. I can see that something big has gone down. I'll take them to the library. You need to see Coachman.'

'I do, but I need to see the Principal first.'

'You're shaking. Need a cuppa first?'

'No, thanks. I need to do this while I'm still on a roll.'

* * *

Coachman, in a blue suit and pale lemon shirt, reclined in his office chair. He tapped his fingertips. 'All Dobbs said was that he'd been rude and that you sent him to the Principal. The Principal, of course, returned him to me. So, what did he say exactly?'

'Why do I have to repeat language like that? It was sexual and demeaning. Isn't it enough that he defied me? You've got the documentation on his harassment. You've seen what the class did to the furniture today. You know I haven't exaggerated the situation.'

'Yes, but it's Dobbs we're dealing with.'

'What does that mean? There should be one standard irrespective of who the kid is. Something has to happen to him beyond detention.'

Coachman flashed his teeth. 'Calm down, Cassie. You women get so easily overwrought.'

Cassie's eyes narrowed as she looked at him. 'Are you going to support me in disciplining him?'

'I'll decide on my course of action after I've investigated the matter. It's a pity you couldn't solve this before it came to a head.'

'Well, I tried. It would have been infinitely better from my perspective if I'd been able to leave you and any other man out of the solution. Is it my fault that all authority figures here are male?'

'I believe you're demonstrating why men hold power.'

Cassie refused to be sidetracked. 'Look, there has to be a line that once crossed has consequences that extend beyond normal classroom discipline.'

'What do you want? A caning? Suspension? Both are extreme measures and used in only the worst circumstance. We do not cane lightly here. The school and community at last year's meeting on discipline sanctioned the use of the cane in special circumstances, exceptional circumstances. We don't want to be called before the courts on a charge of assault, do we? And we can't suspend students without the development of a file.'

'10G are awful everywhere! Dobbs is their leader. The worst of them! There must be a huge file already.'

'You've had them now for almost a semester. How much documentation have you done?'

'Not everything but enough surely.'

'I believe that was the end-of-recess bell.' He consulted a folder of timetables on his desk. 'And you're on class. We'll discuss this at a more convenient time.'

When she arrived at the classroom, Cassie found her Year 9 class subdued and Rajes, in the doorway, waiting for her. 'I'll take them, Cassie. You need a break. There are lollies in my top drawer; help yourself to some.'

'Thanks.'

* * *

Van der Huffen and Selton's conversation finished when

Cassie entered. She moved to her centre table. It was as she had left it.

Both men looked at her when the phone rang. She ignored it and their expectation that she would answer it. It was one thing to reject her mother's role of subservience and quite another to weed it out of her own reflex behaviours.

The phone demanded attention.

Cassie looked at Van der Huffen.

'All right, so I'm the closest.' He arched an eyebrow at Selton but answered the phone. While he waited for the receptionist to switch the call through, he scrutinised Cassie. 'That woman's lost the connection yet again. It's at times like this that I wish the Hitman had got those biddies retired.' He watched Cassie while he waited for the call to be reconnected. 'You look like you've had a passionate embrace with battle. Your eyes are on fire, your cheek aglow …'

'I don't want to hear it! And you can drop the shocked protestations too.'

She felt like escaping but resisted that childhood impulse. Sitting at her desk, Cassie winnowed her thoughts for a course of action. This was just another form of dance. She had to work out the steps.

Her absentminded finger tapping finally resulted in Selton saying, 'Do you mind?'

Cassie looked at him blankly.

'The tapping.'

'Oh, sorry.'

They worked until the next bell in silence. Unnoticed, the men left for class. Alone, Cassie remembered Rajes' lollies. She laughed when she saw the packet of Minties.

For the rest of the day, her expression was one well-known by Keimera students; it said, 'Don't mess with me!'

The trembling set in as Cassie drove away from the school. On the outskirts of the town, she pulled into a parking bay that allowed tourists to appreciate the splendour of the seascape and the contrast of the rural hinterland.

Sick, she had to get out of the car. After vomiting, the trembling worsened. Breathe, she thought as she climbed back into her car, breathe.

Tears streamed unheeded down her face. What a day! Facing west, Cassie watched the rural landscape change as the purple hue of late afternoon signalled that winter was close. Emotions gave way to feeling drained. Realising that she could never accept the status quo, Cassie committed to changing it, somehow.

* * *

Tense, cold days marked the next two weeks. Students were systematically culled from 10G each lesson and interviewed by Coachman. Dobbs guarded Coachman's doorway during those lessons until resolution could be reached, exiting the building by a circuitous route for his other lessons. This kept him away from Cassie.

The class pitied each lesson's victims, worked in silence, and glared at Cassie. Her other classes were subdued also; the effect of the school grapevine, she assumed.

Throughout the investigation, 10G boys were on lunch detention. They lined the upper corridor like palace guards with a changeover at the mid-lunch bell.

By the time Coachman came to a decision, the constraint operating on 10G boys was weakening. During detention, they pushed the envelope of control.

Matt Spence, a boy whose shocking red hair and bad

behaviour made him stand out even among this group of lunch detainees, stood in the alcove between the cleaner's room and the corridor that led to Coachman's office. He gestured at the boys near him, pulling faces and acting the fool. Skinny Rudd, an anorexic-looking boy with a snotty nose, mirrored the behaviour to those near him. Neither boy saw Van der Huffen enter the corridor from the stairwell.

The boys facing the stairwell froze at the sight of Van der Huffen. They took in the cane and his arms tucked wing-like around it. His head jutted forward.

Someone whispered, 'The Crow.'

Matt Spence, mid-grimace, straightened and inched back to his assigned station. The remaining boys froze.

'Hmm,' Van der Huffen sounded as he inspected the line-up on the way to Coachman's office.

Dobbs' attempt at bravado failed under Van der Huffen's piercing stare.

Cassie was in Coachman's office when Van der Huffen entered.

Coachman leant back well into his chair. He closed on, 'The investigation outcomes are as follows: a caning for Dobbs followed by a two week suspension. The remainder of the class are to continue detention until the mid-semester break. At that time, the situation will be reviewed. I have asked Vander to dispense the caning. Miss Sleight, you are expected to stand by for its administration, including a talk to the boys by Van der Huffen and Selton.'

Cassie blanched. 'I'd prefer —'

'This is not up for discussion. I want it clear to one and all that we are aligned with you on this matter. The boys know that caning occurs in only the most serious of circumstances. There will not be any more this year. Now, if you'll excuse me, I have an appointment with the Boss. I'll just ring the staffroom and let Selton know we're ready.'

Van der Huffen called 10G boys from their stations along the two corridors to him. 'Bob down boys, Mr Selton will be along in a minute. We have something very important to talk to you about.'

After a bit of joggling and squirming, the boys settled and focused on Van der Huffen and Selton.

Selton began, 'Between us, Mr Van der Huffen and I have taught all of you at sometime. Some of you are even in my Under 17s football squad. Out of the classroom, we know that you are a good mob of blokes.' Selton, by look, passed the dialogue over to Van der Huffen.

'But in the classroom, well, that's been a different matter, hasn't it? Some of you have chosen to follow in the footsteps of older kids who ended up expelled. What you do not know about those kids is that as adults many of them ended up in jail; their lives ruined. Their parents' hearts broken by the waste and loss of a decent future for their sons.'

In rhythm, Selton continued, 'Recently, we've become aware of the extent of your misbehaviour, of your disrespect to and abuse of Ms Sleight through attitude, language, and volume. Shocked as we are by that, even worse is your squandering of the chance to get an education …'

'An education that could help you into an apprenticeship and then later a trade. What you do at school now is going to affect you financially for years to come.'

Selton said, 'Your behaviour with Ms Sleight has also given us serious cause for worry. Abuse of women is not tolerated in our society! Lack of discipline and its evil twin, aggression, are not tolerated in the workplace!'

'Australia is a society built on the rule of law with a set of laws that apply to everyone. The same goes for schools.'

'Some people call our system the Robin Hood system because the government takes from the rich and gives to the poor so that there is equality in the opportunity to learn and the resources needed for learning. It doesn't matter how poor your family is,' Selton looked at Mick Fryor, 'or how drunk your dads are.' He looked at Dobbs and Skinny Rudd. 'The system is about 'a fair go' for all.'

'Your behaviour with Ms Sleight or any other teacher is not on! You know Mr Selton and I both abhor the use of the cane.' A number of the boys nodded, some a little too vigorously. 'Nonetheless, as in society, there are crimes that result in terrible penalties.'

'Mr Van der Huffen, Ms Sleight, and I hope that this is the worst thing to happen in your lives. That you take pause and consider your actions and where they are leading you. That you choose to make the most of the remaining time at school with Ms Sleight and learn something that can help you get a job and be proud of yourselves. Footy practice is cancelled this arvo, boys,' Selton said to footballers. 'I'll see you on the field Friday arvo as planned.' He left.

'Shall we begin? Dobbs step up to the mark.' Van der Huffen looked at the boy, his eyes downcast but the swagger still in his stance. He was very different from the boy Van der Huffen had taught in Year 7. 'You are at a crossroads, Glen.' The boy looked at him then. 'Although this will hurt, that pain will be nothing to that in your future if you continue on this road. You're a natural leader; don't take the mob down the wrong path.'

The cane sliced the air and impacted on flesh. Cassie fought a rising nausea.

Dobbs' face was anguished.

'You can go to the front office now,' Van der Huffen said, 'your parents are waiting to take you home.'

Van der Huffen spoke quietly to Cassie. 'Kids like Dobbs lack a moral compass. We have to help our adolescent beasts find the beauty in being civilised. Otherwise, they're headed for the horrors of jail.' To the boys lining the corridor, he said, 'Now, I believe that 10G have something to say to you, Ms Sleight.' As an aside, he said to her, 'Beware of misguided compassion.'

In the apology line-up, present flicked to the past triggered by the warning.

* * *

In Year 8, Jake had spent school lunches with his harem. Cassie coped better with his abandonment of her than in previous years. It was only at school after all. Her father joked about Jake's resident status.

Besides, she'd found Jenny. Jenny's family were keen amateur ornithologists.

Jenny saw Tymon Black, at recess, throwing stones into the tree where the birds nested. It was a senseless act, typical of Tymon. He gave new meaning to being a bully. The nest fell just as the bell rang. She knew it had fledglings in it. Her father had shown it to her the previous weekend. Fidgeting throughout Science, she whispered her fear to Cassie in Maths.

That lunch, the girls left the clamour of the playground. Cassie didn't even look for Jake. He saw her though. He might not hang out with her as much at school, but he always knew where she was.

Jenny cried when she saw the nestlings. Two were dead.

One was alive, just. Its featherless wing stuck out in an unnatural way.

Cassie scooped it into her palm. She did not care that the mother would not nurture it. Mrs. Kang, her Science teacher, would. This life could be saved.

The girls were on the edge of the quad when Tymon blocked their way. No amount of bullying would induce Cassie to surrender her charge. They stood toe to toe. Returned glare for glare.

Jenny ran around in futile circles looking for the teacher on duty.

Jake saw Jenny first. Then he looked for Cassie. He saw Tymon smash her hand. Felt sick when he saw Tymon push her aside and her fall. Jake's feet could not cover the ground between Cassie and him fast enough. Tymon would regret this even if it broke every one of Jake's bones to achieve his goal.

Cassie was up quicker than she had fallen. She saw Jenny's tearstained face. Followed her gaze. Saw the remains of the bird as Tymon lifted his foot off it.

Even at a distance, Jake could see the clench in her jaw-line, the tension in her body. She was ready for battle. She would be creamed. His mouth was dry. He was not aware of feet touching ground.

Cassie knew she had a choice: the leaves or the concrete. She chose the concrete. She barged Tymon. He fell back. She heard a sound like an egg cracking. Blood splattered everywhere.

Jake, the duty teacher, and a crowd were instantly there. There was a cacophony of noise and lots of elbows and legs.

The Principal accused Cassie of misguided compassion. He was shocked at her lack of remorse. She was suspended for three days.

After that, Tymon kept Cassie at a distance. She did not hear of any more acts of cruelty. From her perspective, the price she paid was not too high.

Chapter 20

In the distance, Selton's voice rumbled over the microphone as he delivered an HG and Roy styled commentary on the Year 11 versus Year 12 basketball tournament.

There is a rhythm now underscoring my days, Cassie thought as she climbed the stairs.

On reaching the top floor, Cassie became aware of Coachman dressing down one of the men. She wasn't sure who. Ahead of her, Caroline Thompson and Sandra Meyers, the two ringleaders in Year 8's morning campaign of resistance against her, slouched against the walls in front of the staff room. Both girls were bottle blondes, but where one was fleshy the other was bone. Cassie approached them with measured steps. They looked at her resentfully.

'Get off the walls, girls! The time you spend outside this staff room will be dependent on what you have to say for yourselves on my return.'

Cassie nudged the door open with her hip. English and Social Science staff crammed together at the windows, some on chairs, and others on desks watching the game. Four-day-old socks smelt better.

'Selton's great, but he needs a Roy though,' an unfamiliar voice said from the crowd pressing into the windows.

'You're right,' replied an unknown. 'Ever thought of teaming up with him for these matches, Vander?'

'No, doing it for the faculty is one thing and quite another for the student body. I like my image as it is; I've no wish to send a different signal to our adolescent beasts.'

'Well, he's bloody good at it,' he continued, 'I'm a big —'

'Ssshh, time-out's over.'

For once, it would be easy getting into the room.

Having offloaded her work things at her table, Cassie decided on an alternative punishment for the girls – collecting rubbish. There was a lot of it blowing around the school from wind-tipped bins.

Back in the corridor, Cassie was surprised to find the girls gone. She vented in throaty sounds, a behaviour her mother had particularly hated.

'Unable to resist my attractions, eh?' said Talbut who had been leaning against the corridor wall.

Turning, Cassie asked, 'What?'

'The sensual groaning in my presence, the tremulous quiver of desire fired by my touch.' He ran his hands down her arms.

She shrugged them off. Practised now in dealing with the offensive, Cassie said, 'You've got that wrong.'

'Ah, you disappoint me. Then I assume you must be upset over the absence of those two Year 8 girls. As 2IC in this faculty, Cassie, it's my duty to tell you that standing unsupervised miscreants in the corridors during lunch hour is unacceptable. If you wish to punish, then do so, but in your own classroom. I dismissed the girls.'

'You what? You stand students outside the staff room all the time!'

'The operative word in this conversation, Ms Sleight, is supervise. My standing in this school is such that I can supervise at a distance,' he paused for effect, 'whereas you cannot.' He re-entered the staff room as Rajes entered the upper corridor.

'It doesn't take a degree to see that you're upset, Cassie. What has happened?'

'Talbut is such a chauvinistic ass! He dismissed students that I'd placed on corridor detention. He said —'

'His standing in this school was such that he could supervise at a distance whereas you couldn't.'

'How did you know?'

'He did the same thing to Samantha.'

'She hasn't said anything about it to me.'

'I came in on the end of the interaction. It was natural for her to confide in me. It wasn't important enough to revisit with you after the event. Besides, he was right then and is now.'

Cassie frowned.

'The truth is often unpalatable, but you need to hear and accept it.'

'Is that where you've been, Rajes? Dealing with an unpalatable truth?'

'No, I've come from a class in the demountables. The parent-teacher interview was in session one.'

'Coachman sitting in still?'

'Indeed he is.'

'Not going well?' Cassie paused and looked at her colleague. 'You're making me work for this, Rajes. What's up?'

'Fuller made some dubious comments about me to my Year 11 students. Apparently, he resents my allocation of senior classes and his demotion to juniors.'

'From the sound of it,' Cassie glanced up the corridor, 'he's being shredded by Coachman as we speak.'

'He deserves it.' Rajes chuckled. 'Keith takes criticism of his staff personally. It is,' she searched for the right word, 'amusing to see parents backtrack. They seem to have great respect for him.'

'You're not upset?'

'Ignorance is the buzz of an annoying fly; it's squashable.' Rajes smiled at her. 'Besides, Keith takes such delight in my Master's being in my second language. He makes it such a telling point.'

The bell rang.

'Back to the battle?' Rajes asked Cassie, waiting for the men to leave before they re-entered.

'Not me, I'm off for the next two lessons.'

'Me too,' Samantha said, coming to a halt next to the women. Her dress flatteringly revealed her full bosom, narrow waist, and generous hips. 'It was an easy duty today with Selton putting on a show.'

I wish I could be more like Rajes, Cassie thought as Rajes sorted the work on her desk yet again. She liked Rajes' balance and self-possession under pressure. Her skill as a teacher was obvious, seen in the material she shared as well as in her disciplined classes.

'How's it going, Cassie?' Samantha asked, ignoring Rajes.

'So so.'

'How're you handling …? It's awful how everything has innuendo now.'

'You think so too? That's a relief!' Cassie said.

'Why?'

'I was worried I was a prude.'

'Because you're offended at times?'

Cassie nodded.

'That doesn't make you a prude, just inexperienced with working in a male-dominated workplace.'

'I don't understand, Samantha.'

'The values ingrained in language,' Rajes interjected, 'are a part of a patriarchal culture. Most people are not attuned to language and its implications so they miss the significance of the embedded messages and that perpetuates the male culture.' Rajes stood. 'Fascinating though this discussion is, I am afraid I have to shelve it for another time. I'm off to the library to negotiate a research lesson for Year 9.' The door whispered closed behind her.

'Do you think you'll last as a teacher, Samantha?'

'No, maybe, who knows? Steven and I thought teachers had cushy hours, and it worked better for having a family; that's why I retrained. I'm giving it two years, and then I'll make a decision. Why?'

'If it's like this every year, I don't want to be a teacher.'

Silence.

Without looking up from her work, Samantha said, 'So, how's Talbut's mission to win you going?'

'I'm not interested in him.'

'And yet you play the oldest game in the book with him.'

'What?'

'You read Tennyson?'

'What has that got to do with this?'

'You've positioned yourself as Talbut's game. A clever move, I must admit. You are 'the sleek and shining creature of the chase'.'

'Well. I don't want him to ride me down!'

'Play offside then, and you'll get him offside.'

'I don't understand ...'

'Turn the hunt back on him, and end the game. He'll lose interest if you make him a trophy.' In response to Cassie's bewildered expression, Samantha added, 'Join the banter and put the man down.'

'I'm not that sort of woman. Besides, it takes ages for me to think of a comeback. Always has. I revisit an incident a thousand times with things I could have said but when something actually happens, I draw a blank.'

'Well, with Talbut you can predict the intent of the incident so why not plan ahead and have five adaptable lines? No matter how big a man is, he is always vulnerable in the crutch. Sex is power, Cassie. Use it properly, and it'll get you whatever you want.'

'That's pretty cynical.'

'You've obviously not been backed against a wall with a hot-blooded man like Talbut yet. How this plays out can be your choice.'

* * *

A number of the men grouped together near the tea urn, looking at a magazine that Talbut held stretched open in his extended arms. They looked up as Cassie entered.

Van der Huffen and Selton sat at their desks.

Talbut looked at the magazine, angling it and then at her. He assessed her, his eyes travelling slowly over her body. 'Yes, I'd say you resemble this picture.'

The men with him mirrored Talbut.

Cassie crossed to Talbut's side as casually as she could to look at the magazine. It was a nude centrefold. She kept the blush down and thought of Rajes and the coldness in her eyes when she looked at Talbut.

'I'm not as beefy in the thighs.' Her glance dropped for a flicker of time. 'Lost your plastic raincoat?'

Talbut coloured. The other men laughed.

'I believe, PS, that words fail Talbut, a first for this year.'

'A just dessert, VH, his performance has been very ordinary.'

'Paltry.'

'I think puny is a better description,' Cassie said ending their conversation.

Talbut left the room.

Experiencing a high from her first offensive defensive move, she looked at the other men, challenge in her face. Hands up in an offside way, they separated, moving to their desks.

* * *

Satisfaction in the kill and from the cut and thrust banter with Selton and Van der Huffen faded. At first, Talbut ignored Cassie.

In the second week, when the others were engrossed in their work, she looked up to find him staring at her. He licked his lips suggestively. After a shocked moment, Cassie calmed herself with sensible self-talk. Many people have dry lips, she told herself; he means nothing by it. In the days that followed, his behaviour repeated. She read the lewd inference in his behaviour for what it was. After that, she pretended not to see him.

That strategy didn't work for her outside the staffroom. Whenever Cassie came across Talbut in a corridor, he side-stepped into her course. It didn't seem to matter to him whether other people were in the corridor or not. A dance of sorts always followed in which Cassie tried to stay out of his way. He had a stock comment to her reaction. 'I'm flattered, Cassie, but you need to control this fascination with me.'

After a week, Talbut appeared to lose interest in her. That

is until she encountered him in the stairwell on her way to the library when he was supposed to be on class. His hand moved to his trouser front, his hand movement a downward pushing gesture. She shuddered at the thought of his having a hard on. She turned and retreated upstairs, aware that Talbut was on her heels, her heart pounding. They walked off in different directions when they reached the top corridor.

The following day, Cassie arrived at school earlier than usual to get an hour's marking done before the start of the school day, confident in the knowledge that Talbut now timed his arrival to five minutes before the start-of-lessons school bell rang. Halfway up the stairs, she came to a standstill. Talbut was coming down them. She considered retreating but decided against it. Eyes fixed on the upper corridor, in her peripheral vision she registered a hand rub near his zipper. Reflexively, she looked at him. His tongue darted in and out at her.

By the month's end, Cassie felt as if she were a chock under the wheel of a very big truck. With Kate's philosophy in mind, Cassie waylaid Talbut, at the end of the Friday lessons, on his way back to the staff room.

The other teaching staff had left the building. Cleaners moved silently through the school, an invisible crew; the whir of the floor polishers had not yet begun.

Having been delayed by a giggle of flirtatious Year 12 girls at the bottom of the stairs, Talbut now climbed them on a high.

Standing at the top of the stairs, Cassie blocked his path and so had the advantage of height.

Misunderstanding, Talbut said, 'And my day just gets better and better.'

'Not where I'm concerned, it doesn't! I don't like the way

you've been behaving toward me; you're acting like one of the kids in 10G.'

'10G? I'm cut to the quick. By the way, has anyone ever told you that you look even more beautiful when you're angry?'

Cassie looked down at him, her face impassive.

'I'm available for some hand-to-man combat if it'll ease your stress.'

'Cut it out, or I'll lodge a formal complaint with Coachman!'

Talbut chuckled. 'If you think he doesn't see your prudish sensitivity to social interaction for what it is, you're mistaken.'

'Sexual harassment is how you make me feel, not what Coachman thinks of me. Go peddle your wares somewhere else; I'm not interested. In fact, I think you're sleazy and creepy.'

In a surprising turnabout, Talbut retraced his steps and left the building.

Driving back to Madison House, Cassie was very much on edge. Avoiding afternoon tea, she sought the comfort of music in her room.

As she danced to the Eurogliders, Cassie felt uplifted. She'd drawn a line, and despite his bravado, Talbut had retreated. Her issues with him were done and dusted or so she thought.

Chapter 21

Keimera Dance Studios hired floor space at the RSL. Martin Jones, the owner and chief instructor, ran the RSL balls and provided discount lessons to its members. His short stature misrepresented his skill and grace on the floor. A man of sharp wit and temper, he had coached hundreds of dancers whose interest and desire exceeded their talent. He was determined to coach champions before he retired.

The rooms were relatively empty that Friday afternoon. Private classes had begun, but the social dance session for adults did not start until nine-thirty. His senior citizens preferred their social dance on Saturday afternoons.

Studios are mostly uniform in layout: parquetry floor, a range of lights for effect, a wall of mirrors, and good sound equipment.

Martin was on the phone in his office when Cassie entered. She moved with fluid grace. He recognised her immediately. He gestured that he would be five minutes. She filled the time by looking at the studio photos that lined one of the walls.

From the photographs, Cassie realised that Mike and Kate had both downplayed their dance pasts. Waiting provided her with an opportunity to study the younger Michael. He had strength and agility. The photographer had taken great action shots.

'What can I do you for?' Martin asked.

'I was told you run a social dance Friday nights. Can anyone come?'

'It's a first come first served basis. There's usually a queue by eleven-thirty. After that, entry is tied to departures.'

'And you're opened till?'

'Two-thirty.' Martin looked at her closely. 'Didn't you dance with Jake Dominguez?'

'A long time ago.'

'I saw you win the Nationals in '85. A flawless performance! Then you disappeared. An accident or something?'

'The something.'

'And you're here because …?'

'I miss dancing.'

'You interested in competing again?' It was an effort for Martin to control his excitement.

'Not at the moment.'

'See me if you change your mind.'

* * *

Samantha had raved about this particular dress shop. Cassie drifted over the racks of dresses.

A sky blue dress with a simple cut, fluid and flattering, begged to be bought. As she exited, a beige, faux fur edged overcoat caught her eye. It complemented the dress and would keep her warm between the house and the studio.

With the dress and coat safely wrapped in tissue and bagged, the next stop was for a coffee and cake at a nearby café renovated from a Federation house into a business. It was busy. A clump of senior citizens thawed in front of the open fire. People of all ages congregated in nearby booths and tables including groups of Cassie's Year 8 and 9 students.

Their friendly greetings, when they saw her, added to her enjoyment of the afternoon.

Service was prompt.

Contemplating the joy of cream that offset the richness of the mud cake, Cassie looked up to see Mary Selton, heavily pregnant, before her.

'Mind if I join you? There aren't any free tables.'

'Course not!'

'I'm beginning to feel like a beached whale.' Mary laughed as she adjusted the chair to accommodate her stomach. 'At night, I have to wake Paul whenever I want to turn over. Paul says —'

'G'day, Mary,' an elderly Aboriginal man said as he passed their table. 'Pass on my thanks to your man for getting young Malcolm back on track. Havin' Paul as mentor is makin' all the difference.'

'Cassie Sleight meet Ted Perkins. Ted's a highly respected elder in our community.'

'Hello.'

'G'day. You teach my grandson, Ron Spannari. He's enjoyin' English.'

'Is he?' Cassie felt taller somehow.

'See you and Paul on Friday?'

'Sure will.'

A rescuer and helper by nature, Mary decided to take advantage of the opportunity to help her husband if she could. After considering her options, she began with, 'School still tough?'

Cassie was silent as a waitress served Mary.

'The English men really aren't chauvinist pigs, y' know. Did I shock you? No, don't feel you have to pretend you haven't thought so. From Paul's recounts at home even I think they have behaved badly. In their defence, I think their philosophy was: want to live in a man's world then field the hits like a man.'

'But it hasn't been a man's world for a long time now, has it?'

'At Keimera High, it has been.'

'So, why are you telling me this? It's not likely to endear Selton or the others to me.'

'Paul feels guilty that he sat on the fence for so long and doesn't know how to correct the situation.'

'Well, he shouldn't.'

'Oh … And Mark Talbut? What about him?'

Silence.

'He's always been a testosterone-driven ladies' man, Cassie.'

'Not this lady's, and he finally knows it.'

'So you don't need Paul's help?'

'Not now.'

'Then let's talk about something else.'

In the warmth of fellowship and laughter that followed, Cassie gained insight into the Seltons' lives. She felt a bond, yet untested, but nonetheless strong. It was how she felt when she was with Leonie. Regret tinged her departure, her place taken by one of Mary's friends who had been looking for a table.

Belonging is a deep genetic drive. More and more, Cassie felt it. Safe and comfortable with the Madison House residents, her membership in the wider community was extending, weaving itself into the layers of her life.

At the register, a Greek woman said to Cassie, 'We are so happy that you've come to Keimera. Maria talks about you all the time. She loves English! It is good to say, 'Get your head out of that book' and not, 'Why don't you ever read?' Put your money away; it is our pleasure.'

Teaching was like a love affair, Cassie realised on the drive back to Madison House. It had the same highs and lows. The pain in penetrating the student barrier had passed. She would savour the high while it lasted.

* * *

Looking at the kitchen whiteboard, Cassie saw she was home alone. Momentarily disappointed that she had no one with whom to share her purchases, she realised that she was also relieved. She didn't want to go into the story behind her decision. There was also the added benefit that she could play her records as loud as she wanted.

On the way upstairs, she realised that she could also get lost in the warmth of the shower. No time limits that night on bathroom time.

The opening strains of *Black Magic Woman* sounded as she left her bedroom. Cassie surrendered to the music. God, she thought, how I have missed this! The song ended as she stepped into the shower. Her mind went blank as water cascaded over her. Time passed with her unaware of it.

Loud knocking at the bathroom door brought her back to reality. Mavis called, 'How much longer are you goin' to be?'

When she opened the door, Mavis complained. 'There'd better be some hot water left. Looks like it's all gone up in steam.'

'There is.'

'Want to come to the pub tonight?'

'Thanks, but I've other plans.'

'A man?'

'Something better.'

'What?'

'Dance and lots of men.'

'Good day at school?'

'No … but there have been some pluses.'

'See you.'

* * *

Small white lights decorated the trees outside the RSL creating a sense of warmth in the cold winter night. They were the only light source in the stairwell, giving a magical quality to the entrance. Music filled the air.

The studio floor was alive with dancers. They were involved in a progressive, changing partner at some unseen signal that only those initiated into the studio's secrets recognised. Cassie had never seen it done with a Latin American dance before. She concentrated on the dancers trying to understand how it worked.

This was not a simple case of the man leading. A group mentality seemed to be operating, and it was linked to the rhythm. She decided against watching and surrendered to feel. She closed her eyes, opening them when she thought she had felt the signal for a change.

The music was infectious!

She laughed when she finally sensed the change and saw that it had happened.

'What do you think?' Martin asked, having crossed to her.

'How long have you been doing this sort of thing?'

'One of my teachers brought it back from Brazil. Want to dance?'

Martin pulled her to him, and the game began. She laughed every time she got it right. Soon she had had a number of partners, all of them in tune with the group. There didn't seem to be any control over how the new partner was determined. It was random.

Towards the end of the bracket, she changed to Michael. She misstepped at first because she was more conscious of him than the rhythm. After that she relaxed and enjoyed his partnership, however, she missed the next change and stood befuddled for a moment until rescued by Martin.

Two changes later, Michael was back. The conversation that followed did not flow smoothly because focus was on the dance, which by its nature made talking difficult.

'Did you manoeuvre your return?'

'Sure did. You're a good dancer, Cassie, really good.'

'Consider the compliment returned. Can you …'

Michael faked the next change and brought her back to him.

'Clever, Mike. I didn't see that coming.'

'How good are you really, Cassie?'

'I can follow anywhere you lead.'

'A huge claim. Let's see if that's true.'

They negotiated a more intricate series of steps than that previously attempted.

'Very snazzy, Mike. How unchivalrous to try and out-step me.'

'Do you think that's possible?'

'Ah … a challenge. You're on.'

It was an exhilarating game that quickly gained an audience. Joy. It had been a long time since Cassie had felt it at such intensity.

The audience were dazzled. The bracket finished on applause of appreciation.

Martin restrained his urge to press them into partnership. Kate was his bird in the hand. It would not pay to lose her for the one fluttering above the bush. He had decided against telling Michael of Cassie's dance triumphs, concerned that he would be intimidated. Michael had talent and potential but was not yet in Cassie's class. Watching, Martin was impressed with her control. She did not flaunt her skill or attempt to outshine her partner. She was a special woman indeed.

It seemed to be a natural extension of the dance for Michael to stay close to Cassie in the breaks. She liked the pressure of his hand on her back as he directed her to seating. She liked his aftershave.

'Where's Kate?'

'It's her parents' thirtieth wedding anniversary.'

It seemed equally natural that they danced together on and off for the rest of the night. Her other partners had varying degree of skill. The joy of the dance was there, but it reached an almost orgasmic height when she danced with Michael. The boundaries in dance allowed her to feel intense passion safely. She felt a sense of loss as the last dance ended.

'Walk you to your car?' Michael said.

'That'd be good if it wasn't back at the house.'

'How'd you get here?'

'Taxi.'

'Want a lift?'

'If you're not going anywhere else.'

'Like?'

'Meeting up with Kate.'

'We're not a couple, Cassie. We just hang out, mostly here.'

Cassie enjoyed the return drive.

Back at Madison House, they lingered on the darkened landing near their respective rooms.

'This has been a good end to a difficult week,' she said, deliberately choosing the understatement.

'You're having some wins though.'

In response to her non-verbal question, he added, 'Nothing's a secret in a small town. Besides, you're a lot more upbeat at home than when you first started at the school. I put it down to more wins than losses. Tonight was fun.'

'Yes, it was.'

The intensity in the moment made Cassie aware of her own heartbeat. Her senses heightened, she realised she liked everything about him.

Michael found her tantalising. He stepped closer, the tenderness of his tone registered with her rather than what was said. Aware of the strong tactile appeal of his shirt, Cassie ran her hand along the material in his sleeve, aware again of his muscles, as she had been when they danced.

On impulse, Michael leant forward for a kiss.

Aware that she was intoxicated with dance fever, Cassie responded anyway. This type of desire did not frighten her. It seemed a natural extension of what they had shared throughout the night. It was different from the bond with Jake though.

The kiss lingered on her lips long after they separated.

Still holding her hand, he brushed it to his lips.

Cassie's breath caught in her throat. To cover, she said, 'Now I know what Mavis means when she says someone is smooth as.'

'You really are a puzzle, Cassie. So passionate in dance and yet so guarded in life. Good night, beautiful.'

The aftertaste, Cassie's father had once pontificated, is what defines a fine wine.

Using that standard, Michael was certainly a prize. Cassie frowned as she entered her room. Did Michael really think she was beautiful or was he like Talbut and used the cliché to ingratiate himself?

Chapter 22

Sleep came easily, but as the night progressed, Cassie slipped from one phase of the nightmare to the next. Memories of her struggle to survive at work as well as trauma associated with Talbut and from her teens with Jake fractured into a kaleidoscope reality. She tossed in her bed and became tangled in the bedclothes. A voice within her denied the distorted reality, tried to sort the pieces from the jigsaw into a coherent picture.

Cassie wrestled with a stranger, trying to dislodge his weight. Blades of grass spiked her face as she thrashed. She cried out in frustration. He pinioned her arms to the ground. The heat of his hands burned like ropes under friction.

Wake! Wake! The inner voice demanded. Cassie heard the voice and responded to it, aware again of the sobbing as she came back into the present. Halfway between sleep and the conscious state, she wondered who was crying as she struggled to throw off the heaviness.

Heaving her arms free of the bed clothing, Cassie sat upright; her hair matted with sweat, her nightclothes saturated. Her breathing was fast and shallow. It took time to recognise her surroundings.

Tears streamed down her face. She closed her eyes and controlled her breathing, forcing it to slow. Her hands rhythmically controlled the tidal action of her breath. It took time, but she calmed.

After that calming process, she faced the source of her nightmares.

* * *

Saturday 20 March, 1982. The afternoon light glazed the distant hills orange and coloured the creek that meandered through the family property. Jake lolled with her on the unmown slopes of the dam in the north-eastern paddock after a swim.

Sixteen-year-old Cassie liked wrestling. Jake's strength impressed and excited her. They vied with each other, rolling to gain advantage. He toyed with her for some time. She laughed, thinking she had the upper hand. In a heartbeat, he flipped her underneath him, her arms pinned to the grass. His victory crow challenged her. She laughed, confident she would unsettle him. The more she struggled, the harder he gripped. His face, during that frenetic breath of time, contorted. She looked at a stranger.

Jake released Cassie when he registered her distress. Concerned, he caressed the worry from her face. His fingers trailed over her forehead, down her cheeks and over her lips. It was her first kiss. She had thought that kissing might even replace chocolate in her list of delights.

The rest of that afternoon was a jigsaw with pieces missing. Kisses aroused passion. His hands groped her breasts, her thighs, fingered inside her pants. She objected, floundered, a reluctant participant, overwhelmed by the raging flood of his desire. He invaded her, deaf to her tearful protest.

What happened after that remained a blank for Cassie.

Her next memory was of the bustle and laughter of unexpected visitors, who arrived late afternoon and stayed for dinner. Everything seemed surreal to her. Trapped inside an invisible bubble, the voices around her seemed hollow and distorted. Unable to eat, she excused herself on the pretext of a headache.

In the dark of her room, Cassie huddled under her sheets, curled into a foetal position. Her emotions seeped into the darkness. She dared not cry. If anyone heard her, there would be questions she did not know how to answer.

The next day, Cassie complained of feeling sick and stayed in bed until the afternoon. When Jake and Melissa with their respective parents arrived for a barbeque that Sunday evening, Jake's cheerfulness took her by surprise.

'Come for a walk, Cassie?' Jake asked as their parents settled in for a pre-dinner game of cards.

'Mum needs my help here if she's to play cards.'

'You sure?'

'Absolutely. I'm in charge of salads. I've ... I've a number to make as well as dessert.'

Melissa's, 'I'll come, Jake,' gave Cassie pause.

'I could do with your help too, Melissa,' was all that Cassie said.

Throughout the evening and under the watchful eyes of parents, Cassie played the part of Jake's best friend until she could escape.

Monday, Cassie again complained of being sick and stayed home. That day off extended into a week of missed school. When Jake telephoned, Cassie called out to her mother, 'Tell him I'll call back later,' but she didn't.

By the next Saturday, Cassie faced another fear, the possibility of pregnancy. While her family were out shopping, she explored her mother's books on the living room bookshelf. Running her finger along the book spines, she found the one she wanted, *Know Your Body*. Informed now, she checked her nipples. Were they browner? Her breasts fuller? She wished she had been more observant.

Resolute, Cassie vowed she would *not* be like those girls at school who had been forced to leave due to pregnancy. She would *not* marry to suit her parent's view of the world. They would *never* know.

At home and school during the following week, Cassie fobbed Jake off with one excuse after another.

Observing Cassie's increasingly pallid features and loss of appetite, Nancy said, 'If you're not improved soon, it's off to the doctor with you.'

'Okay, if I don't improve.'

At the end of yet another dark week, Cassie asked her mother if she could see their doctor.

'It's what I've been thinking myself, Cassie. And these mood swings … If it's PMS, then we need to do something about it.'

At the doctor's surgery, Nancy stayed in the waiting room, confident that she was contributing to her daughter's growth toward independence.

When Cassie returned to her mother, she felt lighter, having shared her burden and knowing patient confidentiality protected her. In her jeans' pocket, she carried a small packet of tablets dispensed to her by the doctor from his stash of samples. If that failed, she had a referral to a clinic, operating under the defacto system of the time.

Cassie endured another month of waiting.

When her period still did not arrive and having had the pregnancy confirmed through urine and blood tests, Cassie rang the Sydney clinic on her referral and made an appointment.

On the following Monday, with the referral tucked into the front pocket of her backpack, she skipped school and headed for the city. The trip itself was a blur.

In the waiting room, Cassie read censure in the faces of the older women. The receptionist's tone though was soothing. Escorted into a clinically cold room, she shivered as a well-upholstered doctor dialogued with her.

So many questions. Too much detail. 'But can't it be done today?'

'No dear, the procedure needs to be scheduled for next week. You'll need to bring someone with you.'

Woodenly, Cassie filled out the required paperwork before leaving. Who can I bring? Who can I bring? repeated in her head in rising pitch while she was at the surgery *and* all the way back to Richmond on the train.

Waiting in the bus shelter near the station, Cassie nodded at townspeople she knew as they passed. The bubble in which she had been living contracted. She felt devastating shame. Panic clawed within her. She knew one thing only; nothing would put her off the abortion. Who can I bring? Who can I bring?

With minutes left before her bus arrived, Cassie felt an unexpected wetness. She bolted for the ladies' toilets in the park opposite.

Locked in a cubicle, her tears matched the heavy flow of menstrual blood. The relief she felt was overwhelming despite the cramping.

After that, Cassie's relationship with Jake changed. Her avoidance of him was now a concern of their respective parents. That concern heightened when Cassie pulled out of ballroom dancing. Tight lipped, civil, and with her mask in place, she refused to dance.

It took months before Cassie initiated any talk with Jake, longer for her to resume their friendship, twelve months before she returned to the dance floor and their partnership, even longer before she felt comfortable with any expression of intimacy. In time, she accepted his excuse of being overwhelmed by his love for her. Much later, after she had regained confidence in her heterosexuality, she came to enjoy their sexual encounters.

* * *

1988. Dawn came softly though the bedroom window. Staring at the ceiling, Cassie realised that *that* encounter with Jake had defined her afterwards. The ghost imprint of his hands on her body triggered shaking. Cassie cocooned the bedclothes around her. Slowly, the trembling subsided. She thought again of Samantha's comparison of her to Persephone. I will *not* be a Persephone anymore.

Considering her relationship with Michael, Cassie realised that the possibility of romance frightened her. There were too many variables, too many unknowns. The survival dance of school life stretched her emotionally to her limits. She was not prepared to risk a friendship for the pain that came with romance. Sleep eluded her. When her alarm clock sounded, Cassie braced herself for the day ahead.

That bleak winter's day, the staff room windows were closed; the room was smog bound. Van der Huffen chewed on his cigar as he considered the argument in a Year 12 essay. Samantha coughed and said something quietly to him.

Having missed what was said, Cassie caught his reaction in her peripheral vision. He considered Samantha, cigar poised in his hand, and then resumed puffing and marking. She moved her chair as far away from him as possible. The sink blocked her.

Samantha looked back at Van der Huffen, coughed in an exaggerated manner, stood, and moved to the window. After opening it, she returned to her work.

A cold breeze dispelled the smog.

Selton, stubble-faced and looking the worse for wear, wrestled with the Sydney Morning Herald; a broadsheet newspaper printed with exercise in mind as much as information. He fought the paper and the breeze. Cassie's notes and Van der Huffen's pile of essays scattered.

'Why the bloody hell is that window open? Look what it's doing!' Van der Huffen said.

'Much the same as your cigar smoke is doing to our lungs I should think,' Samantha said.

'Uh, like that, is it? Okay, I'll put the bloody thing out.'

'And what about the rest of you?' asked Samantha.

'No law against smoking inside,' said Talbut.

'Yet, but there will be.'

'She's right, mate,' Selton said, 'Ten years ago we all smoked. Who'd have thought …?'

'And we need fresh air now.' Samantha opened the second window.

'For God's sake, these essays are due back tomorrow,' Van der Huffen said, splayed across his desk, 'and it's freezing to boot!'

'And I'm sick of this stench as well as concerned about my health. Don't any of you listen to the news? Apparently passive smoking is on a par with smoking.'

Cassie looked up from where she was crouched, a confusion of her retrieved from the floor in her hands. 'Can I suggest —?'

'No!' was the unanimous chorus.

Talbut looked resentfully at Samantha. Superior bitch, he thought, always a quip to put us in place. He thought about where he would like to put her.

'Okay, okay, and the score is, ladies and gentlemen, Ms Smith ten, men zero,' said Van der Huffen.

Most of the tobacco was stubbed out.

Samantha looked meaningfully at Talbut who ignored her.

'Cut it out, Talbut,' Selton said. 'Even my wife complains about the stench when I come home. She says that it's hard to get out …'

'Said the actress to the bishop,' Van der Huffen added without looking up from his work.

Samantha remained at the open window. 'It's time you guys dropped that tag. The joke's worn out.'

Talbut screwed the butt into the saucer, his eyes on Samantha. 'Anything else I can do to please?' He tongued his lips slowly as she looked coldly at him, unseen by the rest of the staff.

The bell rang, triggering the departure of most staff. Samantha closed the window before grabbing her books and heading off to class.

Only Cassie, Rajes, and Selton remained. They worked in silence for a good length of time. The quiet, almost whispered, conversation between Selton and Rajes snagged Cassie's attention in a way that a loud conversation would not have.

'The earlier ultrasounds didn't pick it up,' Selton said.

'Do they know yet what sort of heart problem?'

'Something to do with a malfunctioning valve. That's why we're off to a specialist in Sydney next week. He has the latest gear and is supposed to be a top specialist. That has to be good then, eh?'

'Early recognition of a problem results in the safer manage-ment of it. Have they said anything about a Caesar?'

'Yes, but Mary had her heart set on —'

'A natural birth, I know. Intervention, however, doesn't lessen the miracle of birth.'

'Tell that to her.'

'If the opportunity presents itself.'

'Opportunity, it has so many different meanings. I hope …' Selton broke down.

Appalled, Cassie did not know what to do: stay, go, or pre-tend she was not there. She chose the comfort of the tea ritual. Resisting the urge to remove the accumulated stains from Selton's mug, she made him a brew that was strong enough to put hair on any man's chest. Selton accepted the mug unaware of its source. Rajes nodded her thanks. Cassie returned to her work.

* * *

Dancing was more than entertainment to Cassie. Her soul opened and fed on the substance of creative expression. Liberated from the stresses and strains of her everyday world by dance, she felt a sweet intensity that was beyond anything else she had ever experienced. Partners were plentiful. Most of them danced well.

Cassie enjoyed being in a threesome. It kept Michael from being too attentive, reinforcing she wanted him as a friend. By alternating with Kate as his partner, Cassie had the oppor-tunity to soar emotionally through dance. It was a relief to Cassie that Kate was not like Melissa. Maybe, she thought, it was possible after all for two women to share a man in friendship.

Celia Cruz' distinctive vocal style signalled the Salsa. Kate critically watched Cassie and Michael on the floor. What made their performance exceptional? The combinations, high in degree of difficulty, were sharp and perfect in execution. Strategically placed breaks heightened the overall impact, provided space and accentuated the rhythm. The dance was intensely sensual; the emotions behind the choreography revealed. As in everything they danced, their movements appeared to create the music rather than respond to it. Were they rehearsing up at the big house? She bit her nails absent-mindedly; she was on the right course; getting Michael away from Madison House continued to be an imperative.

Michael is a superb partner, Kate thought. Thank God, I have a prior claim. She found it difficult applauding the dance-stopping performance, but did so, and then reclaimed her place by Michael's side. The casual ease with which Cassie relinquished him confirmed Kate's ownership.

Marvin Gaye's, *I Heard It Through the Grapevine* signalled The Merrilyn. Although Cassie loved this New Vogue slow foxtrot, she chose to sit it out and watch. It was always hard to dance with other partners after Michael. She liked the limited dance prescription to footwork, alignments and holds because it left scope for dancers to add their own expression through shaping and styling.

For Cassie, the dance was a love story between equals. She liked the intimacy and romance in the synchronised turns, the breakaway, and return. As a couple, they had beautiful body flight. Cassie envied their freedom and longed for the familiarity they had with other dancers in the studio who ceased to treat them as a floorshow. Overall, she thought theirs was an elegant hypnotic performance.

With an artist's eye, Vincent Pearce, Visual Arts teacher,

appreciated the aura of Madonna, the virgin not the singer, as Cassie sat absorbed by the scene. When he asked her to join him in a quickstep, he understood the meaning of a beatific smile. Well matched in height, he was aware that, though a competent dancer, he lacked her skill. She was a joy, uncritical and approving.

Escorting Cassie to her seat, Pearce remarked, 'You're a different person here. I didn't recognise you the first night I dropped in.'

'I've been going through a wardrobe makeover.'

'I didn't mean that.' Pearce hesitated. 'It's been hard to miss the stress the English women have been under.'

'Cassie, La Bamba?' Michael said with Kate at his elbow.

'Excuse me, Vincent. I'd love to, Mike.'

Vincent's eyes followed them as they took up position on the floor. 'Competition, do you think?'

'No.' Not if I can help it, Kate thought, all the more worried now that Vincent voiced her fear.

* * *

There was a developing sameness about the Saturday night pub ritual that tired Cassie even though she enjoyed being part of a community. She enjoyed the walk to and from the pub, the cold air, and being able to talk without having to yell above the general hubbub of the pub. She disliked the passivity of sitting and drinking. She hated feeling like a fly at a picnic when she made the mistake of going with only Mavis and Terry. She also disliked the way Terry's mood changed when other men paid attention to Mavis. As the weeks passed, his jealousy exploded into aggression one Saturday night.

Watching the pub scene, Cassie realised her list of

acquaintances was growing. She liked chatting to people, especially to parents of her better-behaved students.

A man sitting at the bar intercepted Mavis on her way back from the toilets. He stood and hooked an arm around her as she passed, halting her progress. 'How's about singin' my favourite song? You're the reason I come to this hole.'

Unflustered, Mavis smiled up at him. 'I didn't know I had a fan,' she said as she removed his arm. 'Why don't you sit down? I've picked some great songs for tonight. I'm on a break at the moment.'

Other admirers delayed her route back to their table.

'I don't like you flirtin' with men like that,' Terry said.

'I wasn't —'

'I've got eyes!' He grabbed her. 'You mightn't have the ring yet, but we are engaged. I've got ownership rights.'

Possession, Cassie had experienced it with Jake. She did not like it. It had little to do with love.

Mavis, however, seemed pleased.

'You've got nothin' to worry about ...'

'What about a song?' One of the men at the bar had followed Mavis to the table.

'Hop it, mate,' Terry said and pushed him back away from Mavis.

The man reacted. Fists flew. Terry staggered under the force of a blow to his cheek. An ugly red stained the area. He returned a rapid sequence of blows: to the head, the body, and the head. With each contact, the man's head snapped backwards, his body folded. Blood flowed from his mouth, nose, and right eyebrow. The man stumbled, regained his footing, returned blow for blow.

Cassie and Mavis had never seen a fight live. The brute intensity of it shocked them.

Cassie's appeal to men in the crowd to break it up went unheard. Caught up in the blood lust, they yelled advice.

'Someone, stop this, please!' Mavis added her appeal to Cassie's.

No one did.

Mavis hurled herself between the men. It worked in the stories she read; it did not in life. The men shrugged her off. She fell backwards to the ground. The right side of her face tingled from the impact of a fist. Blood from the fight splattered her face.

'You okay?' Cassie asked.

'A bit dazed. How can we stop them, Cassie?'

'Not that way. Don't do that again! Why hasn't a bouncer or the publican stepped in?'

The slogging match continued with neither man giving ground. Fists flew everywhere. The crowd pushed forward.

'Bouncer? There isn't one. As for Jack, he doesn't normally come in until nine.'

Cassie looked at her watch; Jack Fitzgerald was not in sight.

After questioning the barmaid, Cassie headed for the restaurant out the back but met Jack in the corridor that linked each establishment.

'No need,' Jack said to Cassie. 'I've been told already.'

Jack forced his way through the crowd. A heavily built man, he had not allowed for the physical power that rage generated in the combatants. As a last resort, he pinioned Terry's arms from behind. At the same time, spectators held the other fighter off. The fight ended.

The men stood apart now, bent over, breathing hard, bleeding.

Mavis was in tears. Cassie, however, felt strangely detached.

'You okay, love?' Jack asked Mavis. An ugly bruise spread

from her cheek to her eye. Mavis nodded. 'You don't look all right.' Jack turned to Cassie. 'Help her get her man home; I don't want him back unless he has his temper in check.'

Cassie wished they had the luxury of a car. She called a taxi.

It was an unpleasant trip back, Terry all the time challenging Mavis over her commitment to their relationship, demanding she prove it by moving in with him.

As Mavis helped Terry into the house, Cassie followed, trembling from denied emotion. On the stairs, anger elbowed out shock. It was hard for Cassie to repress it as she listened to Terry. He was anything but a victim.

With Terry in his room, the women returned to theirs. 'I know this type of man, Mavis; he'll end up being a … a tyrant. Walk away now.'

'No, you don't! If you want to be my friend, don't criticise my man!' Mavis walked ahead, her hands over her ears to block out Cassie, and slammed her bedroom door closed in Cassie's face.

That angry retreat developed into a rift that lasted two weeks. She pointedly excluded Cassie at mealtimes though the other residents worked hard to compensate for the coldness.

Michael on passing Cassie's room a few nights after the rift began, stopped and asked, 'What's going on with you and Mavis?'

'This sort of thing happens between women from time to time, Michael, don't you know?'

'Yes, but … Look, have I done anything to upset you? You've been … not distant exactly but …'

'No … it's not you. I've just had a lot on my plate.'

'That's why having a life apart from work is important. Don't tell me Friday night dancing is enough. It isn't. Look, I'm going to Sydney in a few weeks. Why not come with me?'

'I can't just take a sickie, Michael.'

'It'll be a Saturday. I'm leaving early morning and intend being back late the same day. Give all this a rest; come with me.'

'I appreciate the thought but …'

'You only want a platonic friendship. I get it.'

Over the next week, Cassie smiled in the face of Mavis' shunning, not knowing what else to do. Finally, she turned to her mother in their weekly phone contact.

'Did you like it, Cassie, when Dad and I tried to stop you making mistakes? Do you remember your reaction?'

'Yes,' Cassie sighed, 'it was the same. I am sorry, Mum, if I made you feel like this. But what can I do?'

'It's not your place to do anything other than be there for Mavis. You don't have to like Terry, but you do have to accept Mavis' choice with grace and a smile if you want the friendship.'

'But we're not talking!'

'Then start. Walls only exist if we see them. You've seen me get past them. You must've learnt something.'

* * *

The brown light of dusk joined day and night. An exuberant rehearsal of Mungo Jerry's *In the Summertime* for the pub sing-along filled Madison House that Saturday.

Male voices chorused with gusto, 'Chh chh-chh, uh Chh chh-chh, uh.' Percussion reinforced the beat.

Mavis' voice sounded throughout the house.

Cassie, on her return from visiting Samantha, trailed the singing to the living room.

Mavis, in a flowing patterned dress and denim jacket, sat

on the lounge strumming her guitar. Her spirit was liberated by the music.

Near her stood Michael, sporting a new stubble beard, wearing a T-shirt combined with a light coloured sports coat, jeans, and sneakers – a young version of Don Johnson from *Miami Vice*. Gary, in a sports coat over his Hawaiian shirt coupled with torn jeans, knelt next to him, beating a tattoo on the coffee table. Terry, in brown trousers with a cabled blue woollen jumper, blew into a large glass jug to provide deep percussive complementary sound. The men had copies of the lyrics.

Cassie stood on the threshold like a swimmer worrying about a dive into cold water. She plunged in, standing next to Michael. During the chorus, she looped arms with him. Enjoying the contact, Cassie remembered feeling this way with Jake. She tensed momentarily at the thought.

Michael sensed Cassie's sudden body change, withdrew his arm from hers, and draped it over her shoulder instead. In that 'drawing to him' gesture, Cassie read mateship, not romance.

The opening line of the chorus worked well for 'Sing along with us,' but Cassie and Michael made a mishmash of the rest of the chorus both distracted by the emotional subtext between them.

'All right?' Michael sang, looking pointedly at Cassie. She replied with a nod, forcing herself to relax, lean on Michael, and be a part of the whole again.

'Great!' Mavis said. 'Let's do it next Saturday night. You comin' then, Cassie?'

'I hadn't planned to.'

'It'd be good if you did. I've missed you.'

'Friends?' Cassie asked.

'Course we are, you silly nong.'

'Get us a cuppa, will you, love?' Terry asked Mavis who complied immediately.

Cassie frowned. She did not like the way Terry assumed it was Mavis' role to serve him. Mavis seemed oblivious to the implications.

'Anyone else want somethin'?' Terry offered.

Channelling memories of her father, Cassie followed Mavis into the kitchen. Terry's offer was less about generosity and more about demonstrating ownership and power.

'Need any help, Mavis?'

'On top of things, thanks.'

'Look … about Terry. I had no right to say what I did. I'm seeing the present in terms of the past.'

'Oh yes?' Finally, Mavis thought, answers to Cassie's failed romance. She perched on a kitchen stool in anticipation. The kettle whistled shrilly.

'I'll take this stuff in, shall I, Mavis?'

Chapter 23

By third term, school life settled into a rhythm that Cassie liked. She knew the students in her classes now and found that teaching really was a dance. When you knew the basics, you coped with people who varied it. She loved teaching Year 7s. Their wide-eyed response to study was akin to her own as a child. Her contentment, however, was shattered toward the end of winter.

Cassie had stayed late at school that Thursday afternoon as part of her plan to confine work to the workplace. The cleaner, dragging an antique polisher, passed the staff room and glanced at her, but he went unnoticed because she was engrossed in marking. The lower and upper corridors reverberated as floors were returned to a high-gloss shine. Slowly, the cleaners moved onto distant wings; silence descended.

As the evening closed in on her, Cassie realised she had stayed later than intended. Packing up, she was conscious that the school was virtually deserted. She saw the lights wink off in the building opposite as it was secured for the night, felt vulnerable but dismissed her fears. Schools were safe places.

Talbut parked in the main quadrangle in the school's ground. Earlier that afternoon, he had returned to his home after a few hours at the pub and discovered he had lost his house keys. Irritated that his plans for hunting were threatened, he had mentally retraced his actions that day. Dimly, he remembered upending his briefcase at his work desk for some reason that eluded him now. So he returned to the high school.

Talbut met Cassie mid-stairwell. 'G'day. I didn't expect to flush a bird from the cover here.'

'What?' Cassie attempted to pass.

'Don't play dumb with me.' Talbut's hand shot out and blocked her path. His breath was stale liquor.

Reflexively, Cassie turned her head away. She thought of retreat but decided against it.

'It's time you shed that virginal innocence. I know what women really want.'

'I doubt that.'

Talbut's other hand dropped to her breast and groped at it in search of her nipple. Outraged, Cassie tried to push it away, but he grabbed her hand and twisted it, forcing her to move backward. Her eyes welled with tears.

'So you like it a little rough? I knew you were hot for it.'

'Hot for your head!'

'Here,' he grabbed her hand and moved it to his genitals, 'feel it.'

'No ... I meant ... Let me go!'

Talbut's other hand pinioned her against the wall. He stepped closer. Cassie yanked her hand from his in disgust. 'Leave me alone.'

'Let that unbridled passion out, m' dear; I enjoy sex in unusual places.' He pressed against her. His mouth sought hers roughly.

With her jaw clenched, Cassie tried to use her body weight to throw him off balance. 'Get away from me.' She flayed at him, but he grabbed her arms and forced them down. His hold on her lessened as his right hand dropped to her thigh and groin. Her hands came up to his face. She clawed him with her nails. His head jerked back in pain. She followed through with a sharp blow upward at his nose. He swore violently at her and tried to pull her to him. Desperate, she kneed him as hard as she could. He doubled, and collapsed on the stairs, writhing and breathless. She stepped away from him. Somehow, she managed to focus her thoughts and breathe out, 'What sort of man are you?' before she left him immobilised by pain.

Shock set in after she parked in the sheds at Madison House. Sweat streamed off her. Her skin burned and tingled. The trembling became seismic. When it subsided, she stumbled out of her car but needed to lean against it for support. The dark added to her disorientation. Somehow she made it to the house.

The laughter in the house sounded distant and distorted. Unable to deal with people, Cassie sat on the verandah steps for a time. With a single focus, she headed for her room, glad that everyone had adjourned to the living room.

The hiss and steam of the shower filled the bathroom. She lathered her arms, her breasts, and finally her thighs in an attempt to erase the touch and the feel of the groping. For a long time, she just stood there, the water pouring over her.

Towelling herself dry, Cassie thought, if he comes near me again … every idea was violent. She decided on carrying a metal nail file in her pocket.

In bed, she curled into a foetal position. Her emotions seeped into the darkness.

* * *

The next morning, Cassie, still in her pyjamas, imagined a number of action plans. With each imagining, she'd been reduced to tears and trembling. Her thoughts were disjointed and her emotions in riot. She could not express how she felt: the depth of the violation. It had been impossible for her to give the specifics of the confrontation with Dobbs earlier that year. This was far worse. She felt such shame. How would she keep her emotions in check?

Staring at herself in the mirror, Cassie wished she had invested in a suit as part of her transformation; something with a masculine cut and the padded oversized shoulders in fashion at that time. Something that men would recognise as a power statement. She looked and felt anything but power-ful. She considered retrieving her old clothes but realised that Talbut would win if he saw that he had intimidated her in that way. Instead, after emptying her wardrobe, she chose a red shirt and a calf-length, black skirt with pleats at the back before heading down the corridor to the bathroom.

Focused on her mission, her face white, Cassie passed through the kitchen. The people there were a blur. Cassie did not hear Minna talking to her at breakfast. She looked through Mavis and was deaf to Michael. After two mouth-fuls of toast, she could not stomach anymore and so excused herself and left.

'Something's up,' Mavis said. 'Do you know what?'

'No, council meeting went later than usual last night. George didn't say anything.'

'I came in late too.' Mavis did not add that she had her own problems. 'I haven't seen her since early yesterday.'

Cassie's car sped into Keimera. She still lacked a plan. Should she see Coachman, given he expected all school con-cerns to go by him, or should she lodge a formal complaint with the Principal? She was shaking when she walked into the school; her prime mover being the emotional steam pent up since the trauma. The place looked quite ordinary, untouched by her personal drama.

On route to the staff room, she realised that Talbut might have arrived earlier. She did not want to see him first, could not stand to be within sight of him. She stopped. She returned to the street to see which cars had arrived. Talbut's car was not there. Coachman's was, as usual, parked in the fourth space from the driveway.

Outside Coachman's office, Cassie still did not have a clue what she was going to say. He was on the phone so she waited.

The receiver slammed into its cradle. Coachman's features were flushed. 'Yes?' he snapped.

'May I speak with you?'

'I've already indicated that you can. Come in.'

Cassie fought for control by steadying her breathing.

'Well?'

'Yesterday, I stayed back at school to work … It was late when I left … On the way out … Talbut came back … I'm not sure why … He was there as I came down.'

'For God's sake, get to the point woman. I'm a busy man.'

Cassie steadied herself. 'I'd like to lodge a formal complain about Talbut's behaviour. He …'

'I'm not in the mood for your thin-skinned reactions to humour or compliments today, Miss Sleight. I've reviewed this failing in you as part of the probation process, have I not?'

'Yes, but —

'You work in a predominantly male environment. I have said it before, but I will say it again; if it is too hot in the work-place, return to the kitchen or the secretarial pool.'

'Teaching has been a female career path since Victorian times. What planet are you on?'

'Primary teaching, m' dear. Women began their assault on the male domain, high schools, only in the mid-seventies.'

'Assault,' Cassie spluttered, 'that's why I'm here … Talbut—'

'Yes, yes, Talbut's behaviour is crass at times, but he means to flatter you. I admit his execution may have the opposite effect. The best I can do is talk to him.'

'But …'

The phone rang.

On the phone, Coachman said, 'Yes? … That's terrible! How long does the doctor say? … Uh huh. Thanks for ringing.'

'Mr Coachman, you don't understand. Talbut …'

'That was Talbut. He had some sort of accident yesterday afternoon and injured himself. He's taken sick leave for the week. I'll talk to him about your concern on his return. Close the door on your way out.'

Cassie refused the dismissal. 'You don't even know the details.'

'Irrelevant. You're upset with his behaviour, and you've had it. I will deal with it. Matter closed.'

Coachman picked up the phone and dialled.

Dismissed, Cassie went to the staff room.

Other staff arrived. Rajes, among others, recognised Cassie's stress and her power dress statement but did not inquire into it. The solution to the ongoing struggle that was inherent in teaching was a measure of character. With a full load that day, the other women had time for little else than a quick coffee before dashing off to their classrooms.

* * *

The school day began. It was like getting on a carousel. Once you hopped on, little was required but to hold on.

At recess, Cassie tried to make an appointment with the Principal.

The Principal's secretary said, 'You do realise that Mr Coachman is your first port of call.'

'Done that; not satisfied.'

'Really?' She looked at her appointment book. 'He isn't here the next few days. You have been reading the education magazine and the department gazettes, haven't you? Lots of changes are in play. Best we could do is Friday.'

Cassie asked the Deputy if she could speak to him as he exited his office. 'No time now. Why haven't you seen Coachman?'

The cliché, 'a dog chasing its tail' had new meaning for her. The unfolding events had little connection to the drama and outrage that she had imagined.

On her way back to the staff room, Cassie resisted the growing sense of helplessness.

'You appear deep in thought,' Selton said from beside her.

Cassie jumped. 'Sorry, I didn't notice you were there.'

'Obviously.'

They climbed the stairs and walked toward the English area in silence.

Selton took hold of her arm, 'Just a minute, Cassie.'

She recoiled.

'Sorry.' Selton frowned; her reaction had been disproportionate. 'I didn't mean to upset you. I just wanted a word before we go in.'

'Well?' Cassie asked him.

'Something's up, what?'

His concern triggered tears, but she tightened her eyes determined they would not flow.

'As bad as that?' Selton said.

She nodded, struggling to regain composure.

'Anything I can do?' Selton asked.

'Got a Rottweiler?'

Selton digested the information. The bell rang. 'I'm available after the next session. Back to the battle.'

Off for that period, Cassie waited until the other staff left before entering. What to do? The police? She imagined the scene and realised that she could not prove a thing, especially with Talbut's story of an injury after work. A restraining order? Again, the proof. Impossible given the workplace conditions. Resign? She had never given in to bullying. At least she did not have to deal with Talbut that day. It was a small relief.

By the time Selton had time for a quiet talk with Cassie, she had rationalised her situation and had her emotions in hand.

'Coachman tells me he will deal with Talbut for you,' Selton said.

'Yes, I know that, but he wouldn't hear me out. Last night—'

'Mary stews over things like that too. When Coachman warns one of his staff, he does it spectacularly. I can promise you that you won't have any more problems with Talbut.'

Cassie nodded and decided to give the whole issue a rest. Why weren't men better listeners? The answer came with a realisation that *listen* is an anagram of *silent*. Men looked for solutions and missed them because they didn't hear a woman out. So it had been with her father. So it was in the staff room.

Cassie consoled herself with the fact that there would be a workplace consequence to Talbut's offensive behaviour. The self-defence course, taken while she was at university, had produced results. Hopefully, he would think twice before he came near her again. Was it possible to debunk Talbut's excuse? Her cheeks burned as she thought about public disclosure. Shame weighed in.

The routine of the day took over. Cassie's classes, not particularly intuitive groups, recognised the telltale signs of a teacher ready to devour them. It was a day of heads down and bums up.

The day passed without time for shared confidence with the women. The week rushed by filled with a thousand distractions that made it easy for Cassie not to revisit her dishonour. She decided some things were too dark for casual conversation over tea.

Defeated, Cassie reverted to her former conservative dress.

Mavis was the only person to comment, her disappointment evident when she said, 'Why are you wearing that stuff? What's up?'

The explanation formed in Cassie's mind, but she could not bring herself to revisit the trauma by telling Mavis. Instead, she chose to say, 'Haven't you ever had down times, Mavis?'

'Sure I have, but never so bad I let it change me.'

With that simple statement, Mavis focused Cassie on the choice before her. Who would she be: the person she wanted to be or someone consumed by her fear, hiding in oversized clothes, avoiding being desirable, failing to discriminate between men?

* * *

After his week on sick leave, Talbut was due to return to work. In the sober truth of dawn, he had realised that he was potentially in trouble. He would have to be careful how much he drank in future. He hoped the medical certificate and the damage from crashing his car would provide corroborating evidence if accusations were made.

On his return, a Tuesday morning at eight, Coachman carpeted him at length. While Coachman sympathised about a workplace without a sense of humour, he used the opportunity to caution Talbut. Coachman emphasised that he did not like the rumours bandied about in town.

Uncertain as to what Coachman knew, Talbut assumed a submissive mask. He had toadied to Coachman for years. It was the reason he was 2IC and not Selton. It was why he volunteered to help the Deputy by doing the early morning casual teacher hire. The credit he earned meant that he could spin himself out of anything. He had been subservient this long, he could keep it up a bit longer. Coachman's support in the promotion stakes was even more important now that a merit system had been introduced.

Pee in enough pockets, Talbut thought on the way to the staff room, and your scent becomes indistinguishable. Beneath his satisfaction, his ego stung. His anger was comparable to what he had felt a year ago, the day his marriage ended. Just a little longer, he told himself, and I'll have payback. It was just a question of the opportune moment.

* * *

1987. Talbut, drained by a week of marking examination papers at the end of the semester, had returned home to find his wife's car boot open and suitcases inside it.

'What the …?'

Entering their modest home overlooking the beach, he met his wife in the foyer. 'Mel, what's going on?'

'I've nothing more to say, Mark. You just don't hear me. I want out of here!'

He reached out for her, thinking this was her usual bid for

attention, but she hit his hand away. 'That's not going to work this time,' she said.

He stepped up to her, pushing her against the wall. 'I've neglected you. I know it, but I'll make it up to you.' His mouth crushed hers.

She resisted him, but his sheer weight fixed her to the wall. Mel surrendered, knowing that if she continued to battle he would interpret that as a bid for love-making. He was already manoeuvring her to the bedroom.

'I've got my period,' Mel said.

He let her go with distaste. 'Shouldn't lead a man on like that then.'

'I wasn't.'

'Listen, baby, if you really wanted to leave you would've done so before I came home.' He corrected his pants, uncomfortable with the tightness. Picking up her suitcase, he was surprised by its weight. In past scenes, the cases were empty.

'I left it till now because I didn't want you on my parents' doorstep. You have to know that this time it's for real. I've had it with waiting for your promotion! It's not going to change anything. Look at you.' She laughed bitterly. 'A middle-aged man content with life in the small arena. The only thing upwardly mobile about you is your prick! You lied to me y' bastard.' She threw an opened letter at him. 'All your posting preferences are for coastal towns like this one! You promised me we'd move to the city. You'll always be a spectator, Mark, on the sideline, wishing you were a player but never taking what you want.'

He struck her; put her in her place, on the floor and grovelling.

Chapter 24

Spring and the life associated with it came late that year unconstrained by calendar dates. Keimera finally threw off the shackles of winter as school life swung into the fourth term. Cafés spread onto the pavement. Umbrellas went up. The town rejoiced in the budding life, celebrating it in large and small ways. The weekend migration of Sydneysiders returned, improving business and reducing available parking spaces.

The tide was out and the volcanic rocks around Black Beach, where the harbour met the township, stood naked to the sun. Holidaymakers scattered across the rocks: fishing, exploring rock pools, collecting shells, and teasing the waves. Cassie watched a flock circle the departing fishing boats as she and Mavis walked around the harbour, Mavis balancing on the retaining wall that shaped the ocean into a bay.

'Well, for special weekends, my parents travelled over an hour just to bring me here. My favourite was the rocket slide. I felt like I was climbin' to heaven. And here we are.'

They sat on grassed slopes that descended from the main road in the town. Mavis wrapped her arms around her knees. Her white shorts contrasted with her tan. Her translucent shirt slipped off her shoulders as she watched the scene.

Cassie lay back, resting on her elbows, studying toes that peeped out beneath her blue jeans. The ricochet of tennis balls from nearby tennis courts mingled with the squawks of quarrelling seagulls.

'I still don't get why you're not dating, Cassie.'

'I've gone out a few times with Mike.'

'As friends. That's not real dating. Aren't there any teachers with romantic potential?'

'Well, there is an art teacher I like, but he seems content with Friday night dancing.'

'Sounds cheap. Ditch him.'

Mavis whistled, and in a voice that carried said, 'Boy, that bloke has got a really cute bum!' Cassie turned her head, following Mavis' line of sight.

Mavis turned to Cassie, her eyes wide and innocent. 'Cassie! You really are forward. You shouldn't say things like that.'

Cassie grinned, realising denial was useless.

The man, an average looking person with brown hair, turned and looked at them. He said something to his male tennis partner who walked off to a seat near the courts.

In a voice that only Cassie could hear, Mavis said, 'Another bloke who's improved with age.'

He moved to them and dropped onto the grass.

'G'day, Mavis. Who's your friend?'

'Peter, this is Cassie. She's a teacher at the high school and new in town. She's not dating anyone at the moment.'

'Mavis!' Cassie said under her breath.

'G'day. Going to the pub tonight, Mavis?'

'I don't know what Terry's got planned yet.' Underneath her light tone, Mavis was worried. Since the last visit to her parents and with the longer hours Terry was working, she had not seen much of him. She would have to work hard to undo the damage. *Maybe I should tell Terry to forget buying an expensive engagement ring. It would give him more time for me*, she thought, *and help the relationship.*

'And what about you?' he said to Cassie, assessing her.

'I'm tied up with a friend.'

'Do I know him?' asked Peter.

'I doubt it.'

Mavis frowned at Cassie, upset by her coldness.

'Peter!' someone called from the court. 'We're on.'

'Beaut!' He met his tennis partner at the court entrance.

'Not goin' to find happiness that way, Cassie. You should've let me set you up with Peter. He's a really good bloke. Not the sort who mimics behaviour in movies, expecting to get laid. He won't bore you talking about his man toys or numb you to sleep by his fascination with himself.'

'Sounds like you've had some bad dates.'

'Some? An ocean full before Terry.'

'Well, I don't need a man to be happy, Mavis. In fact, I think happiness has to come from within.'

'Maybe, but it also comes from mixin' with people and gettin' on with life. C'mon, let's get an ice cream, and we can also catch up on the local gossip.'

As they walked up the street, Cassie only dimly registered Mavis' chatter. Though Cassie was mostly over Jake, part of her was not. She felt like a favourite coat that had been discarded for something updated and trendy. Until she outgrew that, she was vulnerable to the dangers of a relationship on the rebound.

'What sort of ring do you want, Cassie, when the right man comes along? I want a large stone, bigger than that one.' They had stopped outside one of two jewellery shops in the town. 'Terry's doin' overtime to get me a lovely big diamond. Good things are worth some sacrifice.'

'Did you say right man?'

'Uh huh.'

'That's a myth, I think. Otherwise how awful would it be if he was poor and lived on the other side of the world?'

'Don't you believe in love, Cassie?'

'Yes … but the cost that comes with marrying seems too high.'

'It's expensive, but it is a special day and the memories —'

'I was talking about the cost of being married, not just the wedding day.'

'How can you say that when you live with a couple like Minna and George?'

'Because I grew up surrounded by women in unhappy marriages.'

'Are you sure they were unhappy? My gran and pa used to bicker all the time, but he was lost when she died. Mum said it was their way of showing they cared for each other because they weren't comfortable with being seen as mushy. I reckon you're only saying that because you've never really been in love. Hey, wait up!'

After walking in companionable silence for a while, Mavis asked, 'So what's turned you off men?'

'I'm not turned off men; I like them, but getting a man is not the focus of my life.'

'What is then?'

'I am. I don't mean in a selfish way. I mean … it's hard to explain.'

Mavis waited.

'I want to be the best version of myself. I haven't got beyond that yet. I'm working it out as I go. It's harder for our generation than our mums'. Where are our role models?'

* * *

Music, a Bob Marley selection, played softly in the background. Cassie and Mavis lounged across Mavis' bed. Mavis flicked through women's magazines as Cassie read some of Mavis' lyrics in a well-worn A5 manuscript book.

'Well, Cassie?'

'Your lyrics are so different from the way you …'

'Speak?'

Cassie nodded.

'I never wanted to sound like a geek. Besides, how I speak has nothin' to do with how I think or write. So, you like any of them?'

'The way you frame ideas is unique, but …'

'Give me my book back. I can live with you not likin' my songs, but I can't cope with you playin' the teacher with me.'

'Don't ask me to read your stuff if you only want to be flattered. For what it's worth, you …'

'Do you think your hairdresser is as good with colour as he is a stylist? I fancy myself as a blonde.'

'Your eyebrows are too black for it to look natural. Why?'

'Terry was really taken with one last night at the pub. Mind you, she was stunnin'.'

'You can't change just because he admires someone else.'

'Yair, but he always reacts to blondes.'

'Well, I think you'd be a fool to mess with your hair. It's great.'

'Uhuh. Terry and I are havin' a weekend away soon to my parents' farm.'

'Something for me to look forward to.'

Mavis looked at her questioningly.

'The walls aren't soundproofed, you know.'

'Tell me about it; I knew every time you had a nightmare.'

'Oh.'

'I've got to keep him satisfied somehow though. He's forever on about movin' into our own place; I don't want to. Look, we're givin' Gary a month of sleep, and then we'll change back to Terry's room. We'll be like the tide: in and out.'

'That's gross!'

'Cassie!' Mavis threw one pillow after another at her. 'And you used to be such an innocent!'

With the pillows restored to their rightful place on the bed, Mavis continued, 'Babs at work reckons livin' together is a good thing. She says it shows whether you can survive the day-to-day hassles of a relationship before you get married. What do you think?'

Cassie shrugged but added as an afterthought, 'I don't know. Lots of people live together for years but break-up after they marry. It's not really a test unless you have full access to his accounts and share the stresses of maintaining a home.'

Mavis stared into the distance. Terry kept two things to himself: his car and his money. 'Well, Terry's doin' overtime as it is to pay for my ring. We can't afford our own place, not with the weddin' costs. My dress alone …'

'Yes, well … don't expect me to get caught up in the Cinderella experience. It's not what counts. How much effort and talk has there been over the details of your marriage? None, right? Where's the balance?'

'Yair, yair. I don't want another earful.' Mavis looked at her watch. 'Look at the time. Got to run.'

Cassie looked after her; was this how her behaviour had seemed to Leonie and her mother when they saw a truth that she refused to acknowledge? Was there one truth underlying a situation? She hoped not. Otherwise, Mavis was about to make a terrible mistake just as she had.

Chapter 25

Heat radiated from the small of Selton's **back** as he trailed his class across the quadrangle. Eight weeks left before his seed took shape and identity, ending seventeen barren years. Twin boys; he felt blessed.

Selton watched his students lunge into the bus' seats and hang out of its windows. He would be the father he had wished for as a boy. After the last head withdrew, the bus rattled off toward the township.

The telephone rang.

'Morning, English faculty. Cassandra Sleight speaking. How may I help you?'

The speaker was female, her voice strained.

'Sorry, I didn't catch that … Oh, Mary, hi. You've just missed Selton.'

Pain arched through Mary Selton's abdomen; her groan cut across her next comment. Her groan sounded down the telephone line.

'Are you all right? Mary?'

The breathing changed; the short gasping intakes faded and the comment was barely audible.

'But you're not due for weeks yet!'

The breathing was harsh and then eased. Again, the voice was soft.

'But Selton's on an excursion … Rajes? … I'll check her timetable.' The phone cord stretched to maximum. 'She's on class. You should phone for an ambulance … I promise I'll find Selton and tell Rajes. I promise!' Foreboding propelled her into action.

In the middle of her explanation of the Middle East conflict, Rajes paused as Cassie jerked into view, the younger woman's distress obvious. Conscious of her class, Rajes manoeuvred her into the corridor. The class strained to listen.

'Cassie, I'll go to their house first in case the ambulance is already out on a call. Find Selton and supervise his class. My class,' Rajes looked at them as she spoke, 'can be trusted to get on with their work.' They nodded, concerned. 'Try to gain some composure. I'll phone the school as soon as Mary is in medical care.'

The women separated. Cassie was halfway down the corridor when the older woman called. 'You'd better tell the office or they'll want our hide for leaving the school.'

It took all of Cassie's self-control not to run.

Finding Selton was easier said than done. Cassie, in her panic, had left the school without checking the itinerary for the Year 9 History local area study. She was in town before she realised her error. She knew the front office kept a record of each excursion and so sought to solve the problem with a quick call.

The first two public phones that Cassie tried were out of order. With no choice but to return to the school, Cassie took a short cut down Collins and into Long Street. As she did so, she saw a school bus heading in the reverse direction. Her tyres squealed as she came to a halt behind the bus.

'What are you doing here?'

Cassie's prepared explanation evaporated. 'Mary's in labour.'

'Shit!'

'Rajes has gone to the house in case there is a delay with the ambulance. Go, I'll take your class! Oh, oh, oh! Wait! You'll need my keys.'

Back at school and drained by the crisis, Cassie found it difficult to concentrate on her afternoon class. At the end of the day, the English faculty lounged in the staffroom, waiting for news. At five-twenty, the telephone jolted them out of inaction.

'The twins?' The lines in Van der Huffen's face deepened as he listened. 'Mother and child are doing fine. Got it; I'll pass it on.'

The English staff sat with their backs turned on their work, faced inward, inarticulate in the face of death. The bookend boys were the first to leave with mumbled farewells; their departure triggered an exodus. Samantha lingered, concerned about Van der Huffen's distress but uncertain as to what to say. In the end, she left on, 'See you tomorrow.'

'Vander, are you going to the hospital now or later?' Cassie asked still at her desk.

'I'm not going at all.'

'But you're one of his best friends; you have to be there for him!'

'No, actually, I don't. Grief is a private thing.'

'That's the emotional coward's excuse. All year I've watched you and Selton protect each other's backs. You can't let him down now, not on this! God, Vander, listen to me! He will remember your support or lack of it once his grief passes. I know how my dad felt when my granddad died. This is so much worse than that loss. It'll change everything if you're not there!'

'Enlighten me; since when were we close?'

'We're not, but I am indebted to you and Selton for support with 10G, and I intend to repay it now. C'mon.'

The blood-sun hung just above the hills as Van der Huffen's car sped north to the hospital. It was a silent trip with the occupants locked in thought. Darkness closed on the car.

The first thing Cassie noticed, as she and Van der Huffen entered the maternity wing, was the cold caress of air-conditioning. Then she noticed the pastel walls, the filtered light from the cretonne curtains, and the bloom of flowers. It looked like a motel.

Baby Selton was not in the nursery.

Worried, Cassie and Van der Huffen sought out Rajes who waited, steaming coffee cup in hand, outside Mary's room. Selton emerged as they arrived.

Van der Huffen crossed to Selton and gave him one of those three pat-on-the-back bear hugs that heterosexual men reserve for their sex; only physical contact could convey what he felt.

'I'm sorry, Selton, about the loss of the other child,' Cassie said, knowing there was no comfort that could be offered other than the acknowledgement of his loss. To Rajes, she said quietly in an aside, 'And the survivor is?'

'A boy. We had two boys.' Selton took the proffered coffee and looked expectantly at Rajes who said, 'The Perkins are on their way.'

'The baby's not in the nursery,' Cassie asked.

Rajes answered for Selton who struggled with his emotions. She steered Cassie away from him as she spoke. 'The baby's been on the respirator for a few hours. The doctor insists it's only a precaution. A cardiologist has —'

'That's still an issue then?' Cassie asked.

'A precaution given the concerns during the pregnancy,' Rajes replied.

Selton sipped his coffee but tasted fear. Van der Huffen stood by him, wordless.

'What do we do now?'

'Wait,' Rajes said.

The cardiologist, a woman power-suited in electric blue, arrived just after eight and spoke to the parents alone. She estimated Mary to be in her thirties but silently acknowledged that fleshy women often looked younger. Her dark skin had an unnatural pallor.

Mary felt as if her mind was a spring suffering from over-load; the jargon was alienating. Her focus kept switching from the doctor to Selton as he stared out the window.

'Put simply?' Mary asked the doctor, her eyes on Selton's back.

'He'll survive, but intensive care will be needed for some time.'

* * *

Selton's exorcism of grief repelled his male colleagues. They squirmed at their desks, relieved when they could get away to playground duty or classes. The gender stereotype that women were more comfortable with emotional displays than men held true on this occasion. When the bell rang that day, the men hastily left the staffroom followed by a despondent Selton.

'Expecting adult men to provide solace is as productive as asking a six year old boy to do the same,' Rajes replied to Cassie as they organised their work for that release lesson.

'Thank God, I'm off,' Samantha announced as she entered

from playground duty. After checking Selton's timetable on the noticeboard, she added, 'And there's a double blessing because it's a Selton-free session as well.'

Rajes looked reprovingly at Samantha who reacted with, 'C'mon, admit it; his grief is getting to all of us. I wish he'd suck it up. I don't get his need to talk about it.'

'Let's hope you never have an experience that gives you that insight,' Rajes said. 'Compassion costs us nothing, Samantha.'

'Look, what I say to you is not how I behave with him, you know that, but I've been wondering lately if tough love wouldn't be better. Selton's not ridding himself of grief; he's whipping himself and us with it.'

'I've kept ... dark stuff to myself,' Cassie said, 'and it took ages for me to deal with it. I wonder now if I had shared it, if ...'

'So, Little Miss Control has had some ripples in her life pond, has she?'

Stunned and at a loss for a retort, Cassie plugged in her cassette player's earphones, glad she had music to block Samantha out. Though there were friendly moments between them, Samantha's biting remarks kept them from being genuine friends.

'Cassie did not deserve that,' Rajes said. 'What you don't appreciate is that there is a goodness in her, an integrity, a strength. Besides, a person should never be criticised for being compassionate; so few people are these days.'

'True, but there is a line between compassion and encouraging narcissism. We should be focusing Selton on the positives, not the loss.'

'Your reaction says a lot about you, Samantha.' With that, Rajes made a show of being distracted by the pile of marking on her desk.

That lunchtime, Coachman's attempt at consolation, 'The loss of the spare is tragic, mate, but you still have an heir, and you can have more kids. Focus on that!' elicited rage unlike anything Cassie had ever witnessed.

Thunderous silence. Everyone in the room felt the imminence of violence. Selton's colour, like the temperature sensor in a mercury thermometer, rose alarmingly. He shook trying to contain it; eyes wild, face contorted, fists clenched. The shaking increased to seismic proportions; Selton's hands, like arthritic claws, opened and closed as he battled to retain control.

Watching them, Cassie was horrified yet trapped in the moment. Around her, her colleagues formed a tableau of shock. Coachman looked like he expected a blow but seemed unable to retreat.

Action broke the spell.

Lifted up by his coat lapels, Coachman's feet dangled, his face close to Selton's who visibly struggled for self-control. Cassie understood that struggle and recognised the Herculean task to contain its charring heat. What could any of them do now to rescue Selton from his agony?

Selton's struggle to retain control translated itself into trembling, reverberating from Selton through Coachman.

Most of the faculty were frozen. Pothole, more rotund then ever, stood in panic and then sat realising there was no way out. Fuller distractedly reached for his neighbour's sandwich and ate it despite registering the taste was odd. The eating went unnoticed in the shock of the moment. The ceiling fan whirred futilely.

With her eyes closed and crying, Cassie begged the universe, Don't let him be cast adrift. As she opened them, she saw Rajes standing beside Selton, her hand resting on his shoulder, her words inaudible to the rest of them.

Selton, in a finely controlled movement, discarded Coachman in disgust. At the same time, Van der Huffen coolly crossed from his desk to the sink. Coachman disappeared. Selton collapsed into his chair.

Hot water sounded as it flowed into the mug. A teaspoon chinked in the stirring. A mug of tea was thrust into Selton's hands. He was aware he had to hold on; letting go would destroy him. On a subliminal level, it was the first comfort Selton had felt since grief had taken possession of him. He had not succumbed yet, but he felt the pull downward.

'I feel like a shotgun has blown a hole right through me,' Selton, his voice hoarse, said to the room in general.

The bell rang. The English faculty drifted away, ghosts in Selton's world. Silence shrouded the faculty corridors. Heat and anguish crushed staff and students. Coachman avoided the staff room until normality returned.

Chapter 26

Two weeks passed. Terry, Gary and George played darts on the verandah, glad to return to outdoor pastimes. Michael sat on the floor delving into the complexities of Geography. He had three weeks before his HSC examinations. Cassie sat in the window embrasure reading.

The whistling kettle brought Cassie back from the world of *Solomon's Child*. She liked this text much better than Clarke's *The Min-Min*. It would succeed with her Year 8s where the other had failed.

'Cassie, would you mind asking me a few questions on this stuff after supper?' Michael asked. 'You've been a big help so far. It's worth a dinner out once I'm free of the exams.'

'I like working with you, Mike, and don't need repayment. So, where would we go?'

'Fenways on a Saturday night.'

'Fenways? That's too special for … Do you mean as a date, a real date?'

'Why not?' There was challenge behind his smile.

Holding Michael's gaze, Cassie said, 'There are plenty of reasons, but I'd love to anyway.' Marking her place in the novel, she said, 'I'll take your turn helping with supper tonight.'

'Thanks.'

'My pleasure.' Once out of the living room and sight, Cassie improvised a few light-hearted steps, liking being liked. Entering the kitchen, she froze.

Before her, Mavis was a watery mess. Her hair was lifeless and blonde. Minna looked helplessly at Cassie.

'What have you done, Mavis?' Cassie asked.

'Don't say it, I know! What am I goin' to do? I can't let Terry see me like this. I went home to Mum's, but she didn't have any ideas. She was real good about it though.' Mavis started to cry.

Minna patted Mavis' arm.

'What can I do?'

'Maybe a lot of conditioner would get rid of that straw effect.' Cassie sat down opposite her.

Mavis swallowed her tears, 'Mum tried that.'

'Maybe you should leave it alone until tomorrow. You can go back to the hairdressers …' Cassie fingered the hair carefully.

'Mum said that too. She gave me her favourite scarf to wear 'n all.' Mavis started to cry again. 'Isn't there somethin' we can try now?'

'Well, I do have a great conditioner. It's for difficult hair. Without it, I'd look like a clown.'

Mavis smiled at her through the tears. 'Mum's stuff comes from Woollies. Good ol' Mum. She drove my car back to town and Dad followed in the Ute because they were worried about me.' She started crying again. 'What am I goin' to do?'

'Let's try mine. It can't hurt,' Cassie said gently.

'Come on, Mavis. Up you get. The sooner Cassie gets you upstairs the better you'll feel.'

'But where's Terry? I couldn't bear it if he saw me lookin' like this.'

'He's playing darts,' Cassie said. 'Look, I'll go back and

keep an eye on him. If it looks like he's going to head out this way, I'll stop him.'

Mavis nodded.

Back on the verandah, the dart game continued. 'Your turn, mate,' George said passing the darts to Terry. 'I doubt either of you can top my score.'

'The game's not over yet,' Gary said. 'Terry and I are close on your heels.'

'Either of you boys want a tinnie?' George sauntered toward the kitchen whistling.

On her return, Cassie dropped down next to Michael. 'Supper will be awhile … Your mum wants to delay it a bit.'

'I'm not ready either,' Michael answered.

Sitting in an armchair near him, Cassie feigned interest in a magazine but eavesdropped on Terry and Gary.

'You grew up with Selton, didn't you?' Gary said to Terry.

'We lived next door to him, but he's a lot older than me.' Terry lined up his dart and hit the bull's eye.

'What do you make of his drinkin' lately? There's a lot of talk about it round town.'

Cassie frowned. That explained a lot of things about Selton. She wondered how Mary was coping and remembered her mother's suffering as the three of them waited for Tom to come home from work or the pub or the club or wherever he went with his mates or that woman. Cassie knew with certainty that she could not live that life. She considered making phone contact with Mary but postponed the act; Mavis needed help first. Like many good intentions, the thought was never enacted.

'Our dads put us through hell.' The second dart was off target.

'I heard they expected twins but lost one.'

'Wouldn't know. Ask Cassie; she works with him! Our dads

were bloody stupid, selfish old men. I hate drunks! Never gave a shit about what we needed or were goin' through!' The final dart missed the board completely. 'What's it to you?'

'I like him,' Gary said as he removed the darts. 'He's a hell of a swimmer and was in the life savin' movement for years. Don't like to see people like that sufferin' if there's somethin' I can do to help.'

'Sure. What's in it for you?'

'Nothin'. I just thought —'

'He's black and ugly enough to take care of himself.'

Gary looked at Terry in disgust, torn between a desire for knowledge and habitual discomfort in talking about mates or emotions.

Michael's, 'Thanks, Cassie, I reckon I've got any question on that topic nailed,' brought her attention back to him. 'Do you mind asking me stuff off the fact sheet now?'

A panic-stricken scream rent the air.

Minna rushed from the kitchen and collided with Cassie at the foot of the staircase. They rushed upstairs. The men followed.

The upstairs hallway was dark; all the bedroom doors were closed. Mavis stood in the bathroom doorway, wrapped in a striped towel, her hair lit by the bathroom light.

'Look at my hair!' she sobbed. 'Oh, God, what am I goin' to do?'

'Calm down,' soothed Cassie. 'We can't see your hair properly with all that gel in it. Rinse it off; we'll have a better idea of what's wrong,'

'I can't. My hair … it's turned to jelly.'

Cassie now knew what Mavis meant by gobsmacked.

'Don't worry, Mavis,' Gary said. 'You really are a sweetie now.'

The men laughed.

Mavis, aware of Terry, rushed off to her bedroom.

'Don't be so insensitive, Gary,' Minna said. She gave the men a backward look as she and Cassie followed Mavis.

'Oh, c'mon. This is the first time I've been able to get one back on her.' Gary went downstairs parodying *It's A Long Way to the Top*, a song by his favourite rock band, AC/DC. His voice warbled upstairs as he descended, 'It's so hard to bear when your hair has turned to jellooooooo.'

Terry hesitated on the threshold of Mavis' bedroom, hoping Mavis could not hear Gary.

'Jelloooooo.' Gary obviously enjoyed the echo in the foyer.

Beyond comfort, Mavis said, 'Terry'll never look at me again. How could I be so stupid?'

'Nonsense,' Terry said. 'You'll always look beautiful to me. Your hair is just the icing on a very special cake: the sort of cake that doesn't even need icing.' He wiped away her tears.

Her hair wobbled but neither Terry nor Mavis was aware of it.

* * *

The next morning with a scarf wrapped around Mavis' hair in an attempt to avoid the stares of the curious, Mavis and Cassie stood outside the hairdressers'. It had seemed simple the previous night.

'I don't think I can do it,' said Mavis.

'It's this, or shares in a wig factory.'

Silence.

'It's a matter of image,' Cassie continued. 'We have to remain cool and collected. Like any business, they have to stand by the quality of their product.'

The manager, although sympathetic, refused to accept responsibility for the condition of Mavis' hair. His attitude changed Mavis' tears to anger.

'Now, listen 'ere, mate,' Mavis said. She moved closer to the moustachioed man and looked down at him. 'You can drop the false accent. No one here believes you're French. Fix m' hair or I am goin' to be a permanent fixture here. I can give you a taste of what that'd be like right now.' She moved across the salon to an incoming customer. Her Australian accent clashed with her attempt at French, 'Bon joura, madam.'

The startled woman looked at Mavis who had turned to the women seated at the various sinks and chairs around the room. 'Attention ladies! This is a sample of Monsoora Andre's handiwork.' She pulled off her scarf with the aplomb of a magician.

Wet, Mavis' hair had been glutinous jelly. Dry, it was matted straw. Fear of it falling out had prevented her from brushing it.

Intakes of breath. A freeze-frame of coffee cups. The flutter of falling magazines. Women took frightened double takes in the salon mirrors. Their cups clattered. The salon emptied faster than a beer mug in a boat race.

'All right, all right.' The manager dropped his accent. 'We'll fix it.' Cassie arched an eyebrow at him while Mavis continued to look militant. 'Yair, we'll bear the cost. It'll be close cut though. Sit here.'

Mavis looked at Cassie uncertain about being shorn.

Cassie said, 'You've got great cheek bones and beautiful eyes. With the right make-up, you'll look stunning!'

'Terry's goin' to hate it!'

'Mavis, you need to stop defining yourself by Terry's likes and dislikes. Otherwise you'll become a slave —'

'Let up!' Mavis turned from Cassie as she sat.

* * *

There was no quick fix, no short cut in Selton's route through grieving. The landmarks of the journey shaped through use of the tools provided by his culture, support in the wider community, and his wife's faith in counselling.

Weeks passed with the faculty women in tears as they listened to his outpouring. Many of the men became scarce at recess and lunch breaks. Talk about the loss of little Ben peppered other conversations but the people who cared – the women, Van der Huffen, and Fuller – listened in silence with patience.

Still grieving, Selton saw again the world in its absurdities. He smiled occasionally, returned to the games of life. Over time and to the combined relief of the school, he seemed to recover. They did not understand that grief now travelled with him silently.

Selton made time for his wife and child, shared his feelings, and talked about their future. Simple things like the gurgle of Will's laugh or the feel of him resting against him during the burping process introduced normality into their lives. Selton did not realise that Will and his needs denied Mary time for herself. Selton marvelled at his wife's bravery. It helped him in his journey.

Chapter 27

'No rest for the wicked,' Cassie said to George as he prepared the evening meal. 'Van der Huffen says the marking copulates over night.'

Caught up in a French chef impersonation, George replied, 'I spit on this man who speaks to young women in such vile language.' He made an appropriate gesture.

'Too much Monty Python with the boys, George. Catch you later.'

Coffee mug refreshed, Cassie crossed paths with Minna whose head was in a fog of council issues.

'That's considerate of you, Cassie,' Minna said taking the coffee from her.

'But I —'

'I need my head read for working with dim-witted, short-sighted politicians.' She returned to her study.

On Cassie's return from the kitchen with a second cup, the slam of a telephone startled her. She looked at Minna who stamped into the foyer flushed with anger.

'If developers had their way, Keimera would be ruined like Surfers. I need a smoke.' Minna went to the coat closet under the stairwell and returned with a contraband pack of Royal Blunts' cigarellos. She opened one of the windows before lighting up.

'George will suffer from apoplexy if he sees you with that.'

Minna savoured her cigarello and then relaxed into the exhale that she blew out the window. 'What he doesn't know can't hurt me. Besides, I don't do it often. Nicotine is so … soothing.'

'Since you're having a break, can I ask you something personal?'

'Of course.'

'When you got married …?'

'Yes?'

'Were you sure that George was the right man?'

'The right man? There's no such thing. Truth is I've had a number of loves, work being one of them. The older you get, Cassie, the more you realise that there are a number of right men in this world. It's all a matter of timing.'

'Are you telling me you were attracted to men after you married as well?'

'Of course I was. I got married. I didn't die. A good marriage isn't a wedding gift from an unseen guest. It's something you both work and suffer to get. I love George, but there have been times even with him when I thought I didn't. They weren't short spells either.'

'Maybe I should've asked you how you knew he was the man you should marry.'

'Should? I'm not sure that there were any telltale signs.' Memories of that time and her first husband gave Minna pause. 'I chose … to mesh my life with George's because we suited well … loved each other … and I could have the life I wanted.' Not so with Bill who put his career as an overseas journalist ahead of his relationship. 'I've never been the sort of woman who'd let my goals be subordinate to a man's. Have you got someone in mind?'

'No,' Cassie's voice dropped slightly in pitch, 'just wondering, that's all. Mavis and I have talked about it. I just wanted your perspective.'

'Things have changed in so many ways for your generation, yet the pressure on women in relationships remains essentially unchanged. I worry when I see that reruns of shows like *I Dream of Jeanie* are popular and about the preoccupation with body image, sex, and getting a man.' She looked out the window down the hill. 'Do you know if anyone is expecting visitors?'

'No.'

George's distinctive foot tread sounded toward them from the kitchen.

There was a frantic flurry of cigarette disposal. Minna retreated into her study.

George said at the opened door, 'Someone coming up the drive. Know anyone who drives a yellow car?'

Cassie froze.

* * *

Something must be wrong, Cassie thought as she stood on the back steps, focused on Jake's arrival. Why else would he be here? When she saw Melissa with Jake, Cassie knew something was wrong. Leonie in her last phone call had talked at length about Jake's avoidance of his wife.

Getting out of the car, Jake felt drawn to the beauty before him. Had he met her before? His silence cued Melissa who said, 'Oh! Thank goodness! What a long trip! What on the earth have you done to your beautiful long hair, Cassie?'

Cassie was dimly aware of Melissa who continued to chatter, 'When Leonie suggested that I come with Jake to get you, I never realised how far this place was, did you, Jake? Such a lovely town. Perhaps we should look for our holiday house here.'

Jake looked at her sharply. When would Melissa stop peddling the myth that they were still together? He hadn't seen her in weeks, and she still refused to let go.

'What's happened, Jake?'

'Your mother's ill, and your dad wants you to come home.' It seemed natural for Jake to put a comforting arm around Cassie.

'Our families,' Melissa said, 'thought it'd be less traumatic for you and safer if we came and got you. So much better than a phone call.' She displaced Jake's arm gently and replaced it with hers. 'It's all right, Cassie. Really, it is. Your mum's in Intensive Care. She looked a bit pale, but that's natural, given she's had a heart attack. I thought today … well, I think everyday, but today I thought, looking at her, that the medical attention is almost more frightening than the pain, all those wires and the machines. I said as much to Jake, didn't I? Would you feel better if we went inside? I know I would. Perhaps I could have a cuppa while you're grabbing your things. I can fill in anyone who needs to know.'

'We can go now. I just need to let the people inside know. They can take care of things down here for me.'

'Oh, but you'll need clothing. We don't mind waiting.'

'No, I won't. I can borrow Leonie's. She won't mind. Jake, you understand, don't you? I have to see Mum.'

'Come on, Melissa. There's some coffee in the flask. I'm certain it's still hot.'

* * *

The quiet freshness of that October night air contrasted with the heat of the house. A cool change had arrived from the south. Cassie stood on her family verandah, beyond feeling. The emptiness was terrible.

The funeral was a fragmented mosaic of phrases and faces. It had closed with Leonie reading Mary Frye's bereavement verse. The reading echoed in Cassie's mind.

'Do not stand at my grave and weep,
I am not there; I do not sleep.
I am a thousand winds that blow.
I am the diamond glints on snow.
I am the sun on ripened grain.
I am the gentle autumn rain.
When you awaken in the morning's hush,
I am the swift uplifting rush
Of quiet birds in circling flight.
I am the soft starlight at night.
Do not stand at my grave and cry,
I am not there; I did not die.'

But you did, Cassie thought, and I wasn't there. She listened to the wind in the trees, at the left of the house, whisper its grief. It was a restrained lament. Sombre clouds massed in the west blocking out the stars although they were visible toward Windsor. An occasional light flickered from nearby properties.

The opening notes of Robert Goulet's *My Love Forgive Me* reached out into the night. Cassie cringed. They really needed to do something about her father's guilt. Its waves crashed over everyone within hearing. Resisting the urge to drift, she clung to the raft of action; it had carried her safely though that year despite the huge swells in the newly charted ocean that she explored. She hoped now the tidal wave surge of the grief would not drown her.

The song finished, Tom lifted the needle off the next track and returned it to the beginning of the track.

From the bedroom doorway, Cassie watched Leonie pat her left arm as she stared into the dark. Cassie hesitated. Over the last few days they had worn grief separately, unable to cope with the way pain magnified when they came together, even though they talked everyday trivia. Leonie's arm pat increased rhythmically; so did the intensity in hand contact to flesh.

Cassie intercepted the hand as she spoke. 'Don't, Leonie.'

'What's wrong with me? I can't cry ...'

'That doesn't mean anything. I didn't cry after Pops died, the breakup with Jake, or the ab ...'

'What?'

'Not even at Mum's funeral. I've spent a good part of this year in tears; believe me, it's awful. Better not to feel.'

Tom turned up the volume of his record player.

Both women winced.

Leonie said, 'I hate the way Dad wallows in his ... pain. I think he's responsible for my passion for having silence when I want it. Let's get out of here!'

'What about Dad?'

'Mum would want us to be there for him, I guess. How about you tell him we're taking him for a walk. I've an idea of how to end this torture by music.'

With Tom safely out of sight, in the lounge room, Leonie removed the needle from the arm of the turntable. She was tempted to scratch the record but hid it.

Ready and waiting on the verandah, Cassie wondered where both relatives were. After waiting five minutes or so, she went in search of her father. She found him sitting on his bed, spent from an earlier venting at a bedroom rug that had tripped him up. A rug that Nancy had asked him a million times to fix.

'C'mon, Dad. The fresh air will do you good. The southerly's brought in a cool change.' Cassie crossed to his closet and removed a brown drill jacket that he wore around the property. 'Here, I'll help you into it.' Her father responded robotically.

Leonie met Cassie outside their parents' room. She spoke in undertones, 'I've made Dad a coffee laced with whisky. Maybe that and the walk will help him sleep. I can't cope with much more of his night prowling.'

The Sleights walked an eight mile circuit along country roads. Little was said beyond the mundane.

Returning to the house, small figures surrounded by the vast darkness of the night, they found Jake. His mother had sent over an Esky packed with meals for the next week. The ritual of unpacking complete, Cassie watched Jake drive away, a cloud of dust in his wake. She wished she could take time back.

* * *

The carrot-red moon was huge and low. Its gentle light shimmered in the haze around it. The temperature had dropped unexpectedly, sending the populace back into warmer clothing. Three weeks had passed since her return home, but to Cassie, time was frozen.

Rain coming, Cassie thought, drawing the curtains closed. She returned to the lounge on which she and Jake had been sitting. He knelt at the fire, stirring its dying embers.

Uncomfortable with the silence, Cassie said, 'The council in Keimera have banned open fires in new houses. Apparently, the smoke is exacerbating the fogs.'

'Fascinating,' Jake said returning to her.

'Just one of the many gems one gleans when living with a councillor.'

'Travel has broadened your horizons then?'

Cassie laughed. 'Yes, exploring the small arena, the enigma of rebellious boys, the cut and thrust of argument ... It's a dream come true.'

'But not yours.'

'You know how a person feels when the ice cream falls out of the cone onto the ground? I felt like that.'

'So, why didn't you chuck it in and come home?'

'Because ... I've found some things that I like despite the grit.'

Conversation meandered and then petered out. For a while, they sat in silent comfort watching the flames chase each other across the wood.

'So, you've been separated for seven months?'

'I married Melissa for the wrong reasons.'

Silence as Cassie digested his statement.

'I didn't really propose, you know. She misunderstood what I was saying. I found out the hard way. Her parents had mine over for a celebration dinner. Everything snowballed after that.'

Silence. Cassie looked at him in disbelief.

'Sounds incredible, but it's true. The price of playing it hard and passionate with the daughter of friends. You never got jealous, why?'

'I did, but I wasn't going to compete. If our love wasn't big enough to hold you, I wanted none of it. I didn't want a life like our mothers' lives.'

'Oh!'

Silence.

'I tried telling Melissa the truth the week before we married.'

'And?'

'I told her gently ... too gently. She misunderstood, again, and the pit got deeper.' In amused disdain, he added, 'She's such an air-head.'

Shocked by the disrespect in his assessment, Cassie was not sure that she even agreed with it. Thinking it through, Cassie said, 'That doesn't explain you actually walking down the aisle, taking vows.'

'You were gone. It didn't look like I'd ever get you back. Melissa seemed … Anyway, I just couldn't live that farce so I walked out.'

'How did Melissa take it when you told her?' She read his expression, appalled now. 'You just left?'

'I know, I've caused pain to everyone in my world. I do know Melissa doesn't deserve how I used her. Papa was long and loud about that. He went on and on about how marriage is for life and all that other Spanish Catholic stuff!' Jake ran his hands through his hair and held them at the back of his head. 'What a mess I've made! I played stupid and unthinking games and lost who and what I loved. I really love you, Cassie.'

Cassie's eyes glistened, but she kept an iron grip on her control. She would mourn her mother, lost love, and the irreparable tear in the families' fabric in private.

The fire flared along the darkened upper edge of the logs, dancing in its joy. It sang in muted flutings, crackled in delight. Tongues of flame leapt upward and entwined. Cassie's hand rested on Jake's upper thigh. Her head nestled in his shoulder. She felt his arousal and moved away from him.

'Inconsiderate of me,' Cassie said. 'Sorry. An old habit.'

'It's time I went. Get my coat?'

'Sure.'

Jake followed her to the coat closet which was near the front door. He looked at Cassie. She had been his shadow for longer than he could remember. He wanted them stitched back together.

'Well, see you,' Cassie said.

He stood there, arms by his side, looking at her. 'Yair, bye.'

Cassie watched him leave. There was comfort in being with people who shared history and understood without words.

Chapter 28

The road thrum of the bus sounded the sorrow that Cassie brought back to Keimera. The first thing she saw at midday, as the bus came over the rise, was the lighthouse. The second thing was the distant settlement.

As her taxi crawled up the snaking driveway to Madison House, Cassie saw there wasn't anyone on the verandah to note her return. The rear parking spots were empty too. Relieved, she entered the house, glad that she had time to get her emotions in check. That proved harder than expected. She wondered how she had boxed her feelings before.

Alone in her room, Cassie knew fear of mortality. It was like her childhood fear of the creature that lived in the dark. In the shadow of the monster, Mortality, Cassie realised that she had wasted the hours of her life so far on hiding from the turmoil and joy that was life. She had put a wall between herself and Jake rather than drawing a line as her mother had finally done with her father. It did not matter how many 'right' men there were in the world. If she could not get it right with Jake, she never would with anyone. Grief, Mortality's fraternal twin, overtook her, consumed her.

Overwrought but fighting it, Cassie sought solace through music, Ravel's *Bolero*. With the volume up, the music unravelled in its intricate beauty. Unthinkingly, she responded in dance, and in doing so, found her way out of the monster's grip.

Later that day, Michael arrived home. On hearing Enya's

Sail Away carrying from Cassie's room, he sprinted upstairs two at a time to find her lying on her bed.

'Want to escape, eh?'

'Something like that, Mike. The sound is strangely uplifting.'

Assessing Cassie, Michael said, 'When I'm really down, I use music to move me away from where I'm at. Is that what you're doing? Imagining times when you'll be far away from sorrow?'

'Oh, Mike.' Cassie struggled to contain her pain but failed, bursting into anguished tears.

He climbed onto her bed, pulled her to him, cradling her. 'It's okay, I'm here. Let it out. You'll feel better once it's released. You're safe.' And she did for the time she was within his embrace.

* * *

Buoyed by the sympathy and support from the residents of Madison House, Cassie returned to school well after term four had begun. There was solace in the school routine. The student body was subdued under the pressure of examinations, the teaching staff preoccupied with marking and related matters. Apart from a momentary awkwardness over Cassie's loss, they forgot about it. Their distraction made it easier for Cassie to keep grief inside the box she had mentally created for it. So too did the changes at Madison House.

Minna went to Perth for a National CWA conference. Gary took his holidays and went inland to visit his parents. HSC examinations monopolised Michael's time and thoughts. He took time out for Cassie in the evenings, entertaining her with overstated stories about the eccentricities of other HSC candidates. He had a talent for tall tales.

The days stretched one into the other.

Tired and feeling the onset of a headache at the end of the third week since her return, Cassie rested on her bed, listening to *Welcome*, a Santana album. Although it followed the jazz-fusion formula, it was far more experimental than Santana's earlier four albums. She loved it although she knew others, Jake included, did not. She thought of her mother who had also loved this style of music. Maybe there was truth in Mary Frye's bereavement verse.

The front screen slammed.

An angry sounding footfall on the stairs and corridor signalled it was Mavis. Unwilling to lose her current mood, Cassie hoped she could dodge whatever drama was unfolding in Mavis' life. Cassie lacked the oomph needed to help anyone else.

Half an hour later, Mavis knocked on Cassie's door.

'Mind if I come in?'

'What's up?'

Mavis' face flushed. 'Nothing!'

'Didn't sound like it a while ago. Things were fine when you left.'

Mavis' reply was muffled. She moved to the record player and turned it off. 'I don't like this one.'

Torn between irritation and concern, Cassie said, 'C'mon, talk to me.'

'Terry gave me an engagement ring. It's not the one I pointed out to him in the magazine or even the one down at the jewellers!'

'Oh.'

'It was supposed to be a whole carat. I told him I want to be engaged but not with that ring.'

Cassie sat up, stunned. 'Mavis!'

'You wouldn't have liked the ring either. I'm ashamed to wear it. Terry says he's tired of doin' overtime. Said this ring was good enough. Things got out-of-hand, and he lost it.' She swallowed before continuing. 'He … he hit me … Not bruisin' hard, mind you, but it hurt. I'm frightened; what if he calls off the engagement?'

'That's the least of your concerns.'

'What?'

'There's no excuse for hitting a woman. It's you who should rethink the engagement.'

'What?'

'You heard me.'

'I provoked him. I pushed him away. This was really out of character. You've never liked him, not really. This is an old tune you're singing.'

'Nothing excuses violence.'

'Some things do. Bein' a woman doesn't give me the right to dish out behaviour he wouldn't accept from a man. I brought it on myself. He was so pleased when he gave me the box. I guess I was a bit insensitive, but I was shocked.'

'Shallow is closer.'

'You don't understand. The ring proves how much he loves me.'

Cassie thought of the ring Jake had given Melissa. It was the knuckle dragging kind. Too big, too heavy, impractical. 'It shows his income bracket and not much else.'

'It's more than that!'

'I'll say it again. Marriage is not primarily about the Cinderella experience, and the glitter that comes with it. What's more important: the fairytale or the basis of the relationship?'

'I want both. Besides, Terry could've bought this ring

without doin' any overtime. He says he'd rather use the money for settin' up our own place.'

'You need to …'

'Drop it!' Mavis covered her ears and left.

Cassie put her music back on. Thumping on the wall minutes later resulted in her turning it off. And because she did, Cassie heard Terry's return twenty minutes later and the sound of reconciliation.

'I'm sorry, Mavis. I hate myself for what …' there was a break in Terry's voice, 'happened.' His crying sounded awful, wounded.

'Shush. It was my fault as much as yours.'

Uncomfortable with the changing sounds, Cassie fled downstairs. Even though it was late before she returned to her room, the lovemaking was all too clear.

The next night, Cassie felt overtired and as if a cold was coming on. She lounged on the upper verandah in an effort to find respite from the heat. At first, she was unaware of the voices drifting outward from Mavis' room. The voices pulled at her consciousness.

'What?' The shock was evident in Mavis' voice.

'I said I've found the perfect flat for us. It overlooks the southern beach, has generous rooms, and is an unbelievably low price. I put a deposit on it this morning.'

Mavis felt the sting of the hook. She floundered. 'A marriage doesn't work if you're not on the same page.'

'What better way to find it? This way we can see if we are suited. We have issues that we need to resolve. If we can't, we avoid the cost of marriage and divorce.'

Mavis made the mistake of looking into his eyes. The wound from her rejection was clearly visible. She had not valued the attention to romance in his proposal but had tossed it aside like an apple core into the bin. 'You're right. C'mon let's tell Minna and George.'

Minna masked her disapproval but George was direct. 'Living together isn't a valid test. Marriage is a commitment to work at a relationship for better or worse. If you aren't prepared to make that pledge and the legal binding that goes with it then you already know.'

'We are committed; we're engaged,' Mavis said. 'C'mon Terry, we've got to go.'

* * *

'How cool is it, Minna,' Mavis said sitting in the lounge room, 'that Cassie gets all these balloons and a gift, and we get chocolates! I just love romance. This time I'm gettin' to the bottom of it.'

'Now, Mavis ...'

'Mmmmm! These are delicious, Min. Are you sure you won't have one?' Mavis sipped her coffee. 'Melts in your mouth. Really, you should try one.'

'No, no, the doctor is adamant that I stick to this diet.'

'Ooooh! This one is out of this world! These are mine, all mine, do you hear?' Mavis laughed.

'I guess one won't hurt.'

'Great, eh? Listen to this: Paddington chocolates, hand-crafted by master chocolatier, Walter Pulkownik, are made from fresh, natural ingredients and contain no animal fat. I reckon the Creme de Menthe is orgasmic.'

'Well, I wouldn't put it quite that way, but it is sublime.'

'I'm so glad I had a flex afternoon and that I put off moving out till next weekend. Oh!' The liqueur inside the chocolate burst through its shell. Mavis' eyeballs almost kissed with the shock of the alcohol. 'No better way to spend an afternoon!'

'Mavis, I think …'

On seeing Cassie, Mavis crossed to her. 'Out with it. Who is he? When do we meet him? He certainly knows how to get on a person's good side. I can't wait to see what's inside the box.'

Minna intervened, silencing Mavis with a hand gesture. 'Mavis is on a sugar high, otherwise she'd be showing more sensitivity and realise that the gifts could also have been sent to lighten your mourning. Such a generous thing to send the household a gift too.'

'I'll say,' said Mavis, chocolate in her mouth, as Cassie looked at the gift card.

On reading the card, Cassie sat down, missing the chair.

'Looks like she's floored,' Mavis said next to her. 'Unexpected, eh? Have a chocolate.' She picked up the card that Cassie had discarded and read it. 'I want to build my life around you, Jake.' Ooo! So romantic. Can't wait to see what's in the box.'

'Give Cassie some space, Mavis. Come and help me make a cuppa.'

Mavis stood to follow Minna but veered course to the coffee table. 'Just gettin' a few more chockies to tide us over durin' our banishment.'

'Mavis, now!'

'I'm comin'.' Mavis turned in the archway. 'Isn't love great?'

Great was not the word that Cassie would have chosen. Opening the box, she was amazed to find a music box with two miniature ballroom dancers atop it. *I'll be there* played melodically rather than the tinkling sound common to music boxes.

'So …' Michael said from the living room archway, 'Mavis

says your old boyfriend's back on the scene.' He crossed to her. 'Is this something you're giving away too?'

'It's too expensive to do that.'

'And beautiful. Handcrafted by the looks. The dancers significant?'

'We used to be partners.'

Michael nodded, digesting that news. 'Get anywhere with him?'

'First place in the Nationals.'

'What?'

'1985.'

'God! ... I saw you dance then.' After concentrated thought, Michael said, 'Wow! That was you? His wife ... she a dancer?'

'No.'

'He's realised what he's lost and wants you back.' Looking at the gift card, he said, 'And not just for dancing. It'd be hard to turn your back on that.'

'That's my dilemma. We balanced each other in some ways but not everything. A lot of the time we've been in opposition.'

'That makes for a dynamic relationship.'

'I thought so once but ...'

'What?'

'I don't know. It's a control thing that I still have to work out. For a while now, I've been thinking I was part of the problem, not just Jake.'

'Right ... Look, I've got stuff to sort out and a bag to pack. I'm up in Sydney the next two weeks for work and ... investigating career paths.'

'No one has said ...' Cassie felt jangled by the change in energy between them.

'I haven't told Mum and Dad yet. See you.'

* * *

It just did not make sense to Marg as she unpacked boxes into cupboards in Mavis' laminated kitchen. Terry was thirty years old, supposed to have a regional managerial position with Custom Credit, and had boarded for God knew how many years with minimal living expenses. Where, then, had the money gone?

Mavis, after a terrible argument with Terry over the struggle to get their mattress upstairs and through the doorway of the flat, had called Madison House for assistance. The phone rang out. Without another option, she had phoned her father. Both parents came.

Mavis' apartment was on the top floor of a hacienda complex that faced the ocean, south of the township. The main stairwell's exterior wall was glass and provided a sweeping view of the beachfront and the ocean. The rear access, that the men were currently using, was thankfully full brick. The move in was difficult enough without the added hassle of glass.

Marg's mind was on overload. Trevor and Terry were currently struggling with the white goods purchased from a second-hand dealer. They had already moved up good quality, second-hand furniture that was now in place. Again, it did not make sense to elect self-delivery to a third floor apartment when someone could have been paid to do it, someone who did it for a living.

If only she could talk honestly to her daughter! Mothers were supposed to help their daughters peel away the blind of mass-marketed values and the spin of self-serving boyfriends to see what was true. All this talk about the wedding day without thought to the foundations upon which the relationship was built.

Mavis had begun this paired life on assumptions without thought to the details of the partnership. For a small investment, Terry had gained a partner but with very little to lose. Though talking marriage, the man hedged his bets with them living together without legal commitment, thus avoiding the claims on him that divorce entailed. It would be easy for Terry to walk away when the going got tough as it did in all relationships during the life journey. Of course, Mavis could walk at any time too.

* * *

Temperatures reached record levels as November dragged on. Dark clouds massed to the south. Selton watched the sky from the staff room. 'The storm is about to break.'

Cassie finished a makeshift fan. 'It's been like this before without rain. Do you want me to make you one, Rajes?'

'I am fine.'

'No, it's different this time. I hope Mary's all right. She's been really stressed since the clouds started gathering.'

Cassie crossed to the window. 'I can take your class so you can sign out and go home. Your wife should come before work especially now.'

'You're right, but my Year 11s have their first major assessment task coming up soon.' Usually a decisive man, Selton procrastinated. 'And there's the bell. There's only one period left in the day. She'll be right.'

Around the quadrangle, classroom lights contrasted with the bruised blackness of the afternoon. Lightning jagged across the sky and moments later thunder sounded. The wind picked up. Scraps of paper funnelled upwards and then scattered. The yardman scurried from one bin to the next, securing lids and moving the bins to a protected spot.

Watching him, Cassie thought of her mother's grave, vulnerable to the elements. Perhaps Mary was feeling the same. She hoped the storm would not reach that far north. Steam rose from the concrete. Listening to her intuition, Cassie grabbed her bag and headed for the car park.

* * *

The frenetic movement of the windscreen wipers failed to improve visibility. Cassie was halfway down the street before she realised that her destination was unclear. Should she go to the Selton's house or the cemetery?

Located on the hillside, the coastal cemetery bore the brunt of the storm. Cassie's car crawled up the road that led to the children's burial area. Visibility was zero.

The car door cracked open. Cassie eased out, fighting the wind that tugged at her umbrella. She walked toward Ben Selton's grave.

Mary sat sheltering the grave and herself with an oversized, gaudy umbrella – the sort used for cover at the beach. Her right hand rested on the grave mound.

Cassie knelt beside Mary.

'I couldn't bear the thought of him going through this alone. Elaine Perkins has Will. A mother's supposed … supposed to protect her baby.'

'I don't think he's frightened.'

'I know.' Mary started at the grey wall of rain. 'He … he's dead.' Pain extended into her ear.

Cassie wrapped a comforting arm around her. The touch triggered the pain release. It reverberated through them. It was pain that arms couldn't fold on, that kept hands agitated in the verbal outpouring.

'I never … never really told Paul how I felt. He was so broken; he couldn't carry the weight of my grief as well.'

Her mother was a selfless woman too. Cassie corrected herself: had been. She was thankful for the shared grief with Leonie and her father after their initial isolation. The sisters had laughed when they saw one another the night before her return to Keimera; Leonie wore her mother's slippers: ankle Ugg boots, and Cassie her mother's favourite dressing gown despite the incongruity with the weather.

Over time, Mary's keening subsided into sobs, muffled pain, and then silence.

Hesitantly, 'Do you want to talk about… ?'

'He was so small, too frail.' Mary palmed the tears off her face. 'I thought that if we did everything we could during the pregnancy and one or both died … that I'd have no regret. I can't live with this!'

The road of pain was the same; only the travellers were different. Mother mourned son; daughter mourned mother.

Cassie's legs cramped. As she adjusted her position, the wind ballooned inside her umbrella, inverting it, and snapping its ribs. 'Damn!'

Sandwiched between laughter and tears, Mary said, 'Come under this one; we've plenty of room.' Silence. 'Paul seems to find comfort from him being one with the land.' She struggled for control. 'I can't bear the thought of him turning to dust.'

'When my granddad died, my mum said, 'Life is a journey that begins in one womb and ends in another.' That helped when we buried her.'

Waves of rain rippled across the landscape. Time washed away. Cassie was dimly aware of a car nearby.

'I'm ready to leave him now.'

A car door slammed.

'Thank you, Cassie.'

Selton strode through the blind of the rain toward the grave. The last image Cassie had of them that afternoon was in an embrace. It was something she needed too: to be held, comforted, understood without the need for words.

Returning to the emptiness of Madison House, Cassie was uncertain as to whether she felt relief that she had time to collect herself or regret that she had to face grief alone. After a warm shower, she phoned Leonie and then her father. No one answered. With grief pressing down on her, Cassie wished Michael was back from Sydney.

Escaping, Cassie spent as much of that night as she could in the spill of the Madisons' laughter and banter. When they retired, she stayed up with Gary listening to his worries about the surf club shared between ad breaks in a cricket telecast.

At midnight, unable to sleep and with grief claiming her, Cassie remembered the way Jake had comforted her after her grandfather died. Uncaring about the late hour, she phoned him. They talked until she was calm before he set out for Keimera. In such moments of crisis, lives change.

* * *

The next night, balls of light ringed the harbour park and shimmered in the dead tide. Lovers sat on the harbour wall, wrapped in one another. Couples strolled along the curved concrete walkway that connected the two points. Families picnicked on the grassy slopes between the harbour and the main road avoiding the heat of their homes. Children's voices blended with the sounds of the night. Although still November, Christmas decorations heralded the approaching season.

Jake walked with his right arm around Cassie, having spent a perfect day with her. They were so close they shared the rhythm of breathing. That which she had thought lost was found. They stopped at the harbour wall, looking at the ocean. The evening had a hypnotic quality.

Cassie's peace disappeared when she recognised Talbut. He sat on a wooden seat on the edge of the light spill. Vegetation discreetly screened his back and sides. A young woman, someone she faintly recognised, sat on top of him.

The woman's legs straddled Talbut. Her breasts crushed against him. He moved rhythmically under her. She rode him. Her back arched in growing ecstasy. She leant back, revealing her unbuttoned shirt and a flash of flesh.

Cassie turned abruptly to the harbour. Her body felt like it was crawling with ants of fire.

Jake stood, ready to move on, aware of the sudden tension in Cassie. They strolled to the lighthouse lookout. It took the hour stroll from the harbour park to the southern headland and back to town before she felt better.

The soft glow of light in the café augmented Cassie's mood. She watched the swirls on the top of her coffee and replaced her spoon on the saucer.

Jake looked at her from hooded eyes. He watched conflicting emotions play across Cassie's face and waited.

She looked up at him and smiled, her eyes soft and warm.

His heart lurched. It had been a long time since he had seen that particular smile. He sipped his coffee.

'Good, isn't it?' The ambiguity of his comment was not lost on Cassie.

'Yes.' She noticed a clutch of curious Year 9 girls from a nearby table.

'You look like you want to say something.'

'Perhaps, this isn't the best place ...'

Jake looked around, noting the gaggle of girls in the café booths kneeling on their seats and giggling.

He replaced his cup. 'Want to go somewhere else?'

'It'll be the same everywhere, kids I know or their parents. If it's not them, it'll be someone who knows the Madisons. Privacy is an illusion here.'

'There's always my room.'

Cassie felt the opening beat of the tango. She rose to its pulse, moved to its cadence. As they walked to Jake's car, she heard the beat and its subtle brushed hesitation in their tread.

Jake's motel room overlooked the harbour. The surging song of the surf built as the tide rolled in.

Sitting on the edge of the bed, Cassie felt self-conscious for the first time. Jake lifted her fingers to his lips and kissed them slowly, one at a time. His lips were warm and sensuous. She caressed his cheek and faced her feelings. Gently, Jake pressed her backwards.

Looking up at him, Cassie saw the flickering images of the boy she had loved and the man she cared about. The interchange of images stopped; she saw the man. 'Jake, I can't ...'

Immediately responsive, Jake stopped, sitting up.

Standing now, Cassie put distance between them and in a rush said, 'I'm so sorry. I was hurting and didn't think beyond my need. This is wrong for us. We don't complement one another the way ... I'm so sorry, Jake.' She grabbed her things and left, glad that there would not be a repeat of the tempestuous scenes of the teenage years.

A week later, Cassie sat watching the sunlight flicker on the ocean, the work before her forgotten. Engrossed in sorting out her feelings, she was unaware of Minna sitting on garden furniture below, listening to a delegation of councillors who wanted Minna to run for mayor again. She missed George's concerned expression as he paused on the verandah steps, watching his wife. Did not register his comment, 'Too devious to be trusted.'

Though she saw Gary stride from the lawns to the verandah, his complaint to George about poor leadership at the surf club was lost on her.

The telephone rang, but Michael was the only one who seemed to hear it. Cassie did not hear his opening response but did register his angry reply, 'No, mate, she doesn't want to speak to you. You've got a wife. Go back to her!' Michael's support mattered to Cassie as did his lack of questions probing beyond what she had been prepared to tell him.

As the afternoon sun sank and orange coloured the landscape, Cassie realised that she was angry. Angry with Jake. Furious with herself. It demanded expression.

When Michael meandered onto the verandah with coffee for two half an hour later, she was gone.

In isolation on the grassed cliff north of Madison House, the strengthening onshore winds buffeted Cassie who stood, staring out to sea. Lacking words, she expressed her anger in movement. Arms in swift opposition formed one sharp grotesque pose. A series of sharp, forceful gestures followed and then extended into a misshapen, bizarre dance. The twist and angular nature of the multi-directional movement became monstrous. It ended in feet pounding earth in a series of circles decreasing in size until she came to a standstill.

Chapter 29

'Hope you don't mind, but I need a lift home,' Michael said to Cassie, standing beside her car outside the school. 'My car is in the workshop for a few days. It's too hot to walk back.'

'Course I don't, but I need a caffeine fix first and not the instant coffee kind at the house. I'm whacked!'

'Upset you made a mistake breaking with your boyfriend?'

'No, it was the right thing. I think it's just the letdown after a crisis. That and the usual stress of teaching, having to put up with allusions to Jake at work, from Gary ...'

'Dad's told him to put a lid on it. Not much is missed, Cassie, in a small town. The interest'll subside soon enough.'

'Bye Miss,' some students called, walking toward town.

Cassie waved at them before climbing into her car.

'Those kids seem okay.'

'Yes. I wish all the kids in my classes were like them. Look, I just need some quiet ... no offence.'

'None taken.'

Cassie drove the short distance into town in silence, taking care not to jerk the gears. They were in luck, finding a space on their first circuit of the street.

'You're looking awful white, Cassie. Maybe we should go to the doctor's.'

'No, I usually feel drained an hour or so after school though not to this degree.'

'Inside or out?' he asked, already heading for a shaded spot.

'Inside, out of the glare.'

With orders taken, Cassie waited for Michael while he waited for her. It was one of those moments where two people are trying to be courteous but end up being awkward.

'Get it out, Michael. Whatever you think, just tell me.'

'Martin wants me to take up competition again.'

'And that's it?'

'He suggested I ask you.'

It was a still moment before Cassie responded. 'It's tempting, but it wouldn't work.'

'Well, that didn't get much consideration. Why not?'

'You've seen what my workload is like. Besides, you won't have time. You'll be at uni.'

'I'm having a year off study before I commit to a career path.'

'To be honest, Mike, I don't want to …' How could she explain it?

'Not good enough, eh? Forget it then. I'll pay the bill. No, it's my shout.' He left.

Appalled at his interpretation, Cassie sat motionless in amazement. How could Michael think her guilty of such ego?

Brought back to her surroundings by the waiter who asked, 'Can I get you anything else?' Cassie collected her things and walked to her car.

On her return to Madison House, Cassie saw Michael ahead of her. As the car approached him, it slowed. 'Let me give you a lift at least, Mike. Don't ignore me. C'mon, this is silly.'

'That's a matter of opinion, Cassie. Thanks for the offer, but I prefer my own company.'

* * *

As Cassie knocked on Mavis' flat door a week later, she heard Mavis rehearsing, 'Wishes come true but they come false as well …'

Sounds of the guitar being put down followed by the approach of footsteps. Mavis opened the door. 'Cassie! I'm so glad to see you.' Mavis flicked a glance at the clock. Five o'clock. Terry wouldn't be home till six-thirty.

After a quick tour of the flat, Cassie sat at the small breakfast bar while Mavis began the dinner preparation.

'Are you sure you don't want to stay for dinner?'

'I'd love to but can't. It's the English faculty night at La Scala.'

'Oh, they've great food! It seems a lifetime since I went somewhere that nice.'

'What?'

'Terry can't see the point, not when I'm such a good cook.'

'And you're okay with that?'

'Cassie, it's a great compliment. A woman has to keep her man satisfied and content otherwise he'll wander.'

'What were you singing earlier? It sounded so sad. One of yours?'

'I wish … it was a Dolly Parton song.'

'Geez, that's a big change in style.'

'You learn a lot about song if you're diverse in your repertoire. I haven't found my style yet, but I have been workin' on my lyrics. There's one in particular I'd like your thoughts on.'

'Are you sure you're ready to share. Last year …'

'Yair, I know … I'm over being precious.' Mavis disappeared into her bedroom.

The rattle of keys in the door signalled Terry's arrival. As he entered, he threw his suit coat onto an armchair. 'Mavis, I'm home!'

'Hello, Terry.' Cassie swivelled round to greet him.

'G'day, Cassie, didn't know you were invited over.'

'I wasn't. I popped in. You don't mind, do you?'

'Course not.'

After pulling off his tie, Terry slung it over the armchair as well. 'Mavis!'

'Comin'!' With the sound of a toilet flushing in the background, Mavis entered, flustered.

'Would you like a drink, Cassie? Oh … you've got one. Mavis is usually on the ball with that sort of thing. Has one ready for me when I walk in.'

'And I would've now if I'd known you were comin' home early.' Mavis hurried to the kitchen, poured a Scotch and coke, grabbed a napkin, and crossed to Terry.

'Thanks, love. If you don't mind, Cassie, I'll put the TV on.'

Cassie's reply was lost in the sudden blare of *The Price is Right*.

After picking up Terry's clothing and the shoes he'd just kicked off, Mavis hurried to their room. She reappeared with some magazines and a small A5 sized book.

'I thought you'd like some light reading while I'm busy in the kitchen. Terry doesn't like waitin' for his dinner. It'll only take me a tick to get it on. I'm interested in your thoughts on the ones I've bookmarked.'

'Terry,' Mavis called, 'can you turn it down?'

Terry neither answered nor responded in any way.

Uncomfortable, Cassie focused on the lyrics.

Mavis looked at Terry and seemed to debate repeating her request. After obviously waiting for a good few minutes, Mavis chose to ignore his inaction. Her frustration expressed itself in the way she worked. After having browned the meat for the evening casserole, she asked, 'Well?'

'I really like this line in *Time Watch:* In the orchestra of life, every instrument has its sound, scale, and part. Where did the idea come from?'

'Just … stuff happenin' while I was waitin' for Terry one night. Have you read *Lifesong*?'

'Not yet.' Cassie flicked through the music manuscript notebook.

'Second from last.'

In the time it took for Cassie to consider the lyrics, Mavis had prepared all the vegetables.

I've heard the words *The Singer not the Song* somewhere.'

'It's the title of a Stones' song … They use discord to show that it's not the song but the singers; they can sell anything.'

'Really? … These lyrics are really beautiful, Mavis.'

Pleased, Mavis said, 'You think? It's taken me ages. There was so much I wanted to say. Getting it down tight was hard, really hard. I thought that, bein' a dancer, you'd see what I was talkin' about. What's your take on the meaning?'

'It's elegantly simple.'

'Oh!' Mavis' disappointment was clear.

'No … no, I didn't mean it that way. It's a really deep subject, and you've cut to the heart of the matter. I've thought about it a lot too but not in terms of my relationship to dance or yours to song.'

'Then what?'

'Couples and marriage. I've thought it was the singers and the song that were the problem. Looking at it from this perspective, I can see …'

'So it's clear I'm talkin' about somethin' bigger?'

'Very. Can I hear it?'

'Another time when Terry's not home. He thinks …'

'How much longer, Mavis, to dinner?'

'Thirty minutes or so.'

'It's six already!'

'I know, but this stove is old and slow. If you agreed to buy a microwave oven …'

'I don't want untested new technology in my home. Heat comes out of ovens; it stands to reason the same applies to microwaves. We're not havin' one till it's a standard item in homes and the jury's in on its safety.'

'Well, I'd best be going, Mavis.'

'I'll see Cassie out, Terry. Everything's on simmer, Terry … Nothin' is going to burn.'

'Good to see you, Terry.'

'Sure.' Terry remained on the sofa and flicked through the channels.

As they walked to Cassie's car, Cassie asked, 'Everything all right with Terry?'

'Yair. He's just in one of his moods.'

'And living together?'

'It's hard workin' full-time and runnin' a home let alone doin' something on the side like music.'

'Regrets?'

'Not really … I just wish … Dad says, When people assume, it makes an ass of you and me.'

'And you feel that it has?'

'It's nearly the nineties, Cassie. All the magazines say: Get the ground rules right before you move in. I never thought about what was involved when you shacked up. I'm an idiot!'

'Don't be too hard on yourself.'

'If someone asked you … to move in or get married … you'd nut out the detail before decidin', wouldn't you?'

'Yes … most probably … but I've issues with what's expected of a woman when she becomes the female part of a relationship. I really like your idea that for the beauty of the song to be realised, the arrangement and the skill of the performer are important.'

'It's what I meant at least.'

'I couldn't remember your words. You know, Mavis, it's a waste not to do something with your music beyond singin' at the pub.'

'Terry wouldn't like it.'

'If it were me, I wouldn't be letting him call the shots on my life.'

Chapter 30

The sheets lay crumpled at the foot end of Cassie's bed, kicked there earlier in one of a hundred attempts to relax and cool down that summer night. Picking up her dressing gown, she strolled onto the verandah.

Light streamed out from the house. Strange silhouettes danced across the lawns. The lower screen door slammed. From the sound of it, George had brought out drinks for Minna.

Cassie considered joining them but decided against it. She drifted along the verandah. Stars festooned the sky. She danced using her dressing gown as a prop, playing with the strengthening breeze. Waves hushed over the rocks. The ocean glistened in the moonlight.

Rounding a corner, she smelt tobacco, not the scent from George's pipe or that of Minna's cigarellos.

'What are you doing here?' Michael asked, looking up.

'I didn't know you smoked,' Cassie said at a distance from him.

'I gave it up but needed one tonight.'

'Sorry to disturb you.'

'You haven't.' Michael remained seated.

The breeze brushed her silk nightdress against her body. Flustered, Cassie put on her dressing gown.

'Don't do that on my account,' he said. 'It's hot enough without adding more clothing.'

'Oh, it doesn't make it hotter.'

She leant against the railing and looked at Michael. 'What's wrong?'

'Nothing much; just another frustrating day.'

A thin line of cigarette smoke reached for her as he exhaled. His face camouflaged his inner turmoil. His cigarette became a stub and then ashed.

As he moved out of the shadows, Cassie noted his red patterned boxers and the lustre of his skin in the moonlight. Conscious of his closeness, she swallowed, aware of the intensity in the moment. 'We can talk about it, Mike, if it helps.'

'Ever thought you finally got it right only to discover you hadn't?'

This was so close to recent events with Jake that Cassie thought Michael had changed the subject to her. 'Everyone makes mistakes, Michael.'

'I hate my job, Cassie.'

'What?' Cassie almost laughed from relief but didn't. Thinking quickly, she said, 'Once you've got qualifications, it'll be different.'

'In some ways, but not the endless pressure to spin events into news that sells. I'm heading off north over summer. Things are always clearer when I'm labouring. Besides, the money will come in handy for uni when I eventually go.'

'You entitled to leave yet?'

'I'm taking leave without pay from now till the end of January. The short version of the rest of it is that I want you as my dance partner.' Michael took hold of her, turning her to him.

The energy between them changed. To Cassie, each movement and gesture seemed slow, stylised almost. Flustered but not frightened by it, she drifted. For a moment, she thought he might kiss her or she him.

'Sorry. Didn't mean to frighten you. I'll get out of your space.' He returned to his bedroom.

Alone, Cassie watched the lighthouse beacon probe the ink-black darkness. In relationships, had she become a wallflower, the past choreographing her present steps?

Passing Michael's room on the way to her room, she saw the light still on and, impulsively, knocked on the screen door.

'Come in,' Michael said in answer to her knock. He sat on his bed, leaning against the bed-head, smoking still. 'Well, what do you want?'

Standing just inside the room, Cassie steadied herself. 'George would have a fit if he knew you were smoking, let alone that it was in bed. I'll be your partner on one condition: I have an equal say in everything that affects us in dance.'

Michael's eyes were dark slits. 'Any other ultimatums?'

'It's a condition, Mike.' Uncomfortable, she turned toward the door.

'It's a deal, Cassie. Shake.'

Cassie turned to find him crossing the floor. When he reached her, he pulled her into an embrace instead. Again, she was very aware of his physical appeal. 'I wish my mum was alive to see us dance.'

'She'll be with you in spirit, I'm sure.'

The screen door banged behind Cassie. She returned to the cool verandah and danced on the breeze. Michael stubbed his cigarette out, turned off the light, and scrunched his pillows. Sleep evaded him.

* * *

January, 1989. Wee Waa in summer was mercilessly hot. Rows of cotton seedlings stretched for miles. Travellers remember the straightness of those rows, the greyish-brown dirt, and the treeless, shadeless plain.

Field workers, their backs bent, toiled up the rows, chipping random weeds in the fields. Michael stood and arched his back. He removed his wide brimmed hat and mopped his forehead. It was hard work, bloody hard, and boring. His mates had thrown the job in after three days. They'd been replaced quickly. It was a sign of the economic times. He didn't have that luxury because the money he would earn was equivalent to a year's casual work at home. Uni, if he went, was expensive, and he wanted to avoid the HECS tax.

Michael resumed his position and resisted the urge to roll up the long sleeves of his flannel shirt. Other shirts were too thin in that heat. Sweat streamed down his baggy trouser legs. When it built up, he would feel better. His boots, already worn from the coarse soil he trudged, were covered in a skin of dust.

He'd been out in the cotton fields since dawn and had a few hours left before the heat became impossible. Boredom. It was soul sucking.

His mind drifted to his future. A career in the air force had seemed attractive as his discontent at the paper grew. He especially liked the prospect of changing jobs every two years or so and the fact that a degree through the Defence Force Academy did not attract a HECS tax. Canberra, though, seemed a long way from Keimera.

Surprised at the thought, he pondered it. In the three years of study at ADFA, Cassie would move on to another partner. He wasn't sure what he felt about that. Had he been irresponsible in beginning that partnership? Should he have mentioned the possibility of it to her? His future lacked certainty. Crossing bridges before you got to them was always a bad idea.

Ten o'clock. The workers piled into open trucks. He was

wedged between dust and sweat. The convoy of trucks arrived at the tin sheds that housed the workers. He grabbed an ice-cold can of beer and headed for the shade side of the huts. Inside was a furnace.

Siesta.

After sunset, they would return to the fields and work in the pools of light provided by the trucks. It was unbelievably dark at night, darker than anything he had seen before. His thoughts channelled to the future. It had been months since the recruitment testing and ages since his other applications had been submitted.

* * *

Summer haze shimmered over north Richmond. The sun scorched the paddocks, yellowing the grasses, sapping energy from humanity and animals alike. The radio, switched on in the middle of a newsbreak, carried to the girls who were wilting in the shade of the verandah. Both were listless and disinclined to talk.

'This drought promises to be worse than the one in 82-83. The rural community and its economy are devastated. Fires rage in South Australia, Victoria, and across New South Wales.' The radio was switched off and replaced by Tom Sleight's newest toy – a CD player. New music, *September Morn*, soared with the heat. Leonie's beam made Cassie laugh.

'What's so funny out here?'

His daughters, dressed in shorts and contrasting T-shirts, exchanged looks. 'Just a sister thing,' Leonie said.

Tom wiped the sweat off his forehead with the back of his hand. 'This is our last day of heat. We're having air-conditioning installed tomorrow. Should've got one years ago.'

The family mood plummeted. Nancy had lobbied for it for years.

'Better late than never, Dad,' Cassie said.

'Feel like scones?' Leonie asked. It was something her mother would have offered him if she had been there.

'No thanks, love, it's about time I lost some weight.'

Afternoon faded into dusk. Disinterested in activity, the Sleights languished on the verandah so they were in a good spot to see a car rumbling down the dirt road into their property.

'Got to get that driveway fixed,' Tom said. 'Know anyone with a four-wheel drive, girls?'

'It might be Mike Madison.'

'Cassie, where are you going?' called Leonie following Cassie into the house.

'Bathroom. Won't be long.'

* * *

Tanned and unshaven, Michael jumped out of his car. His shirt sleeves, although short, were rolled high in the fashion of the time. He strode across the distance separating his car and Tom Sleight. 'Hope you don't mind me dropping in like this, but I was on my way home, and somehow, the car ended up here. You must be Cassie's father.'

'Indeed I am. It's always a pleasure to meet one of her friends. So where have you come from?'

'Wee Waa. I left early this morning.'

As the men shook hands, the screen door swung open. Leonie crossed to them. 'Mike …?'

'Wow!' Michael said, thinking he spoke to Cassie, crossing to her. 'I would never have thought of you as a blonde. As for the length …Who'd have thought … Don't get me wrong; it's great!' Unable to contain his emotions, he kissed her before saying, 'You're looking great, Cassie! Taste good too.'

'I'm not ...' Leonie said, laughing, from within his embrace.

'Wrong girl, lad,' Tom said amused. 'This is Leonie, Cassie's sister.'

Michael released Leonie. 'Sorry about that,' he said, obviously embarrassed.

'Don't be. It's not like it hasn't happened before.' Seeing Cassie now on the verandah, Leonie added, 'Though once you really know us, you'll wonder how you could make such a mistake.'

'Hello, Michael.'

'Geez, it's good to see you, Cassie,' Michael said, taking in her white cotton trousers, the white, body-shaping bandera, the curve of her bare shoulders, and the sheen of her skin. 'And you look ... fantastic. Hope you don't mind me dropping in.'

'Of course not,' Cassie said.

There was an awkward silence.

Aware of the tension, Tom said, 'C'mon inside.'

The Sleights led the way through the house to the large kitchen and breakfast area.

With pleasure dripping from each word, Michael said, 'You don't know how good it is to see all the trappings of civilisation. Hello fridge! Hello ice dispenser! Mind if I help myself to some ice and water?'

'Of course we don't,' Leonie said.

Tom said, 'There's beer if you'd prefer it.'

'No, water and ice are fine. Oh, the luxury of it! You don't realise how lucky you are until you have to go without, do you?'

'No,' Tom Sleight said. 'Please excuse me. I've just

remembered I have to ...' He was gone, an upsurge of emotion threatening to spill over the walls of his control.

Exuberant, Michael planted a quick smoochy kiss on Cassie's lips.

'Michael, calm down,' Cassie said, laughing.

'Can't help it. I haven't seen an attractive woman for an eternity. I feel like I've been fasting.' He planted another smoochy kiss on her cheek. 'You're edible.'

'Is there anything, apart from Cassie, that you'd like?' Leonie asked. 'We were about to have supper.'

'Leonie!'

'Well,' Michael hesitated.

'Go ahead, ask,' Leonie encouraged.

'I'd love a bath and a shave. Not even my air-conditioning could make a significant dent in today's heat.' Then before Cassie could stop him, he had her pinioned in an underarm wrestle hold and roughed up her hair. The manoeuvre completed, Michael said, 'Don't worry, Cassie. You'll find me a different man after that bath.'

'That can't come too fast for me. Leonie, will you help him out? I've something I need to do.'

On Cassie's return to the kitchen, Leonie said, 'You never mentioned him. Why?'

'He's just one of many people in my life in Keimera.'

'A significant person from the looks of it, especially given you changed clothes. Is he why you've been so down this summer?'

'That's an odd thing to say given how much has been lost recently.'

'Maybe. I've thought for a while something else was going on with you though. I'm flattered anyone could still make that old mistake; it means nothing.'

'Really, I don't care.'

'Cassie? You okay?'

'Fine.'

Sometime later Michael emerged, cooled, refreshed, composed and with his emotions collected.

Cassie recovered her brightness as Michael entertained them with stories about the cotton fields and the people he had met there. The cadence of the evening seemed well-matched to the background music.

'Why don't we show your family what sort of dance partnership we'll be?'

'You're dancing again, Cassie?' Tom and Leonie spoke in unison.

'Uh huh.'

Tom was on his feet, pushing furniture back. 'Leonie, put on a Foxtrot.'

'Something Latin would be better for this space,' Cassie said.

Strains of Salsa filled the night.

'You're attuned as a couple,' Tom said. 'There's promise.'

Well-versed in Cassie's dance skills, Tom in a private moment with her said, 'It's good you're dancing again, Pumpkin, but I don't like to see you lowering your standards. Mike has potential, undoubtedly, but it'll take work to bring him up to your class. Do you want to waste that time? Wouldn't it be easier to come home and resume your partnership with Jake if you want to compete? He's filed for divorce, y' know.'

'No, Dad, it wouldn't.'

As they separated for the night, Cassie said to Leonie, 'I'm glad you get that dancing is about more than winning.'

'Don't worry about what Dad says. As a couple, your timing and the complexity of steps are great and you express the essence of the dance. That's what's important in Latin, isn't it? Doesn't that trump whatever's missing?'

'Some people would argue it did. In the end, it all depends on the judges.'

'So, what's happening off the dance floor?'

'Nothing. I'm not making that mistake twice.'

'You can't live life if you're afraid of passion.'

'I'm not afraid, but I have learnt from my mistakes.'

After that night, Michael headed home.

With his departure, Cassie became restless. She blamed the heat, the disappearing days of the summer, and a realisation that she needed to organise for the beginning of another year's teaching. She spoke of the gala event in the town – the annual bush dance held at Madison House and run by the Country Women's Association. The funds raised that year were for drought relief in rural New South Wales and for the Disaster Relief Fund previously depleted by a twenty thousand dollar donation from State Executive to victims of the devastating Natal Flood. Tom and Leonie weren't surprised when Cassie left for Keimera before the Australia Day weekend.

Chapter 31

Madison House was ablaze with lights. People spilled from the wide verandahs onto the lawns around the huge portable dance floor built the day before. There was an air of expectancy as the bush band tuned their instruments. While they readied themselves for the first bracket, the fiddlers maintained a light, witty patter that entertained the young who were impatient for the dance to begin.

To the right of the dance floor, round, plump women in floral cotton dresses, protected from stains by obligatory aprons, stood serving at the tables, their faces baked by years of relentless summer sun; moisturisers were unheard of among these women and make-up was a rarity. Their talk was of families, weddings and funerals, of backbreaking work on a thirsty land, the effects of the recession, and of mortgages paid and unpaid.

Nearby, the traditional sausage sizzle flared into life. Its billowing smoke stung eyes and caused the men, who habitually stood near the kegs, to move to the southern end of the verandah out of range.

The middle-aged and elderly divided into two camps, the women and the men. They came together irregularly and, for the most part, preferred their own kind.

Flushed and exhilarated from the reel, Cassie left the dance floor a few steps ahead of her partner, a man with a shiny head. She paused on the top step of the makeshift dance floor. Michael came up from behind and draped his arm over her shoulder.

While they talked, Cassie looked around for Mavis. She saw Terry first. For a moment, Cassie did not recognise Mavis. They stood apart from the crowd of men at the kegs. Even from a distance, Cassie could see that she was subdued, drained of all her usual vivacity.

From Terry's body language, it was clear they were arguing. He berated Mavis who remained impassive. Cassie chewed her bottom lip, unsure of what she could or should do to alleviate her friend's obvious distress.

Terry stormed off. Mavis fled into the crowd near the house. Cassie looked back at Michael and realised that his attention was elsewhere.

'Hey, Kate's back. I thought she was away till February.'

'Go ahead, I want a word with Mavis.'

He was gone. Cassie considered this greeting, comparing it to his recent visit to her home. It was much the same.

'So you prefer boys, Cassie?' Talbut asked, appearing seemingly from nowhere. 'Or is it the status of his family that attracts you?'

'What?' Cassie stepped away from him in reflex.

Talbut disappeared into the swirling masses on the dance floor.

'What's such a beautiful face doing with a frown?' a deep male voice asked.

'Vincent!'

'You'll have to let me capture you on canvas some day.'

'A winning line if I ever heard one.'

Chuckling, Vincent replied, 'So I've found; most women want to be immortalised. I'd ask you to dance, but I'm dying of thirst. Later?'

'Love to.'

* * *

Mavis sat on the lowest step of the rear verandah, her shoulders stooped, crying. Assuming a casual air, Cassie sat down beside her. They sat in silence for a while.

'It's not workin' out, Cassie. Nothin' is! We should never have stayed with my parents over the Christmas break! Mum was polite, but her lips just got thinner and thinner! Dad hardly spoke to Terry.'

Cassie passed her a clean handkerchief, which she always carried, a habit passed from mother to daughter.

'It wasn't much better when we came back. Terry's so moody. If he gets the promotion to the Sydney office, he wants me to come too but not to work or even study at the Conservatorium like he promised once.' Mavis blew her nose, the trumpet of the distressed. When she was calmer, she continued, 'Mum said … Terry looks so different once he's worked up!'

A memory flickered but faltered, unclear. Cassie tuned back into Mavis.

'Just when I've decided to chuck him over, he does somethin' real sweet and repentant. So I stay.'

Cassie touched Mavis' arm reassuringly. She flinched. 'I … er … jarred m' shoulder changin' the furniture around the other day. So, what do you think, Cassie?'

'You have to tell Terry what you want and find the compromise.'

While they sat, Cassie could hear snatches of dialogue from inside the house but significant pieces of it were drowned by bursts of laughter from passers-by and the bush band.

'George, I think you should really consider what I've been saying about Mike and that girl.'

'Min, they're old friends. That's it!'

'There's a lot more than friendship in it, at least on Kate's part! Did you see her tonight? He'll get trapped here.'

'No one's ever trapped. That's just an excuse not to make the tough decisions. Mike's not of that ilk!'

A noisy foursome passed the rear verandah and the speaker's comments were lost. Cassie did, however, hear part of George's rejoinder.

'Stop worrying, Min, he'll find his way.'

Mavis blew her nose loudly. The voices from the kitchen receded, and the kitchen lights switched off.

* * *

The fiddles duelled at a frenetic pace. The dance floorboards reverberated with the tread of hundreds of feet.

'How about a dance, Mavis?' Cassie asked.

'Aw, I don't know. I don't think this would be a good time to ask Terry.'

'Terry be damned! C'mon, be my partner in a reel. It'll make us feel better.'

Mavis hesitated.

'Where's that independent free spirit we all know and love?'

'I don't know.'

'Just listen to the music. How can you resist that?' On impulse she broke into song, 'C'mon, Mavis, c'mon, c'mon.'

'Okay, if you stop singing. You really can't, y' know.'

They walked to the dance floor, arms linked.

Mavis saw Terry sitting by the kegs, apart from the other men, talking to Gary. Experience told her that it was best that she kept herself out of his reach, at least until his anger died. It was unlikely that he'd seek her out.

The set was wild and lusty yet even graceless dancers observed the boundaries of its code. As Cassie was swung off her feet by one man and then another, she realised that the energy and emotion was a means of expression usually denied everyday people; in an inarticulate population, music and dance said what words could not.

During the dance, Michael and Cassie came together. Their time together in dance, fluid and uplifting, was short-lived. They separated but re-joined as the set repeated. When it ended, Michael hugged Cassie.

'You mine for the next set, Cassie?' Vincent asked.

'She's with me ...'

'I'd love to, Vince.'

* * *

At midnight, celebratory fireworks off the southern Point burst above the skyline. Each burst illuminated the crowd of onlookers who oohhed and ahhed in rapture.

Tired of the role of carefree partygoer, Cassie waited for the fireworks to end and then retreated to the upper floor of the house. It was deserted.

From the verandah, Cassie could see the Seltons, Chandrans, and baby Will. He was a treasured child. Watching the couples sitting on the lawns below, Cassie realised she envied their 'pairedness', the expression of love visible in their interactions.

Memory flickered like a television set before it's tuned in properly. The approaching clump of footsteps interrupted Cassie's train of thought. She shook off the past.

'I thought it was you up here,' Michael said.

Cassie smiled at him, seeing him with sudden clarity. Like his father, Michael was not a taker. She knew her trust in him was not misplaced.

'Anything up, Cassie?'

'I'm worried about Mavis.'

He listened without interrupting her.

'Don't worry about her. Nothing can keep Mavis down for long.'

With his arm around her, they watched the distant lights of the township blink out. In the comfort of contact, Cassie wondered if her mother was right. Nancy had said, 'People were what they were; it was fixed as were the roles they played.' Cassie hoped not.

* * *

With the enthusiasm of the condemned, teaching staff entered the school library for the first meeting of the school year. Watching her colleagues, Cassie realised that she did not want to become like the majority of people around her.

'I say, VH,' Paul Selton said in undertones, 'does this august assemblage remind you of a cattle drive? Just look at the way Doggy is behaving. It's strongly reminiscent of a cattle dog.'

'A sheep dog would be a more appropriate description, PS, given his shaggy hair. It obscures his vision and ours for that matter, not that that's a loss.'

The people around them laughed.

'This doesn't look good, mate,' Van der Huffen leant across to Selton. 'Coachman has goofed, erred, blundered …'

'Just as well the staff room issue is resolved. This doesn't look good for the faculty in the scheme of things, the wheel of life, the—' Selton's comment was lost in a scuffle of chairs and the knock of the chairman's gavel.

The staff meeting was stupefying! The Principal and then his Deputy spoke so long that somnolence spread its protective wings over most of the audience. Many staff sat with their eyes open but their minds asleep.

Two and a half hours after the meeting began, it finished. The school staff shook themselves, shrugging off sleep in much the same way as a wet dog shakes off water. Selton and Van der Huffen ambled out of the library and resumed their repartee.

'Didn't know our Deputy Doggy was capable of stringing that many words together in a single utterance, VH, did you?'

'Floored me, PS. The man's verbal dexterity astonished, astounded and even stunned me. It was a masterful display of one and two syllable usage.'

Looking over his shoulder to ensure confidentiality, Selton continued, 'I thought Coachman did remarkably well maintaining an obsequious profile …'

'In the face of such tantalising bait? Doggy is living proof that Neanderthal Man did not die out.'

'Exactly. Coachman's humiliation will undoubtedly require a massive massaging of ego or a display of his power …'

'Speaking of sycophants, PS, where do you think Coachman stands on the challenge to Talbut's position as 2IC?'

'Rajes has the credentials, VH.'

'As do you.'

'Yes, but I don't want that particular position, VH.'

'Meaning?'

'Coachman's price is too high. Servility is not my style, nor is it Rajes.'

* * *

Having adjourned at the end of the school day to a harbour café, Rajes updated Cassie and Samantha on her interview with Coachman.

'His paradigm comes from a different culture from ours. I didn't expect the position.'

'If you think that, Rajes, why apply?' Cassie asked.

'It is time Talbut gained some perspective.'

'Take him down a notch or two, you mean,' Samantha said. 'You should appeal Coachman's decision under affirmative action.'

Rajes laughed, 'Not for a 2IC position! It's not worth it *this* time.' A woman waving at them from a table across the room distracted Rajes. 'If you excuse me for a moment ...'

'Van der Huffen said the same thing to her, Samantha.'

'Really? That's out-of-character for him, isn't it?'

'No, not really. He gives credit where it's due.'

'Or where flattery will win him favour.'

Cassie looked at Samantha amazed at this pot calling Van der Huffen's kettle black.

'The masks those men wear are quaint, even funny at times.'

'You need to take them seriously.'

'Oh, I do! Rajes is wrong about this, Cassie. When limitations are placed on you because of your gender, getting what you want, however you can, is worth it every time!'

'That attitude is potentially destructive.'

'To barriers, absolutely. To someone unwilling to manipulate the situation, perhaps.'

'But it backfired on you with Talbut, didn't it?'

'Yes, but he was the exception not the rule ... Besides, isn't it why you changed your appearance?'

In response to Cassie's questioning expression, Samantha added, 'Don't play the innocent with me. Men respond to women who are packaged well; it's easier to get what you want.'

Silence. At times like this, Cassie wished she had the gift of the cutting reply.

'So, Cassie, what's this I hear about you taking up competition ballroom?'

'How do you …?'

'It's a small town, Cassie. Besides, I know Kate Denford.'

'Oh.'

'From what I hear, you're not above playing games to get what you want either.'

'What!'

'Kate says the only reason Mike Madison picked you over her was because you have the role of Demure Woman off pat.'

'Well, she's wrong!'

'Hit a raw nerve, have I? Well, personally, I thought it was good you'd finally wised up. Then I realised you'd been playing that part last year as well. You're good, Cassie – even I was deceived.'

'I'm not like that!'

Samantha laughed, 'Well, you'd better be. You don't get anywhere by standing up to those in power.'

* * *

The comfort Cassie felt with Vincent at the dance studio and school was absent as they sat on the restaurant terrace, waiting for the second course.

Painfully aware of the moment's awkwardness, Vincent distracted her with an explanation of the place's history. 'Fitzgerald was a well-known character in the area and used to run a café in the main street in the 1950s. He was a local war hero. He and his wife expanded the café into this restaurant in 1961. It's as renowned as Robertson Pie Shop or The Paragon at Goulburn. All the staff are apprenticed and trained in house. The current chef has worked here since 1985. He's a mate of mine.

He only uses quality local produce and seafood. The photos around the room chronicle the family business journey; they're also an interesting window into Keimera's past.'

The second course was expertly cooked and beautifully presented. Vincent was knowledgeable about wines, an interest developed in his student days when he had subsidised his study by working as a bartender and waiter.

Relaxation came with the second bottle of wine. They talked and laughed over shared school experiences but found little in common beyond that and dance.

Back at Madison House, Vincent walked her to the rear verandah.

'It's been fun,' Cassie said.

'Worth repeating?'

'Yes.'

Vincent's lips reminded her of wine; the aftertaste lingered pleasantly as she climbed the stairs to her room.

After changing, Cassie sought respite from the heat on the verandah. There was an unnatural stillness about the night.

The screen door to Michael's room swung open. 'So, how did the date go?'

'A gastronomic delight.'

'I wasn't asking about the meal.' Michael leant on the verandah railing and looked at the town lights to the south.

'Vince is great company and a true gentleman.'

'I saw his ... farewell. Passionless is an apt description for it if you ask me.'

'I didn't. What's put you on edge?'

'It's the heat, mostly. That and an argument with Kate.'

'Over our partnership?'

'Yep.'

'I've been wondering about that. Did you choose me over her because you think I'm The Demure Little Woman?'

'Whatever made you think that? You're a better dancer than Kate will ever be. You shouldn't listen to her.'

'So the choice was about your ego?'

'Geez, where is all this guff coming from? It was a decision based on the fact that you're the superior dancer.'

* * *

'I can't go through this again!' Samantha said to Cassie as she stomped into the staff room. 'Those kids are animals!' Tears released some of the emotion pent up behind her anger. She collapsed into her chair. 'I thought all that teen rebellion and argument with Coachman was behind me. If it's like this every year, I'm going to chuck it in!'

Cassie passed Samantha the cup of tea she had just made, poured another and passed it to Rajes. Cassie said, 'I was just saying the same thing to Rajes.'

'The pack mentality really frightens me. Yuk!' Samantha looked at her tea. 'Milk? I hate the stuff!' She walked to the sink and poured the tea down the drain. 'My Year 7s, in the short time they've been here, have already found their negative role models.' Samantha made herself a coffee. 'The parody would be funny if the result wasn't so scary! Who knows where this sort of disorder leads?'

'To anarchy if it goes unchecked,' Rajes said. '*The Lord of the Flies* shows that as did my experience when my husband and I were expelled from Uganda in 72.'

'You experienced the brutality of Amin's boy soldiers first hand?'

'Yes, his sadism was like an oil slick.'

'Your class shouldn't be left unsupervised,' Cassie said. 'Do you want me to take them?'

Tempted, Samantha looked at Cassie's timetable. 'No, you've got Year 9 next. They're worse than my lot! You won't survive them if you take mine. Thanks for the offer though. I'd better get back before they strip the display work and posters off the walls, again! I don't even understand why they do that! It's senseless.' Samantha checked her make-up in a hand mirror taken from her top desk drawer. Looking now at Rajes, Samantha said, 'Are you comfortable talking about your Uganda experience? My Year 11 History class are studying Power and Authority; it'd be great if you'd be a guest speaker. Would you?'

'Perhaps. You know, Samantha, Keith demonstrated faith in your ability when he overruled Talbut and assigned Year 11 and 12 History classes to you. Keep that in mind when you're dealing with the little beasties in Year 7.'

'Faith or a need to flex his power muscle in the faculty given his subservience within the executive this year. Well, wish me luck. I'm off.' She left.

* * *

'Watch it!' Cassie called out, avoiding being imprinted on the kitchen wall by the force of Gary's entry a week later.

'You okay?' Gary asked. 'Didn't realise anyone was there. I'm awful sorry. You hurt?'

'I'm fine, just tired.'

'Are you sure, Cassie? I've seen stunned mullet look better. I reckon you need an icepack.'

'It's bony there so I don't think it'll bruise.'

Gary peered into her eyes. 'The eyes are supposed to show if someone is concussed, but I forget the sign. Do you know?'

'Stop fussing! The whiteboard doesn't show you're home, Gary.'

''Bout to do that now. You're home early.'

'I've had a headache all morning. In the end, I just had to leave.'

'And I've made it worse. Sorry. So you don't feel up to talkin' to Mavis then?'

'Did she call?'

'No, but I was at her work today to see Big Dave about nominating Ken for the captaincy. I wanted his support. It'd be an act of protest over the captain's failure to organise meets, schedules, and surf patrols.'

'I don't see why—'

'Of course you wouldn't bein' a woman. Anyway, I thought I'd see Mavis while I was there.'

'Gary, I was asking why this can't keep.'

'Mavis has been real sick lately. She's missed heaps of days and she's thrown in singin' at the pub.'

'That's … unlike her.'

'That's what I thought. So, I called round the flat. She spoke to me through the door, wouldn't let me in. Considerin' how Terry acts when anyone shows an interest in her, it sort of made sense. Then again …'

'What?'

'Nothing. Give her a call now, will you?'

'You think something is wrong?'

'I'm undecided. Just call her!'

After counting ten ring tones, Cassie hung up. 'What's behind this, Gary?'

'A bloke can't talk about people's private affairs. I've always liked Mavis even if I did give her curry most times. Wouldn't like to see her … well … so many women cut themselves off from friends when they get involved with a man. A mistake if you ask me.'

'Gary ...'

'Look, Cassie, if Mavis isn't at work in a week, will you come to her place to make sure she's okay?'

'Sure but ...'

'No buts. In the meantime, would you keep contact with her? Let me know if you think somethin' is up. You look terrible. I hope it's not the flu or something or the hit on the head. Shit, look at the time! I have to get back to work.'

Chapter 32

'Do you know who this Macbeth guy is that the top classes are studyin'?' Tony from 10C asked Cassie as the class unpacked for the lesson.

'Course she does, Chook. Miss knows everythin,' Stella, an acne-scarred girl, said.

'No one knows everything,' Cassie replied, 'but Macbeth was a brave general who allowed greed and ambition to take control of his life, and he lost everything he valued.'

'Which war, Miss? The last one or Vietnam?' a voice, in the process of breaking, squeaked.

'Hundreds of years ago, Ben.'

'The play sounds cool.' Tony turned to his peers. 'It's got witchcraft in it too.'

'It does, but not the sort you …'

'Do you reckon this bloke Macbeth is the one in *The Goodies* last week?' asked Carl, a square set boy with chewed hair.

'Is that old show still on reruns?'

'It's not old, Miss, I ain't seen it before.'

Matt Winston, a deep voiced lothario from the centre of his female court, said, 'I'd like to get it in the re-run. I vote for doing it. Who else?'

Hands shot up around the room.

'We could I suppose, but you should know Shakespearean language in the play is very different from anything you've read at school so far.'

'Aw, she thinks we're vegies!' The front legs of Tony's chair slammed into the floor.

'No, I don't. Even the top classes complain about the language. The characters talked very differently from the way we do today.'

'She's tryin' to talk us out of it,' a disembodied voice said from the side of the room. Cassie looked to see who had spoken.

'She's not!' Stella said. 'Miss is always tellin' us that if we work hard and keep goin' at things then we'll succeed.'

It could have been any one of three boys so Cassie spoke to the class. 'Okay, we'll do it once we finish this unit, but the first word of complaint, and we stop.'

* * *

As hot summer nights go, that Saturday was a record breaker. The senior Madisons, in formal grandeur, had left for a fundraiser. Gary had wandered off an hour or so earlier to the pub. Cassie and Michael had escaped the house's heat and now enjoyed the oncoming sea breeze in the fading light of the day.

'Want another drink, Cassie?' Michael said, standing.

'As a matter of fact, yes, but I can get it myself.'

'Of course, but is there any harm in letting me do it?'

'Guess not.'

'You've been very toey of late, especially about being independent. Why?'

The sound of an approaching car distracted Cassie.

'Visitors by the look,' Michael said. 'Hang on, I've seen that sports car before. Where?'

'It's Jake.' Secure about the well-being of her father, with whom she had spoken earlier in the evening, Cassie took a shortcut across the side verandah to the rear of the house where Jake was now parking.

Michael debated following her but entered the house instead, empty glasses in hand.

In the kitchen, he congratulated himself on thoughtfully clearing up the kitchen clutter for his mother. Eventually, Michael gave into his curiosity and stood near the screen door with a view of the couple outside.

Cassie and Jake stood close together, too close in Michael's opinion. His view was partially obscured by Jake's car. Their conversation, a murmur, did not carry to him. After an earnest exchange, Jake left at a slow crawl, leaving very little dust in his wake.

'So what did he want?' Michael asked as she walked toward him and the house.

'To be more than we once were.'

'And that was?'

Looking, it seemed to Michael, through him, and toward the driveway south, Cassie said, 'A dream once,' as she passed him.

* * *

Nearly an hour later, the plaintive call of a blues guitar intruded on Cassie's consciousness, enticing her from her hot room.

Downstairs, the lounge room was empty though the large French doors had been thrown open and curtains billowed. A pile of records were stacked on the player. After unsuccessfully fingering through some of the covers to identify the song she'd heard, Cassie found Michael on the verandah, smoking.

'I thought you'd given it up.'

He stubbed the cigarette out. 'Old habits and wants die hard especially if you make the mistake of tasting them again.'

'What were you playing a while ago?'

'Blues.'

'There was one track ... the guitar solo was beautiful. Who was it?'

'Don't know.'

Silence.

'And you don't particularly care, Mike?'

'That's about it.'

Silence.

'Dusk on the sea is beautiful, isn't it?' Cassie asked.

Silence.

'Since it's cooler, why not experiment with dance, Mike?'

'No ... I'm already putting extra time on improving my technique with Martin. Dancing just makes me aware of the gulf between us.'

'I was thinking of trying something different ... improvisation ... We could do it out here on the lawn ... I used to ... It's a fun way of improving the dialogue between a couple.'

'I'm not in the mood ...'

'Maybe something more upbeat will change that.' Cassie returned to the lounge room, fingered through the eclectic collection, decided on a 70s oldie, *Eagle Rock*.

By the time the opening refrain had concluded: 'Now listen, Oh we're steppin' out ...' Cassie had returned to the lawn and surrendered to the energy and joy of the song, dancing solo in the spill of verandah light and the shadows that engulfed the wider lawn. Michael resisted the urge to join her for the next two tracks.

'No, Mike, not ballroom. Do your own thing. Improvise. See if somewhere in that process, we can find ... movement that fits together somehow. Stop worrying about technique.'

For the next hour they danced mostly in contrast, sometimes

in laughter after mistiming and colliding, occasionally finding a dialogue that disappeared whenever Michael tried to control it.

'I suppose Jake was great at this?'

'No … I always had to complement his lead. Our teacher said it put a ceiling on our creativity.'

'Hard to believe that. In '85, you were amazing!'

'There's more to dance than winning … at least for me. We need to stack some more records if you want to continue that is.'

'I'll do it, Cassie, but this time, how about we begin with a mirror exercise but swap lead at points in the song. Like in Salsa at the RSL that first night you went there.'

* * *

At times, life is like the images in the distant heat haze. Distinguishing the real from the imagined requires scrutiny.

'That man is despicable!' Samantha hissed.

'Coachman?'

'Talbut.'

'What's brought this new insight, Samantha?'

'Tina Schwartz brought three of her friends to see me yesterday over …'

'She's one of the mature aged students enrolled this year, isn't she?'

'Yes. Anyway, Talbut has the girls in 2 Unit Related English. He's been running additional lessons early in the morning for kids who were behind in skills.'

'So? Lots of teachers do, Samantha.'

'That's not the issue.'

'Then what's the problem?'

'The girls don't like his special brand of attention.'

'He's coming onto them? Individually or as a group?'

'Nothing overt. He sits way too close. Uses instruction to be up close and personal. His pants are too tight. That sort of thing. They want to drop out of the extra lessons without repercussions but can't work out how to. So they came to me.'

'Why didn't they see Coachman or the Deputy?'

'They tried, Cassie, but he ...'

'Went to the solution without actually listening to the full story.'

'Yes ... Anyway Coachman spoke to Talbut but the whole thing has backfired on the girls. So they came to me; I have them for History.'

'What did Coachman say when you spoke to him?'

'As far as Coachman's concerned, Talbut's timetabled extra classes for senior kids for years without complaint. It's how he gets such consistently high results. As for his relationship with senior girls, Coachman says it's common knowledge they exploit his attraction to them. He pointed out we all get emotionally close to the kids we invest time in. He says Talbut would never cross the line though. The interview backfired on me. The Hitman is looking for a scapegoat, and we're it. Apparently, and this is almost verbatim, we're feminists contaminating the view of impressionable female students who would otherwise not take offence.'

'What are you going to do?'

'Nothing much. I've informed my immediate supervisor. He carries the blame if he's wrong.'

'And the girls?'

'Will skip the extra lessons on the pretext of being sick.'

'Talbut's a dangerous man.'

'Crass and objectionable definitely, but dangerous? I don't think so ... Not really ... He can be stepped on.'

'I don't know. I never told you the full story of last year. He—'

'Came onto you? Was offensive? Me too.'

'He tried to assault me, Samantha, and no one would listen to me.'

'I don't recall any signs that …'

'Because Talbut called in with some story about an accident and took time off work. Besides, like these girls, I didn't have any credible witnesses to prove his lie. How can you let this slide, Samantha?'

'As you just said, lack of credible evidence. The whole sexual harassment issue is a really grey area, especially because, in this instance, the girls admit to flirting with Talbut initially. Coachman puts their complaint in the same category with boys who end in a fight after starting a game of mock battle. He actually told them, 'Don't offer what you're not prepared to deliver.' Don't you read the papers, Cassie? Getting women's rights upheld in court is something else altogether.'

A rap on the door interrupted the discussion. Though Selton looked disbelievingly at the women, he accepted Samantha's explanation that the door latch must've slipped.

Unable to settle on work and unwilling to accept Samantha's defeat, Cassie headed for Coachman's office.

'May I speak to you?'

'Not if it's a continuation of the Schwartz complaint.'

'Oh … It is.'

'Then you can go.'

Cassie pulled out the chair facing Coachman's desk and encamped.

Ignoring her, Coachman made a show of work.

Twenty minutes passed with Cassie unwavering in her focus on him.

Unable to concentrate under her stare, Coachman said, 'All right; out with it.'

'You can't dismiss this complaint. There is a duty of care here.'

'And you've read *The Crucible*. Girls have personal agendas when they make such accusations, and good men can have their lives ruined because of it.'

Keep this a discussion, Cassie thought. 'Yes, that can happen, but it's not a universal truth, is it? Has it occurred to you that Talbut could be a wolf in sheep's clothing.'

'Rubbish! I've known him for years. He's a good man.'

'I'm sure that's the face he's let you see.'

Coachman returned to his work. Ten minutes passed before he looked at Cassie again. 'Do you seriously think I'd miss something like that?'

Cassie had pondered the how of that question herself for some time. 'Yes, because I think you assume other men have your values.'

Silence.

Minutes later, Cassie broke the silence. 'A wolf in sheep's clothing gets away with it because his disguise is a good one. Surely you've heard gossip?'

'I don't listen to gossip. It's mostly spread by small-minded people with little to occupy them other than the salacious. That sort of person sees dirt where there isn't any.' Coachman returned to his work.

'Is it possible that Talbut's changed, and you haven't noticed it because the change has been gradual? Or maybe the times have changed, and he hasn't.' Cassie waited for a reaction, but none was forthcoming. 'The girls and I can't be the only people who have challenged your view of him. Geez, I've seen him having sex in public. I can't be the only one who knows stuff like that about him.'

Coachman leant back in his chair in thought, recollecting a series of comments he'd heard around and about the town in the past eighteen months. 'Accusations aren't evidence though, especially when girls are known to be sexual teases, and these girls are.'

With a calm that she was far from feeling, Cassie replied, 'I don't know about that, but I do know their distress is genuine.'

'If anyone needs protection, Miss Sleight, it's Talbut.'

'If you want to see it that way, then yes, someone in this situation needs protection.'

Coachman leant back in his chair, deep in thought, his fingertips together. Later, when the end-of-period bell rang, he came out of his reverie. 'All right, I'll move the girls.'

'Thank you.'

Coachman returned to his work, troubled.

* * *

The next day in her free lesson, Cassie checked the book room to see if there were enough copies of Macbeth for her class. She discovered a massive supply of all things Shakespearian. Re-entering the corridor, she witnessed two separate scenes. To her right, Talbut in Coachman's office gesticulated forcefully, his argument an underscore to a discussion nearer her. To her left, Chris Williams, a boy with dark curly hair and a slight build, argued with Samantha.

'I'm not going back to his class, Miss! I can't stand him! His dick interferes with lessons all the time. If I can't be in your class … If I can't be in your class then I'm gunna leave!'

'I understand your feelings, Chris, but you need to give Mr

Talbut a fair go, and you need to give yourself time to adapt to teaching ideas. 'Sons and Lovers' is a challenging text …'

'It's not the book that sucks! It's him. He's a prick! Besides, I don't want to adapt. I was doin' good in your class after I settled down last year, wasn't I? Please, let me stay!'

Samantha considered the boy and looked toward Coachman's office. 'I'll see what I can do, but I don't think it'll do any good.'

Cassie called from the book room doorway, 'Ms Smith!'

Samantha replied, 'Ms Sleight?'

'Can I use Chris to help me get some texts to my classroom?'

'Yes, but after that he must return to class.' To the boy, Samantha said, 'If you challenge Mr Coachman's authority in this, he won't consider our request. Chris, will you do as I ask?'

'Okay,' his reluctance clear.

'Come back next recess for Mr Coachman's decision.'

By the time of Cassie's return, the matter had been resolved. The end of Coachman's discussion with Talbut carried clearly to Samantha who waited at the top of the stairwell.

Talbut said, 'By supporting this kid's defiance, you're undermining my authority in the school.' As he walked passed her, Talbut looked at Samantha; there was malevolence in his expression.

'Mrs Smith,' Coachman called.

Cassie left for the staff room, disturbed by the revelations from the incident.

In his office, Coachman's face was grave. 'My decision in this case will be the exception not the rule. Chris has been an underachiever until you developed a relationship with him last year. He has great potential. I hold you responsible now for his Year 11 and 12 results. You may go.'

Returning to the staff room, Samantha felt the weight of

Coachman's charge. She had not expected that burden when she undertook Chris' defence, being direct just did not pay. She had not wanted that responsibility.

'So,' Cassie asked, 'is Coachman going to do anything about Talbut now?'

'He says he doesn't take Chris' complaint seriously, but I don't know if that's true. All he said to me was that the girls have Talbut's measure. Women-in-training he called them. When I pushed it, he said he'd look into the matter discreetly, but he thinks Chris exaggerated the situation for his own gain.'

'But if you put this in context of the Year 12 girls' complaints ...'

'Coachman'd be aware of the implications just as much as we are. He's a smart man and takes pride in the fact that he is. For him to accept what we say is happening, he'd have to acknowledge he'd been duped. Not an easy pill for a man like him to swallow. We'll have to be vigilant as we move around the school. Has Talbut bothered you lately?'

'No, but then I avoid him. You?'

Samantha laughed. 'No, he's quite clear in his dislike of me now. He avoids me. I've nothing to fear from him.'

* * *

'I can't understand this, Miss!' wailed Stella. 'Not even a bit!'

'Aw, shut up, Stella!' Tony was equally appalled, but he had committed himself to the task and was not retreating. 'Miss warned us. Ignore her, Miss, the rest of us want to do it!' He eyeballed the class daring another complaint. He had told his girlfriend they were studying the play; he was not prepared to lose that new respect.

'You'll find the audio cassette reading more helpful now that we've read the first few scenes, and I've explained what the words mean. We'll go over it again, okay?'

Cassie paused the tape at the end of scene three. Her class looked depressed. Their limitations were now glaringly obvious.

Feeling like she was climbing Mount Everest with a bus on her back, Cassie said, 'Okay, I'll try to explain what happened. The most important thing about this scene is that Macbeth is an amazingly fearless soldier who is not put off by the odds against him, an olden day Rambo. How many of you saw that movie? Good, so you know the sort of man I'm talking about. You're having difficulty understanding what Shakespeare is saying because you don't get the comparisons he's making.'

The bell rang; the class waited for dismissal.

'It'll get easier as you get used to the language.'

Her class doubted that truth and expressed it in disheartened mumblings.

'Everyone will get used to the language, I promise.'

Chapter 33

A cool autumn breeze played with the living room curtains of Madison House. On the verandah outside that room, Vincent Pearce finished his last A3 sketch and turned to Cassie who stood to his left at his shoulder. 'Well, what do you think of this series?'

'They're great! You really are an artist!' Impulsively, Cassie hugged him.

After she released him, Vincent said, 'Don't tell me you believed that guff that those who can't do teach?'

'Of course not, but Vince, these are masterful. You've captured everything that Shakespeare painted orally. I am so grateful for your help. Is there is anything I can do to repay you?'

'Some evening delight later?'

'That's … okay.'

The clock in the living room chimed six.

'Look, Cassie, I'm not going to have time to get home, change, and get back; I made the reservation at seven. Given our plans why not get ready at my place?'

Cassie hesitated.

'I've got instant hot water, and you can go first.'

'With such an unselfish offer, how could I not? Give me ten minutes?'

'Sure. Get whatever you need to feel comfortable.'

As it turned out, it took Cassie fifteen minutes before she descended.

With her black leather barrel bag in hand, Cassie passed Michael on his way up.

'Where're you off to, Cassie?'

'Out. About.'

'With old Pearce?'

'He's not old.'

'He's so far north he's almost at the Arctic.'

'To boys maybe. See you!' Cassie said blithely.

Michael stood on the verandah outside his room, watching Cassie drive off. He decided to go for a run and work off his pent up energy.

* * *

Vincent lived in a real studio apartment: a bedroom and a living area, overlooking Surf Beach. It seemed cramped with his easel and tools set up in the living area.

Wrapped in a bath towel and with her back to the door, Cassie felt uneasy.

'Never did I see true beauty until tonight.'

Turning, Cassie felt herself flush. Vincent stood in the doorway. Aware of her vulnerability, she asked, 'Where'd you get that line from? It sounds like one of the romantic poets.'

'Don't know. It's not a line; it's the truth.' Vincent crossed to her, obviously at ease.

'Yes, well ...'

'I was serious about painting you. Nothing more beautiful than a naked woman. How about I order dinner in and we start tonight?' He ran his hand over her bare shoulder. 'Your skin is like velvet.'

Cassie swallowed nervously but worked for a casual response. 'Sounds like one of Year 7s' poetry attempts:

Your skin is like velvet
You smell like a rose
I like you a lot
So what goes?
I'd rather go out as planned, thanks.'

Vincent slipped an arm around her, pulling her to him. 'A putdown, Cassie? Surely not.'

'I feel really uncomfortable like this,' Cassie said, disentwining herself.

'We're in synch as usual, Cassie. Of course, it's in your hands ...'

Cassie's mental, Yuk! translated itself into a grimace.

Vincent released her, surprised 'I've misread the situation? I thought back at Madison House ... Never mind.'

With her mind racing for an exit line, she remembered Coachman's dismissal and adapted it to this situation. 'Close the door on the way out, will you, Vince? I won't be long.'

He left.

Dressing quickly, Cassie ran a comb through her hair as she practiced appearing nonchalant. She considered cancelling dinner with him but realized she needed to let him save face. So instead, she planned chitchat for the drive from his flat to the restaurant.

When Cassie actually came face-to-face with Vincent, she became flustered and tongue-tied. Vincent seemed nonplussed and worked to put her at ease. Within the security of the crowded restaurant, her composure returned.

Throughout the meal, Vincent's pleasure and knowledge in all things gourmet continued as in past dates to dominate the conversation. When that avenue was exhausted, his conversation shifted to shared turf: school.

'You've got to admit, Vince, blocking exits to simulate the

collapse of sections of the building was a bit excessive for a fire drill. In the end, Selton gave up and decided it was easier to be incinerated.'

'Irresponsible is what my lot thought. It just prolonged the soap opera. As for Van der Huffen's commentary … well, his cynicism undermines the system.'

'Well, I thought he was funny. I really liked his description of Cameron as a Colossus astride centre stage.'

'I didn't, and I wasn't the odd one out in this. The people around me were loud in their agreement with Talbut when he told Van der Huffen to shut up.'

'They make great Strawberries Romanoff here,' Cassie said.

As they drove back to Madison House, Vincent said, 'Was it just me or was the meal the only thing of substance we've shared tonight?'

Cassie laughed, at ease for the first time. 'That's a tactful way of putting it. I'm sorry. I …'

Vincent laughed. 'Just want to be friends? That's usually my line. Women usually want to tie up a relationship like some parcel.'

After parking at the rear of the house, Vincent opened the car door for her and said as she swivelled out, 'I'd prefer if this didn't become fodder for Selton and Vander Huffen.'

'You really don't know me if you think that's a possibility. Good night, Vince. Thanks again for your help.'

As a final gesture, Vincent kissed the palm of her hand before leaving.

As Cassie watched his lights cut a path into the night as he drove off, Michael stepped out of the shadows.

'How's love with the teacher going?'

'You scared me, Mike, I didn't realise you were there.'

'Obviously.'

'Vince is a really nice man, generous in more ways than I can describe but he's not my type.'

'And that is?'

'I'm not sure there is one.'

* * *

The dance sessions tantalised and frustrated Martin Jones. There was something intangible that burred the couple's dancing. He stood on the rim of the dance floor, frowning as he watched them.

Though Michael's movements were strong and forceful, the dance lacked the liquid ease of the previous week's work. It was replaced by something primitive.

This dance reminded Jones of something. The image was strongest when he concentrated on Michael. It eluded him when he watched Cassie.

Michael's outstretched arm snapped Cassie to him. The force of the move stunned her. She became a rag doll in his arms.

The image crystallised. Jones saw a French riverfront cafe, men in berets with horizontal striped shirts and tight trousers, and their dance partners: women in black satin skirts split to the hip.

What is that dance style called? He searched his memory. Ah! The French Apaché. It was a Bohemian dance from the early twentieth century, politically incorrect but highly dramatic. Not typical of the usual dialogue between this couple.

Jones stopped the music.

Cassie straightened herself. 'Okay, what's wrong? I know we're working on precision, but you've given a new meaning to execution.'

'I need a break.'

'Is that all you've got to say?' She followed him from the floor and sat on the bench behind Jones, making a point of being separate from Michael.

'Righto, m' boy, what's the problem?' Jones rolled a cigarette while he waited.

'Can we get a coffee first?' Cassie asked.

The ritual of the commonplace introduced a surface calm.

Cassie's energy drained as the cups did. Having pushed herself throughout the previous year, the stress of trying to do too much in this first term had left her bankrupt. She looked at her mug. Jones' coffee was the type that put hair on the chest, and she suspected it had a similar effect on the mouth.

'From where I stood, the problem's with Mike.'

Martin's wife called him into his office. 'Sort it out!' he called back over his shoulder to them.

Cassie sat on the floor next to Michael. 'What's wrong?'

Terrible timing, Michael thought. He had met Cassie too soon. 'It's good news really. I didn't tell anyone at home, but I applied to join the RAAF last year. They phoned today. I've passed the first stage of the process. A confirmation letter should arrive soon with details of the next Officer Interview Board. If I do well there, I'm in.'

Cassie manufactured enthusiasm. 'That's great!'

'It is, but I have other options that I'm investigating.'

'Options?' She messed her hair in a tired gesture. 'Journalism?'

'If I went to Wollongong uni, we'd be able to continue dancing and be together.'

'I thought you'd decided against that. Anyway, our dance partnership shouldn't be a deciding factor.'

He took her hands and held them. 'It's important to me.

You are too.' He leant forward and kissed her, lightly with a hint of intensity.

Cassie felt light-headed. 'Mike, I don't want … Your career should …' She was tired and lacked the energy to deal with the deeper issues of life and relationships.

'I know. We're nothing to each other off the floor.' He kissed her again. She lost her centre, lost her sense of separateness in the undertow of the kiss. Cassie was unaware that she'd initiated its end. Reluctant to release her, Michael responded anyway. The separation was slow and, for a moment, seemed not to eventuate.

'I might not pass the Board. I've got to think through the long term consequences of what I choose.'

Jones returned. 'Let's call it quits for this evening.'

Cassie said, 'I've a shocking headache. I feel faint.'

'I'll ring George and get him to drive my car home while I drive yours.'

* * *

The morning light-tide swept darkness from Cassie's room. It lapped against the wall of her unconsciousness, pulling her into the day. She pushed herself up onto her elbows and looked over the bed. It seemed much larger. I should get up, she thought, but she sank back into her pillows and rolled over, heavy with a weariness that was far worse than tiredness.

Her alarm clock was gone. The bedclothes clung to her like water to an emerging swimmer. She found it under her bed. Wading through the silence and down the stairs to the phone, the need to notify the school of her absence gave her impetus to get to the foyer.

The school phone, when Cassie rang, was engaged. She sat

on the bottom stair, mustering energy for a trip to the kitchen. What did Minna and George say last night? She wondered. Where were they going? She drew a blank. Am I alone home? She shook her head. No, home alone. The need to lie down was greater than the need to eat. She drifted into an uneasy sleep.

Patterns of light teased her back to consciousness. She shivered; it was surprisingly cold.

Flushed, she gained the upper corridor and laboured toward her bedroom. She stumbled over to the dressing table and hauled out a woollen sweater and some thick socks. She barely made the bed and collapsed onto it, drawing up as many of the covers as she could.

* * *

Michael hated entering closed houses; they breathed heat. Coming home for lunch had seemed one of the perks of working for the local newspaper.

Halfway up the stairs, he heard retching.

Cassie sat on the floor of the bathroom, vomiting into the toilet, wearing a padded jacket. Her face was tearstained, her colour heightened.

Michael knelt beside her.

'Don't, Mike. This is too revolting. Could you get me a bowl and help me to my bed? I want to die in bed.' Crying, she said, 'And I haven't let school know that I'm not in.'

He felt her head. 'You're not dying, Cassie. It's more like a good case of the flu or maybe some virus. I'll get you to bed, but first I'll get a bowl. As for school, they'll have worked that out for themselves.'

'Would you phone them anyway and let them know I'm sick?'

'When I've got you back in your room.'

It had seemed simple. He had lifted her many times but had not appreciated the contribution of momentum in those lifts. The cramped conditions limited the depth to which he could sink. Cassie clutched her bowl and put her free arm around his neck.

His biceps cramped. Pain cut into his shoulder blades. He rolled her out of his arms and onto the floor. He tried again, this time his back to the wall. Scooping her into his arms, he rolled her back against his body. Their level changed momentarily. He staggered slightly but found the gravity pull of their combined bodies worked against him.

Consumed by the struggle, he only subliminally noted the searing contact of her body. He tried inching up the wall. His thigh muscles knotted. Cassie was fractious and difficult to hold. Michael leant back against the wall, gathering his strength. At the same time, Cassie wriggled in his arms. Her vomit bowl spilt on him.

'Awh!' Revulsion brought him upright with one arm holding her. She slid to her feet. 'I'm sorry. You'll have to walk.' He fought to hold her rag-doll frame up while he stripped off his shirt. 'That felt bloody awful! Come on.'

'I can't. My legs are jelly.'

'C'mon.' He propped her against him.

'I can't. Just leave me to die.'

'Geez, you're ill, not dying.'

'You don't know how bad I feel. Everything hurts.' Her cheeks burned red.

After a few faltering steps, she tried to lie down.

'No, you don't,' he said, forcing her to remain upright, 'it's not far to your bedroom.'

'It's miles away.'

He stumbled with her down the corridor.

'I need to lie down. It doesn't matter where, just as long as it is flat.'

'Not bloody likely …'

'Of all the mean …'

'Don't waste energy complaining, walk.'

'No, you don't understand. I can't make it to my room.'

'Yes, you can … oops …'

Cassie's body went limp. The plastic bowl clattered onto the floor. Her dead weight was significantly heavier. She flopped in his arms.

Michael muttered under his breath and altered their stance. Standing behind her, he linked his arms under her armpits. Her body tilted back resting on his. He used his feet to propel her feet forward. They made the room. He flopped her forward onto the bed. Her legs dangled over its sides. He swung her over so that she was no longer lying face down. He sat on the edge of her bed, recovering from the exertion, and considered his course of action.

The first thing was a shirt. The second, take Cassie's temperature.

Sitting on the bottom stair, Michael waited for the receptionist to put his call through. Doctor MacIntyre had been the family doctor for as long as Michael could remember. After a brief exchange of pleasantries, he briefed the doctor.

'Forty-two degrees Celsius is real hot, huh?' Michael said.

'The most important thing is to get her cool. Give her three Panadol tablets and strip her down. We need to be careful, high temperatures make a person vulnerable to … no need to worry you about that now. If possible, get her into a cool bath. I'd come up now, but I've a full surgery. I'll be finished here in a couple of hours, maybe sooner if there aren't any more complications.'

'Do you think I should bring her down to you?'

'No, you'd still have to wait. We have a few emergencies here. Your friend will be all right if you follow my directions. The main thing is to get that temperature down. I'll come as soon as I'm free.'

Armed with Panadol, he returned to her bedroom. 'Okay, Cassie, I want you to take these.'

She swallowed the tablets under protest.

'Doctor Mac says we've got to get you cool.'

'I'm freezing.'

'That's just the temperature. Now, be a good girl and co-operate. We've got to get rid of these blankets and peel all this winter clothing off you.'

'No way!' She was defeated by her own lack of energy. All she could do was harry Michael.

'C'mon, sit up and get those layers off.'

Cassie scrunched further under the covers of her bed. 'Of all the hard-hearted … No, don't touch those covers!' She refused to release them. 'I'm cold … Don't pull the sheets back! Listen to me. Noooo!'

He prised them from her grasp. 'Now, off with these layers. My God! You're about three sizes bigger than normal! C'mon, sit up.'

'Nooo!' She hit at his hands but lacked the power to resist.

His patience dwindled with the peel of clothing.

'Don't open those windows wider. I'll catch pneumonia.'

'For God's sake!'

He turned to find she had pulled some bed clothing up. 'Blast you!' He yanked the covers out of her hands and dumped them on the floor. 'Maybe you should worry about dying … from having your neck wrung.'

'I wish my mum was here. She wouldn't be so hard-hearted.' The thought brought the tears.

'I'll be back in a tick.' He disappeared into the corridor. He needed a bowl of cool water, some face washers, and lots of cool drink.

An hour passed. Cassie's temperature remained at forty-two degrees.

'Doctor Mac said I was to put you in a bath if your temperature refuses to come down. I've got the bath running now. It's tepid, not cold.'

'Oh no! No way! What … what are you doing?'

He hauled her up. 'This is as hard for me as it is for you.'

She pulled against him, trying to return to her bed. 'Sssure it is …' She spoke through her teeth. 'Leave me alone! Otherwise I'll … I'll …' She was unable to finish her threat.

Drawing on super human strength, he pulled her into his arms. She pulled at the remaining bed sheet which tangled his legs. He cursed her and kicked it off.

'Okay, okay, I'll co-operate … I promise … Please, please don't put me in the bath. I'll be good. Really I will.'

He jolted her onto the floor when they reached the bathroom. 'Be a good girl, it's for your own good. Hop in the bath and stay there until the doctor arrives.'

'No.' Her teeth chattered involuntarily, 'There's no way I'm going in that bath, and you can't make me. You need my co-operation if I'm to undress and get in, and I won't!'

'That's what you think!' He picked her up and leant over the bath. It was the old-fashioned kind, deep and built for giants.

He released her. The waters swelled. She spluttered her protest, but it was too late. He'd won.

'I'll never forgive you!'

'That's fine with me,' Michael said, walking out.

Wallowing in the bath water and her misery, her nightdress

ballooning around her, she yelled out, 'I don't love you any more.'

He returned. 'What did you say?'

'Mike? Come here for a minute.' Her voice was subdued and her demeanour passive. 'There's something I should tell you.'

Tenderness in his voice now he asked, 'What?'

'Could you come a little closer?' Her arms rested on the top rim of the tub.

'Well?'

'Just a little closer, I haven't got the energy to talk any louder.'

He knelt close to the bath. She plunged her arms into the water, creating a tidal wave that covered him and the floor.

'Bitch!' He stood up, drenched, 'That's bloody petty!'

'I know.' Cassie reclined in the bath. 'But I'll die happy.'

* * *

Gary arrived at the house that afternoon feeling like he had done a good day's work and thinking about a nice cold beer. As he drove up the driveway, he passed the departing local chemist delivery van.

'What's up?' Gary asked when he came upon Michael slouched against the stairwell wall and his legs blocking access to the first floor.

'Thank God someone is home! Can you take over for me, mate? I've had it!'

'Take over what?'

'That woman is the most … the most … words can't do justice to what she is.'

'And you're talking about?'

'Cassie. She has to have two Panadol at five-thirty and an

antibiotic again at seven. She's a lot better now. Her temperature is still up, but it's not as bad as it was.'

'Whoa! Back up a bit.'

'Cassie's sick, and I've been the only one here. I've been hanging out for someone to relieve me. I need a swim.'

'I'm not good with sick people. How long will you be?'

'The doctor said to keep the room aired, the bed clothes off her, and to keep the liquids up. I told the school; you can tell her that if she asks. Tell her the doctor said she'll be off the rest of the week. I'm out of here. Good luck!'

He headed to his room to change. Uncertain, Gary followed.

'If there's one thing I've learnt this afternoon,' Michael said, 'it's that I'm not suited to the medical profession. If all patients are as difficult as Cassie, then they deserve a lot more pay. Did I tell you not to let her pull up the bedclothes? Or to close the windows?'

Gary nodded.

Cassie lay passively watching the afternoon breeze dance with her curtain. She looked up as Gary entered the room.

'You okay, mate? Mike's passed you over into my care.'

'He's been really cruel to me. I'm cold, and he won't even let me pull up a sheet.' Tears rolled down her face.

'Can't see how that could hurt. I'm getting' a beer. Feel like a cuppa?'

'Please.'

'Okay then, it'll only take a minute or two. Hey, what about some of Minna's teacake? Food always makes me feel better when I'm sick.'

'Oh,' Cassie shook her head, 'I couldn't come at the cake. I'd puke.'

'No need to share that with me. Won't be long.'

Cassie tentatively pulled up the sheet and snuggled into it.

Michael poked his head in through her door as he headed off to the beach. 'Cassie! You promised; get that sheet off!'

She jettisoned it.

He searched upstairs for Gary and then headed downstairs. 'Isn't anyone else responsible?' he muttered. 'Man, you can't leave her alone. Why do you think I was sitting on the stairs? Not for comfort. You need to be within earshot.'

The late afternoon sun streamed into Cassie's room. Its warmth was a welcome caress.

Gary returned with a tray stacked. He sat on a chair after having propped Cassie up with pillows.

'A bit hot in here, don't you think? How about I draw the curtains?'

Cassie opened her mouth to remonstrate and then thought the better of it. She was no longer freezing, just unwell.

'Boy, Mike's in a bad mood. Any idea when the others get back?'

Cassie shook her head.

'Lucky I'm here then, eh?'

* * *

Voices on the stairs woke Gary who lay sprawled on the floor at the top of the stairs.

'A really witty article, Mrs Madison.'

Gary stretched, easing out the cricks in his body.

'Thank you, Rajes. I've been concerned about women's issues for some time, but other agenda meant I wasn't able to write about it till now. It's amazing how many people are poorly informed.'

'Beaut!' Gary said as the women came abreast of him.

'Cassie's all yours, Minna. I won't burden you with the drill Mike gave me. I'm outta here!'

Concerned, Minna entered Cassie's room. 'How do you feel?' The gentleness in her tone brought tears into Cassie's eyes.

'Terrible. I've never been sick like this before, never!'

Minna read the direction on the medication boxes. 'Well, you've a visitor.'

Rajes, carrying a briefcase, materialised.

'Don't cry. It will only make you feel worse.' Rajes straightened the bedclothes and did her best to make Cassie comfortable while Minna tidied the room. The women fussed over Cassie like aunts fuss over young children at Christmas. The shrill note of the kettle sounded. Minna left.

'It's so nice of you to come, Rajes.'

'When you didn't call in sick today, there was such a fuss! No one was home when Paul came here this morning.'

'I must've been asleep.'

'Then Coachman received a call about two this afternoon. He was going to drop off this marking for you, but since I was coming, he gave it to me.'

'I can't cope with that.'

'That is what Paul and I said to Coachman, but he was immovable. We did manage to get the work modified.' Rajes opened her valise and pulled out a box of chocolates and then reams of mid-semester exam papers.

'Oh.' Cassie sank into her pillows and slipped down under her sheets.

Rajes laughed. 'It looks much worse than it really is. You had the Creative Writing section, but Paul swapped it for the multiple choice comprehension instead.' She rummaged in her bag. 'Here are the answers. It's purely a mechanical task, tedious but not mentally demanding. The deadline has been put back till your return. If you can't … well, we'll cross that bridge when we get to it.'

* * *

On the Saturday, Cassie woke, conscious that she was feeling better. Relieved to be freed from her room, she spent the morning on the front verandah, marking. It was a boring task, a simple matter of checking off responses on a sheet and tallying scores.

Picking up the binoculars, she scanned the distant rocks and then looked at the surfers on the northern beach. Wet-suited, they were indistinguishable from each other. The beach was almost deserted. As she sat with her chin on the palm of her hand, she wondered at the despondent cries of seagulls circling the harbour below.

'Why so dejected on such a beautiful day?' Michael asked as he came up from behind her. He had been working on his car at the back of the house most of the morning. George, on the way to bowls, had mentioned that Cassie was ensconced on the front verandah. Michael had continued working on his car and initially ignored George's none-too-subtle hint that this would be a good time to clear the air. 'And why are you wasting it on paperwork?'

'I have to finish it before I go back,' Cassie's tone reflected her oppression. 'The English staff need the marks for the reports.'

'Whew!' He fingered through the piles of papers. 'Need a hand?'

'Yes, there's not much to it, but accuracy is important. Isn't there something else you'd rather be doing though?'

'There are plenty of things, but if you need, no, if you want help, I'd like to share the workload. Your choice.'

'I'll make a second answer sheet then,' Cassie said.

Michael sat down and picked up the binoculars while he waited for her to complete his copy of the answers. 'What or, should I ask, who were you looking for?'

'No one … nothing really. Just looking for a distraction from the marking.'

They worked silently for a few minutes.

'Um … about the other day … the day I got sick.'

'Yes?'

'I'd like to apologise for being … for being a little difficult.'

'A little?'

'Very difficult then.'

'Apology accepted.'

Cassie returned to her marking, and Michael followed her lead.

'Did you mean it, Mike, when you said I was a bitch?'

'At the time you were.'

'You're not going to take it back then?'

'No.'

'I was really sick though.'

'Yes, and petty.'

'You're right; I was.'

The rhythm of the marking continued for a time.

'Is that the reason you haven't been to see me, Mike?'

'No, I've had a lot on my plate and needed space to sort things out.'

'Have you?' Cassie asked, concerned.

'No.'

'I'm a good listener.' In response to his expression, she added, 'when I'm well.'

In the silence, Cassie wondered if other women found it difficult to accept derogatory remarks, no matter how valid, from men they liked. Liked? She avoided that line of thought. 'Mike? Gary's worried about Mavis. Any idea why?'

'He's upset she gave up singing at the pub. You know how much he liked being a part of that.'

'Do you think that's it? Singing for Mavis is like dancing for us. To give that up …'

Michael considered the situation before answering. 'The reason would be huge … Jealousy, do you think?'

'Terry is that … Do you think he gets status from the fact that Mavis is so fine, and he owns her? When he stops her doing stuff, is it so he can show he's master of her fate?'

'I don't think so. He just has traditional expectations.'

'Hmmm. I promised Gary I'd visit Mavis if she was still off sick. He says she hasn't been back to work since we last spoke. Would you come with me?'

'Course I will, Cassie. Just tell me when.'

'You're not going to tell me I'm being silly?'

'Not my call. If you're worried, justified or not, we need to do something about it. And if you're right …'

'Can you make it Monday at four-thirty?'

Chapter 34

'Maybe Mavis isn't home,' Cassie said having rung the doorbell twice without a response.

'Nah, she's here … has to be …' Gary said. 'She wasn't on the beach. The apartments are too far away from anythin' for her to have walked. Besides, when I talked to her boss he reckoned somethin' was up.'

Michael opened his mouth to speculate but Gary cut him short with, 'Her boss doesn't think she's pregnant. He said that given the sort of clothes she'd been wearing that …'

'Well?' both Cassie and Michael asked.

'Don't want to go there. The important thing now is to see Mavis. Not talk to her through the door mind, actually see her.'

'Where's all this stuff coming from, mate?'

'At the pub when we talked, Terry stopped referrin' to Mavis. He just talked about It. For a long while, I thought he was talkin' about his fear of becomin' like his dad. I'm not sure when I twigged he was talkin' about Mavis. His hate freaked me out.' The urgency in Gary's knocking increased. 'C'mon, Mavis, open up. It's Gary, and I've brought Cassie and Michael.'

'Mavis? If you're in there, please open the door,' Cassie called, memories of Mavis' talk about the inner beast surfacing.

* * *

Mavis moved gingerly from the sofa. With each footstep, her body and head ached. Her brows creased in the effort to make the door. Her scalp was tender as was the rest of her body. Each step, no matter how she placed it, jarred. The room spun. Some evil genie played with her life, setting her up for disaster while she thought she was doing the right thing. She opened the door.

One side of her face was swollen. Her forehead had an ugly gash across it. A large, ugly bruise of a hundred hues ringed her throat. Her arms were grazed and bruised. She could barely walk.

Shocked, Cassie said, 'Oh! What's happened?'

'The mongrel! The bastard!'

'Cool it, Gary!' Michael said.

Mavis folded in front of them, but Gary caught her and carried her to the sofa.

'Cassie, find some bags and put what she owns in them!' Michael said. 'We're taking her out of here.'

Gary fumed, 'I'd like to give him a taste of it. Struth, Mavis, I never, never thought it'd be as bad as this! God Almighty!'

'Shut up, Gary. You're upsetting Mavis. Go bring the car around. You ready yet, Cassie?'

'Struth.' Gary knelt at Mavis' feet. 'That's the last thing I want to do, you poor old thing. It's just that I knew he blamed you. That the blame was turnin' into hate for a while now … I feel it's me that's let this happen … I should have said some-thin', done somethin' a long time ago. Can you ever forgive me?' Gary was close to tears himself.

'Cassie?' Michael called.

'I can't find her guitar.'

Mavis tried to speak. Her voice croaked. 'Terry smashed it … I'm … I'm … so … glad …' She passed out.

'C'mon, Cassie! We'll file a complaint and get a court order for the rest of her stuff later. She needs to see a doctor.'

'I'll carry her, Mike.' With that, Gary scooped Mavis into his arms.

Outside, thunder reverberated overhead. The breaking storm was one that they'd remember. The trip to the local hospital, though short, was fraught with hazards: blinding rain, overworked wipers, slick roads, and diminished speed. Nerves stretched to their limit.

Glad of Michael's calm take-charge manner, Cassie and Gary found Mavis' clinging dependency heart-wrenching as they waited with her in Casualty. When she was released, they considered taking Mavis to her parents' house despite the distance. The storm was the deciding factor against that journey.

* * *

Kate sat on the floor waiting for Gary, enjoying the roaring fire, the first for that year. Plans for the surf club's activities were splayed out before her on the coffee table. She chewed her pen and occasionally amended the plans. George sat in his armchair, talking to Minna.

George said, 'The hardest thing, Min, has been convincing medical staff that they are carers for the aged rather than hospital staff and convincing the Board to increase the amount of personal space for each resident beyond a bed and a bedside table.'

Minna surveyed the possessions that she loved in that particular room. 'We've spent a lifetime working for all of this. To lose it, just because we got old and infirm.' She shook her head, thinking that it would be heart-breaking, soul destroying. 'I…'

Mavis' arrival brought everyone to a stand in a concerned

hubbub of noise. While Gary helped Mavis into a chair, Cassie explained the sequence of events leading to the rescue. Michael brought up the rear with the few things Cassie had packed.

A wave of nausea hit Mavis. Her legs shook as Cassie helped her to the bathroom.

'But why?' asked George.

'Does it matter?' asked Kate. 'Does anything one person does justify violence; let alone this sort of abuse?'

'I just don't understand how this sort of thing could happen,' Minna said.

'Terry's a good bloke, but ...' Gary said.

'We can see how good!' Kate said in derisive tones.

'Nah, he is,' Gary spoke to the Madisons. 'He lived here for ages, didn't he? It's just ... well ... I don't really understand what it was Mavis was doin', but it set him off.'

'What! It's Mavis' fault that he beat her?' Kate said to Gary as Cassie returned.

'Where's Mavis, Cassie?' asked Minna, ignoring the argument developing in the background.

'She wanted to lie down. The medication is taking affect. She's in her old room.'

'I'll check on her later then,' Minna said.

Gary continued, 'I reckon anyone's capable of it given the right circumstances. You hear about good blokes being set off by some trigger all the time.'

'No, mate, you're wrong, there,' Michael said. 'Anyone capable of this was never a good bloke. He just pretended to be.'

'And what did the police say?' asked Minna.

'They are reluctant to get involved in domestic violence even though they have the power to do so.'

'Why, for God's sake?' Minna asked.

'Experience,' Michael said.

'What does that mean?' George asked.

'Dad, Sgt Evans said that they prefer the woman to lay the charge. That way, they know she's fair dinkum about pursuin' it. They have the power to charge the bloke themselves, especially when the woman has occasioned actual bodily or grievous harm, but he said in ninety out of one hundred cases when they did that, the woman would renege and refuse to testify when the bloke ended up in court. Apparently, blokes who do this sort of thing suffer a lot of remorse once the incident has passed, and the woman usually drops the matter. He said women aren't usually vindictive.'

'Vindictive? For Christ's sake!' Kate stood and walked to the window overlooking the sea.

George asked, 'Well, what did Mavis do?'

Gary answered, 'She signed a formal charge of assault and took out a restrainin' order.'

'I'm surprised she was up to going to the police tonight, Gary,' Minna said.

'The doctor called them. He said any delay would complicate the matter.'

Kate asked, 'Did the doctor suggest counselling? More than her body's battered.'

'You're right. She's not the same person. I'm worried about her nausea. She can't seem to stop heaving.'

'Distress can do that to you,' George said.

'That's what the doctor said,' Cassie replied, worried.

'Well, if it doesn't settle down, we'll take her back to him,' said Gary.

* * *

Fifty slow minutes passed in the doctor's waiting room as the warmth faded out of that early winter's day. Cassie flicked through a magazine, her thoughts elsewhere. She yawned, crossed and then uncrossed her legs, leant forward on her chair, and looked through the curtains that shielded patients from the curious glances of passers-by. The look became a stare.

Mavis emerged from the doctor's rooms dry-eyed but distraught – a hunted creature fighting the clawing panic within. Cassie knew the emotion behind that expression and followed her out.

'Mavis?'

'Not here, Cassie.' Mavis fled to the car.

'Well?' Cassie put the key in the ignition. She touched Mavis' shoulder. 'Well? How can I help?'

Mavis looked out of the car window; the shops and people were a watery blur. 'You can't. No one can.'

'What did he say?'

'He said … he tested to make sure …' Mavis rocked in her misery, 'I'm pregnant!'

'How?'

Mavis looked at her, the answer obvious.

'I mean … I know how, but why? This sort of thing can't happen in this day and age. Contraception is supposed to be …'

The expression on Mavis' face suggested the impossible.

'Mavis, you were taking the pill, weren't you? I mean, it couldn't have been a moment of passion. You were living with him.'

'No.'

'Why for heaven's sake not?'

'It gave me headaches. I thought a condom was just as good, and Terry pulled out before he came.'

Cassie clicked her seat belt in and drove out of the car park.

Mavis did not look at her, glad that Cassie had to concentrate on the road.

'It's not that bad, Mavis. Not nowadays.'

'For you! I don't want to be pregnant, Cassie. I'm not gettin' married, am I?'

'Nowadays that's not an issue.'

Silence.

'There aren't that many options. You have it and keep it, have and put it up for adoption, or you don't. That's it!'

'I know. The doctor said as much. He gave me a referral to a Sydney clinic if I … You've seen the anti-abortion protests on the news, Cassie. I don't think I can go through that ever.'

'Adoption then?'

'I'd have to have the baby. Everyone would know. Cassie, it was hard enough at work, livin' with the side-looks and the whispers when I'd go in after a fight.'

'Maybe the ugliness of the protests is media beat up. Anyway, the relief when it's over would, I imagine, be like having a collapsed lung inflated. There're good counselling services too. The post trauma, I've heard people say, comes from the conditions associated with falling pregnant. It depends on how you think about the foetus. Is life from conception, only after the quickening, or somewhere in between?'

'Quickenin'?'

'The first movement of the foetus in the womb felt by the mother.'

'You know a lot about this.'

For Cassie, her experience had been a lifetime ago. 'I used to know a girl who faced the same choice.'

'And?'

Past and present flickered, but the images did not resolve. 'She decided on abortion.'

'And?'

'Her story *then* shouldn't define yours *now*.'

'Things like that do though, don't they? We see life through the filter of experiences – ours and other people's. That's why you warned me about Terry, isn't it?'

Cassie didn't respond but pondered on what Mavis had said, seeing a truth in it.

'What happened to her, Cassie?'

'She got on with her life but for a *long* while became what circumstance made her.'

'What do you think she'd tell me?'

'Whatever you do, it has to be *your* choice, not just a reaction.' Cassie paused.

Corridors of sunlight streamed through the bare winter trees in the passing rural scene. Regret in both women tinged the silence in the car.

Finally, Cassie broke the silence. 'All right, let's deal with this afternoon. What are you going to say when we get back to Minna's?'

'Do we have to say anything?'

'Course you do! They know I took you to the doctor's.'

'I don't want anyone to know.'

'Then, think about it on the way there.'

'What would you do?'

It'd been a terrible, lonely time for Cassie. 'What I would do is not important. We have very different backgrounds. As I said, you have to make a choice, not mirror what someone else chose or would choose. I've learnt things are not that simple when it's happening to you. Not when it's your whole future at stake. I don't know what I'd do if I was pregnant now. There is one thing really important in all of this; you are not alone. Lots of people love you and will stick by you, me included.'

As is often the case, the imagined outcome has little connection to reality. When Mavis entered, Minna took one look at her face and said, 'You're pregnant, right?'

Mavis nodded.

'I thought so. Your reaction to kitchen smells was a giveaway. It's not the end of the world, Mavis.'

Chapter 35

'A successful team beats with one heart,' Martin Jones had said and yet Michael and he stood in the dance studio unconsciously aligned, excluding Cassie from the creative dialogue.

After numerous attempts at input, Cassie picked up her towel and rehearsal bag and left. Angry but with a veneer of calm, she decided on a shower. When she was cool, she would remind them that coming together was a beginning. Communicating together was progress. Working together was success. She would not cast them as chauvinists strong though that impulse was.

'What the …?' Martin said.

Michael followed, catching up at the door of the lift. 'Hey, wait up. What's got into you?'

'Nothing a little respect won't fix.' She pushed her anger down. 'I have no idea what it was like for you when you danced with Kate, but we agreed to collaborate. That was the deal, remember? Don't give me that guff 'the man leads and the woman follows'. In social dancing, sure. Not when you are part of a team and in the choreography stage. In competition, it's a dialogue. I'm not dancing any more tonight. I'll speak to you and Martin when I am not so hot!'

Michael blocked her exit. 'You're behaviour is really immature. Storming off doesn't solve the problem.'

'Again, a matter of interpretation. I saw it more as a time

out to cool down. You need to decide if you want a partner or a life-sized doll.' Cassie pushed the lift button again.

'You're overreacting …'

'Don't tell me I'm overreacting, you insensitive clod. I am your partner; that means I am treated as an equal. I am out of any relationship, platonic or otherwise, if I'm treated as a possession or the silent little woman.'

The lift doors opened, and she pushed him out of her way. Michael put his hand and foot in the door to stop its closure.

'And don't try to control my behaviour.' She kicked him in the shins.

The doors closed. Tears of frustration welled in her eyes as the lift descended.

* * *

Not a car in sight, Cassie thought, regretting very much the manner of her exit. Returning to the lounge, she flicked on the television. She zoned out as the news played in the background. A tearful Bob Hawke in interview snagged her attention. Crocodile tears, she thought. If he were serious about his infidelity, he wouldn't be making a bid for sympathy now. Disgusted, she switched the set off.

Drained, Cassie read Minna's newspaper article about systematic anomalies in land valuations in the region.

'Well, do I need armour?' Michael asked from the doorway.

Embarrassed, she said, 'No, you're safe. Look, Mike, I …'

'Me first. I'm sorry that we didn't give you input, Cassie. Don't bite my head off! I forgot about our deal. My only excuse is that I brought the pattern of my dance relationship with Kate to ours. I am sorry.'

'Kate must have really changed. I can't imagine her being a bystander in the creative process.'

'Well, she was.'

'Thanks for the apology. I am so sorry I kicked you, but, for the record, don't try to control me.'

'We're both at fault.'

She looked at his leg. 'Does it hurt very much?'

'Not after the surgeon finished with me. Look, Cassie, I get now that collaboration means more to you than information sharing. Right?'

'Yes,' Cassie paused, wanting to get her part right, 'and I need to speak up before I get upset especially if I feel imposed on.' Memory flickered. She concentrated on it but could not see through to its meaning.

Squatting with his hands on her chair, he said, 'I'm sorry I've put that frown there and even more sorry about today. Will you be my partner?'

She looked at him, trying to assess the subtext to what he said. She was undecided and could feel anger welling up within.

'Well?' Michael asked.

'Speaking of that, how could you ask me to partner you, knowing you might join the RAAF?'

'It wasn't and isn't set in concrete.'

'You should've told me from the start. That was the deal! Anything that affects the partnership, I have a say in!'

'Geez, I didn't see that switch coming! What happened to "Our dance partnership shouldn't be a deciding factor in my career path"?'

'Men always think there are excuses for putting their wants first! If that's the way it's going to be, I'd be better off with Jake.'

'Is that what his call last night was about?'

'Among other things.'

'Which one of us are you playing, Cassie?'

'Neither of you. Jake and I are … I don't owe you an explanation!'

Silence, long and intense.

'You have a point, Cassie. I was selfish. If I concede you have a say in any future decision, can we call a truce?'

'It's a deal.'

In her rising, Michael pulled her forward and kissed her, a brush of lips. They lingered and then she pulled away gently.

'Michael …'

'The kiss of friends sealing a deal, perhaps you'd prefer to toast the agreement with a cuppa.'

'I think …' Cassie was tired of her confusion. Life was too short to waste on waiting for another's lead. Her father, a poker player, would have said it was time to call on his hand. 'What's going on with us?'

It was a difficult moment for Michael. This was the last thing he had expected that evening as he left the studio. He cared about Cassie, wanted the relationship, but knew there would be pain for them both if he took up the RAAF option. Was it fair to either of them?

In the silence, Cassie added, 'Is there something beyond friendship here?'

'If there was, how would you feel about it?'

'Relieved. I've spent the past trying to protect myself from hurt. It can't be done. So I've decided to get the most out of the moment and relationships. The future can take care of itself. And you feel …?'

'I care for you and want to be a couple on and off the floor.'

Cassie stepped in to Michael, her face upturned. He kissed

her forehead and then her lips, a series of gentle caresses that increased with passion. Sensitive to Cassie's signals, he held himself in check and separated from her in a lingering kiss.

'I'm a little uneasy about telling Minna and George and the others.'

'Don't be. They're quick. They'll see how things are. We should see Martin and work out how to make this partnership work.'

* * *

Settled in the lounge room an hour later, George considered Minna.

Looking up at him, she asked, 'What?'

'Nothing.'

'I can see it's not. Out with it.'

'I don't want an argument.'

'It's serious then.'

'I was shocked listening to you and Trixie. I never thought you were the sort to deny aging. I'm disappointed in you.'

Minna frowned; he had never voiced such sentiments before.

'Ditch the long sleeves. You look great! If anything …'

About to interrupt him and explain herself, Minna lost her train of thought as she absorbed Cassie and Michael's entrance.

'You're like a rare wine; age has only increased your value.' George turned to see what had gobsmacked his loquacious wife. He took in the handholding but finished his sentence.

Minna looked beyond the handholding to the difference in Michael. Unsure of what to say, she chose to protect the ground hard won since his return. 'Very nicely said. Hello you two, have a good practice?'

'Great!' Michael replied. 'Who's chef tonight?'

'Gary,' Minna replied. She looked at her husband, concerned at the effect of his silence. 'Do you feel like dusting off this old bottle and taking it out for dinner?'

'So that's why he phoned earlier and apologised about letting everyone down at dinner,' George said. 'Why don't you take your girl out for the night? I'm going to wine and dine mine.'

On her way upstairs, Minna worried about the implications of the relationship and its impact on Michael's future. He was not the sort to be content with life in the small arena. Would he put that at risk and come to regret the choice and resent the cause?

Like Minna, George also worried about the future. Aware now of Michael's career options; either choice, Air Force or journalism, meant huge demands on time as well as focused application. That did not marry with a long-distance romance. Then, what a man found attractive at twenty-one was different from a decade later.

* * *

'I've been worryin' about Macbeth's decision all night,' Matt Winston said from amidst his bevy of tarted up beauties. 'He's wrong about bein' in the middle of the river of blood and returnin' bein' as hard as goin' on. Dad and I was talkin' last night about the play and how battle affects soldiers. He says that over time they become desensitised to the bloodshed. They stop thinkin' about other solutions and battle on, reflex like, until it's over or they're dead. Do you think that's what's happened to Macbeth?'

Surprised by Matt's personal response to the text, Cassie began, 'Well …'

'If he was desensitised, he wouldn't be considerin' his direction, now would he?' commented Chook as he moved his bag down to one of the front desks, 'and he wouldn't have been shocked by Duncan's death ...'

'He was shocked by Duncan's death because it was ...' Matt answered, 'what was that word?'

'A base act is what you're tryin' to say, Matt. Isn't that what you said, Miss?' offered Stella. 'It went against his code. It was who he killed and what that meant and not the actual killing that got him.'

'I reckon Dad and Stella are both right,' Matt said. 'Look at the way he hacked his way through the battlefield when the play first started. He didn't lose his nerve then. I reckon he only ever sees one way out of conflict and that's combat.'

'Then explain his stoppin' in the river, you nong!' Tony said exasperated.

'I think,' Stella said jumping in, 'that this play shows everyone is capable of evil if the right buttons are pushed. Remember how respected Macbeth was at the beginning.'

'Nah ...' another student said. The discussion seesawed from one issue to the next.

Disturbed by Stella's insight, Cassie wondered if the universal truths so often attributed to Shakespearean plays applied in Terry and Talbut's contexts. Gary had believed Terry to be a good man yet he had not turned out so. Coachman believed Talbut was a good man. The jury was still out on a verdict about him. How did anyone see beyond the masks that people wear? This was something to talk over with Michael when he returned from Sydney. His openness to such discussion was another thing she valued about him.

Returning to the staffroom, Cassie realised that she loved it when 10C's mind-wheels turned. She could almost hear them grinding in the problem solving tasks before them. Most of all she loved discussion. There were many days now when she almost floated upstairs carried by the exhilaration of the work. She might just stay a teacher after all.

* * *

Dishevelled and numb, Mavis sat under a canopy of trees near Madison House, rugged in a thick blanket, unable to face the horrors of sleep and the fears that hung in her room. The pearl grey of winter's dawn contrasted sharply with the textured darkness of the leaves overhead.

She watched George walk up the driveway. He moved slowly, wearied by his night vigil over a dying friend. She remained silent, trying to meld with the shadows, separated from him by more than age.

George sensed rather than saw her. He hesitated on the lawns, aware of her crisis but reluctant to coerce her to his view. He decided against acknowledging her presence and slowly climbed the verandah stairs. He paused again once he reached the verandah.

His silence added to Mavis' isolation. She altered her position, curled, and looked inland toward the mountains. She looked vulnerable in the half-light.

Compassion carried him to her side. Solicitude motivated speech. 'You're up early. It's too cold for you to be out here.'

'I couldn't sleep. It's easier to think out here. Besides, I feel more in touch with life out here.'

'What about?'

'I was just wishin' I was a kangaroo.'

'Why on earth would anyone wish that?'

'If I were a kangaroo, I'd be able to suspend the pregnancy until the time was right for me to have this baby.'

'Can they do that?'

She nodded. 'It was on an SBS documentary last week.'

George chose his words carefully. 'Life rarely happens when we're ready for it, Mavis. I fell in love and married long before I planned. Retirement caught me unawares. Life is untimely. Fighting against it makes things worse.'

She was silent.

'Look at me two years ago. I was lost; I felt trapped. I searched for a solution. Prayer helped.'

'God's turned his back on me, George.'

'It's man who separates himself from God, Mavis, not the other way around.'

The morning birds called to one another. Waves whispered to the rocks.

He stood, 'I looked into death's face tonight; can you shoulder its burden? I want to comfort you, but I can't. What you're contemplating is against everything that I believe.' He moved away from her, paused and then added, 'I'm praying for you.'

As he entered the house, George felt bitter about the petty politics and fiscal interests that hampered his vision of life for the elderly. The old and infirm were not empty Cornflake boxes, something discarded into a holding area until disposal. Care with dignity meant nourishment of the spirit as well. The right to life issue elicited such passion for the unborn. Why was there indifference when it came to the aged? Fred's end is not going to be for nothing, George thought, as he trudged up to bed. I will make a difference, so help me God!

* * *

Four rings of students from 10C dotted the oval, that windless winter's day, with a student in the centre of each circle. It was pleasant outside, more like the autumn. Students on the perimeter called out promises, attempting to lure the centre person to them. The activity was loud and interspersed with laughter.

Eventually, with the problem solved, Cassie had her class come together, bobbing down or sitting on the grass as they listened.

'What won you over, Chook, and why?'

'At first, I thought I wanted money and a fast car, Miss, and my group battled over how much and the type. Then Stella offered me my mum and dad back together. I was tempted and so I started walkin' towards her but realised it wouldn't be any good because it would be goin' back to the way it was, so I stopped.'

'But you chose Stella in the end?'

'When she offered me a happy, loving family like the Waltons.'

Moved, Cassie and the group were silent.

Matt Winston broke the silence. 'At first, Miss, it was fun playin' with the power to give Tony things we all wanted. After a while, it got borin' because we couldn't get him to take more than a few steps before he changed his mind. We stood around for a while thinkin' this was a dumb thing to be doin'. Then I remembered Tony wanted his girl to talk to him like she does the kids in her class: ideas and stuff. So, I offered him that. He came to me like a shot.'

'What does this tell us then about the class' belief that the witches made Macbeth murder Duncan?'

'The spell at the beginning is a false lead, isn't it, Miss?' Stella asked. 'It's more about letting the bad things in life come to the surface than putting a spell on Macbeth. The witches told Macbeth and Banquo the same thing, but only Macbeth chose murder to get it.'

Excited, Tony said, 'So the kids in the circle were like the witches?'

One of the girls began to sing *I'll Put a Spell on You* and a few boys and girls joined in, but the song faded because they didn't know all of the words.

'Okay, now given what Tony has realised, what does that mean about their influence on Macbeth?'

The class looked expectantly at Cassie in the belief she would provide the answer.

'Matt and Stella, how did you win the person to your side?'

Matt's brow furrowed in thought. Stella, used to giving way to the boys, waited until she was sure Matt did not have the answer. 'We used what we knew about the person.'

'Good. Was Macbeth under a spell when he chose to kill Duncan and the others?'

Matt answered, 'Yes.'

'No,' Tony said, 'the witches used what they knew about Macbeth to make him think about taking the throne. He was a man of action and not the sort to wait around.'

'You're wrong, Tony,' Matt said. 'Remember Stella said that the witches spell was general and meant to let bad things come to the surface.'

'I didn't say surface,' Stella said.

'You should of then,' Matt replied, 'the spell allowed the bad side of Macbeth to come out. It made it possible for him to be conned by the prophesy.'

'Thoughtful answers, Matt and Tony. On the way back to class, I want you to decide which explanation you agree with. Also, think about the meaning of the words: conned, tempted, corrupted, and decide which word describes how Macbeth was influenced. You can talk it over on the way back if you want. When we get back, I want you to reflect on what you've learnt from studying the play and from the activities we've done, in a journal entry. Don't forget I'm interested in your reasons.'

'One thing I learnt,' Matt said to Tony as they walked a few people behind Cassie, 'is that some people shouldn't take their clothes off. Those witches in that Polanski movie still give me nightmares. I never thought being naked could be ugly!'

Seeing Talbut as they passed, Cassie realised that he, like Terry, was accountable for his choices and behaviour as were they all. She wondered about the motive underlying his behaviour.

Chapter 36

The **Board President** of the RAAF Officer Interview Boards came to the door and asked each candidate to return.

Michael walked to free his body of its growing agitation, occasionally leaving the Pitt St, Sydney waiting room to stretch his legs in the corridor. Finally he was called in.

'Congratulations, Michael. We're going to recommend you for an appointment as an officer.'

'How long before I know what's going to happen?'

'Within the next six to eight weeks, you'll receive a letter offering you a commission as an officer cadet. Once you formally accept, you'll be given formal joining instructions for the Defence Force Academy.'

After the hand shaking, Michael had walked back to the parking station. He had felt terrific.

Back at Madison House, the complexity of his situation dampened his high. Minna and George had been thrilled, embracing him, asking him to go back over the whole experience in minute detail. In the lounge room, they discussed the logistics of his move. Neither of them asked what would happen to his relationship with Cassie. Three years was a long time to be separated, and long distance romances rarely worked out.

There were many things that Minna wanted to say to Michael but did not. It was a matter of trusting Michael's judgement. Of being sensitive to where their respective lives overlapped. This was not something on which she should comment.

* * *

The blood sun that afternoon seemed unnaturally close to Cassie as she walked with her class on the dry sand avoiding the winter-cold waves that lapped the shore. She was really pleased with her students' draft products from the writing excursion into town and the landscape exploration along the foreshore.

Glad to get off the noisy school bus at that Friday's end, Cassie had been engrossed in marking students off her roll, collecting their work, farewelling them, and so missed at first Michael standing next to her car.

All the things that Michael had planned to say were, in the end, left unsaid. He delivered the news to her simply before she climbed in her car.

'Great,' Cassie said, looking over the car, trying to be genuinely pleased for him.

As the car grumbled into life, Michael asked, 'So that means you're okay with me accepting the offer?'

'Yes.' There was nothing else she could say, knowing that she would not accept his input if the situation was reversed. 'Feel like a coffee? I do.'

He agreed, not knowing where the mood would take them.

'Harbourview?' she asked. She was a jangle of emotions and did not really know what she truly felt.

'Are you sure about this, Cassie?'

'I was wrong before. I don't think anyone has the right to make choices for someone else, and no one should be asked to give up things that are really important.'

Sitting outdoors at the sidewalk café, the camaraderie of the passing community gave Cassie the time she needed to process Michael's news. After he was gone, what would she do? Stay in teaching? She didn't think so. Go back to Sydney? What then?

'Look, this can be worked out,' Michael replied.

'It's good Martin's away at the moment,' Cassie said. 'I don't feel like dealing with his reaction just yet.'

'Forget Martin. On the way back, I realised I don't want to be separated from you. There are schools in Canberra. Come with me.'

Cassie reached for a glass of water, having gulped her cake.

'While I was waiting for the Board results, I was talking to this married guy. He said that he's moving his family to Canberra for the three years. The RAAF provide rental assistance so while you're looking for work we'd make ends meet.'

'It's such a big thing. We haven't even …' How could she approach the sex thing? They didn't even know if they were compatible that way.

'Marry me.'

'What?'

'Hardly the reaction I expected. We're either in love or not. Which is it?'

'There's more to my life than …' Cassie stopped. Before she became part of a relationship, there were questions she needed answered. She knew one thing for certain: she could not be a Melissa or a Mavis, embracing the tedium of household chores and servility. 'There's a lot more to getting married than being in love. That can wear out in living together.'

Perplexed and hurt, Michael said, 'If you think that …' He stood, half turned, hesitated and then left.

* * *

Using family as an excuse, Cassie returned home for the weekend.

In that long Saturday night at home, Cassie realised that her deepest fear was that she was inadequate. Jake loved her yet she had not been enough for him. Would the same be true of Michael? His career path by necessity involved separation. Turning on the bedside light, she was glad now that Leonie no longer shared with her. She read for a while and then discarded the book. Uneasy in mind and heart, she decided on a camomile tea.

Standing at the bench waiting for the kettle to boil, memories of her mother flooded Cassie's vision. The kitchen had been Nancy's domain. The terracotta floor tiles had been a reminder of her parents' honeymoon in Mexico. The hanging plants reflected Nancy's love of gardening. Like a mirror reflecting into many mirrors, images of their family life in the kitchen, joyful and heartbreaking, repeated and replayed. Her head ached. She sighed from frustration.

In an attempt to ease the headache, Cassie pulled her short hair back and up to lessen the tension, then slumped to the floor.

The kettle's whistle woke Leonie.

'Oi!' bellowed Tom Sleight from his bedroom. 'For God's sake, turn that kettle off.'

Leonie hesitated as she stood barefooted in the kitchen, her flimsy nightwear a contrast to Cassie's beige and blue striped short pyjamas. 'Cassie? Can I help?'

'Oh, sorry, I didn't mean to wake you.'

'I couldn't sleep anyway. Too excited about tomorrow's interview and the prospect of a job in Paris. Ahh! Now, why are you up?'

As they talked, Cassie realised that sharing thoughts was like sorting cards in a game of Patience.

'I've thought of myself as Cassie, the teacher, or Cassie, the dancer, never Cassie, the housewife. As for Cassie, the lover, she was inadequate, a loser.'

'Not a loser, Cassie. Jake wants you back. He's grown up.'

'For how long? I really don't know how to hold someone … Mum said Dad's other relationships were about good sex … I thought the sex was good between Jake and me but he wandered anyway.'

'Do you seriously think Mum understood Dad or even herself? Think, Cassie! Dad's other women didn't hold him either. Personally, I think it was more about power and ego. That's something the men we grew up with shared, that and being selfish. None of the men we know really committed to their wives. They never shared anything significant: not money, not decision making, and as for interests – token time. Michael doesn't sound like someone who does the talk but not the walk.'

'He's not; he's like his Dad.'

'Two rare men then. So what's his parents' relationship like?'

'Different, a loving one based on equality and respect; at least that's what it looks like.'

'Then you can have it all.'

'Is that possible, realistically? I've a hard enough time fitting in dancing with school work. If I try to be everything: teacher, wife, housekeeper, lover, maybe mother … Even listing it makes me feel exhausted and inadequate. And in that list, there isn't any consideration of being me, meeting my needs.'

'Well, there's your answer then. Choose career, stay single but not celibate. Career and romance … What more can a girl want? That's what I'm going to do.'

'I don't think that'll work for me. Seriously, will it for you? I see sex … intercourse … as more than the satisfaction of a demanding appetite or an addictive impulse. For me, the oneness and unity that comes with it engenders soul.' She did not add that soul, that mysterious, positive, powerful force at the core of her being, was too valuable to give away again lightly. 'Isn't that what you felt with John?'

'No. I see now he was Mr Right for Me Then. I'm a bit confused, Cassie. If you think like that, then your job isn't as important.'

'No, it has to be. There's more to me than being half of someone else's coin. I think that's how Mum became Dad's shadow and lost herself. I don't want to be like that.'

'Then you won't. I've been thinking about this for a long time. I really believe there is synchronicity in life; that it's a matter of making the right choice and then everything else falls into place. Look at how things have worked for you so far and all because you chose to walk away from Jake; and for me because I walked away from John. God, I might land a job in Paris in fashion! I never thought that would happen a year ago. You look terrible. Why not stay up here a few days while you sort things out?'

'I do have a headache. Maybe …'

'I'll get Dad to call your work and let them know.'

Chapter 37

The morning was fog-bound. Cold fingered Meri Bennett's bare arms. She regretted leaving her school jacket at home. She had overslept and almost missed the bus.

The weather forecast had said it would be a warm day without the usual onshore winds. On the trip down from the hills, she thought that the fog looked like an animal, crouched low, lying in wait for its prey.

Seven-twenty. Meri hated these early lessons with Talbut now; regretted choosing 3- Unit English. The cut off point for Year 11 students to change subjects had passed ages ago before the recent problems with Talbut had surfaced. When he looked at her, her flesh crawled. Touching her texts made her skin crawl.

Her footsteps echoed in the quadrangle.

The seniors' common room on the ground floor was also empty. It was a spacious room, furnished with grey modular armchairs and coffee tables. Disused Styrofoam cups lay where yesterday's users had left them.

Meri looked at her watch. It was possible the others had arrived, made a cup of coffee, and headed for the classroom. They found comfort in being en masse and would have been uncomfortable risking a tête-à-tête with Talbut for tardiness. As she hurried after them, Meri hoped she could avoid the perils of that one-to-one meeting. She'd been pawed enough.

The usual entry to the building was locked. Strange, the

cleaners usually leave it open, she thought. Hurrying from one end of the building to the other, she tried each entrance as she did so. Maybe it's a sign. The last door was open. Damn! It wasn't a sign.

The stillness and silence within the building reinforced Meri's isolation. As she walked, she listened for the sound of her class but heard nothing.

Outside the room, relief flooded her. It was empty. Maybe Talbut was away. If that was the case, why hadn't anyone been in the common room? Meri took a step she would live to regret.

'Only dull people are late, Ms Bennett.'

'Sorry, sir.' Meri was relieved at his displeasure. This mood usually meant biting sarcasm and not the amorous advances of his lighter moments.

The prettiest girl in Year 11, Meri's hair reminded Talbut of fire. From her behaviour with her last boyfriend at breaks, he suspected she was hot in other ways as well. Talbut had hungered for her since she had matured in Year 10 but had kept to his rule of no one under eighteen beyond the game of innuendo and other forms of flirtation.

Then, of course, there had been Kara. She had pursued him. Her flattering attention had done much to salve his ego wounded by his ex-wife's ridicule and the behaviour of his female colleagues. Kara's need for overt sexual displays had become tedious though. Year 12 girls, the pick of them, had been a refreshing diversion from Kara. That game had been going well until Samantha's intervention. That bitch would get hers one day!

'There's no point in a lesson, is there, sir, with the others away?'

'Nonsense, if I thought that, I'd have cancelled class when I looked at the Geography excursion list yesterday.'

'The excursion!' How could I have forgotten it? The argument with her father the night before and the tension that morning had meant that she had broken the ritual of checking her school diary for notes.

'We can discuss your last assessment task. Mr Selton was most impressed with your perspective on Lear. It was an unconventional response with some unorthodox views that I'd like us to re-examine. Don't dally in the doorway.'

His work-like attitude allayed her fears. She moved to a desk.

'Can't discuss it from there. I've only one copy.' He moved his chair closer to hers. Too close for Meri's liking.

Her jaw clenched. Wary, she widened the distance between their chairs.

'Now, let me see …' He scanned her work, looking for the issue in question. 'Here it is. A most unusual interpretation of Cordelia's behaviour.' He angled her paper. She could not see it from where she sat.

'Can I read it, sir? I don't know which bit you're referring to.'

'Move closer. I need to see it too.'

Meri searched for a plausible excuse to leave. She did not move.

'If the mountain won't come to Mohammad then …' Talbut deftly moved to her. Finding the closeness disquieting, Meri tensed.

'Something wrong?' He put his hand on her knee.

'Sir, don't … please!' Meri pulled away and stood.

'Don't what? Meri …'

'It is clear, Mr Talbut,' Samantha said coming into view at the doorway, 'that Ms Bennett is distressed. Meri, you are free to leave. Wait for me in your common room.'

Tears spilling down her face, Meri left, 'Thanks, Miss.'

'How dare you!' Talbut said.

'The same could be said to you. Issues of trust are obviously not high on your agenda. I'll be seeing Coachman about this.'

Samantha left.

The common room was empty when Meri returned. She fumbled with her locker keys but managed to open it. She shoved her folder in and grabbed her purse. As she closed the locker, she caught her reflection in the small mirror hung inside. Her mascara had run. She had to get out of there. She needed to feel safe so she left hurriedly.

* * *

Concerned with Meri's wellbeing, Samantha lost time looking for her before heading for the Principal's office.

The receptionist, working the before school shift, directed Samantha to the chairs outside the Principal's office. Waiting, Samantha noticed the fine grain in the panelling around the reception cubicle, the texture of the tiles, their sheen, and the clock ticking.

The door opened and Talbut strolled out, his loathing directed at Samantha.

'You're next, Mrs Smith.'

Sunlight streamed in behind the Principal as he leant back in his swivel chair. His grey, cropped hair contrasted against the dark shadows that covered his face. 'Revenge is a nasty business, Mrs Smith.'

'What?'

'Mr Talbut has updated me on the situation. Your inexperience understandably led you to misinterpret the scene. Over the years, I've heard scores of scorned girls who have tried to wreck a teacher's career because he rebuffed them.'

'It isn't …'

'Infatuation with a male teacher is part of adolescence. I won't listen to slander.'

Shocked by his reaction, Samantha left the office. Despite the pressure of a full day of classes, she went to Coachman.

'What is it now?'

Having heard Samantha out, Coachman said, 'I'll speak to the boss and organise for Talbut to be taken off classes and given … I don't know, something meaningful while we sort this out. Talbut has a right to tell his version just as you have a responsibility to express your perception of events. Meri is the key to this. In the meantime, say nothing.'

'Shouldn't we call the police?'

'That's up to Meri and her parents if they have a complaint.'

The rest of that day was like any other. Talbut seemed indifferent to the morning's events and pleased to have been assigned curriculum matters to work on instead of teaching. Samantha considered discussing the matter with Rajes that afternoon but decided against it. She decided to wait until Meri filed a complaint with the Principal. Meri was absent from school for the remainder of that week.

* * *

'Did you forget, Cassie?' Mavis asked anxiously after Cassie parked at Madison House the Monday morning of her return. Michael and Gary stood behind Mavis on the verandah.

'The court case,' Michael said with a strained smile.

'Oh, I did. Sorry!' Cassie looked at her watch. 'There's time for a coffee, isn't there?'

'What about letting your work know?' Gary asked.

'Oh … I put the leave paperwork in ages ago.'

'C'mon then,' Michael said, 'you can get a coffee in town before we go to the courthouse. Since your car is out, Cassie, —'

'Okay.'

Michael manoeuvred Mavis into the front passenger seat while Gary and he took the back seat.

Driving, Cassie looked at Michael through the rear-vision mirror. His eyes were fixed on the passing landscape. In the background, Gary maintained a banter that to Cassie was just noise. This was not how she had imagined her return.

* * *

Midmorning light streamed in through the glass windows of the courthouse foyer between the two magistrates' courts. Cassie and Mavis, and then Gary and Michael sat on the red vinyl seating along adjacent sides of the foyer.

Finally, the court constable called Terry. He then spoke in undertones to Mavis, directing her into the main body of the court.

Inside the court, Cassie, Gary, and Michael sat on one of the long benches in the gallery at the back of the room. A coloured partition, waist high, separated the gallery from the body of the court. Mavis stood before the bar, between the court constable and stenographers' boxes. Terry stood in the dock to Mavis' right behind the bar. He looked pale and haggard.

Everything in the room was maple. It was windowless and claustrophobic. By contrast, the atmosphere was informal, something Cassie had not expected. She had thought the magistrate and court officials would be dressed in wigs and gowns. Too much *Rumpole of the Bailey,* she thought. The court officials were relaxed, and the situation was unintimidating. Their joviality and conversation jarred.

The court constable stood and read the charge. 'That Terry Kirkby did unlawfully assault Mavis Mills on Sunday 7 May, Wednesday 17 May, Thursday 18 May, and Sunday 21 May 1989.'

The Magistrate looked down at Terry and after having asked him whether he understood the charges asked, 'How do you plead?'

'Guilty.'

The Police Prosecutor then read the facts, 'Your worship, the complainant and the defendant were in a defacto relationship and resided at Beachview apartment 412 where the following incident took place. About seven pm, Ms Mills returned to her home after a visit to her parents' farm. The argument occurred over Ms Mills' taking the defendant's car earlier that day and a subsequent accident.'

Mavis stood below the bench, her body closed, her eyes downcast.

'On Sunday 7 May, the defendant repeatedly struck Ms Mills with his fists, finally knocking her to the floor. He then dragged her across the floor of their apartment, throwing her out of the home. The abuse continued in the hallway. When neighbours attempted to intervene, Mr Kirkby was abusive and removed Ms Mills back into the flat. Further acts of violence were reported on Wednesday 17 May and Thursday 18 May by neighbours but without any complaint being filed at the time. The final assault took place on Sunday 21 May when Ms Mills tried to leave the relationship. Ms Mills sustained a deep cut to her right forehead, severe bruising to her neck, face, shoulders, and breasts. Her arms suffered carpet burns and additional bruising. There was older bruising over her body indicating previous acts of violence. No internal injuries were sustained.'

The magistrate then turned to Mavis and asked if she had anything further to add. She did not. She was pale and clearly intimidated. She shook her head. The court constable asked her to state her response for the court stenographer. She did so; her voice was little more than a whisper.

The magistrate addressed Terry.

Mavis dashed away tears before she turned and looked at him.

'It hurts me your honour … that I've done this to Mavis … I don't know what came over me. I won't touch her again … see her even. There's nothing to keep us together. No reason for us to continue the relationship.' Mavis started. She looked fearfully at Cassie who willed her friend to remain calm. Terry continued, unaware of Mavis' reaction, 'I'd cut off my hands first.'

The magistrate considered the information before him.

The case concluded with Terry placed on a good behaviour bond and issued a fine. It was a first offence and the magistrate was reluctant to impose a severe sentence. He did, however, warn Terry that further contact with and abuse of Mavis could result in confinement.

'Is that all there is to this?' Cassie whispered to Michael.

He shrugged.

'He should've been locked up,' Gary said, audible to all.

'Sgt Evan,' Michael said, 'told me that was unlikely given Terry's assurance that there wouldn't be any further violence, that he accepted that the relationship was terminated. He said that we need to put this into perspective.'

'Perspective! Look at Mavis!' Gary said. 'Is she the woman we know and love?'

'A fine?' Cassie added, 'God, what was the point?'

The courtroom emptied.

Chapter 38

Cassie switched on the dance studio radio as she waited for Michael and Martin Jones to arrive for rehearsal; both were late. She did not recognise the music.

For Cassie, dance was the broken love affair restored. It had survived her separation from it and was sweeter because of the reunion. She loved the sweet intensity of the track. Her movement was improvised, a solo composition of arresting gesture and motion. As she danced, Cassie thought about the cool friendship that Michael now maintained with her. Her carefully prepared explanation to bridge the gulf between them remained unsaid.

With the change in music, Cassie tried to shake off her regret. Refusing to think about the future, she soared on the music's currents.

Ticked off at the delays that had caused him to be late, Michael came to a standstill in the doorway. Cassie seemed oblivious to his presence as she circuited the floor. He studied the dance and then joined her, complementing her form, exploring the transference of weight. This was not a matter of follow the leader. They surrendered to their natures, to the yearning heart, to the dance of opposites and ancient rhythms. They moved as if they were melody and counter melody.

The Jones heard the music as they climbed the stairs. They stood at the entrance of the studio enthralled by the dancers before them.

'Wow!' Martin's wife said to him as they arrived at the studio, 'They really are fantastic, aren't they? Where did they learn that?'

Martin watched them. 'I don't think they have. Watch. They're like musicians in a jam session.'

The couple's movement was now like song and echo. Then it changed to one long soaring melody balanced by one clearly-defined harmony. The exploration of pattern and rhythm was spellbinding and increasingly sensual.

'I see now why you were so excited, Martin.'

The dancers crisscrossed the gleaming parquetry floor, their execution faultless.

'A marriage of grace and beauty. It looks like they've sorted out the problem of the last few weeks. Let's give them some privacy.' They hovered out of sight.

The last bars of the music lingered in the air. Michael swirled Cassie away from him and then brought her back into an embrace. She looked at him then, disturbed by the loss of bliss. The dance ended.

He leant forward and kissed her. Senses reeling, pulse pounding, the dancers came to an awareness of their surroundings with the Jones' spontaneous applause.

Realising too late their intrusion, the spectators withdrew completely.

Pulling Cassie into a private corner in the room, Michael asked, 'Well? Decided yet?'

'No,' Cassie said shyly, 'but I think I'd like to make love anyway.'

* * *

'Anybody got chalk?' Van der Huffen entered the staff room

in a hurry. 'Third week of term two and supplies have run out! Either there's too much chalk and not enough talk, or someone forgot to put in the order.'

'Thanks,' he said to Cassie who had passed him a few sticks. He turned and stepped into Fuller.

'Sorry, mate,' Van der Huffen said.

'Wait till you hear what's happened!' Fuller's voice was full of news.

Van der Huffen re-entered the room.

'I was over at the front office, working on Year 11 reports and having a lot of trouble, I might add—'

'Get on with it. I don't have all day. I've a class waiting.'

'Sorry, Vander. Well, as I was saying, I was over at the front—'

'Yes, yes,' Rajes said, 'we've been through that! What happened?'

'Who should walk in but the Regional Director, one of our Year 11 girls, and her parents!'

'Go on!' Van der Huffen said.

'What?' asked Cassie.

'They disappeared into the Principal's office. I made an excuse to hang around as did everyone else in the office at that time. Boy, some people are nosy!'

'My God, what's going on?' Van der Huffen asked.

'Something to do with staff impropriety,' Fuller replied.

'What?' the men chorused, and then sat down, shocked.

'Who?' Van der Huffen asked.

Fuller said from the phone table, 'Must be someone in our faculty because I heard the receptionist phone and ask Coachman to come over.'

Cassie looked at Samantha and mouthed, 'Talbut?'

Samantha nodded.

Van der Huffen said, 'Get on with it, man. What happened?'

'Don't know.'

'What! Why didn't you wait?' his audience chorused.

'I ran out of reasons to be there. I asked Amber to give us three short bursts on the phone if there were any more interesting developments.'

'Well, well, well! I'm speechless,' Van der Huffen said, retreating to his class.

Seconds later, Coachman put his head into the staff room. 'Mrs Smith, the Principal wants you in his office right now!'

* * *

'Anything you can add that might cast light on where the truth lies?' Principal Cameron asked Samantha.

After a quick glance at Meri and her parents, she said, 'The women of the English faculty found Talbut's behaviour offensive throughout last year.'

'Yes,' the Principal said, 'know all about that. Anything else?'

'Last year, Talbut tried to … he made a sexual advance when we were alone in the textbook room.'

'Did you file a complaint?'

'No.'

'Then how do I know your version of whatever happened is the truth?' Addressing Coachman, Cameron asked, 'How credible is Mrs Smith's version? There were rumours that she and Talbut had an affair, one that ended badly.'

Shocked, Samantha said, 'What?'

Coachman replied, 'That seemed to be the case, but I have no idea what happened between them. Of the two, she never expressed malice. As for the welfare of senior girls, she has appeared to act with genuine concern.'

* * *

'Well?' Selton asked Samantha on her return to the staff room.

'It's an inquiry into Talbut's misconduct with Meri Bennett.'

'But Tina and her friends were moved!' Cassie said.

'Meri's in Year 11,' Samantha said.

Selton and a number of the men were shocked at the double disclosure.

'When and how did his flirtation become improper?' Fuller asked.

'What?' Selton asked, appalled at the implications of Fuller's comment.

'While I realise that I have the reputation of a dirty old man to uphold, there are some things that go beyond the pale, Selton, so don't look at me like that!'

'You never said anything about Meri,' Cassie said to Samantha.

Redirecting her frustration at Cassie, Samantha eyed her coldly. 'Like telling you would have made a difference.'

The telephone startled Fuller who spilt his coffee.

'You actually witnessed something, Samantha?' Selton asked.

'I thought I did but not anything strong enough to corroborate Meri's accusation beyond the fact that I believed Meri was in danger. There was nothing else on record against him except for Cassie and my objections to his behaviour last year. That's been dismissed as irrelevant in this schoolgirl matter.'

Cassie considered seeing the Principal herself to establish that this incident was one in a pattern. Where was her verifiable proof? She tuned back into the faculty conversation and heard Selton say, 'The thing is we don't really know what happened. There is reasonable doubt. You know the rest.'

* * *

'What are you all waiting for?' Coachman said from the doorway. 'You have classes to teach, and rumours to dispel. Talbut's taken leave until this matter is sorted out.'

The staff gathered their materials and left without a word.

Walking down the corridor, Cassie realised how close she had walked to danger. The stairwell scene returned to her vividly.

At the end of the day, the staff came uneasily together in staggered returns from their classes. Caffeine steadied concern.

'I've been thinking,' Selton said, 'about the implications of working in a world where actions are interpreted through a Talbut distorted glass!'

'I know,' Fuller said. 'It's enormous!'

'The school system is built upon the integrity of a teacher's word. If that foundation is removed …' Van der Huffen said. 'Imagine a school where credibility is undermined and accusations and student interpretations are treated as fact.'

'So you want to retain the status quo?' Cassie was incredulous.

A firm, 'No!' was the collective response.

'What then?'

Selton chose his words carefully, 'We have to be thoughtful in the sort of culture and environment that we allow to develop. We all contribute to it.'

'That's deep,' Fuller said. 'We need time for that to penetrate.'

'As the actress said to the bishop,' was the communal response with the exception of Van der Huffen. He said, 'I question whether we can hear from the actress anymore.'

The Principal called an urgent meeting of the Parents and Citizens Association. It had record attendance. The meeting was heated. The executive staff back-pedalled defensively over staffing and refused comment on Talbut's departure, citing the court as the appropriate venue for that matter.

Chapter 39

It looked like any other suburban street of inner Sydney. The houses, built in the first quarter of the century, were brick and semi-detached. The street was narrow and not designed for the heavy traffic that passed daily.

Mavis unfolded the piece of paper taken from her denim skirt pocket. She was in the right street but at the wrong end. A thickset man, working with a jackhammer, looked at her. She told herself that he could not possibly know her purpose and hurried away from the noise and dust.

Looking at the street barriers, Mavis assumed it was a sign of roadwork. She stopped and checked the address.

At the end of the street, a noisy group had gathered with placards. Mavis looked at the house number where she had stopped and mentally counted the house numbers to the protesters.

A bus slowed and stopped. The driver looked at Mavis. 'Are you gettin' on or what?' He shook his head when she failed to answer and drove off.

A woman of indiscriminate age, who'd been sitting on the front step of her house, moved to the fence. 'Are you all right? You look lost.'

'No, I know where I'm goin'. Thanks.' Mavis moved on.

One house from the protesters, Mavis saw an elegant, middle-aged woman standing apart from the protest making notes. A camera operator was with her. The trio watched a young woman – head partially shaven, nose-ringed, flimsy dress and heavy shoes – pass through the path cordoned off by police.

The crowd seethed and pushed at the barriers. A missile flew from inside the crowd and splattered red on the woman's feet. Splotches of red covered her legs.

The barriers broke. The corridor to the clinic door closed as the crowd boiled around the woman. The police were scattered like flotsam in rough seas, battling the swell of protesters around her. Placards tilted and waved in the air. Noise reverberated in the street.

The woman was elbowed, knocked over, kicked. She surfaced, clawed her way to the surface. She gasped, screamed for release. The police fought to regroup. They managed to form a single line around her. Safe, she changed course and fled. The crowd cheered.

The police conferred and in the quiet that followed restored the barriers.

Mavis walked around the perimeter of the crowd looking for access. She saw a gap and moved forward. A policewoman, too small in build for this mob, asked Mavis her intent.

'I want to go in.'

'We'll try and shield you. It's not going to be easy.'

'Gettin' to this point was hard. I didn't expect anythin' different now.'

Two rows of blue figures ringed her. They moved forward.

Empowered by their earlier success, the crowd's energy increased. The chanting was unintelligible. The faces were warped, grossly distorted with rage. Something wet hit her face. Mavis palmed it off. Red, thick and clinging. She stared at it. Lost her footing. Went down. The police buoyed her up. Activity around her seemed fast forwarded while she moved in slow motion. The faces leant in at her. She knew their judgement. She waded through it. Her determination infuriated the crowd. It pressed in. Placards. Elbows. Hate. The path closed. The police and Mavis moved forward, ploughing a way to the door. She fell in.

The waiting room was empty with the exception of a receptionist. Mavis was surprised by how ordinary it looked. She looked at her watch. Fifteen minutes early.

The receptionist said, 'The bathroom's that way.'

Back now in the waiting room with her face clean but stain still on her clothing, Mavis picked up a magazine and flicked unseeingly through it. She checked her watch again. It had stopped. She flicked through one magazine after another. She started when she heard her name and fumbled with her handbag.

The consultant looked like she was someone's grandmother.

Mavis answered mechanically at first.

'Are you sure this is what you want?'

'Want? What I want?'

'Dear, you have a choice.' The woman noted Mavis' reaction on her questionnaire. 'I'll walk you through the procedure then, shall I? We'll talk again later.'

The room was small and sterile, the walls white, the furnishing functional. The guide showed Mavis the instruments and explained the procedure.

They entered another room, a typical suburban living room: a lounge, a couple of armchairs, and television. The wall pictures were rural and serene.

'You and a friend wait here for a while after the procedure before you're allowed to leave. Take this pamphlet. Read it carefully. You'll find it's comprehensive.'

They returned to the interview room.

'Now dear. Are you sure this is what you want?'

'I don't have a choice.'

'As I said before, we are about choice.' She stood. 'I know there's a counsellor free; it's been slow the past few weeks.'

* * *

Protected from the steady fall of November rain, Mavis sat in a taxi shelter on the corner of the shopping complex located near Keimera Rail Station. When she saw Cassie's car approaching, Mavis stood, her umbrella flexing in the driving rain.

The wind threatened to snatch the closing car door out of her hand. Mavis battled with it and a suitcase as she climbed in.

'Where have you been, Mavis?'

'Sydney. I did it.'

'What?'

'I went up to an abortion clinic. It doesn't just deal in abortions though. It deals with a whole range of women's needs.'

'Go on.'

'There were protesters outside the clinic. Real awful it was, much worse than seeing at a distance like on TV. Why do they want women to go to back street abortionists?'

'I don't think they do. They've forgotten abortion predates legalisation. What did you do?'

'I went in anyway.'

'And?'

'Isolation's a horrible feeling, Cassie. I never want to feel like that again.'

The blast of a car horn startled both women. Aware that she had been blocking access to the taxi rank, Cassie pulled out into the traffic. Her windscreen wipers worked overtime as she drove across the main street to a parking space at the foot of the road that led to Madison House. She parked.

'What happened?'

'Oh, I had my appointment and spoke to a counsellor for ages. I never realised it before, but I've reacted to stuff happenin' around me without really thinkin' it through, y' know, like a choice with options.'

'Mavis, what did you decide?'

'Oh, haven't I told you that yet? I decided not to. It wouldn't be right for me. Why are you cryin'?'

'I don't know, relief, I guess.'

'You want to know somethin' else?'

'What?' Cassie rummaged through her handbag in search of a handkerchief.

'It made the whole thing real for me … not just a nightmare. Things are so much worse when you can't see the way out.'

'I know.'

'I'm goin' to see a counsellor down here and get help sortin' out my feelings.' She paused. 'Cassie, get a grip.'

'Oh, Mavis … you just seem so different!'

'I am. There's one thing I'd like your help with though.'

'Yes?'

'Would you come with me when I go to tell my parents?'

'Of course I will.'

That weekend, having latched the paddock gate behind Mavis' car, Cassie climbed into it. In the distance, the women could see Trevor slowly following the cattle to the milking sheds.

'That's Dad.'

'I'd worked that out.'

Mavis laughed.

Trevor waited, one foot on the lower rung of the wire fence, watching the approaching car.

'I don't know why Dad doesn't replace the gates with cattle grids,' Mavis added as Cassie climbed out of the car again, 'it'd be a darn sight easier for him and visitors than this to-and-froin' every time someone wanted to leave the property. Mum's usually out with him this time of day. I wonder where she is.'

Trevor looked critically at his daughter. The signs of abuse and the thinness were no longer evident.

Mavis linked arms with him, assured him that she was well, and changed the topic to the scandal at the school. Her energy emphasised his weariness.

Walking on his right, Cassie noted the run-down fences and the house's state of disrepair. The ground under foot was dry. The disintegrating remains of grass turned to dust under their feet.

The steps into the house were new as was the verandah.

'The proper work on the house will start next month,' Trevor said. 'Developers paid me a tidy sum for some land on the eastern side. Things are lookin' up for us.'

Mavis grimaced at Cassie.

'Hi, Mum, this is Cassie.'

'Good to meet you. I thought we'd have tea on the veran-dah; that is unless you feel like a cold drink instead.'

'Tea will be fine,' the women said in unison.

'Cassie, I'll put our stuff in the bedroom.'

On Mavis' return, the group sat companionably, enjoying what there was of the afternoon breeze.

'It's so much drier here than on the coast,' Cassie said.

'It's a tinder box all right,' Trevor said. 'Remember, water's precious when you bath tonight. Well, those cows aren't goin' to milk themselves. We'll see you girls when we get back.'

'Before you do, I've somethin' important to say.' Mavis took a breath, looked at Cassie for encouragement, and continued. 'I told you, when we arrived, that I was well, and I am.' She looked helplessly at Cassie. 'There's no easy way to say this so here it is: I'm pregnant.' For Mavis, it was like a spill gate opening, 'I'm havin' a baby and not an abortion. No use goin' there if you are thinkin' about it. Terry's out of m' life and that's the way I want to keep it. The boss says I can work as long as I want, but I'm comin' home to have it if you'll have me. After that … well, I don't know. We'll work that out I guess when we get there.'

'If we'll have you?' Marg was in tears. 'Of course we will!'

Trevor fished out a worn handkerchief and blew his nose hard and loud.

In the privacy of their bedroom later that night, the Mills lay awake unable to sleep. 'I'm frightened, Trevor, that we'll get this wrong. I don't want to lose our daughter again.'

'Been thinkin' that myself. We've got to work this out carefully.'

'Bringin' up another child at our age is goin' to be hard.'

'If we think like that, we'll be makin' our first mistake. We're the support system. It's Mavis who's doin' the bringin' up. It's real important we don't overstep the boundaries.'

'How're we goin' to manage?' Marg cried silently for all that had been lost.

'Don't know yet.' Trevor did his best to comfort his wife.

'Another generation trapped on the land. I had such high hopes that Mavis would fulfil her dream.' Marg sobbed quietly into her husband's shoulder.

'Shush, she'll hear you.'

Unaware of her parents' concerns, Mavis sang on the return trip to town the next day. It was the first time that year that her heart had been full enough to do so. On their return, they saw Gary on the verandah with a gift that wrapping could not disguise.

'A guitar, Gary?' Mavis squealed, not even out of the car. 'Oh, you shouldn't of!'

* * *

Despite the cool of that spring evening, Cassie and Michael dined al fresco in the motel restaurant overlooking the southern end of Black Beach. They nodded at people they knew, indifferent to the interested glances.

Inside the restaurant, a band played contemporary dance music. With the opening bars of *She's like the Wind*, a slow rumba, Cassie and Michael joined the crowd on the floor. Their dance had an erotic quality with exaggerated slow hip movements and sinuous arm gestures that caressed face and body. As the trumpet solo reached its climactic height, Michael drew up from the floor, his hands a breath's brush from Cassie's body. Their splayed hands meshed near her face, a still moment of intense passion. When the final notes of the song sounded, they kissed slowly, a taste and promise. Their seductive dialogue moved from the dance floor to the motel room.

Undressing was not the rushed strip of lust blinded by the frenzied rush of kissing but rather a slow pleasurable peeling away to a natural state. Kisses were small open-mouthed caresses that covered lips, face, lobes and neck. Michael fondled her thigh, squeezed it, and luxuriated in its firmness. Cassie relaxed under his hands, hungering for his flesh.

The dancers lived in the moment, attuned to the communication of contact. In the soft glow of the room, Michael trailed a hand slowly down Cassie's neck to her breasts. He unbuttoned her shirt, pulled it out of her jeans. Her skin was silk, soft and supple. Her black lace bra contrasted against the milky whiteness of her flesh. He nuzzled her breasts, nibbled her nipple, and gently sucked it upward, kissing it after he released it. He trailed his hands over her breasts, sending shivers of delight through her body.

Her hands traced the muscles in his shoulders, fingered his biceps, wandered down his back, gripped his buttocks and pulled him closer. They rolled over. She straddled him and slowly unbuttoned his shirt, kissing his chest as she did so. Her tongue traced the circle of his navel. She sat up and savoured his tanned torso. She undid his jeans, fingered his body hair, tantalised his genitals. Smiled.

His hands cupped her breasts, fondling them slowly. She moved to his side. He peeled her jeans. Their thighs entwined. Her hips arched slowly, rhythmically. He lowered into her, gently, carefully, slowly. Liquid fire raced through their bodies. They moved in unison to the surging pulse of primeval music.

Chapter 40

That same night, darkness claimed rooms across the school as cleaners, the invisible people who battled the aftermath of an adolescent tide, worked at a frenetic pace. Cost-cutting measures meant that there were too few cleaners for too many classrooms. Every morning and night, it was a race against time. School corridors reverberated as the floors returned to a high gloss shine. Lights flicked off and gloom engulfed sections of the school.

Samantha knelt, bottom protruding from underneath her desk. In her agitation over the time, she had upended her handbag. Its contents lay scattered under her desk. She was supposed to meet her husband for dinner at six and here she was still at school.

Difficult did not even come close to describing her day. First the argument with her husband that morning, then pushy parents taking up her one session off that day, and now finally her bag. Absorbed by her feelings of distress, she missed the quiet footfall of someone entering the room and the whisper of the door closing.

What an arse! the man thought, deflected momentarily from his purpose. Waggling at and tantalising him. Firm from the looks of it, ripe, on offer. The skirt slit previewed the inner fruit. The clothing would be easy to peel. Its juice held promise of heat and biting spice. He closed for the picking. His hands tested the plumpness of cloth-covered flesh.

Shock jarred Samantha's head into the desktop. Pain and fear blocked her thought. Protesting, she tried to withdraw from under the desk but found herself imprisoned by legs astride her. Her skirt was hauled abruptly upwards. She struggled against its lifting trying to free herself. Blind to her assailant, Samantha lashed backwards futilely. She could feel the pound of his heart against her, his heat. She fought back.

His hand muted her scream. He pulled her into him. Grabbed her arms and pinioned them. Forced her head sideways and crushed it into the edge of the desk, his fingers entwining her hair.

Tears and blood mingled. She thrashed with her legs.

The head thump to the floor deadened her.

He took her violently from the rear, uncaring as to the tunnel. In the violence of that taking, she slipped into a semi-conscious state. The pace of his passion increased. His rasping groans climaxed. He exulted in the power. Sated, he rose from her.

Her stillness failed to interest him. Past experience with his wife, still life when it came to sex, had conditioned him to expect it. His efforts to arouse her had had the reverse effect. She was the inadequate one!

The mess concerned him. It was over his legs and, if he wasn't careful, it would stain his trousers. He cleaned himself at the sink, thinking nothing about his misuse of the tea-towel. He'd have to put the trousers in at the drycleaners. Looking out the window, he saw lights turned off in the building opposite. He restored the furniture displaced by his passion.

Returning to his purpose, he collected his things. As an afterthought, he rifled through desk after desk in search of keys to the storeroom where he thought high-priced, portable technology and electrical equipment were stored. There had been enough risk to make this adventure exciting without any real danger of being caught.

Thwarted in the now ransacked room, he took the few things of value. With a glance at the woman, he thought, This job hasn't been a total waste of time. He left as quietly as he had arrived.

Samantha lay inert on the floor.

* * *

The hum of the floor polisher reverberated in Samantha's head like the buzzing of angry bees. She heard the sobbing and wondered who it was. Slowly, she pulled herself together, managing somehow to get to her feet. She collapsed onto a chair, staring at the wall opposite her, seized by shaking. Her legs were useless. She wasn't even aware that she was sitting.

Her face was numb. Her lip was swollen and bleeding. Her groin ached from the jarred opening of her legs. Her skin felt clogged with the grime of seed.

She raked her fingers through her hair, freeing it from the bun chosen earlier that day. It tumbled down, obscuring much of her face.

She stood, straightening herself as she did so. Her hand felt the tear in her skirt. Tears bottlenecked in her throat. She needed to vomit. She had to get out of there.

* * *

The blaring crescendo of a horn brought Samantha back to her surroundings. She pulled the steering wheel sharply to the left, avoiding impact with an oncoming truck, coming to a jarring halt off the shoulder of the road. The shock of near collision released a flood of emotion. Sandwiched between tears and hysteria, she fought for control.

'Are you all right, Miss?' An old male face peered in through the driver's window at Samantha sometime later. He had a torch. 'Terrible when you see that sort of thing happening, even if it is from a distance. That bastard did not even stop! For a moment there, I thought my pacemaker was going to leap out of my throat. Bloody expensive to get that fixed again.'

His wife peered in at her as well. 'Did you bang your head on the steering wheel?'

'Travelling far?'

Samantha shook her head.

'Can my wife drive you there? I can follow in the truck. Not a good idea to be driving in case you're in shock.'

'No.'

'Anything we can do for you?'

Samantha shook her head.

'Well, we passed a café up the road. I reckon you need a break before going further. Drive careful now.'

Looking into the mirrored walls of the café as she entered, Samantha saw the bruised and bloodied face of someone she thought she knew. She was oblivious to the stares of the people behind the counter. Slowly, Samantha realised she was looking at herself.

The coffee was terrible like it was made from coal dust. Aware now that she was trembling, she sat there.

Customers came and went.

With darkness shrouding the earth, Samantha walked to the public phone outside. She called her husband, endured his anger at being stood up, and, crying, asked him to come and get her. She did not know how she would tell him. The first time, she thought, will be the hardest.

* * *

Steven Smith listened in silence as the Casualty doctor detailed the extent of Samantha's injuries, all of which the doctor had documented.

'I've given her a sedative injection and here's a prescription for antidepressants. I'll call you if there is any problem with the test results.' In response to Steven's blank look, the doctor added, 'Venereal disease. She'll have to come back for Aids testing.'

Silence as Steven absorbed that possibility. 'Did she say much to you about it? All she did was cry on the way here.'

'Survivors of sexual assault react and eventually heal differently. It depends on the situation and the person. The disconnection that she's going through is a form of shock. I think the third person references to herself and what happened are part of the disbelief that many women experience. Your priority should be to make her feel safe. It's not advisable to leave her alone. Be prepared for nightmares. I'm afraid sedatives aren't much help there. She'll need counselling. You both will. I've called the police; your wife seemed okay with that. The sooner she lodges a complaint the better. They'll have to investigate the crime scene. See if there are any clues to the attacker's identity.'

* * *

In the shadows of his bedroom, Steven sat in a chair brought in from his living area, absorbing his wife's torment. At times, he spoke soothingly to her, reassuring her that she was safe. When that failed, he woke her.

In the waking, Samantha struggled to move from

nightmare to reality. Even in that waking, the terror stayed with her. Unseeing, she thrashed at her husband until she knew it was him.

Calming Samantha was difficult, but Steven managed it somehow. Yes, he thought, if he got his hands on the bastard, the low-life would pay. There would not be anything left for the courts.

As night paled into dawn, Steven realised that others were accountable. Ignoring the hour, he phoned his mother and arranged for her to take his watch. She arrived at seven.

* * *

Having been contacted by the police the night before, Principal Cameron and his Deputy Barker were at the school by six that morning to instruct the cleaners not to enter the English wing. They met Coachman at seven to develop contingency plans.

At seven-thirty, the police arrived.

Steven Smith arrived at eight. Unexpected though his presence was, Cameron dealt with him immediately. Cameron took him into his office, organised a clerk to get him tea, and asked Barker to join him as a witness.

'Why aren't there security measures in place to protect people working in the school after hours? Even the school phones are turned off. Why, when you know staff are still working? I want to know who was on the grounds that afternoon and evening.'

In a tone meant to calm, Barker said, 'The majority of staff here prefer to work in the security of their homes given how late they have to work. Nothing like this has happened before. It is unreasonable to expect us …'

'Unreasonable! I'll tell you what's unreasonable! My wife

has been harassed since she got here last year. And I know that other women and girls here have suffered as well so don't pretend otherwise, and you bastards didn't do anything about it!'

Barker looked at Cameron.

'You are entitled to this anger. We fully understand where you are coming from. The matter is in the hands of the police. They have instructed us not to say or do anything that could affect their investigation.'

'This is typical of you mongrels. All lip service, no action.' Steven slammed out of the office.

Chapter 41

On a high when she arrived at school that day, Cassie was puzzled by the four police cars parked outside. In the main quadrangle, she found staff and students clustered in their respective groups. Even more curious, Coachman waited on the steps to the English wing, directing them to Home Economics Room 3 where a special meeting was to take place once everyone had arrived.

Shocked, Cassie and other English staff sat at student desks listening to Sergeant Quirk who outlined the sketchy details of the attack on Samantha. Cassie felt sick. She flicked a look at Talbut. What was he doing here? He looked as appalled as the other men.

Sergeant Quirk continued, 'The staff room and the upper floor are a crime scene and so are inaccessible.' In answer to a question from Selton, Quirk said, 'I don't know how long the investigation will take.'

The news was mind-boggling, incomprehensible. The random nature of the attack and the robbery was disturbing.

The sergeant ended on, 'It is inadvisable for any woman to remain in the school grounds after hours until the perpetrator has been caught.' He handed the meeting back to the Principal and then left.

The Principal explained the security measures for female staff and student safety. He ended on, 'A letter will be sent home to parents warning that a rapist is at large and precautions need to be taken.'

Then Coachman outlined how they would deal with classes that day and the days that would follow. 'It is important that the days are as normal as possible; routine is the key. Classes will be held in the multi purpose centre and teachers are to work in year teams. Talbut's been recalled from leave to take Samantha's classes. We're lucky to have him pitch in; thanks, mate. Speculation and gossip are to be discouraged.'

After the meeting, the English staff filed out in silence to the school assembly where the Deputy spoke to the student body about theft and an attack on an unidentified teacher.

Although the carousel of school life continued that day, it did so haltingly. Conversation in staff rooms was scant in breaks in contrast to the horrified titillation of students in the playground. Everyone felt the shock of the invasion.

The dead tide of the day ended during the last teaching session when student runners arrived with sets of letters from management to parents. That explanation triggered a burst of fevered discussion as people left the grounds. Phones rang off the hook throughout the week. Meanwhile, police came and went each day, a silent backdrop to the returning normalcy of school life.

On her return to Madison House, Cassie was relieved that the news was already out but weighed down nonetheless by a repeat of the day's events. Minna's disillusioned comment, 'Who knows what corruption lies in the heart of men,' resounded in Cassie's thoughts that night and in the days and nights that followed.

Being with Michael kept the wolves of fear at bay, but they lurked in the shadows of Cassie's mind until she faced them. She did so, sitting alone one Saturday afternoon on the front verandah, the chilling weight of memory offset by the warmth of spring. In the background of that day, the rituals of weekend life at Madison House played out.

Thoughts tumbled in her mind from the strongbox in which she had stored them years before. Groping hands. Weight, oppressive and unbearable. The thrusting grunt of invasion. Pain. Fear. Her eyes widened with the dawning realisation. Rape. Jake had said it was love, but she knew better now.

She thought of all the people she had met. Some wore masks that disguised their real intent. Others remained oblivious of the impact of their actions. A number rang true like quality crystal. She was lucky to know the difference now.

* * *

The interviews in the Deputy's office were constructed to test the male staff. Sergeant Quirk watched each person, fascinated as Detective Sergeant Robertson from Nowra conducted the questioning.

As part of their training, police were introduced to the psychology of behaviour. Quirk had found the subject intriguing and had read further into it as a matter of personal interest. Duty in a country town, however, did not provide the police with opportunities to develop their investigatory skills so Quirk was eager to benefit from this case.

Detecting deception often stumps the most experienced police officers, forensic professionals, and judges. Robertson didn't like his chances at breaking this case. The evidence appeared to be limited. The task before him was twofold: collect the facts and identify any deception.

Quirk puzzled over the difference between the truth and a lie. Would a liar be more nervous than a truth-teller?

His voice pitched higher? Did a liar press his lips together more tightly? Was he unable to make eye contact? Robertson remained focused on collecting the jigsaw pieces.

Cleaning staff were known to be on the premises. Four male teachers were seen the night of the rape. Five male students had been seen on school grounds.

* * *

As Robertson interviewed Talbut, he noted that the man was relaxed, cooperative, and confident. Talbut made direct eye contact with both policemen present.

'Your car was sighted at the high school that afternoon.'

'Yes, before sunset. It was a beauty that night; the sort that makes you take notice.'

'So what were you doing there? You were on leave, weren't you?'

'I came back for some possessions I'd forgotten to take with me when I went on leave. I'd submitted my resignation effective the end of the term and wanted to get my things without a fuss. I hate farewells.'

'Please outline what you did when you entered the school.'

'I parked the car, entered by the path near the multi purpose building, came upstairs and then remembered that Coachman had said he'd moved my things into the faculty storeroom downstairs. I went to his office, took the key off the hook near the door and retrieved my things. I left the same way I had entered.'

'See anyone while you were there?'

'Just the cleaner finishing off. He was gone when I came back down.'

'How long did this take?' Robertson said, looking at his notes.

'Five minutes or so.' Talbut offered up, 'Cleaners have to work hard and fast here. Overworked and underpaid if you ask me.'

'See anyone or hear anything on the way out?' Robertson asked.

'No. Anything else?'

'Not for the moment. Thanks.'

* * *

In the safety of the night, Samantha lay next to her husband, comforted by the warmth from their contact. There was security in the way he held her protectively. She stared into the darkness. She hated the approach of the day. Panic took possession then.

Sealed in the apartment by day, she jumped at every sound, and rang Steven a hundred times. The sound of his voice sustained her, but she worried that his patience would end and so struggled for self-control.

Over the past weeks, depression had piled up around her. Cups and plates littered the sink. The order of life swamped in the discards of the day, week, and month: clothing, washing, books, mail, Steven's paraphernalia.

At counselling sessions, Samantha sailed the troubled oceans of assault.

'You're in a double prison, Sam,' the counsellor said. For someone who listened to the troubles of others for a living, May Schwartz' face was surprisingly serene. Her long hair held in a bun featured two large decorative pins. She preferred black and white in her dress given the world she worked in was grey. The scent of lavender burned in May's rooms.

'I prefer Samantha, thanks.'

That small act of assertion in reclaiming identity led the counsellor to say, 'And it's time you returned to life.'

Samantha frowned.

'The first step is the hardest, but it is the small steps that are the most important. You need structure to your day. Look through these brochures and find something for the morning and the afternoon. It's in the ritual of the commonplace that you will find your old self.'

In the burn and stretch of the Body Balance session, Samantha found her centre. She thought of the two Samanthas. The former energised and organised. The present one overwhelmed, barely coping with claiming time for self and defeated by the tedium of housework. She wondered why she should even make an effort if Steven was content to live as they did.

* * *

From the interviews, Robertson learnt that two of the Science teachers regularly worked back late in the pattern of Mrs Smith. They left at five-thirty true to their pattern and had seen two cars parked in the designated English staff area. As they left, they had warned three boys off the premises. The boys had come down to shoot baskets on the courts near the car park. The Science teachers had watched them leave and only then left themselves.

Another male teacher, one of the PE staff, had been organising sporting fixtures and schedules. From his staff room, he could see into the English faculty. As he was locking up, he noticed a male in the English staff room: medium height, no other discernable features because of the distance. The cleaner in his area verified that the PE teacher had left around five-fifty and exited by the nearest stairs in his wing and away from the English area.

The two remaining boys in question had been taking a short cut through the school and had seen the PE teacher exit through the downstairs doors into the school quadrangle and walk to the car park. It was those boys who had seen Talbut leave the English wing some time after the PE teacher had left.

Background checks on the boys ruled them out as likely suspects.

On interviewing the cleaning staff, Quirk had learnt that the supervisor had been inspecting the work completed in the lower level English classrooms and had sighted a man on the final stair of his descent from the upper floor. The supervisor, Jack Johnson, was new to the town and didn't know any of the teaching staff beyond those he dealt with on the job. The description he provided was one in profile. He was confident he would recognise the man again.

From the upper floor cleaner, Quirk learnt Talbut had physical conflict with one of the female English teachers the previous year. The cleaner also repeated rumours that Talbut pursued relationships with students that had not always been welcomed.

These disclosures triggered Quirk's memory. He remembered that a complaint about Talbut had been lodged by parents after they had withdrawn their daughter from the school.

Back at the station, Quirk reviewed past files and found what he had been looking for. The student in question had been Meri Bennett. At the time, after a discreet investigation, there wasn't anything that the police could do beyond record the complaint. The evidence was ambiguous though the girl's trauma had seemed real. The teacher who'd witnessed the alleged inappropriate interaction was Samantha Smith. When

Robertson walked in later that afternoon, he found an excited Quirk awaiting him.

'Well, set up interviews with the remaining women then. We'll interview them separately but have them called to the Principal's office at the same time. In the meantime, we need to investigate the suspect's background.'

* * *

Standing outside Samantha's flat, Rajes said to Cassie, 'Words can lift the spirit or push it further into darkness. I know you want to help her, but I am increasingly uneasy as to how we can.'

The answer became more difficult when they saw her. Consumed by her fears, Samantha had been too full to eat. She was bone thin.

Indifferent to her surroundings, Samantha removed piles of washing from the seating in response to Cassie and Rajes' hesitation and stared around blankly, in a quandary as to where to plonk the clothing scooped into her arms. They sat reluctantly on the edge of the cleared lounge.

'Would you mind if I made us tea?' Rajes asked Samantha after an awkward exchange of civilities.

'Help yourself.'

The kitchen showed signs of effort but different types of mould mired the teapot. Rajes scoured it with a soap pad and then scalded it three times with boiling water.

Cassie wished she knew a cleansing ritual for the soul. She and Samantha talked of commonplace things: the mundane detail of school life, dancing, the approaching Christmas, and Samantha's new interests. Rajes brought the teapot, milk jug, sugar pot, and mugs to the magazine cluttered coffee table on a tray.

As Rajes poured the amber liquid into the mugs, she said, 'This is a beautiful teapot. It's so rare these days to get a spout that doesn't spill but pours to one spot.'

'I tested every pot in the shop before I bought this one. You should've seen the assistant's face.' Samantha laughed at the memory. 'I really love the handle as well. It's long enough for you to get your fingers through but thick enough for a firm grip.' She inhaled the fragrance of the tea. 'I'd forgotten this simple sensual pleasure.'

Their talk meandered.

As the visit ended, Rajes asked, 'Do you think you'll continue teaching?'

'I'm not! I can't!' Samantha's fear charged the atmosphere.

'How can we help?' Cassie mouthed to Rajes. They had come to see if they could help Samantha rise phoenix-like out of the ashes, not to add to the destruction.

Samantha's anguish translated into agitated hand fluttering. Rajes moved closer to her and held her hand.

'I remember this feeling,' Rajes said, 'although the cause was different. When my first husband died as we tried to escape from Uganda, I was lost for a long time. My friends, thinking they were sensitive to my grief, left me alone with it. The grief was like a blanket that I wrapped myself in, a shroud of sorts. It was so thick, layers of it, and I was alive somehow deep within, one of the living dead.'

The image appealed to Samantha. The emotional fog, in which she had been lost, thinned slightly.

Rajes continued, 'For me, the problem with trauma was that I couldn't avoid it because I couldn't escape myself; it was within. I've learnt that there is only one way to heal the spirit and that is to reclaim what has been taken. The hardest thing is working out how you were robbed and of what beyond the obvious things. Personally, I think you need to return to school even if you eventually resign.'

Though listening, Samantha remained unresponsive. The suggestion was huge, too big to taste let alone consume.

'Counsellors have told me there are four steps to recovery: recognising the need, wanting the change, making the effort, and persisting until the hour, the day, the month meant something to me.' Rajes did not say that it took her a long time to peel away the shroud.

The visit ended without resolution but with the suggestion left on the table. Walking downstairs, Cassie asked, 'Do you think she'll recover?'

'She let us in, and she listened. She's also made herself get out of the house and is trying to get involved in life again. All big steps.'

Thinking of her own past trauma, Cassie said, 'It might take years.'

* * *

When the message came through that they were wanted at the Principal's office, Cassie and Rajes were in class. Both women were shocked by the summons. Coachman and Selton provided relief cover for them so they could attend the interviews. In the staff room, Fuller continued to man the phone.

Rajes' demeanour and concise recall of observations impressed Robertson. The men had been at times offensive: bawdy jokes, leering, and innuendo. The women had felt physically harassed by students and some of the male staff, Talbut included. She referred to the extenuating circumstance of the earlier staff room which she felt had contributed to unwanted close contact. She thought it common knowledge that Samantha Smith worked back late at the school as did Cassie.

Quirk's notes from his interview with Cassie corroborated Rajes' observations to Robertson. When asked about the fray with Talbut the previous year, Cassie had been shocked. She outlined events as she recalled them. When asked why she had not reported the assault, she replied that she had attempted to complain to management, but realised that she lacked a witness to corroborate the incident. Pausing at the office door on her departure, she asked, 'How did you know?'

'From interviews, one of the cleaners witnessed it from a distance.'

Robertson whistled through his teeth as he listened to Quirk's report. 'The circumstantial evidence points to Talbut. Let's get him back in for another interview. Tell the Deputy we'll need the office longer.'

* * *

Robertson sat on the edge of his desk and studied Talbut. Quirk sat to his right. Robertson was impressed by Talbut's calm under pressure. Robertson began, 'Do you read the papers?'

'Yes.'

'Then you've heard of Desmond Applebee?'

Talbut was unable to trust his voice so he nodded. He remembered reading that Applebee was the first person in Australia to be convicted of rape using DNA evidence.

'When Mrs Smith attended hospital after the rape, the doctor extracted blood and semen samples from her body and clothes. We have witnesses who contradict your statement with respect to your whereabouts in the school that evening. I'm going to get a court order for a blood sample and semen to be taken from you so that your DNA can be compared to the samples taken by the doctor. You can, of course, provide those samples voluntarily.'

Talbut blanched. He swallowed. 'I believe I am entitled to legal consultation.'

You fucking prick, Robertson thought. 'By all means. You may make the call from here before we take you back to Nowra for formal charging.'

* * *

'Doesn't it make you mad?' Cassie asked Samantha. 'It does me. It wasn't your fault this happened. It could just as easily have been me. The longer you live like this, the bigger Talbut's victory.'

'I've filed charges,' Samantha said, her voice flat.

'How can you stand up to him in court when you can't even stand in the place where it happened?'

Samantha was silent.

'I don't claim to understand the depth of your feelings, but both Rajes and I have suffered violence, different from you, but the effect was the same. Depression. Not wanting to feel because it hurt so much. It took us years to get over it. The longer it takes, the more things that matter are changed, maybe forever. When things got tough last year, anger seemed to sustain you, got you through the battle. You are a fighter. It's really important not to shut down. Be angry about that. Take your life back. Come back to work.'

'So ... Miss Never Loses Her Cool Cassie thinks she knows

all about it. How dare you equate the piddling events of your life with what I've been through! You fucking bitch! How dare you say that to me! I'll show you take control … Get out! Get Out!'

'I'm so sorry. I didn't mean it that way. I just wanted to …'

'Get out! Piss off!'

* * *

Distressed beyond words, Cassie returned to Madison House. The hum of life there sounded hollow and seemed distant. Shaking her head to an invitation to join in a card game with Gary, Minna and George, Cassie headed upstairs. Arriving at her bedroom, she paused and changed course to Michael's.

'Mike?'

'What's up?'

Cassie stumbled over the beginning.

'Slow down, Cassie. Start at the beginning.'

Sitting on his desk chair, Cassie recounted her visit to Samantha and the motivation behind it, including the dark events of her own life.

'I've made such a mess of it, Mike! What can I do?'

A long silence.

Michael thought he knew Cassie but now realised that he did not. Abortion!

'Mike?'

'Sorry, just trying to digest all of it.'

'Any ideas on how I can fix this?'

'It happened, Cassie. I don't think it can be fixed. Shit, this is terrible!'

'I know.'

An incredibly long silence.

Watching him, Cassie wondered, If love grows out of the joy of knowing each other, is the corollary true? Could Mike fall out of love with me? Another voice answered her. No, your trust in him has not been misplaced.

Michael left his bed and crossed to her, kneeling down so they were on the same level. 'I don't know how you got passed all of that. If it'd been me, it would have been the lens I saw the world through.'

'Is it the lens that you now see me through?'

Gently, he pulled her to her feet. 'It means a lot that you shared this with me. I get your procrastination now. I *love* you; nothing in your past can change that.'

Chapter 42

Blustering winds, blistering heat, and impossibly high temperatures had made life difficult for people on the land, in townships, and in the city. Water restrictions were upgraded. New South Wales was straw-dry and disaster-ready.

Cassie drove down the south coast toward Keimera, conscious that her life was about to undergo another change. She shook herself and concentrated on the road.

The road turned and gave a sweeping view of the coast. As far as the eye could see lay a wide belt of smoke that extended inland toward the Dividing Range. This was not the spring smoke of shire-workers who cleared unwanted growth from roadsides. It did not come from farmers clearing their land, nor was it the smoke from volunteer bushfire brigades who cleared away potentially lethal pockets of bush before the onset of summer.

This was a full-fledged bushfire; wild, unruly, raging out of control, hungrily consuming the dry, straw-like grasses of summer, licking up trees, leaping along treetops, billowing in its fury, enveloping the landscape.

The south coast had ignited. Only the coastal settlements, protected by onshore breezes, were spared from the devastation.

Cassie could not see the firebreaks, but she knew they were there; barren scars, void of trees and grass – a rebuffal to the fiery breath of the conflagration. She drove toward Keimera, listening to the bushfire update on her radio.

'The State Emergency and Parks and Wildlife Services have joined with fire fighting contingents from the Defence Force. They are locked in a desperate attempt to save the rural industry and bushlands of the south coast. Stock losses are feared to be heavy. Hundreds of homes in the foothills are endangered. At this point, many people are remaining on their properties and taking the necessary precautions to combat the blaze. This is a terrible blow to farmers already battling the recession. Public halls, schools, and churches along the south coast are being used as evacuation centres and emergency accommodation. The Country Women's Association has extended its role beyond fund raising and is part of a mammoth community effort in providing for the evacuees. Community volunteers also staff field kitchens for the fire fighters across the region. Despite the mind-boggling scale of the fire, no injuries have been reported as yet.'

The usually congested road was deserted.

* * *

Cars choked the sweeping driveway up to Madison House so Cassie parked on the lawn. The stifling heat hit her as she emerged from the air-conditioned comfort of her Celica. She was glad she had invested in the air-conditioning at the beginning of that summer. The return journey would have been intolerable otherwise. Heat pushed in at her from all directions, searing her as she trekked across dry grass to the house. She raised her hand to cover her eyes, shielding them from the fiery glare of the sun.

The verandah was a hive of activity, littered with women

and men of all shapes and sizes. The windows and doors of the house were flung open in an attempt to maximise the onshore south-westerly that brought relief and protection to the coastal township.

The house had become the headquarters for fire relief support to complement the work of the Rural Fire Services. There were groups for all contingencies: transport, accommodation, bedding, meals, clothing, and even toys for the children. As Cassie neared the front verandah, the workers responded to a call from within. They crowded through the front door and French windows leading into the main living room. Cassie followed.

The living room was a crunch of people. Some sat on the floor while others squatted or knelt behind them. Only the people in the foyer stood. Everyone crammed for a better view of the television and the breaking news.

The male newsreader immediately crossed to the reporter at the scene, Mark Burrows, for his update.

'The Commander of the Rural Fire Service has called for more volunteers to assist with fighting the fires across southern New South Wales. Volunteers are to report to their local depot. Those responding will be transported to relief areas and work under seasoned officers. Volunteers should wear overalls or similar clothing, sturdy footwear, and a cap or hat.'

'Mark, how long before this fire is brought under control?'

'They can't say at this stage, Kerry. The main fear here is that the fierce updrafts caused by strong winds above the fire will carry blazing debris and ash across the firebreaks, extending this burning plague. Inhabitants of townships and farmhouses across this region have widened firebreaks around their homes in a frantic attempt to halt the fire. Only human initiative and the indomitable Aussie will to beat the odds will bring this blaze under control.'

'Thanks, Mark, we'll speak to you again in the next news break.'

Normal programs resumed. The house buzzed with reaction. Cassie moved among the crowd looking for familiar faces. She saw Minna near the kitchen doorway locked in heated discussion with George.

'Nonsense, Min! You heard them. They need more volunteers. They are not going to quibble about age.'

'Listen to reason. You'll be of greater help here co-ordinating relief activities than you can be in battling that blaze. No, do not cut me off; I have not finished! Fighting fires is the work of younger men. Admittedly your health is good, but think for a minute! Think of the wasted time, if you're wrong and can't endure the battle. You'll be more —'

'All right, you've made your point; I'll stick to what I've been doing as well as the shuttle service.'

'Exactly. Cassie! I didn't know that you were back. Any trouble on the trip?'

'No, but you should see the fire. Where's Michael?'

'Gary and he dashed upstairs to change,' George said. 'I'm taking them and other volunteers out to the mustering point.'

Cassie's heart jolted. She turned on her heel. Edging her way through the crowd, Cassie came face-to-face with Samantha near the stairs.

'Oh,' Cassie said, 'Samantha, I ...'

'It's all right. I'm ... I don't really know ... Steven's in the volunteer fire brigade. I couldn't stand it at home so I came here to help. We'll catch up later?'

On impulse, Cassie hugged her. 'I never meant ...'

'It's okay ... really.'

'G'day, Cassie, glad you could get through,' Gary said from

the bottom of the stairs. Then to Michael, 'Meet you outside.' Gary's excitement was barely suppressed.

'Mike.' Cassie lacked words, crossed to him, calming herself in his embrace.

'Everything will be all right. See me off?' He gently disentangled himself. 'I have to go. C'mon.' He wrapped his arm around her as they walked outside.

The last of their kisses lingered on Cassie's lips long after Michael had driven out of sight.

* * *

For the next week, Minna and Cassie watched the newsbreaks in growing apprehension. Minna filled her waking hours with work to assist the evacuees. Cassie helped after work. Eventually, the crisis resulted in the early closure of the school.

Fire crews worked in shift rotations. They came in blackened and tired, ate, and returned to the blazing cataclysm. Rest breaks were scheduled throughout the twenty-four hour cycle with crews returning to camps set up for the crisis. Cassie, like other volunteers in the field kitchens, worked tirelessly in the plethora of work associated with supporting those involved in the defence of life and property.

At a distance, Michael watched her as she worked. He saw the way people responded to her and she to them. When he came up to her, they shared precious minutes and then he returned to his group. How many women are like her? he wondered. Not many, was his answer.

Looking at Michael as he sat with his crew, Cassie realised that he could augment her life and she his, making them both the richer for the union.

In the evenings, Cassie returned to Madison House; her

clothes saturated with sweat and the all-pervading smoke of the bushfire.

In the weeks leading up to Christmas, the battle shaped the pattern of life. Thoughts of Christmas and its related preparation were non-existent.

The inhabitants of Madison House returned home in breaks for rest, watching television reports in shocked silence. Horror pictures flashed across the screen, testimony to that summer's inferno. News commentators across the south coast gave updates for their regions. The television report also focused on the empty caravan parks, the evacuated holiday areas, and the negative impact this natural disaster was having on both regional and state economies.

The report closed with a long-range weather forecast, 'The outlook is critical for the next few days. There won't be any relief from the unrelenting heat. However, meteorologists are tracking a storm, massing out at sea as well as a rain-bearing front extending across Victoria and moving slowly north. There is hope that there'll be fire-quenching rain by the weekend.'

Exhausted by the strain of working close to the fire and by her dread, Cassie overslept Friday morning. She woke mid-morning and was appalled by the lateness of the day. After hurriedly donning serviceable clothing, she raced down the stairs two at a time and bumped into Minna.

'Oh, why didn't you wake me? I've missed the truck out for the morning shift. They'll be short-handed now.'

'You needed sleep. You've been pushing yourself too hard, doing too many shifts. I called Kate and asked her to take your place this morning. I want you to take the whole morning off.'

'How can I?'

A flash update signal on the TV interrupted their

conversation. They moved as one to the living room and stood transfixed by the report.

'The south coast of New South Wales is on the brink of catastrophe. A wall of flame, hundreds of kilometres in length, is steadily eating into the remaining bush and town-ships along the coastline are under threat. Fire continues to spread in all directions, leaving little refuge for the fleeing wildlife trying to stay ahead of the flames. It is impossible to avoid the smoking stench of this fire; it is in everyone's nostrils. Major road and rail links have been cut. The people here are isolated and stand now with their backs to the sea on a strip of land that is no more than fifty kilometres wide. Reports from the north tell of a firewall running through the bush at a terrifying pace.

One man, living near the inland town of Robertson, stayed to the very last and was surrounded by flames. He jumped into his swimming pool and watched in horror as fire balls passed overhead and devoured his home. Further south, two children were also rescued this morning after a terrible ordeal in which fire consumed the family home. The children's father is marooned in Sydney and was unable to assist in the fight for his property. His wife and children assumed the mantle of battle, only to flee at the eleventh hour to sanctuary in a nearby cliff. After securing her children in a rock cave with wet towels and a bucket of water, the mother took shelter in a rock crevice lower down the cliff. While the children were found at midday in shock but unscathed, the mother was not.'

The telephone rang and the women returned to the foyer.

'Oh hello, Marg. What's wrong? The fire hasn't turned toward your place has it?' Minna listened. 'Good! You sound upset. Is Mavis all right? … What! … I'll come to the hospital straight away. Of course, I don't mind. Don't worry;

Trevor's as strong as an ox. He'll be fine, just you wait and see … Sorry I missed that. Say again.' Minna's face registered her shock. She covered the phone mouthpiece and spoke to Cassie, 'Mavis is still at the house.' Minna then resumed her conversation, 'Look, I'll call and get her to come in too, shall I? … . You've tried? … The phones could be out; I don't know …'

'I'll go out and get her,' Cassie cut into Minna's train of thought. 'I've nothing else to do.'

The sun was an angry red ball, abnormally large and terrifyingly close to the landscape as Minna watched Cassie drive out of sight. Minna looked at the smoke, black as ink, which drifted upward, attempting to erase the sun itself. Smoke and massing storm clouds out at sea merged. She shuddered and prayed that the rescue was not too late.

On route to the Mills' farm, Cassie passed numerous detours. Firemen stood vetting traffic. Only bona-fide residents and authorised people were permitted to pass.

The sky was lost in smoke. It filled the air, blocking the usually spectacular view gained from the road upon which she travelled. If it had not been for the heat and the smell, Cassie could almost have believed it was winter and that the cloud cover had dropped. She was within five miles of the farm when she came to a roadblock.

'Sorry, Miss. The winds have changed. The fire's headin' this way. I can't let anyone past.'

'But you have to! I've a pregnant friend stranded up at Mills' farm. Her family have sent me to bring her out.'

The man used his backpack radio, seeking advice.

'Did you say you were headin' to Mills farm? We didn't realise anyone was left up there. We thought they'd all evacuated early yesterday mornin'. I could've sworn I saw them go through. Be quick about it. Keep your eye on the colour of the smoke and direction of the wind.'

* * *

Darkening billows of smoke loomed on the near horizon. Mavis watched the smoke along the ridge and knew it was nearly time to evacuate. The wind had changed direction. The homestead stood in the fire's path. She wanted to scream, to run, but she couldn't. This was her baby's heritage. Their future depended on the survival of the cattle and the homestead. Her father had been brought to breaking point by the recession and drought, had rallied, and persevered.

With unspoken and unacknowledged regret, her father had sold pieces of the land that for generations had defined him and their family so that she could follow her dream. It was not right for her to give up now, not when her family had battled for so long against the odds, not in the face of her father's sacrifice. Not while he still struggled for life. She would hold what was left for him.

Mavis felt dizzy and bone-weary from the effort of moving the cattle across the river and of setting up a protective net of sprinklers over the homestead. Her final awkward lumber up the ladders to the roof to check that all the gutters were clear had almost led to a disastrous fall. Her concentration had broken in the climb; her foot and grip had slipped and, for a second, fear of broken bones had replaced her fear of fire.

Sitting on the bottom step leading into the house, Mavis now was too tired to move. She had done all that she could. The cattle were safe. It was time to leave.

The asthmatic wheeze of the stalling EH Holden dwindled into silence; Mavis sat behind the wheel, appalled. Pushing away her fear, she pulled the bonnet release catch. She hoped that knowledge gleaned from years spent with her dad as he tinkered on old cars would help her now. Damn the lack of money! Blast the penny-pinching! If only I had a reliable car!

Cassie arrived as the thought finished.

Torn between laughter and tears of relief, Mavis rushed to her.

Winding down the window, Cassie yelled, 'C'mon, we've got to get out of here; we don't have much time.'

As she crossed to the passenger door, Mavis looked up the driveway to the distant road. Glowing, ember-embedded smoke consumed the exit road. Behind it, a molten firewall roared in its approach. She shook her head in disbelief. 'Look behind you; we can't get out by that road.' Fear lumped in her chest, spilling into her throat. 'It's important we don't panic,' she said as much to calm herself as to reassure Cassie. 'We can find a safe place; we've got time.'

'The house?' Cassie asked. It was hard to breathe calmly with so much smoke in the air.

* * *

Time stretched to eternity and back.

Mavis looked at the trees in the gully below the homestead. Fire had not reached them yet, but it was close. She could hear it; see the pinkish orange glow to the smoke. She could smell the burning gums; it tingled her senses, scraping them raw. She coughed repeatedly, gagged, and fought the rising nausea. Sweat, heat, and fine ash grimed her face. She attempted to wipe her eyes with the hem of her cotton dress. Her throat stung as did her eyes. She pushed her hair, lank and wet from the sprinklers, back off her face and looked toward the milking sheds, waiting for Cassie. C'mon, c'mon, she thought. What's keeping Cassie?

Mavis wanted to scream, but she did not. She refocused on the trees in the gully below and worked on her breathing. The acrid smoke stung her nostrils and eyes. Her taste buds felt as if they were singed. She went inside with the intent of making makeshift masks for Cassie and her to wear.

Returning to the verandah, Mavis looked at her surroundings. She could not see the flames yet, but the smoke glow was increasing in colour and intensity as was the roar. Keep calm, she thought. The fire's close, but we have time to make the river.

Mavis heard Cassie calling between coughs before she saw her. She emerged out of the smoke and lumbered toward Mavis.

'What are you doin' with those fuel cans, Cassie? Why did you bring them?'

'I didn't know what else to do with them. I've filled the generators. Are you sure that it'll keep the pumps and sprinkler system going as the fire passes over?'

'Yes, fires mostly pass quickly; their flames don't usually destroy homes. It's the embers or the radiant heat from the fire or material left near the house that can catch on fire and explode.'

Cassie looked at the fuel cans. 'I shouldn't have brought these!'

'Right. Now where can we … Listen to that! The fire's almost here! Oh God!'

The fire's roar grew louder with frightening speed. They could feel their adversary's scorching breath.

Mavis' fear drove her; she stood. 'The river! We have to make the river!'

'We wouldn't make it! You don't move that fast. We'll be all right here.' Cassie hoped she sounded as confident as she felt. 'The sprinklers have a wide arc. You've had them going all day. Everything's drenched. Even the ground's saturated. Look, we're standing in mud! Nothing can catch alight here, only our imaginations. We've got to keep them doused too. Is there anything else we should do?'

'I … the house … we …' Fear tightened its grip on Mavis. She fought to free herself from its crippling hold. Her eyes stung. It was difficult to breathe. She remembered the masks and passed one to Cassie. 'We need to make sure the doors are closed. The windows should be … we should … oh God, Cassie,' Mavis started to hyperventilate. 'We can't stay in the house. It's too big a gamble. The windows could shatter in the heat.'

'But I thought it'd be the safest place. Isn't that what's recommended by fire authorities? I never really understood why you were so insistent about getting to the river.'

'Think about it! The house's ringed by fire.' Mavis tried to keep her panic down. 'It's burning inward. The heat's getting worse … It's too risky … What if … what if the fire dries the house out faster than the sprinklers can wet it? What if the hoses from the river become damaged? The sprinklers will stop and we'll …' Horror broke Mavis' speech. She struggled to keep out of that monster's mouth. She spoke with a forced calmness. 'We need to get in a ditch … under cover somewhere and as wet as we can make it. Our best chance is to let the fire go over the top of us.'

'But where?' Cassie was close to losing control now.

'Where?' Mavis stared into the orange smoke that obscured land and sky. She considered their options. 'The outhouse! Dad was diggin' a new hole when he got sick. It's pretty wide, really deep, and a huge mess of dirt surrounds it. Nothin' can catch fire there. We need protection of some sort as a cover and water.'

'We could set a sprinkler over us. What sort of cover?'

'I meant water for drinkin'. If we used the sprinkler, we'd run the risk of drownin', or worse, boilin' … We'll use the woollen rugs out of the livin' room and my bedroom as cover … In case embers fall on top of us.'

'Maybe we should wet them too.'

* * *

Mavis sat on the step breathing hard and seized by another coughing fit. Above her, black streamers of smoke swirled in thick red and orange clouds. She stared at the rugs as Cassie dumped the third bucket of water on them. The faces of both women were grimed and covered with a fine, wet film of ash. Their clothes clung to them, saturated by a combination of sweat and river water.

Cassie raced through the house to the kitchen where she filled the buckets to overflowing. Her return was made difficult by the weight of the buckets, and her repeated slipping on the spill. Exhausted, Cassie looked at the rugs that squelched to the touch of Mavis' feet.

'Okay,' Mavis exhaled. 'Let's go! We don't have much time.' Smoke over what had once been the lower pastures momentarily shifted. It was a grotesque world in which trees writhed and groaned as fire consumed them. 'Oh God! Oh God! We have to get out of here. Now!' In her panic, Mavis strained in an attempt to lift one of the rugs. 'These are as heavy as cement!' She collapsed, panting onto the steps. The panting changed to coughing.

'Don't even try and lift the rug. I'll bring them.'

'How can you?'

'One at a time. Don't argue.' Cassie looked around them. The fire roared in its hunger. 'From the sound of it, we can't have much time left. C'mon, Mavis, up you get.'

'Cassie …' Mavis' voice broke in fear.

'We can't afford the luxury of hysterics. I know how you feel. I'm screaming on the inside too, but we have to stay calm otherwise … otherwise …'

'Don't … don't finish it,' Mavis said as she pushed herself to her feet. 'Let's just get to the hole.'

Cassie tried for a cheerful tone, 'Lead on, Mills.'

Mavis covered the distance between the house and the outhouse hole faster than Cassie who dragged the first of the rugs. They overshot the hole and then had to fan out in a careful search of the ground.

'We're close, Cassie, it's … here … somewhere …'

The coughing worsened as they explored their sectors. Cassie kept her thought focus narrow in an attempt to maintain her self-control.

'Isn't this typical of me?' Mavis yelled over the fire's roar. 'I've got into so many holes without even wantin' too, and now I can't find one when I want it.'

'Eureka!' Cassie's relief was evident even though Mavis could not see her.

'You've found it, actually found it? Now, where are you?'

Cassie voice-lead Mavis to safety.

'Okay, hop in while I get the last rug. Pull the rug over your head.' The sentence trailed off into the red haze. The only indication as to Cassie's location was her coughing.

Mavis stared at the hole, mesmerised by it. Dear God, help me! Fear reached for her, ready to pull her in. I thought I was through with pits. Her vision blurred. Her head ached. Her eyes stung. Her throat felt raw and constricted.

Holding onto the ragged shreds of control, Mavis looked over her shoulder, searching the changing smoke screen for Cassie. The fire sounded like a freight train now; that sound was interspersed with explosions.

Mavis eased herself down into the hole and then peered over its edge in the direction of the house. She sobbed as she watched visibility change. At times, she couldn't see past a few yards. At other times, when the smoke cleared, she could see Cassie's silhouetted figure struggling with the second rug. Molten gold blazed behind her.

Mavis heaved at the sodden rug, attempting to cover herself with it. It sagged over her while its weight dragged its ends into the hole. Her neck ached from its saturated weight. Grit from the dragging sprinkled over her; it caught in her eyes. She rubbed them trying to remove it.

Cassie dragged the last rug down to the hole and disappeared again before Mavis could stop her. Bloody hell! Where's she gone now?

Mavis had her answer as she heard Cassie return, groaning faintly under the strain of buckets. She emptied them around the hole and glanced quickly at the approaching fire, frightened by the closeness of a series of explosions. The world glowed through the black red smoke; sky and surroundings boiled.

Cassie looked at the pit and the sagging rug in dismay, 'The rugs aren't going to work. We need something hard and really long. Something big enough to cover the hole and strong enough to bear the rugs' weight.'

Mavis' words became audible even though the sobbing continued, 'There's some corrugated iron lyin' against the milkin' sheds.'

Cassie was gone before Mavis finished.

Mavis called after her, 'The left-hand side.'

Fear overtook Mavis.

'No time to look!' Cassie panted, lowering herself into the pit. It was deep but not wide enough for both women to sit comfortably.

The fire's roar was deafening. It drowned out the noise of the falling timber.

'Cosy?'

'About as cosy as a chicken before roastin'.'

'We're going to survive this, Mavis. We are!'

The world around them turned into molten fire.

Mavis fought the sobbing, but it won.

'C'mon, think of something that's given you comfort in the past. Focus on that.' Sweat ran between Cassie's breasts. She pulled lank, ashen hair off her face.

Both women struggled for control. Mavis gripped Cassie's hand, her bones clearly visible.

Mavis' voice was faint as she recited the only psalm that she knew as a prayer. 'The Lord is my shepherd … I shall not want. He makes me lie down … in green … in green pastures.' Tears and sweat coursed through the ash covering her face.

Cassie crouched closer to Mavis. The comfort was double edged.

Mavis continued, 'He leads me … beside …'

A deafening explosion made them cringe. Sobs jolted out of both women.

'Keep going.' Cassie knew she'd spoken but didn't recognise her own voice.

Mavis sobbed but clung onto the ragged ends of her control. 'He leads me beside still waters.' She swallowed and forced herself to focus. 'He restores my soul. He leads me in paths of righteousness for His name's sake.' Her nails cut into her palms, but she wasn't aware of that pain. 'Even though I sit … amidst flames and destruction, I … I fear no evil; for thou … thou art with me.'

The fire roared, its hunger unsated.

'Thy rod … thy rod and thy staff comfort me. Thou preparest a table …' Fear blocked Mavis' thought.

'You anoint my head?' prompted Cassie.

'No, thou preparest a table in the presence of my enemies.' Mavis closed her eyes and leant against Cassie. 'It's so hot!'

The grandfather of all explosions rent the air around them. They cringed, distancing themselves as much as possible from the firestorm raging around them.

Cassie wondered if they could survive the passing inferno. She was too frightened to think let alone have a revelation about life.

* * *

Distraught from waiting, Minna turned off the TV and rushed to Michael as he entered the room. Blackened by ash, his hair was singed, and his right arm was bandaged.

'Oh, Mike, thank God someone's come back.' She was pale and haggard. 'It's Cassie.'

'What?'

'She went out to the Mills' property to get Mavis, and I haven't heard from her since. She should've been back hours and hours ago! Mike … I'm frightened! I've been watching the television since she left.' Minna was in tears, 'I let her go right into it. I didn't know.'

Fear balled in Michael's stomach as he headed out west to the Mills' property. He pulled the sun visor down in an effort to block the glare of the bloodied sun. She'll be safe. She will be safe, he told himself. They would not have let her go through if there had been any danger. Dear God, please let her be all right! If anything happened to her … The thought was intolerable. Past issues were extinguished. He pushed the accelerator to the floor, determined to drive through the inferno if necessary. Ahead of him, the fire broiled in its rage.

Chapter 43

Television images from the fire front ended with a cross to a reporter at the scene. 'The rain began five hours ago, lightly and with ear-shattering thunder at first. Then it built into a torrential downpour. That noise,' the reporter paused, allowing the microphones to pick up the pounding on the tin roof, 'is the sound of salvation. I was at a firebreak filming this war between man and fire when the rain started. I didn't realise what it was at first.' The reporter's voice wavered with emotion. He paused before continuing, 'I've never seen or felt anything like it before in my life. It was molten rain. Red, grey, black rain – fiery ash falling from the sky. It was hot at first, and, for a moment, this reporter thought it was fire.' His voice broke with raw emotion, 'I can't describe to you how I felt. Then I realised it was wet. Exhausted and close to defeat, the fire-fighters found themselves revitalised. They battled on, aware that fire and its enemy were locked in mortal battle. I learnt once that, great fires by their very nature create great winds, and that rains sometimes come in response to the cataclysm. I didn't believe it then; I do now. Today was such a day. This is Mark Burrows reporting for Eyewitness News. Back to you, Katrina.'

Unable to stand the strain of isolation, Minna left Madison House. Undecided as to her destination, she drove through the town. Everything was closed. What should she do? Where could she be of help?

* * *

The western sun glared at the world on the edge of the distant horizon from behind storm clouds. It was a strange effect; smoke haze heightened the aura surrounding the clouds.

Cassie and Mavis waited at the roadblock. Mop up operations barred passage to Keimera. Cassie stood, impervious to the rain, at the barrier forcing herself to be patient. In the tedium of waiting, her thoughts wandered to Michael and her future.

At times in life, there are unanticipated events beyond our control that winnow chaff from wheat. So it was with Cassie now. She loved Michael, knew she would survive without him, but did not want that end. There had to be a way to stay together. How? She could not be a military groupie, following her man around, a shadow again as she had been with Jake. There were so many careers possible for Michael – would it be so bad if she asked him to rethink his choice?

Stymied, Cassie moved restlessly along the barrier without an answer. Introspective, Cassie saw that in spite of her growth she was still risk averse. Wary, but no longer afraid, she knew how to love but had yet to learn how to live with it. There was an answer. She would find it. Until then …

An odd noise caused Cassie to turn. She scanned the vicinity and, unable to discern the cause, walked back to her smoke-licked, duco-blistered car to check on her friend. Despite the rain, ash and soot covered the car.

Mavis sat with her head back and eyes closed, remembering the smoking ruins of her home. She was past grief, past horror. There'd been a time earlier that day when she'd thought the world had turned to sweat and had collided with the sun. She was ill and looked terrible.

Cassie looked back at the barrier. The man on duty had returned. If only she could impress upon him her growing sense of urgency.

'Excuse me, do you have any idea how much longer this'll be? My friend … she's the pregnant woman in the car over there … She's ill and I …' She'd never understand herself. Of all the times to cry! Why now when she was safe? Tears lined her cheeks. 'I really need to get her to the hospital.'

'Well, why didn't you say something earlier? Look, I'll get on the radio and find out.' He moved across to his land cruiser and radioed his base. Cassie strained unsuccessfully to hear what was said. He returned, 'Look, they're still clearing the road, but they said to send you on through. Be careful!'

* * *

The bush was black, charred and smoking. As Cassie travelled through the mop-up operations, she glimpsed fire fighters beating out the remaining spot fires. She closed all the vents and windows of her car in an attempt to block the bitter fumes and thick smoke-laden air.

The windscreen was streaked with rain, ash, and a fine spray of mud from the dirt road. She looked across at Mavis; tear trails had dried creating a curious effect on her mask of ash. Mavis' silence worried Cassie.

Visibility diminished despite the rain. Cassie pressed the washer button. The last spurt of water smeared the screen, obscuring her vision completely. Damn! That's all we need. She slowed to a halt on the edge of the road.

'Mavis? Mavis?' Cassie leant forward and listened to her breathing. It was steady.

Cassie reached across to the glove box, searching for a box

of tissues. The box was empty. She removed the keys from the ignition and opened the boot of the car. Her old sweater would have to do.

The roar of an engine disturbed her. She looked up and recognised Michael's car as it shot past them. She waved her grimed sweater, attempting to get his attention in his rear-vision mirror. His car slid to a halt one hundred yards down the road. He backed up at breakneck speed.

A few feet from her, he yelled through his open window, 'Thank Christ, you're all right! You don't know how worried we've been! I was stuck forever at the roadblock back at the crossroads. The only reason I got through was because I knew the bloke in charge of operations at my end.'

Cassie fell into his arms. 'Oh, I'm so glad to see you. I thought I'd never see you again. That fear was so much worse than …' The anguish and stress of the day released itself through tears.

'It's okay now. You're safe! Everything's going to be fine.' Michael crushed her to him in his relief, covering her in kisses.

After calm reclaimed them, Michael asked, 'So, how close did the fire get to you and Mavis?'

'Mavis! How could I have forgotten about her? She's ill, Mike. Her breathing got real shallow while we were …' She could not bring herself to talk let alone think about their time in the pit. 'I need to get her to a doctor.'

'Don't you think the hospital would be better?'

'That's what I meant!'

'What's wrong with your car?'

'Nothing much, considering what it's been through. The screen's muddy. I'm out of water.'

'No sweat. I've got a jerry can in the back. Pop the bonnet, and I'll fill up your washers. You can follow me to the hospital.'

* * *

Chance often separates people, but, at times, it brings them together. As Michael drove up to the casualty area, Cassie saw Minna and Marg sitting at one of the sheltered tables outside the hospital cafe, drinking coffee and watching the evening rain. Shaken by the bedraggled appearance of Cassie and Mavis, they followed the trio into the casualty ward.

At first the junior nurse on duty, beleaguered by fire victims, argued that Cassie should take Mavis across to the maternity ward.

'But she's not in labour! I'm not dragging her around this hospital because you're uncertain if you should take her here!'

'C'mon, nurse, have a heart. Can't you bend the rules?' Michael asked.

'What's going on out here?' queried a white coated woman.

'These people have brought in a pregnant woman, Doctor Forbes. I've been trying to tell them that we don't handle that sort of emergency here.'

'I'd say these people have been through enough today. Flexibility isn't going to hurt us, and it won't hurt the patients.'

* * *

'Mavis will be all right, Marg,' Minna said.

'What if … what if … I've passed birthin' problems onto her? How can I face her if I have?'

'Let's pay interest on the problem if it comes due. The

positives are Trevor's gallstones are treatable and not as bad as the heart attack you feared. The girls are safe. Look, there's the foetal monitor. It won't be much longer now.'

Marg crossed herself in prayer. Waiting: Marg had spent a lifetime doing it, that and scrimping on the fumes of income. That lifestyle had appeared over, their fortune changed.

The casualty waiting room looked like a tableau. Cassie sat, eyes closed, in Michael's embrace. Minna and Marg stood like sentinels at the nurse's desk, waiting for news. Clusters of people with a range of injuries surrounded them, each in their own island of pain. Nursing staff, calm and focused on the routine, went through the ritual of care.

In hushed undertones, Michael asked, 'So why won't you marry me then?'

'It's hardly the time …'

'When then?'

Silence.

'Cassie, I've only a few weeks left before I start at the Academy. We have to sort this out!'

'Not here.'

Michael stood and pulled Cassie to her feet. 'C'mon, outside!'

Cassie went with him reluctantly.

'Well, Cassie?'

'Okay … when you proposed, how did you see the relationship working?'

'What? Is this the big barrier? It's nothing compared to—'

'To me it is, Mike. How do you see the relationship playing out?'

'Mostly that we'd live out life together; the usual thing when people are in love.'

'Oh.'

'Not enough for you?' They stood apart, tense. 'And you see it as?'

'I want a partnership of equals, like in dance: no male or female work, just stuff to be done and shared. A joint life – but with space for self.'

'Geez, Cassie, how could I see marriage any other way with parents like mine? The best thing about your career is that it's portable. Who knows what opportunities are out there for you?'

The portability of her career had not occurred to Cassie before. 'Oh.'

'So we're getting married, right?' He stepped closer.

'Yes, I guess we are.'

'I guess, Cassie?'

'No, we are! It's just … hard to get my head around the shift … in perspective. It's not that I don't love you … I do … Whoa! We're getting married!'

'Bloody fantastic!' Michael pulled her to him in a passionate embrace before releasing her. They returned to the Casualty waiting room.

Jargon. Minna frowned. Did all doctors do a course in being obtuse? She looked at Marg, growing paler by the second.

The weight on Marg's chest made her feel sick. She just didn't understand. Tears spilled down her face. She had thought losing her daughter to that man and his excluding influence was the worst pain she would suffer. This was the punishment metered out to mothers who failed.

* * *

The white ceiling glared at Marg. She had difficulty focusing and so closed her eyes for a second and tried again. There wasn't much improvement. Concerned, she forced herself to concentrate on the ceiling, the walls, and the end of the bed.

Bed? Where was she?

Sedation held Marg in its firm grip; she struggled against it and forced her eyes open. It was like looking through a thick smoke haze. They had lost everything, Mavis as well! All she had was Trevor; where was he?

Her outstretched hand moved slowly as if cutting through dense air. Hair? She fingered it and wondered who it was before slipping back into sleep.

Hospitals are such noisy places, Minna thought. The whir of the floor polishers filled the corridors. Nurses scurried from ward to ward. Minna wondered how patients could sleep with all that noise. From her experience, early morning was the noisiest time in hospitals. It did not make sense to her, that and the overweight state of many of the nursing staff.

Standing in the doorway to Marg's room, Minna debated waking Mavis who was asleep; her body slumped on her mother's bed, Marg's still hand on her daughter's head.

'Mavis?' Minna gently roused her. 'You need your rest. I'll call you when she wakes. George and I thought you and your parents could move into Madison House for the interim. The CWA has money for emergency situations like this, and yesterday the government announced a special compensation package for people who have lost their homes.'

'Thank God! That's such a relief!'

'Who's there?' Marg's voice was strained. 'Mavis … is that you?'

'Yes, Mum, I'm here. The baby's fine. Dad's on the mend. Things are on the up from now on.'

Chapter 44

March 1990. The scenery on the trip to Canberra was mostly a blur that Friday afternoon. Cassie was preoccupied with the reunion. She feared an anticlimax based on experience of past longings.

The Hume Highway was narrow and single-laned. The sharp change in landscape as she drove into the Southern Highlands, its lushness and the depth of green, snared Cassie's attention for a while. The kilometres hummed in tune with her progress, and she slipped back into reverie.

Lake George, a tranquil sea of blue that lapped the road for twenty-five kilometres, was beyond her imagination. She pulled into a rest area to enjoy its dappled brilliance.

As her car crested the hill after the ACT border, she caught her breath at the vista: treed urbanscape in the distance ringed by pastoral lands, a spaceship styled tower dominating the skyline, and the blue Brindabella Mountains. The multi-coloured fall of autumn, for which the region was famous, would not occur until much later.

The city struck Cassie as more town-like than cityscape. From the main road, the CBD was visible, but where was the big shopping mall? She could not wait to explore the nation's hub. She thought, This must be how Leonie will feel when she lands in Paris. On reflection, Cassie realised that Leonie's excitement would definitely be greater.

Waiting at the Park Hyatt Hotel for the arrival of the

Madisons, Cassie's adventure began with an exploration of it. She liked the art deco design. Outside, she walked to the parklands surrounding Lake Burley Griffin. Although it was a beautiful place, did she want to move here for the three years of Michael's training? Her third year in teaching promised to be great given her class allocation.

* * *

The Saturday morning of the Chief of Defence Force's parade for ADFA cadets was crisp with a forecast for a hot day. After breakfast, Minna in black crepe pencil trousers and an elegantly cut, white silk, hip length shirt waited in the foyer for George and Cassie. Minna had two concerns when she saw Cassie: her thinness and her vulnerability to sunburn given the green cutaway summer dress. She wished she had brought an umbrella; she knew Cassie would not use sun cream. George, already regretting the need for a suit, arrived last. He worried about parking and seating availability.

The military organisation underlying the parking arrangements was a pleasant contrast from the free-for-all that George had expected. There was an air of suppressed excitement as uniformed officer cadets and midshipmen from the three Services rushed about on appointed duties. The tuning of the Academy band gave pitch to that excitement.

The manicured grassed parade ground, the array of plastic chairs on the verge of the terraced lawns adjacent to the dais, and the ushers alleviated George's second worry. With twenty minutes to the parade, the Keimera group read the program with interest.

Sitting next to Cassie was a careworn, thin woman struggling to keep her two boys, seven and five year olds, settled in the chairs next to hers. She had the usual paraphernalia that characterised a forward thinking parent: colouring pencils and books, an assortment of toys, drink and food.

The younger boy, unable to see beyond the chairs and adults in them, punctuated the silence at intervals with, 'Is Dad there yet?'

The mother's reply was reflex rather than thoughtful and informative. 'Soon, Danny.'

Aware of her boys' impact on the people around her, the woman said to everyone in general, 'I hope the boys aren't troubling you too much. They haven't seen their dad for weeks.' To Cassie, who appeared the only sympathetic listener, she said in a sotto voice, 'We thought moving down here while my husband was on course was for the best. Being uprooted has been hard on the boys and even harder on me. I wish I'd stayed where I had a support system. You live here?'

'No, but I'm thinking of moving down.'

'Take it from me; following your husband when the conditions are controlled by study and training is a huge mistake.'

'I'm not married.'

'Then it's a gamble, isn't it? Your boyfriend won't have much time for you. Not with full-time academic studies and military training for three years! And you're what … twenty something? Not much between you to keep you together.'

'Mummy,' the older boy drew his mother's attention, 'Danny's crawled off toward the back somewhere.'

The woman stood, scanned the filled area behind her, sighted her offspring, and set off after him, calling back to her older son, 'Don't you dare move!'

On the parade ground, the Warrant Officer called, 'Markers!'

A hush of expectation fell over the crowd.

Cassie stared unseeing across the parade ground.

The formality that announced the commencement of the ceremony established sharply that this world was different from that in which the first year officer cadets and midshipmen had grown up. The military haircuts, bearing, and split-second discipline stamped that fact on the audience.

The parade itself was intensely emotional. Minna and George had pride in Michael's achievement and relief that the detour in his adolescence had not kept him from realising his potential. Cassie's eyes filled with tears as she recognised Michael in the march-past.

As the last flight exited the parade ground, family and friends milled in search of their officer cadet or midshipman. Frustrated, the Keimera group decided to let Michael find them. They waited on the external landing of the Cadets' Mess.

This, thought Minna, was worse than waiting for George to return from Korea. The entry point then had been controlled; she had not needed eyes in the back of her head. As in all things, when you focus your energy in the waiting, time stretches.

Minna saw Michael first, rushed to him, and embraced him. George was close on her heels. He gave Michael a bear hug. Cassie stood back allowing the family space. Michael extracted himself, walked to her, and pulled her into the security of his arms.

'God, how I've missed you!' He leant in for a passionate kiss, but she pulled back, conscious of her surroundings.

Disappointed, he looked at her critically. 'Nothing's changed has it?'

'No, it's just …' She stretched up and kissed him then; more passionately than she had intended given the audience but less than he had wanted.

'I'm famished,' Minna interrupted.

'This way, Mum.'

Inside the crush of the Mess, Michael manoeuvred his group to a table that had just been freed. 'Cassie and I'll wait here while you get served; can't afford to let this table go.'

To their far right, a band: drums, guitar, keyboard, and sax provided atmosphere and entertainment.

With his left arm encircling Cassie, Michael relaxed. 'It's been …'

'Anyone else sitting with you, mate?' a solid, squat Army cadet asked.

Cassie recognised the woman and the two boys he had in tow.

'Just my mum and dad, Rick. If you find some chairs, we can move up.'

'Great!' The cadet turned in search of chairs, but his wife stayed him with a comment inaudible to those nearby. With a hand firmly on each boy, she held them in check while she talked in stressed undertones to her husband.

Observing that interaction, Michael said, 'It's been tough for Rick; no time for his family and guilty that he insisted they come down from Queensland.'

Minna and George returned as Rick spoke to Michael. 'Jane wants to push off. The boys need some play time.'

Delayed through the courtesy of introductions and the ritual of chit-chat, Jane lost contact again with the younger boy who used the opportunity to investigate something.

Panicked, she looked around. The older boy said, 'Mum, Danny's walking on the ledge outside.'

'Excuse me. Rick?'

'Catch you later.' The family left.

'I'm glad I'm not in Rick's shoes!' Michael said, unthinking of the implications.

Cassie wore a practised smile, one that did not extend to her eyes.

Crowded venues are the last places for matters of the heart. When Cassie and Michael returned from the smorgasbord, talk centred on Michael's course, Minna's vision as mayor to avoid the higgledy-piggledy growth of towns, and life in Keimera.

The conversation around Cassie fragmented. True to her life experience, the greater her anticipation the larger her disappointment. Her plan to move to Canberra was evaporating.

In the background, the opening bars of *Sway* by Perez Prado sounded, leading into a duet.

Michael pushed back his chair. 'Dance, Cassie?'

Looking up from her reverie, Cassie focused on his outstretched hand.

'I don't think the organisers planned on dancing when they hired the band,' George said.

'Maybe not, but that's no reason to waste good music. Cassie?'

'There isn't a dance floor, Michael,' Minna said.

'Wherever there's music, we'll make a dance floor. Cassie?'

Stepping into position, Cassie looked back over her shoulder at the Madisons and said, 'I don't want to be a wallflower.'

* * *

Music Acknowledgements

Reference is made to the following works:

Ravel	*La Valse, une poème choréographique*
	Le Jardin Feerique
	Sonata for Violin and Piano in G Major
	Bolero
Beatles	*Come Together*
Blondie	*Heart of Glass*
Bill Withers	*Lean on Me*
Santana	*Black Magic Woman Welcome* album
Mungo Jerry	*In the Summertime*
Marvin Gaye	*Heard It On The Grapevine*
Celia Cruz	*Sugar Sugar* Cuando Sali De Cuba
Daddy Cool	*Eagle Rock*
ACDC	*It's A Long Way To the Top*
Robert Goulet	*My Love Forgive Me*
Credence Clearwater Revival	*I'll Put A Spell on You*
Neil Diamond	*September Morn*
Enya	*Sail Away*
Rolling Stones	*The Singer not the Song*
Jackson Five (written by Hal Davis, Berry Gordy, Jr, Willie Hutch & Bob West)	*I'll Be There*
Dolly Parton	*What a Heartache*
P Swayze and S Widelitz	*She's like the Wind*
Perez Prado	*Sway*

LIFE SONG

Can a single mother have it all?

'Could Mavis live the rest of her life as she'd been living? She couldn't, not now she'd glimpsed another world, fleeting though that vision had been.'

Mavis was born to be a songbird. Her parents named her after one, a bird with a distinctive song worthy of poetry. With her wings clipped by circumstance, Mavis spent six years of her life grounded and her dream of soaring flight almost forgotten. Unexpectedly, Mavis discovers she has a choice: accept a life that is ordinary or be among the one percent that shine.

It is a long way to the top in the Australian music industry and more than a name needs to change in order to succeed. It is a grueling challenge with exhausting demands and subtle traps for the uninitiated. Can Mavis make it? Can she build a better life for herself and her son? Can she have it all?

The themes are discovery, reinvention, triumphing against the odds, disparate families, parenting, friendship, and the nature of love; themes that resonate with all ages.

SONG BIRD

I'm not Mavis anymore.

For years, songbird Nikki Mills (aka Mavis Mills) dreamed of the freedom and lifestyle that came with being a platinum record artist. To get there, she put her career and son first and her love life on hold.

Now an international singing sensation, Nikki discovers her reality is very different from what she had imagined. Determined not to be caged by the fan and media circus, Nikki struggles to protect her son, their relationship and lifestyle. That struggle is complicated by her desire for a love life.

The unearthing of Nikki's dark past, known only to her inner circle, creates a paparazzi whirlwind that threatens to destroy her. Can she find the courage to withstand the media storm? Can she transcend her past? How will she resolve matters of the heart?

Set between 2000 and 2002, the themes in 'Song Bird' centre on discovery, belonging, transformation, dealing with adversity, and matters of the heart.

www.ingramcontent.com/pod-product-compliance
Lightning Source LLC
Chambersburg PA
CBHW051936020726
47501CB00001B/154